LUCY LIED

LUCY LIED

A NOVEL

BY

M.J. DASPIT

www.fireshippress.com

Lucy Lied by M.J.Daspit

ISBN-13: 978-1-61179-321-5(Paperback)
ISBN -978-1-61179-322-2(e-book)

BISAC Subject Headings:

FIC014000FICTION / Historical
FIC022000 FICTION / Mystery & Detective / General
FIC033000 FICTION / Westerns

Cover work by Christine Horner

Address all correspondence to:
Fireship Press, LLC
P. O. Box 68412
Tucson, AZ 85737
Or visit our website at:
www.fireshippress.com

Dedication:

To my dear husband and best pal, Gary.

Acknowledgments:

Thanks to Morgan Hunt, Mary Maher, Sorena Fee Pansovoy, Deborah Rich, and Denise Tierney, all of whom have struggled through my manuscripts and offered me their critical comments and kind words of encouragement. I am deeply indebted to Jean Huets, author and founder of Circling Rivers Press, for her close reading and editorial remarks with regard to restructuring the manuscript of LUCY LIED. To Will Howarth, the male half of Dana Hand, author of DEEP CREEK, I appreciate your willingness to assist me as a new author and tolerate my flagrant imposition on an old friendship in asking you to read this book in one of its earliest versions. Will's astute comment about my anachronistic use of the word "fibrillation" led me to discover the National Museum of Civil War Medicine, an indispensable resource for those interested in medical practices of the nineteenth century. Terry Reimer, Director of Research of this invaluable institution, provided detailed documentation in response to queries out of the blue from an unknown writer. Thanks to John and Ryan of Downtown Books and Coffee of Auburn, New York, for being the first to publish one of my short stories, thereby giving me something to offer in the way of "writing credits." And last, but by no means least, thanks to the G-man for tolerating my long hours in isolation tap-tap-tapping at the keyboard.

Chapter One

The young Negro everyone called Steadman's boy was a cautious driver. He'd made good time on the coast road, but slowed to a walk when he turned onto Talbott's place. He let the horse pick his own way along a rutted track through the tall grasses of the oozy mud flats Talbott had been draining and clearing for sugar beets. Four Chinese laborers were at work at the southern end of the property. They looked up at the approach of the wagon. Their four sets of eyes seemed to move in unison as the wagon jolted past. Steadman's boy, who didn't care much for Celestials, took one quick look at them and then kept his eyes down. He thought of ravens flapping off a carcass to avoid a traveler, then settling back on the carrion again.

He reined in at a crude adobe shack with bare brown patches in the whitewash and a wattle roof. The front door stood open, and a chicken came through and took a listless peck at the threshold. He hitched the horse to the pump handle and called across the yard, "Mr. Talbott? You all here? I got your new wheel you ordered for your wagon." He listened intently for any response, but was answered only by the hen, that clucked and peered at him with her head cocked to one side, the way the clerk at Ortin's store was wont to do when tallying a bill.

1

Lucy Lied

Considering how far it was back to town and how angry Steadman would be if he came back without the money for the wheel, the young man had determined that he would not leave before he found Talbott. He walked toward the open door of the house with a feeling of dread.

The shack had but two rooms. In the front room were a trestle table and a pantry with plates and cups, a round Spanish-style fireplace, and two chairs. A door stood open onto the back yard. He could see an outdoor oven, a worktable with a mortar and pestle, some pots and cooking things. A second door led to the back room, with a bedstead and a chest of drawers and pegs for hanging up clothes on the wall. Again he called out, "Mr. Talbott?" as he came through.

He had never been in a white man's bedroom before. It seemed wrong, ill-advised. But he moved one foot in front of the other as if drawn by a magnet to the other side of the bedstead. The shack had a board floor, probably because the ground was soggy. The boards creaked as he stole along the foot of the bed. He kept his eyes down, away from the pillows where if he looked he might imagine the man and his wife, their arms entwined about each other, old Talbott on top of the red-haired woman. So he saw it right away, the farmer's shoeless foot, blue the way white skin looks when it's cold, and still.

Talbott was lying in the narrow space between the bed and the wall. He lay face down wearing only his long johns. The black man peered at a gash about three inches long and an inch or so wide behind Talbott's left ear. He ran one finger across the blood on the floor where it had seeped from the wound. It was dry. The victim's right hand clutched a belt.

Steadman's boy told it just like that to Sheriff Taylor. "I reckon he took his belt down from the peg and got hit from behind," he said. His eyes looked wild and he was out of breath.

Taylor considered the question of whether or not the buck had done Talbott himself, and pocketed the money for the wheel. If he had, it wouldn't make sense for him to come straight back to town and inform the sheriff. But if the boy hadn't done it, Taylor knew he'd have to get off his ass and find out who had.

"You all go on back to Talbott's. Tell Steadman I said so. You keep an eye on things so nothing goes missing."

"Yes, sir," the black man said. He seemed calmer for having told his story to someone else. His eyes didn't seem as crazed as when he'd first appeared, ranting about a murdered white man. Taylor never entertained the idea that a nigger might play the idiot to avoid being accused.

"And take a horse up to Doc Garrett's. Tell him I need him to ride out and have a look at a corpse."

Steadman's boy put his hat back on and took his leave with a tug on the brim. He did as the sheriff said, and a little after noon, Doc Garrett found himself standing over the body of the dead man with Taylor.

"What do you make of it?" Garrett asked. "The belt, I mean."

"Reckon he turned toward the wall to take it down from the peg and got hit from behind," the sheriff said.

"Reckon so," Doc replied, "but it's odd he didn't have his pants on yet. You usually reach for your pants first and put them on, then get your belt."

"Yeah," Taylor agreed, "but who's to say what a contrary cuss like Talbott would do." He pulled off his hat and scratched the top of his head. "Can you tell me when he was killed?"

"Give me a few minutes." Doc squatted down and picked up Talbott's left hand by the wrist. He waggled the fingers to assess the flexibility of the joints.

"I'll be out back," the sheriff said. He settled his hat back on his head and left the room.

Doc continued to note the effects of rigor until the lawman was gone. Once alone with the corpse, he examined the head wound and then scrambled to his feet. He did a slow three hundred and sixty degree survey of the room, then dropped down on all fours and looked under the bed. There was a clean-swiped patch amid a thick fur of dust. Taylor called in from the back yard. "Doc! Come on out here. I found something."

His stomach clenched as he stepped outside and saw Taylor standing with a rusty tool in his hand. "Found it buried in the ashes in the oven," the sheriff said. He handed the short iron bar to Doc. "You reckon that's what did it?"

Doc examined the bar as if he'd never seen one before. "One end has blood on it," he said. "And it matches the wound for size. I'd say this is what killed him without a doubt."

Taylor retrieved his evidence from the doctor's hands. "One of them pry bars the Chinamen use to take abalone off the rocks," he said. "Guess I better corral them Celestials out in the field yonder and see what they know. Might be one of them had a labor dispute with old Talbott." He frowned and hefted the bar. "What do you s'pose happened to the wife?"

"Probably ran off scared," Garrett replied.

"Most like," Taylor agreed, "but the buckboard's still in the barn along with the horse."

"Buckboard's got a bad wheel. Steadman's boy was bringing out a new one."

"Yeah, but she coulda got on the horse," Taylor said.

"Scared of horses," Doc answered. "Remember a couple weeks ago, Talbott brought her into town all banged up? Horse kicked her."

"Shoulder came out of joint? Was that it?" The sheriff gazed up at the gray sky. "Damn high kicker." He sighed. "Well, she can't have got far on foot. I reckon I better gather up some boys and go out looking for her. Won't nobody much want to slog around these sloughs, but that's what's got to be done."

Garrett fought to keep anxiety out of his voice. "I'll be getting back to town, then."

"What about the time of death?"

"Hard to say. Yesterday sometime. Talbott had to have been struck by a right-handed fellow, somebody about his size or bigger. I'll make you out a report."

"Much obliged," Taylor said. "You think you can haul the body back to town for me? I'd have Steadman's boy do it but that boy's so skittish around the deceased I figger he'd faint dead away unless you were there to keep him settled." He shook his head and grinned. "I swear I never thought it possible for a nigger to blanch,

4

but that boy was right pale when he come to tell me he seen Talbott dead."

"Most like he managed the effect for your benefit," Garrett muttered. He'd seen the Negroes enact such shenanigans often enough. A smart man could manage a dull boss by playing the fool, where cleverness would only get him a few more stripes.

"What's that?"

"I said I'll manage the body. I'll drop it by Peabody's when I'm done with it so he can start making a coffin."

"I appreciate it. I got to speak to the field hands yet."

The next morning a special edition of the Monterey paper lauded the sheriff for the expeditious way he had the suspects "jailed before supper." The article gave the names of the four Chinese being held for the murder, without bothering to say why four were incarcerated when the murder looked like the work of only one villain.

Reading such claptrap made Matt Clancy feel anything but sanguine as he finished up his breakfast at the Washington Hotel. The jail next to the gray stone building known as the site of the state's first constitutional convention wasn't much of a stronghold. It occurred to him that four Chinese suspected of killing a white man wouldn't be safe there for long. Citizens stirred up by liquor and brash editorials had been known to tie up the sheriff and bust prisoners out, not to free them but to string them up to the nearest tree.

Clancy made his way to the jail without further delay and found Taylor on his feet to greet him. Taylor's draw hand was poised over his sidearm. "What brings you out this way, Clancy?" he asked. "Got all them troublemakers in the San Joaquin toeing the line?"

The four Chinese sat on the low bunk at the back wall of the cell, separated by a set of bars from the room where the sheriff and Clancy stood facing each other. Clancy nodded toward the inmates. "Them," he said. "I've come to speak to you about letting them go."

"Well, I sure do appreciate your taking an interest," Taylor said, "especially if you've got evidence to exonerate these prisoners." He smiled. "Friends of yours, are they?"

"I know Quong Mai and Ham Tung pretty well. We play *pok kop pew* at the Chinese gambling house down on Washington Street. The other two are Tim Lee and Hoy Wong. I don't know them so well. But I do know all four of them are innocent."

"How's that?" Taylor asked.

"I was reading how Talbott got his skull bashed in with an iron bar."

"That's right. One of them snuck up when his back was turned."

"How's that? Why would any one of them want to kill the man who pays their wages?"

"Reckon they didn't like what they was being paid. Talbott used to brag about how he got paid four dollars a ton in advance for that beet crop of his. Said he agreed to pay these ones seventy cents a ton to split up amongst themselves. My bet is they figured out they could do better if they was to cut out the middleman."

"Why, that makes no sense at all, not if Talbott got paid in advance. You think the beet factory would pay for a crop twice, once to Talbott and once to the Chinese?"

Taylor drew himself up. "Listen here, mister, I don't get paid to figger out how the sugar beet industry works. All I got to worry about is I got a crime on my hands and I got four suspects in jail for it. Don't make a hill of beans if you think it's right or not. Now you take those six-guns of yours and git outta here. Git on your yellow horse and ride back out to the Vásquez place or Leese's boardinghouse or wherever it is you hang your hat these days. Go on down to Washington Street and smoke opium with a yellow whore if you please. But you leave this thing to me."

"I don't know that I can do that," Clancy said. He watched Taylor's little eyes harden. Taylor had pig's eyes. Pigs could be dangerous when they were cornered.

"You will if you value your health." Taylor moved his hand to his gun.

Clancy did the same. He kept watching Taylor's eyes, the sheen of sweat on his face, and the damp straggle of hair that lay matted on his brow. The Chinese were silent. The room was so quiet he could hear his own heartbeat. His palms all but touched the cool handles of the long-barreled Colts, waiting for the sheriff to make the first move. It wasn't a sure thing. He wasn't sure the other man had the guts to draw, but with somebody like Taylor it wasn't a matter of guts so much as stupidity.

The door behind Clancy opened. It was all he could do to resist an ingrained response to turn and fire. But the figure that stepped into his peripheral vision on the right wasn't armed. Doc Garrett stopped short and stood stock still, waiting for the bullets to fly. Clancy was the first to stand easy, then Taylor released his gun and let it slide back into the holster.

Taylor growled, "What is it, Doc?"

"I got that report I promised you," Garrett said. With his hands poised to draw his guns again, Clancy watched Garrett reach into his breast pocket and draw out a piece of folded paper.

Taylor gave a nod toward his desk. "Put it over there."

"Your report," Clancy said, "does it say anything about the person who hit Talbott the lick that killed him—the kind of person the sheriff here ought to be looking for?"

"It does," Garrett replied.

"Read it," Clancy said.

Garrett unfolded the paper, cleared his throat and read. "From my examination, Talbott's attacker was a right-handed man, fairly strong, and about Talbott's size."

Clancy jerked his head toward the cell. "Any of those ones he's got locked up fit that description?"

Doc glanced at the Chinese in the cell. "No. That's what I'm saying."

"Now see here, Doc," Taylor began, "you can ask anybody in town about Chinese laborers, how strong they are in spite of their puny little bodies."

"Oh, they're strong, all right," Garrett agreed, "but my examination revealed that the wound was inflicted by a person about six feet tall. You won't find many Celestials of that height. Only one that I know of."

Doc had not implicated anyone by name, but Taylor knew the Celestial that Garrett was thinking of, a wandering vendor people called Chinaman Joe. Always walked around with a cat on his shoulder. The lawman seized on the suggestion and summoned to mind Joe's favorite haunts, places where he camped with the oddments he peddled up and down the coast. Joe was mild-mannered and wouldn't be hard to bring in, but the sheriff wasn't one to give up easily on a bird in the hand. "What makes you so sure of the size?"

"You can tell from the angle of the blow. I'll show you, if you bring the murder weapon over to where they got Talbott laid out."

Taylor reddened. "You'll swear to that in court?"

"I will."

The sheriff pulled a key from his pocket. "All right, then. The two of you get out of here and take these damned yellow bastards with you."

The doctor and the gunman held their ground until the sheriff had unlocked the cell. The four astonished Orientals left at top speed, but did not omit to bow before Clancy. He nodded and said something in Chinese.

"You speak their gibberish?" Doc asked, as he followed Clancy to the street.

"Learnt a few words back when I ran a railroad gang."

"What did you say to them?"

"Told them I'd see them on Friday night for *pok kop pew*. The Chinaman doesn't have many faults, but he dearly loves to gamble."

"And smoke a pipe, I hear."

"A little opium's no worse than a couple shots of whiskey."

"I got enough vices without adding another," Doc said.

The gunman smiled as he stepped into the street. "Guess I'll leave you to them."

Chapter Two

Chinaman Joe sat at the defendant's table and dreamed of his funeral. The Chee Kong Tong would take up a collection as he had no money himself, nor any relatives that he knew of. The Tong would buy fireworks and pay for a procession of gongs and drums. Along the route to the cemetery there would be an altar where his friends would pay their respects and leave offerings of food. Oranges, red-paper-footed roast suckling pig, cakes, chicken, and rice wine. There would be incense burning and prayers hung to flutter in the breeze. The men would braid their queues with blue and white ribbons as a sign of mourning. Joe had no possessions to burn at the gravesite, but they would torch a pile of sticks, and the smoke would carry his spirit to heaven.

He worried about his cat, whether they would make sure to kill it kindly and then put it on his chest, so the two of them could be buried exactly as they slept together every night. Some years later their bones would be dug up and polished to a gleaming white, and shipped back to China in a small square box.

It comforted Joe to think of this peaceful end, as one white man strode across the floor ranting before another in a black robe. The man in the robe was a judge, and the striding man was the prosecutor. Joe understood it was the prosecutor's duty to be his enemy, and Joe bore him no ill will because it was part of the balance of the universe for everything to have its counterpart in opposition. But he did wish that the judge would help Quong Mai. She stood captive in a small box to the left of the judge with tears streaming down her face. The prosecutor was berating her, pointing to Joe and demanding, "Is this the man you saw crossing Talbott's ranch from time to time? Answer me! I charge you to answer me truthfully!"

"Yes!" Quong Mai's voice choked with sobs. "But not that day. I not see him that day Mr. Talbott is kill."

"Well now, what a surprise." The prosecutor stopped pacing and smirked at the twelve people seated on the side of the room. "Gentlemen of the jury, I have no doubt Joe could have ridden by on an elephant and this woman's answer would be the same."

A titter ran through the audience and the judge slammed down his gavel, causing Quong Mai to weep afresh. "Order in the courtroom. Order." He frowned furiously and the merriment retreated behind coughs and hankies. "Mr. Langley, can you control this witness? Either control this witness or I'll dismiss her."

"I have no further questions." Langley took a seat at the table opposite the one where Joe was sitting.

The judge addressed the man next to Joe, the man charged with his defense. "Mr. Blake?"

Defense counsel, a good-looking man with gray hair meticulously parted down the middle and a bristling mustache and sideburns, cleared his throat. "No questions, Your Honor." From the tone of his voice it seemed he might slip naturally into buttery rumblings of Shakespeare. It was a schooled voice, kind of fancy. It made Joe distrust him immediately. Joe's misgivings increased whenever Mr. Blake saw fit to grasp his hand as it lay on the table, in a gesture that was supposed to convey friendship or perhaps consolation.

"The witness may step down," the judge said, "and we'll take a ten minute recess." He banged the gavel once more and swept out of the courtroom. A chattering immediately arose among the spectators as if to fill the vacuum.

Isabel Vásquez and her cousin Rosanna Leese were in court that day. They talked behind their whalebone fans. "The Triads," Rosanna hissed. "Also called the Tong." She nodded to the handful of soberly dressed Chinese who sat bolt upright with their broad shoulders touching, a wall behind the defense attorney. In their Western-style black suits they looked almost like beefy clerics, except for the long queues hanging down their backs from under their black felt hats. "They're here to remind the defense attorney that regardless of what the jury finds, he'll have them to deal with."

"I don't understand why Judge Nearing allows such brutes in court," Isabel said. "Besides, what do they care if a crazy Chinaman is hanged for a murder in Monterey? That one, that Joe, I hear he is the one who walks the beach with a cat on his shoulder. One day north, the next day south. He peddles things he finds along the way. Now why would he be of interest to these *hombres* from San Francisco?"

"You should ask your neighbor. I hear he has been in San Francisco many times lately. They say it is his doing the Triads are here." She pointed her fan again. "There he sits."

In the row of seats behind the Triads, Isabel spied Matt Clancy's back. His head was bare and his coat was slung over the chair next to him.

"I hear he has a special feeling for their kind," Rosanna continued. "It was all the talk at breakfast, how your neighbor contacted those in power among the Chinese in San Francisco, how it was his doing that Joe has a lawyer. They say it isn't beyond the power of the Tong to bribe jurors."

"They talk like that openly in front of you?"

"As I fill their coffee cups they spill their secrets. I wear a black dress like a priest, so they think I will keep their confidences."

Isabel raised an eyebrow. "Any worth knowing?"

"If I were Clancy I would take care. He has roused much ill feeling by these dealings with the Tong."

Lucy Lied

Isabel frowned at Clancy's back. "How would one bargain with such devils? Do you think he made terms with them over a pipe of opium?"

Rosanna Leese pictured the gunman's stern face, with the gray-green eyes never a degree above the temperature of the coastal waters. "It is Clancy's special gift, dealing with the devil."

"It's warm in here," Isabel said. "I'm bored."

"There are stockings in at the Mercantile," Rosanna said. "We should go now and look at them before they have been pawed over."

Isabel was about to agree when the chatter in the courtroom died and the judge reappeared. "They're coming back in," she whispered.

Judge Nearing assumed his place on the bench, smacked the desk with his gavel, and addressed the prosecutor. "Mr. Langley, call the next prosecution witness."

"Prosecution calls Sheriff Jedediah Taylor."

Taylor came to stand in the dock and obediently repeated the words of the swearing-in with his hand on the bailiff's good book.

Langley began. "Sheriff, on the tenth instant you arrested the man called Chinaman Joe for the murder of Flynn Talbott. Can you tell me, sir, is this the Chinaman you arrested?" He pointed at the defendant once again, extending the whole of his arm.

"Yes," Taylor said ceremoniously. "It is."

"Tell the court on what grounds you arrested him, please."

"Well, sir, Chinaman Joe wanders up and down the coast. Every few days he turns up at Point Alones and then a day or two later on the mud flats to the north; and then some time later he'll be back down south, sometimes as far as Point Lobos. He picks up stuff along the way wherever he goes, things people throw out mostly. He's a scavenger, like. He hauls his finds with him and makes a bit of money here and a bit there peddling the stuff to folks on the other end of his route. Anyhow, according to Dan Ortin, Joe came into town a couple days after Flynn Talbott was killed, with a piece of fancy patchwork he was fixing to sell at Ortin's store. Dan took a look at it and figured one of his ladies would probably snap it up right away and finish it out into a right nice baby quilt. So he bought it off Joe and put the thing in his window. There it stayed for near three weeks, when one morning Doc Garrett spies this piece of patchwork in Ortin's window and reckons he knows it. He goes over to take a closer look, and sure enough, he's seen that patchwork before. It's a scrap that Mrs. Talbott used to bind up an injury to her arm Doc had treated."

"Your Honor," the prosecutor paused to hold up a piece of patchwork, "this is the fabric taken from Ortin's store as evidence. Sheriff, is this the item Doc Garrett told you belonged to Mrs. Talbott?"

"Yes, sir, it is."

The defense attorney was on his feet. "Objection! Hearsay!"

"Sustained," Nearing groaned.

Langley's face registered nothing. "Continue your story, please."

"Well, ain't much left to tell. Garrett went on inside and asked Dan where he'd got the piece. Dan told him it came from Joe. Garrett come and got me. Said he thought there might be some connection between Joe and the murder."

"Exactly what did you think the doctor was suggesting?"

"He got me to thinking it might have been like this: Joe is coming south through the sloughs and takes it into his head to investigate Flynn Talbott's farm. Peddle some stuff there, maybe."

"Talbott's place is located where?"

"Off the coast road along by the Rincón De Las Salinas."

"Continue."

"Anyway, Joe comes up to the house and sees Flynn Talbott's wife in the yard. He decides to go talk to her, but she goes inside. He follows her into the house. See, Joe's not bright enough to know folks just don't go following other folks into their houses. Maybe he was just asking her for food or maybe he wanted to get friendly."

"Go on."

"It figures Mrs. Talbott ran into the bedroom where Flynn was just getting dressed. The Chinaman came on into the bedroom after her. Maybe he meant mischief toward Mrs. Talbott and he didn't think Flynn was still in there. But he gets scared when he sees Flynn take one of his belts off the wall. Joe has an abalone iron in his kit and pulls it out. He hits Talbott with it, once across the face, and then when Talbott wheels around he finishes him off."

"With a second blow to the back of the head?"

"That's right."

"Then what happened?"

"We reckon Talbott's wife ran off scared. She weren't nowhere on the place when we got there."

From his seat at Langley's table, Jason Garrett followed the pacing of the prosecutor. As an expert witness, Doc had testified in court often enough to find it routine, yet this time he was aware of the larger than average crowd of spectators, of their eyes upon him as he sat waiting to give his testimony. Blake was a pretty sharp customer. But Langley was no slouch either, so it didn't look like there was anything to worry about, at least not so far. It was troublesome, though. Garrett saw her in his mind's eye, that day on the beach, her fine hair blowing about her face. He hadn't been sure she was capable of it, not till he saw how that iron had stove in Talbott's thick skull. But he'd never dreamed she'd run away. Anyone with a lick of sense would have seen it was self-defense. She needn't have run.

And it was as if the Almighty had sanctioned his plan, the way Joe had gone straight for that patchwork blowing in the wind from where Doc had secured it on a driftwood snag that lay athwart Joe's route. It seemed almost as if the Almighty were saying, "Go on. Hang the Chinaman. It's just crazy Joe anyway. If the court whacks a few years off his life it ain't likely he's going to notice much." Garrett knew his old black mammy would say it wasn't the Almighty who'd spoken.

From behind the impenetrable veil she wore in public, Sally Locke watched Jason Garrett. He sat on the right side of the courtroom, the side closest to the jury. She watched him fidget with one side of his drooping mustache as he rocked his chair back on the rear legs. It was odd, she thought. He was, after all, accustomed to providing medical evidence in cases of death due to unnatural circumstances. She thought he relished this side of the job, in that he received a fee in legal tender for his time. But this case troubled him, she could tell.

Sally had a way of discerning more about people than she wanted to know. It wasn't just the secrets that men mumbled in their sleep or the truths that emerged from their wild eyes in the throes of passion. There were glimpses into the hearts of girls who came knocking on her door at first light, when the last of the clients had gone and she was ready for her own solitary bed. There were sharp-edged images of women thrashing away all their strength in childbirth and others in fevered delirium after taking the abortionist's concoctions. There were drunks with the gift of tongues upon them and the terminally ill, whispering at the last from the far end of a long tunnel. It was her fate to bear witness to all of these conditions, and to carry with her the knowing of other souls.

And so it was, looking at Garrett, she came to realize that this case was different for him, different from all the rest. What she saw was a face all closed, expression snuffed out. She knew the anguish beneath the frozen surface and discerned that somehow Doc was dangerously involved in a personal way. The trial was a backdrop against which his professional camouflage was, to her eye, slipping. To her eye, his anxiety painted him bright as an orange and black butterfly mounted on a pin.

Adrian Fiske sat in the first row of spectators, close enough to where Doc sat to hear him heave a ragged sigh. The melancholy was on him; that was clear. And with good reason. Even the painter had felt his own good cheer waning, from the moment he stepped into the close air of the courtroom and beheld the hapless Chinaman with his placid eyes and serene face, guileless as a shirt button. How could anyone assign malice to such a face? And how could the faces of the spectators in the gallery look so animated with anticipation, as if they were about to witness a spectacle that would fill them with surpassing joy? It seemed horribly distorted, an illusion that came of sitting in this tired, over-breathed air. He wanted to be outside next to the sun-sparkled sea where he'd often seen Joe plying the beach with the cat on his shoulder. Poor Joe, he thought, looking once more at the large, quiet hands that had so sweetly stroked the old cat. His hands, smoothly folded, lay one across the other flat on the table, as unmoved as the wood itself. Everywhere else the tension in the room was like that before a thunderstorm.

"Prosecution calls Doctor Jason Garrett."

Doc went through the testimony by rote: the disposition of the corpse, time of death, cause of death a blow to the back of the head by a pry bar, that same one entered into evidence.

"And this piece of patchwork," Langley continued, "are you familiar with it?" He grabbed the evidence off the table and held it for Garrett to examine.

"Yes," the doctor replied.

"Is it one that you gave to the murdered man's wife, Lucy?"

"It is."

The prosecutor thanked him and yielded the floor to the defense.

"We will take this opportunity for a brief recess before the cross-examination," the judge declared. "Witness may step down, but you will remain in court."

Chapter Three

Garrett left the witness box for his chair at the prosecution table, grateful that Langley had stepped out for a breath of air. He wanted to be left alone, to remember the thrill of that day.

He remembered climbing the stairs two at a time and pivoting around the newel post at the top, heading to the left, to the door of the room he used as an attic. He had been so afraid that she might run away. Talbott's redheaded woman seemed so wild, a doe with a broken leg. He threw open the lid of the old cedar chest. It had belonged to a great-uncle whose sidearm and boat cloak still nestled close to the bottom, beneath pieces of patchwork that were to have been joined together and stitched to batting and backing, but never were. Perhaps the maker of quilts had died. In any case, once the work was interrupted it was never taken up again. He moved aside a packet of old letters, one edged in black, and grabbed up a gray woolen blanket and one of the patchwork squares. These he carried downstairs, approaching the parlor doorway carefully and peering in. She was still there. "I've brought you something for a sling," he said, "and a blanket to wrap round you on the way home."

He laid the blanket on the divan and came to where she stood. "Turn around and hold your hair aside," he said. She raised her good arm, gathered the mass of red hair that hung to the middle of her back, and held it up off her neck. He caught her profile in the glass that hung on the adjacent wall. She stood like a savage goddess, with her white marble skin and finger-combed hair and breasts all but visible beneath the sweated cotton of her smock. He folded the patchwork square on the diagonal and passed the triangle under her injured arm. She quivered at his touch. "Don't worry. I'll be careful. Just a minute." As he knotted the sling, he glanced down the back of her smock and saw new welts sawing across the white flesh. His hands froze. He'd never seen a white woman with whip scars. At the sight of the stripes, he lurched back in time to when he'd first beheld a returned runaway wench facing her punishment. The two moments were meshed together now, part of his secret erotic life.

Garrett had draped the gray woolen blanket over her shoulders and watched her cross the porch and climb up onto the seat of the buckboard next to her loutish master. He warned Talbott, "I have business in the valley. I'll be calling by to check on her."

The Irishman never responded, but took the brake off his conveyance and turned the horse's head. She had looked around once to catch his eye, but then she was gone.

Doc had felt oddly peevish all the rest of the afternoon, but pulled out all of his old medical journals and busied himself reading up on female maladies. Over the next several days, he visited the other practitioners in the county to obtain texts on the subject and whatever observations their experience provided. In this way he developed a list of disorders which might explain, either one by itself or several together, the girl's inability to speak. The list included hysteria, uteromania, leucorrhoea, uterine hemorrhage, falling of the womb, cancer, spinal irritation, convulsions, haggard features, emaciation, debility, mania and a nervous condition known as *un triste tableau*. The uterus and ovaries, being connected to other organs by a network of nerves, were involved in most women's complaints. Further, many of these complaints were brought on by masturbation, the root cause of unhealthy excitement of the sex organs. He was hopeful that he might discover if a predisposition to this secret sin was evident in the shape of Lucy's skull. He had written away to order a china phrenology head from San Francisco, with twenty-seven traits clearly mapped to the glazed surface of the cranium. From the cranial map, he saw that a prominence near the nape of the neck could indicate the dominance of amativeness. The language area was in the lower ocular orbit. Lucy's troubles might stem from either of these regions. But prior to any definitive diagnosis he would have to take measurements of her skull with calipers and then compare his findings to the porcelain head. It was, without a doubt, the most exciting prospect he had entertained since coming to Monterey.

A rustle of people rising from their seats signaled the reentry of Judge Nearing. He assumed his seat and smacked the desk with his gavel. "Court will now come to order. Dr. Garrett, you are still sworn. Mr. Blake, you have the floor."

The doctor returned to the stand as the defense attorney, Mr. Blake, rose from his seat next to Joe and strode ostentatiously into the center of the room, his highly shined black shoes catching the sunlight that sparkled the dust in the air. "You say the time of death was within twenty-four hours of discovery of the body, give or take another four hours," he said, repeating the doctor's phrase without preamble. "Does that mean, sir, that you cannot tell the difference between a body killed fifteen minutes ago and one killed twenty-eight hours ago?"

Garrett stood straighter in the witness box. "Why, sir, it doesn't mean anything more or less than I stated. There was rigor in the limbs, lividity, and dried blood on the floor, none of which provides us with a precise measurement of the time elapsed since death occurred."

"If you had to be as precise as possible, would you say Talbott could have been killed fifteen minutes before he was found?"

"No. I would say a minimum of two to three hours had passed between the time of death and the time Steadman's boy discovered the corpse."

"Very well. The record should reflect that the doctor has altered his testimony. Now it appears that death occurred between twenty-eight and two hours prior to discovery, which would make it sometime between five o'clock the previous morning and seven o'clock that morning. Would you agree with that, Doctor?"

"Yes."

"Now, Doctor, the prosecution has presented this court with a story of how Mr. Talbott met his end. According to Mr. Langley, Chinaman Joe was passing in the area of Talbott's ranch on his usual walk from somewhere to the north of town to somewhere to the south. He came to Talbott's property and decided to walk up to the farmhouse, maybe peddling something or begging. Then he's supposed to have seen Mrs. Talbott in the yard doing chores. We can imagine him jabbering at her, and she being the skittish type, she fled inside. Now the prosecutor asks us to imagine that Joe followed her right back to her bedroom where her husband was still getting dressed. Isn't it true the deceased hadn't yet put on his pants?"

"Yes. His pants were still on the peg."

"The bed was slept in, so it could be assumed Talbott was getting up, not retiring?"

"Yes."

"Then, sir, it seems to me that we must again narrow your estimate of the time of death somewhat. Is it not reasonable, based on the scenario that the prosecutor has described, to state that death must have occurred between the hour Talbot got up and two hours prior to discovery?"

"I suppose so."

"Now when do farmers get up, doctor?"

"Before daylight, I believe."

"Yes. They rise before the sun. We can assume, I think, that since the Chinese laborers gathered at first light to begin their work on the land, Flynn Talbott was usually up for a couple of hours by then, taking care of the livestock and having his breakfast."

"I believe so."

"And Mrs. Talbott, would she have been out back at the stove making up the cooking fire at about the time her husband was getting dressed?"

"Yes, I think that's likely the case."

"And it's fair to assume that this was before first light?"

"Yes, I believe so."

"Then, sir, if it was dark and Joe was passing some distance away, how did the sight of Mrs. Talbott draw him to the house? How could he have made her out under the circumstances? Are we to suppose that the Chinaman is a creature of such a lascivious nature that Joe can smell an attractive woman and follow his nose to her?"

Garrett gave no answer as the defense attorney wheeled in front of the jury with his hand outstretched toward the Chinaman who looked on, uncomprehending but obediently attentive.

"Now, sir," Blake continued, "did you not also state in your findings that the blow that killed Flynn Talbott was inflicted by a right-handed person of about Talbott's stature?"

"I did."

"And that the blow to his face was inflicted first, then the one to the back of the head?"

"That's correct."

Blake let an expression of confusion dwell on his face for the benefit of the crowd, so they might too begin to feel that something was amiss. "That is to say," Blake said slowly, "that Talbott took a blow to his face and then turned his back on his attacker."

Doc nodded.

"But how is it possible, Doctor? If a man your equal in size came at you with an iron and struck you across the face with it, would you turn your back on him? Can anyone here imagine a more unlikely course of action? Would you not instead lunge for the weapon or your attacker's throat?"

"Are you asking what I would do in the circumstance, sir?"

"Yes. For the purposes of illustration, imagine that Joe was coming at you with this iron." Here he seized the pry-bar and held it up menacingly. "He's a big boy, exceptionally large for a Chinese. He strikes at you once, but not hard enough to break the facial bone below the eye. What do you make of that?"

"Sir?"

"Why, if he intends to kill you, does he start by playing patty-cake?"

Langley was on his feet. He had come to the belated conclusion that Blake was eating his expert witness alive. "Objection! The defense is calling for conjecture."

"I withdraw the question." Blake smiled, knowing that he had planted a powerful image in the minds of the jurors. Patty-cake, indeed.

"Now, Doctor Garrett, as the esteemed prosecutor has asked the court to disallow your thoughts on this question, permit me to speculate for you. I believe that if you knew there was a weapon, such as a gun, behind you that you could reach by turning around for an instant, then in fact you might risk putting your back to your attacker. Would you agree that this might explain Talbott's actions?"

"It would seem likely," Garrett replied cautiously, unsure where Blake was leading.

The defense attorney cradled his chin in his hand for a moment and appeared to ponder. Crossing the floor, he shared his mental processes. "But Talbott had no weapon to reach for—nothing behind him except that belt hanging on the peg, isn't that right?"

"I can testify to the fact that a belt was found clutched in the dead man's hand," Garrett answered.

"Yes, and we don't know whether he reached for it before or after he was hit in the face, but I suspect that it was after. Why else would he have turned his back? Why else would he have given the attacker the opportunity to hit him on the back of the head?" Blake let the shadow pass over his features again, as if he were on the horns of a dilemma. "How can we explain this? Why would he reach for a belt?" He paused and looked squarely at Doc, suggesting to the jury that Garrett must know.

Doc returned Blake's stony gaze, saying nothing, thinking with cold precision. *You know why! Because he'd used it so often on her and it always worked. But if you think I'm going to tell you that now you're wrong, you bastard. Maybe one day I'll whisper it to you in a quiet corner of hell.*

Blake was nothing if not a student of physiognomy. He read the doctor's face with satisfaction, noting the tightness of the jaw and the flare of color in the hollow of each cheek. He knew he'd struck a nerve, and knew that the jury saw it too, saw the doctor on the ropes, and were at that very moment asking themselves why he would act so defensive. Could it be he knew more than he was willing to say? "No more questions," he said contemptuously.

"Mr. Langley, have you any more witnesses?" Nearing asked.

"Prosecution rests, your honor."

"If the defense has no objection," Judge Nearing said peremptorily, "I suggest we take this as an appropriate point at which to recess for fifteen minutes. Court will reconvene at 2:30."

Starved for air and coolness, the spectators fled the courtroom en masse, leaving small personal articles to save their seats. The attorney for the defense rose from his seat and waited until he could safely speak without being overheard. "Mr. Clancy," he said, as the gunman stood to his full height and stretched.

"Mr. Blake," Clancy replied.

"After this adjournment the judge will call upon the defense to present its case."

"Things progress apace," Clancy observed.

"Where's the woman?"

"We haven't located her as yet."

"What? May I remind you that without the woman there is no case for the defense to present? I agreed to represent Chinaman Joe based on your promise to furnish her. Respectfully, sir, I should wring your neck."

"There are men all over the docks looking for her," Clancy began.

"You said it would be no problem," Blake interrupted.

"It won't," Clancy replied evenly. "I expect they have her spotted but are biding their time so they can snatch her clean."

"Oh, for God sakes. Observing the niceties, are we?"

Clancy bristled. "It's not your job to concern yourself." He paused to tamp down his anger. "Your job is to make sure the trial runs to another day."

"Extend the proceedings into tomorrow? With Nearing up there simmering in a puddle of sweat? He'll send this case to the jury as soon as we reconvene since I have no witness to call." Blake extended a hand toward the dock in exasperation. "I suppose you think I should get up on the stand and lead a sing-song?"

"I'll do it," Clancy said. "Put me on the stand." The gunman dropped his voice as a few spectators began to dribble back inside to assume their places. "I can testify to Talbott's character."

"Too thin," Blake said. "The pot calling the kettle black."

"It'll buy time."

Blake nodded and broke off the conversation. He turned away and sat down to wait for the laggard hands of the clock to come to half past. Finally Nearing gaveled the court back into session.

"Mr. Blake." The judge opened his pocket watch and placed it squarely before him on the bench. "Please call your first witness."

Blake stood and shuffled through a sheaf of notes on the defense table.

"Mr. Blake." Nearing peered down impatiently. "Let us get on with it." He inclined his head toward the jury. "I'm in no mood to keep these good people from their supper."

"By no means," Blake agreed. He seemed to have gathered his thoughts sufficiently. "Defense calls Matt Clancy."

A collective gasp from the gallery made manifest the amazement of one and all as Clancy rose and walked with slow deliberation to the dock. The bailiff brought the Bible. The gunman laid a hand on the Holy Scripture. As Clancy swore to the oath, mildly as you please, all eyes watched waiting for the Almighty to ignite a flame under his murdering hand.

"Proceed," the judge said, in that way that seemed to imply that so far he found the witness as boring as buckram.

"Mr. Clancy," Blake began, "please tell the court your place of residence and occupation."

"I hale from back East originally, as most of us do, I expect. For the past twelve years I have worked for the Southern Pacific, as was the Central Pacific when it started. I ran a crew laying rail through the Sierras directly after the war. More recently, I've been working in the San Joaquin as sort of an intermediary between the railroad and the settlers. I have a spread out in the valley between Monterey and Salinas. Used to belong to Felipe Vásquez till just recently. There's a shack near the highway they call the little house. That's where I've been living of late when I'm not away on railroad business."

"And what is the nature of your acquaintanceship with the deceased?"

"From time to time I come into Monterey for a bucket of beer and a bath. Stay at Leese's Boardinghouse for the night when I do. Oft times I play cards at some of the saloons on Alvarado Street. I first saw Talbott at the Washington Hotel. It's a fair game there, but filthy as a sty. You'd be best advised not to eat unless you fancy the green apple quickstep."

Blake waited for a burst of laughter to die down. "And how often did you see Talbott at the Washington Hotel?"

"A few times. Four or five."

"And Mr. Clancy, what did you observe about the deceased upon these occasions?"

"First off, that he was filthier than The Washington."

The crowd thoroughly enjoyed this remark and wouldn't quit giggling until Nearing gaveled them to silence.

Blotting his beaded upper lip with his handkerchief, Blake wiped away the grin he'd put on to signal his sympathy with the spectators. "What of Talbott's character did you observe?"

"One evening I was there and I heard Talbott bawling about how he'd just been up to San Francisco to settle a debt with some Mick. Talbott said he'd paid the freight for this fellow's sister to come out all the way from Ireland to marry him, but then once she got to San Francisco she'd fallen in love with another. So Talbott had to take a different woman instead. Charity case these Irish had taken in somewhere out in Utah. Brought her with them on the immigrant train. Talbott said she'd been working as a laundress on the docks. He said she was clean. I remember that in particular. All that soap and water, he said, as if it was some kind of a joke."

"Are we to gather from this story that Talbott got his wife, a redheaded woman by the name of Lucy, as payment of a debt?"

"So he said."

"Then, am I to understand that this woman's status was little better than that of a chattel slave?"

"I believe so."

"From your observations of Talbott, is there anything else you can tell the court about his character?"

"Yes, indeed," Matt Clancy said. "I observed him once to anger at another patron of the bar. Talbott had been droning on about his beet farm and how rich he'd be in five years. This other—sad to say I don't know his name—expressed some doubt that the profits would be as grand as Talbott claimed. So Talbott cracked him across the jaw with the butt of his whiskey bottle. The man was flung back off balance and Talbott seized him by the back of his shirt collar and drove his face into the bar so the man's open jaw came down full on the leading edge. The blow dislodged several of his teeth and produced a quantity of blood. That done, Talbott let him drop to the floor and warned all present that if anybody would raise a hand to help the poor sot Talbott would give him the same."

"Talbott was a fierce fighter, then?"

"When he sensed there were others at the bar more drunk than he was. Apart from that, I expect most of his ferocity was taken out on that woman he'd bought to keep his house."

"What more can you tell us about Talbott's conduct that you observed?"

"He was a one to bite. I remember he almost took off Monty Foster's finger that one time. Monty Foster's the barkeep at the Elkhorn Saloon."

"And what provoked this attack?"

"I don't know it was anything in particular. Just that Monty was a good talker and Talbott disliked him on principle."

"Talbott was quick to anger, would you say?"

"He could get into a fit of rage faster than a distempered dog."

"And so, is it likely that Talbott had many enemies in town?"

"Objection!" the prosecutor yelled. "Defense calls for the witness to speculate."

"I'll allow it," the judge responded, "provided Mr. Clancy adheres to observed fact."

"I saw a pair of drovers threaten Talbott with a whip one time," Clancy said. "They claimed he'd cheated them at cards. Another time it was the foreman of his labor gang. Talbott hadn't paid up. They settled their dispute outside. I don't know as it was by cash or by fist, but I do know not long after Talbott hired on a new gang of Chinese."

"So from your observations we might conclude there were at least three persons ill disposed toward Talbott, persons who might want to do him harm."

"Four, if you count Monty. He still has little use of that digit that Talbott nearly severed."

Blake stole a look at the clock hung on the wall over the judge's head. It was just past three. Still plenty of time to send the case to the jury unless he had another witness to call.

"Anything more for Mr. Clancy?" Nearing inquired.

Blake shook his head. "No, Your Honor."

"Does the prosecution wish to cross?" the judge asked.

"No cross," Langley said, half-rising.

Nearing pulled out a handkerchief and mopped his brow. "Mr. Clancy, you may step down. Call your next witness, Mr. Blake."

As he returned to his seat, Clancy glanced purposefully at Blake. Blake rose to his feet. "Your honor," the defense attorney began, "I must beg the court's indulgence. My next witness is not in court at this time."

Nearing scowled. "I can grant a ten-minute recess if that would help in procuring him to our presence."

Blake looked embarrassed. "I fear that would profit us little, Your Honor. My next witness is indisposed."

"Who is this witness?" Nearing asked.

27

"Monty Foster," Blake replied.

"The same Foster that Mr. Clancy testified was bitten by Flynn Talbott?"

"It is he," Blake replied. "His injury continues most vexatious and he resorts to ardent spirits to dull the pain."

"Am I to gather," Nearing sputtered, "that your next witness is still soused from last night?"

"Your Honor, I might take issue with your choice of words, but, in short, I must answer in the affirmative." Blake hung his head for a moment to give the judge time to savor his consternation. "If it please the court, I request a continuance until tomorrow morning. At such time my next witness will be in full possession of his wits."

Nearing folded his handkerchief. "Let the record reflect that the bench is entirely put out with the defense attorney, but having run out of patience on this sultry afternoon is inclined to accede to his request. Continuance is granted, but I warn the defense that insobriety will be entertained as an excuse only this once. Court is adjourned. We reconvene tomorrow at ten sharp."

Nearing smote the desk with his gavel and swept away in his robes, leaving the gallery wanting more.

Chapter Four

The spectators burst from the doors of the courtroom like floodwater through a weak spot in the dam.

Crevole Bronson was in haste to get to the newspaper office to scribble down his impressions of the trial's first day while they were still fresh. *Lawyer Langley offers lascivious motive for murder ... Chinaman Joe's inscrutable face typical of his race...* He'd expected to put the story in the paper due out at the end of the week, but now that there would be a second day of testimony he wondered if it wouldn't be worth a special edition. *Defense carves up prosecution medical expert... calls murdered man's character into question...*

Rosanna Leese and Isabel Vásquez joined the press of humanity headed toward the Calle Principal. Rosanna frowned in the expectation that her staff had taken advantage of her absence to shirk their assigned duties. "Come along," she said to her cousin. "Hurry up."

"Stop running. It's too hot," Isabel answered.

"Is that what I should tell my boarders when they want their dinner? Oh, I'm sorry, it was too hot. It's a good thing you are married to a *ranchero*. You have no head for business."

"Oh, really? If I were in charge it's the servants who would be running, not the boss."

Rosanna smiled. "Shall we trade places one day? I would like to see you in an apron serving breakfast."

"And I would like to see you servicing my goat of a husband."

"Is he doing any better?"

"No. He continues to weaken. Truth be told, Felipe needs me only to spoon laudanum into him."

Rosanna chuckled. "Truth be told, it's Ramón who sees to his needs. Am I right?"

"You disapprove of me, cousin? You think I should have stayed home today to hold the old man's hand?"

"Don't be absurd. I would have no one to sit with at the trial if you stayed home."

"What do you think? Will they hang the Chinaman?"

Rosanna considered the question. "It's down to who the jury likes better; Doc Garrett or Clancy. Which one would you choose for a champion?"

"You know I hate Clancy for stealing my land, so it would have to be Doc."

"But Clancy is the stronger of the two, I think," Rosanna said, in that thoughtful way of hers that made Isabel feel childish and naïve. "Clancy's eyes never flinch. When I look at the doctor's eyes I see small fish darting in dark waters."

"You don't trust Doc because he is handsome. He must have thin blood, I think. So pale. Consumptive, like a poet." Isabel grinned. "Do you remember those stories my mother used to tell us, about the ghosts who would find naughty children and steal them from their beds?"

"I suppose you'd like that," Rosanna replied, "if Doc Garrett stole you from your bed."

"What if I said yes? What if I said the idea heats my blood? Would that make you jealous?"

They crossed the porch of the boardinghouse and Rosanna opened the door before she answered. "Go upstairs," she said. "I will come as soon as I've seen to things in the kitchen. We will talk more about what heats your blood."

By the time Isabel was climbing the stairs to her room, Doc Garrett was leading Adrian Fiske toward their favorite saloon. "We should have gone by Jefferson," Fiske complained. "It's shorter. We are going to Simoneau's, are we not?"

"I'd rather avoid the herd," Doc replied.

"Ah. Stated with your usual benevolence toward your fellow man."

"My fellow man can kiss my foot."

"Unusually dyspeptic after your day in court," Adrian observed.

"I don't want to talk about it."

Adrian laughed.

"I amuse you?"

"Of course you do. Why else would I keep such sour company?"

"Exactly what do you find so funny?"

"All that steam blasting out from your ears. You think by not talking about it you escape the heat, but it's just not so. Talking will take your brain off the boil. You should try it."

"Why don't you leave me alone and go paint your infernal cypress tree. Or did you perform your daily ritual before the commencement of today's legal fiasco?"

"I did not," Adrian said, as they took the bend onto Polk Street. "I fancy painting the scene after dark this time. Supposed to be a full moon tonight. You'll be out howling, I expect."

Doc kept his mouth shut until they reached Simoneau's and then opened it only briefly. "Whiskey, Frenchie," he said as he and Adrian passed the patron behind the bar on their way to their usual table.

By the time the bottle and glasses were in front of them the place had filled up with others who'd come from the trial. Each new arrival seemed to seek out Doc with his curious gaze. Doc kept his eyes on his glass.

"You have a following, it seems," Adrian said. "Know any of them?"

"Husbands of some of the Methodist ladies," Doc said.

About that time one of the recently arrived made bold to speak to Garrett. He carried his drink to the table Doc shared with Adrian and knocked it back before he spoke. "Evening, Doc. I'm Silas Fletcher. Don't know if you remember me, but you came out to the place to see to our daughter that time she had the grippe," he said. "I was at court today."

Doc took his sweet time raising his eyes to Fletcher's expectant face.

"I just wondered," Fletcher continued, "why that Blake fellow made so much of the time Talbott died. What in tarnation does that have to do with anything? It don't change who did it."

"Seems like you'd want to ask Blake since he's the one who raised the issue," Doc replied.

The other men had edged forward to surround Fletcher, prodding him to ask this or that. "Seems like," he continued, "that defense attorney got the best of you."

"Well," Doc replied, with a grim smile, "we physicians are trained to fight injury and disease, not to spar with attorneys. You'll forgive me if I did no more than my training equipped me to do."

It was a fair answer, Adrian thought, yet he saw that it did nothing to win over the circle of men.

"So long as justice is done," Kevin Hennessy said, "I s'pect you need not regret the day."

This made Doc raise his sardonic gaze to the eyes of the man who had spoken. "Regret? Why should I? I daresay you and your ilk will continue to call me out in the dead of night to attend your ills and then pay me in fatback and shelled corn. It's nothing to me, is it, one way or the other."

Adrian observed a few hostile glances thrown back as the clutch of men melted away. "I don't think you endeared yourself with your comments," he said to Doc.

"It's of no consequence. They've hated me since the day I first set foot in this town. I can't say I care one way or the other. Why is that, do you suppose?" He sipped his drink and considered the situation. "You're more objectionable by far than I, yet they seem to bear you no ill will."

Adrian Fiske tasted the liquor and mulled Doc's statement for a moment. "They know what to make of me," he replied. "They know me as an artist and chalk up all my foibles to that one central aspect of my character. You, on the other hand, confuse them. You are allied with the Methodist ladies and act the role of an Eastern gentleman. You exhibit professional competence and sufficient manly charms to win you the exquisite favors of Sally Locke. All this serves to make you a paradigm of virtue in their eyes. Yet, you constantly seek the company of such a disreputable figure as myself. This leaves them in a quandary. They are left undecided as to which side of the blanket you belong on and this indecision causes them discomfort. Thus, you are unpopular; not one of the boys."

Doc Garrett recharged both their glasses. "To hell with the boys."

As Doc spoke, Sally Locke was making her way up the steep flight of steps leading to the front door of her house at the corner of Washington and Franklin Streets. The door was opened by her man Louis, a towering South Sea Islander with fierce tattoos, who stood by to receive her hat and gloves as she doffed them. "Please tell Rose to bring me a pot of chocolate," she said as she moved across the foyer to the apartment she occupied.

Louis conveyed the order to Sally's Chinese maid, adding, "Madame is tired."

Rose made the chocolate and put it on a tray along with an exquisite bone china teacup, a silver spoon, and an opium pipe. She carried the tray to Sally's door and noiselessly admitted herself.

"The court today was most interesting?" Rose asked as she set down the tray on the table in front of the green velvet divan where Sally sat fanning her damp face.

"He lives, at least for one more night," Sally replied.

Lucy Lied

Rose poured out and handed the cup of cocoa to her mistress. "You will go tomorrow again?"

"I haven't decided yet," Sally said. "If it weren't hot as the devil's blush in the courtroom I surely would, but ..." She shook her head.

"You wish to bathe?"

"*Pas maintenant,*" Sally said. "I'll ring." She went to the sideboard for the brandy decanter and poured a dollop into her chocolate as Rose withdrew. She sipped then put the cup aside and flung herself across her bed. She imagined how Garrett would behave if he were there, with his single-syllable responses and his smoldering looks. Nothing would coax him out of his dark mood, not cigars, cognac, nor any delicacy her kitchen could provide. When she took him into her bed he would forget himself in the act of love, and then sleep for a time only to wake in a cold sweat, terrified by a nightmare. *Why do I trouble myself over such a difficult man? Why does his absence cause me such discontent after ... how many years? Six, is it? I should have tired of him by now. Can it be that he has tired of me?*

She lay thinking until she could stand her thoughts no longer. Then she pulled the bell cord at the head of the bed. A moment later Rose appeared. "Yes, Madame?"

"You may prepare my bath now. I will be meeting the clientele tonight in the upstairs parlor. Set out that sherry that just came in and *quelque chose de délicieux. Du fromage et du jambon. Pralines, oui?* We will pretend we are back in New Orleans. This is a house of pleasure, *n'est-ce pas?* We must be gay. *Enfin, on droit faire un effort.*"

By the time Sally began her bath, Rosanna Leese had finished organizing the work of her kitchen staff and gone upstairs to the room where Isabel was waiting.

When Rosanna entered the second floor room she set aside for her cousin's monthly visits, Isabel Vásquez was sitting in her corset and shift at the table in the center of the room. She was reading the newspaper and idly twisting in her long, white fingers the string of pearls around her long, white neck. Behind her through the window, a string of heavy-bellied clouds labored over the dull bay, waiting to be delivered of squalls. Held at bay by an offshore breeze, they provided no relief from the unaccustomed heat that had settled over the land. On the table was a bottle of brandy she had brought to share with Rosanna.

Rosanna regarded the new bottle and smiled. "You play the naughty child, pilfering from your husband's stock when I have brandy at the bar downstairs."

"It isn't as much fun drinking your brandy. Felipe will fly into a rage when he sees this bottle is gone and accuse the servants of stealing. They know it is I who have taken the bottle, but no one will say so and get a worse beating for speaking against me."

"Felipe still sees you as the little angel your father promised him when you were only thirteen."

Isabel opened the bottle and poured two glasses. "What took you so long? I'm dying for a drink but I didn't want to start without you."

"You scruple at starting without me! Such a lady! I'm surprised you even touch the stuff."

Isabel grinned and raised her glass. "With the gusto of a hound at his dinner!"

They touched glasses and downed the liquor in one draught.

Isabel produced two cigars from the drawer of the sideboard and handed one to Rosanna. "We need a candle."

Rosanna reached into the pocket of her apron and took out a box of matches. "A good hostess always has a light."

Rosanna joined her cousin at the table. "Is there anything of interest in the paper?"

No. It is a week old. I have read most of it before. So, will Clancy dine with us?"

"He will. I sent bath water up to his room, but afterward he will meet us downstairs. He said it would please him to dine with two such ladies."

"I'm no lady." Isabel rose and walked to the dressing table mirror where she unpinned her hair. "Come, unlace me."

Rosanna loosened her cousin's stays, admiring the fall of hair, dark and shining as a raven's wing, flowing to Isabel's shoulders.

"I also read earlier that the mercantile has just received brand new cut-paper dress patterns—the latest styles from Berlin and New York and Paris. Perhaps you would like a new dress."

Isabel pulled the corset down and let it fall to the floor.

"I don't want a dress. I want to be the man." Isabel kicked the corset aside. Her eyes met Rosanna's in the mirror. "Have the seamstress make me a horsehair mustache and a pair of tight pants with a concha belt and high-heeled boots. Just like the old vaqueros."

Rosanna smiled behind her cousin's petal pink ear. "I don't think you'd like herding cattle. Those vaqueros, they stink like cow shit, you know."

"Maybe I would be a soldier, then, not a cowboy. I would go off to conquer new worlds. Like Cortez, Balboa ..." Isabel turned away from the mirror and dropped into a chair at the table. She filled their glasses again.

Rosanna joined her. She opened the newspaper and read out loud. "Listen to this. Dr. Morgan the metaphysician speaks of the effects of light on the body and mind. Swiss valleys where direct sunlight never reaches the people as they go about their daily occupation, have a hideous prevalence of idiocy and inhabitants who are deaf, blind, misshapen, or incapable of articulate speech. Do you know what this means? Felipe must have been raised in the shade!"

Isabel did not laugh. "You should not speak of *el infermo* that way. It's very bad luck."

"You surprise me, cousin. After all the bitterness you've poured into my ears about how your father was a monster for marrying you off to a man old enough to be your grandfather! I swear as Christ died for sinners, you look sad."

She bristled at Rosanna's mocking. "I never cared for my husband, but ... he struggles so. It's horrible. Frightening. You should look death in the face before you call me a hypocrite."

"I pray I'll be spared a lingering illness," her cousin answered.

"Better to be shot charging over a hill at the enemy," Isabel replied, recovering her high spirits.

But Rosanna was curious to see a remnant of sympathy behind her cousin's roguish smile. "I think you have grown to care for old Felipe over the years."

"Perhaps," Isabel said. "When I married I was too young to see the wisdom of the match. I had no thought of crops, cattle, the ruin that came with the droughts of '67 and '68. My father found for me the one don who would not mortgage my dowry land to the eyes. You're right. I cursed him for it. But that was before I saw my friends put away their satin dancing slippers and live out their youth on dirt floors."

"Well, this is a new tune from a bird I thought I knew well. Have you also forgotten how the old man turned out to be a fool who gambled away your land, that part with the creek on it? Does any of that ring a bell?"

One of Isabel's eyebrows arched with disdain. "I'll get my land back." She rose from the table and went to look out the window.

Rosanna laughed. "Get the land back from Matt Clancy? No wonder you've been talking about soldiering."

Isabel ignored her jest. "You'll see."

"You can ask him later on, over dinner."

"Let's say no more about the land until then."

As Rosanna spoke there was a knock. She sprang up to answer it. A black face appeared where she cracked open the door. It was her hired man, Sam. "Well?" she asked, nettled by the interruption.

"You said you wanted to know about Mr. Clancy."

"Yes?"

"He checked out after his bath."

"Do you know why?"

"He got a telegram. Said he was sorry to miss having dinner with you."

"See that his room is made ready for the next customer," Rosanna Leese replied before shutting the door. "Well," she said to her cousin, "it seems we will have to wait to sound Matt Clancy about your land. It would be railroad business, I expect. The

Southern Pacific sends him to evict settlers in the San Joaquin. Always a squabble over land."

Isabel raised her glass. "To the settlers. Perhaps one of them will shoot him for me."

Chapter Five

The evening brought a brace of salesmen from Saint Louis, a San Francisco journalist by the name of Parker who had come to Monterey to chronicle the Chinaman's ordeal, and an assortment of local revelers who made their way to the whorehouse, having drunk too much to go straight home but not having yet had their fill of adventure. The bewitching Sally Locke appeared in her usual style, that of the cultivated courtesan. She glowed with moist heat amid the admiration of her devoted clientele, her up-swept black ringlets set off by a dress in a particular shade of gold flattering to only one in a thousand women.

"Tell me, Mr. Parker," she said, lavishing her attention on the journalist, "what is it about the trial of a Chinaman for murder that brings you to our town? Surely there are plenty of the same in San Francisco to keep you busy scribbling."

"Oh, that there are. But I wanted to see the Old Spanish Capital for myself."

"Why, pray tell? You make us sound so musty."

"There's a persistent rumor that The Big Four have plans to run a rail spur down this way. Now that I've had a look around, I can't believe there's any truth to the story. Apart from your establishment, Miss Sally, the charms of Monterey can be appreciated within the space of a fifteen minute walk, after which one's shoes are thoroughly coated with dust."

"I hardly think the Southern Pacific would list my house among the advertised attractions in a travel circular."

"More's the pity."

From the corner of her eye, Sally caught a glimpse of Garrett entering the parlor. He looked unusually pale and drawn, his dark eyes cast as black hollows beneath his brow by the brightness of the chandelier. She put her arm through Parker's and walked him away from the gaggle at the refreshments table. "Let me ask you," she said, as they approached the window with its view of the moonlight on the distant bay, "do you think the Chinaman is guilty?"

"He'll hang, most certainly," Parker replied without hesitation.

"Because he had the patchwork goods belonging to the Talbott woman and was known to walk in the area of Talbott's place?"

"It isn't much, but it's enough when the accused has a yellow skin." Rose came around with the sherry tray as Parker finished speaking. He placed his empty glass on the tray and took a fresh one. "Not that I've got anything against the Chinese," he hastened to add, "but you see, Blake has offered no alternate theory of the crime. If he's to win an acquittal he must tell the jury a compelling narrative in which someone else delivers the fatal blow. Do you see what I mean? The defense must come up with a yarn that gains a foothold in the minds of the jurors, a story that gains greater credibility than that of the prosecutor. Only then will the defense establish reasonable doubt of the Chinaman's guilt."

"It's no wonder so many people find trials fascinating," Sally said. She took the reporter's arm again and turned to face the spot where Doc stood across the room. Feigning surprise at seeing him standing near the double doors, she excused herself to go and greet him. As she crossed the room, she made a point to stop by the pier glass to appraise her image.

A familiar voice sounded behind her. "You'd best beware lest you fall in love with your reflection like Narcissus."

Sally continued gazing as Doc stepped into the shining space enclosed by the gilt frame. "I admire not so much what God has given me as what I did with it by dint of my own cleverness," Sally said. "When I look in the mirror I see an entrepreneur, a musician, the female companion of a congressman at one time. A hundred years ago they would have dueled for my hand. But that would have been a different life altogether."

"You don't regret not marrying a rich man?"

"Trade my freedom for bondage? I hardly think so." Sally smiled and turned to face him. "My goodness, sir," she said in her public voice, "I did not think to see you tonight. It's well past your usual hour. Would you care for sherry?" Sally glanced at Rose who came around with her tray of drinks.

Garrett took a glass and sipped. "I must wait until dark lest my doings in The Badlands be seen and reported to the ladies of The Grove who provide for my housing. They would, I think, take offense."

"It's been dark for hours," she said lightly.

Garrett waved his wineglass toward the other side of the parlor. "What's this to-do about?"

"Nothing in particular. We received a case of inferior sherry. I thought I would have a party to get rid of it before I served it by mistake to someone with a good palate."

Garrett put down his glass. "I prefer cognac myself."

Sally shrugged. "I am not serving any, I fear."

"I'll take it in your rooms," he replied.

She left the parlor and went downstairs to wait for him in her apartment. A few minutes later he knocked. She opened the door herself and welcomed him with a kiss. "I am glad you came to my rescue. All the talk of the trial was beginning to bore me."

"It was a devilish day," he said. He left her embrace to flop across the green divan with one arm thrown over his eyes.

"You are not well?"

"Play me something," he said.

Sally sat down to the piano and leafed through her sheet music.

41

Lucy Lied

He waited for her to begin a piece, admiring that combination of disparate elements that made her so fascinating. This same wanton—who loved nothing better than a bawdy joke unless it was the undoing of some pompous Spanish don—played Mozart like an angel, with her back straight and her competent hands bent just so over the keys as if they were waiting for Continental kisses. How liquid she was, yet precise and contained as the measures she played, wasting neither motion, time, nor sympathy.

As she began one of his favorite sonatas, he rose and helped himself to her cognac. He paced and sipped while she played. He liked the feel of her green carpet under his boots, the way the pile kept an impression of his sole. "Louis took me aside when I came in tonight. Said you got a new shipment of cigars."

Sally raised an eyebrow at him. "Louis talks to you?"

"We're boon companions. Didn't you know"?

"It isn't like him to be anything but surly to the clients. He must want some free doctoring."

"Doubt it. He looks hale and hairy enough to pull down the pillars of Dagon's temple." Doc smiled briefly. When the thin smile went away it left his face looking quite bleak.

"Why are you so sad?" she asked.

"I was just thinking about a Negress worked in our kitchen, name of Althea, who made the best damn strawberry pie. Isn't any other pie I've ever had as good as hers."

"Is that why you come here? Because I remind you of the house slaves from when you were a boy?"

He recognized her sarcasm, but he was struck by the truth of it, how he felt at home with her. Sally often said things that were true, things mined from an atavistic capacity for witchcraft and second sight. He sat down next to her with his back to the keys.

"I come here for you," he said. He slipped his arm around her. She abandoned the ivories for his caresses. He hiked her skirt and stroked her long smooth thigh and her round rump. His lips brushed the top of one breast as he inhaled her perfume.

But she felt there was something perfunctory in his attentions. "What is wrong, *cher*?"

He rose from the bench and sighed. "I've been thinking of death."

"Death! But why? Are you—"

"You wouldn't ask why if you'd spent a couple years working in rail yards, tending to men who'd been crushed between cars or parted from their legs in some switching accident. Why, haven't you heard? Death's a popular alternative to surgery. Better than fixing up a man with stumps so he can knuckle his way ape-wise through the rest of his life. Death is the cure-all that never runs out or loses potency, the one thing I always carry in my black bag."

"So ... death comes to us all. There's no doctoring can stave it off forever. It has nothing to do with you."

"It's not that," he said. "Just the notion that a man's life comes down to sinews and phlegm and erections. What he had, what he did, what he thought—none of that matters."

She started playing again, knowing he would go on and eventually say what was really on his mind.

"When I was in medical school and playing too much with ether, I found myself at the end of my first year in danger of being chucked out—rustication. The dean called me into his office. Tried to set my moral compass to true north. 'There are those who come here because they have an abiding interest in the science of the body', he said. 'They want to know about the function of blood, bile, and lungs. They would ask the quintessential question—from what does life arise. Others enter here because they wish to alleviate the sufferings of their fellow man. They are driven to do good in much the way our clergymen are. Regarding these men, I have no doubt of their motivation to learn nor of their ultimate success as medical practitioners. But you, sir, are not a man of either type. And I fear for your soul.'" Doc flopped down on the sofa.

"It is not your soul that troubles you; it is only that the defense lawyer made you look like a fool today," Sally observed, with her usual candor.

"You're a marvel of understanding, Miss Sally. Your concern for my worried mind is truly touching."

Lucy Lied

Her hands came down on the keys in a jangling discord. "What would you have me tell you? Fast and pray and recite the rosary?" Anger heightened her color, beckoned him to take her to bed in that instant, which he did.

That night he dreamt of his old mammy's voice echoing up from the bottom of a recollected Sunday as lifeless as Spanish moss. *The Lord don't answer the prayers of the unrighteous, but the devil surely do.*

Chapter Six

They didn't wait for the cover of darkness, but came for her in late afternoon, just after she and Molly had returned from the laundry and were totting up the day's wages and Molly was talking about what to make for supper. Thinking back on it, Lucy realized that Molly had seemed uneasy, and her color had been a bit off. But as Molly was with child, her color was often off and her mood could swing from tempers to tears in the middle of darning socks. She had changed, Lucy had thought, far beyond the physical swelling of her belly. She seemed not the waggish girl of their time together on the immigrant train, but an anxious soul, aging fast with worry, always fretting about how they'd afford to feed a baby. Her husband Jess had quit his ship and had only odd jobs about the docks. He seemed content to live off Molly's laundress wages and was all too eager to take in Lucy as a lodger as it would increase his family's income without his having to lift a finger. "Jess O'Keefe knows a good thing when he sees it," he was wont to say, grabbing his wife under one arm and the redheaded lodger about the waist with the other. Lucy feared his drunken leering would mature to drunken advances as poor Molly came nearer her time. She was on her guard whenever Jess was in the house, but it came to her later on that she had feared the wrong one of the pair. It was Molly who'd betrayed her to the Chinese for twenty dollars.

Lucy Lied

Molly's face had been taut with expectation that day, but when the big men came through the door and seized Lucy up from her chair, Molly's expression was not one of fear, only irritation at their having made her wait. She had not called out for a policeman nor taken up the poker by the fire to fend them off. All she did was sweep the money that lay on the table toward her as if she'd just won a poker pot while the Chinese bound Lucy's hands. "It's five dollars more for the dress," Molly had said. "It's one of my best and hardly worn. I give it to her only yesterday as what she had on weren't decent to wear on the street." She'd seemed apologetic toward Lucy. "Didn't expect me to trade you straight up for that rag you was wearing and an old piece of patchwork, did you?" Lucy had thought it uncommonly generous at the time, even though Molly had doubled in girth since the day she'd last been able to fasten the buttons.

Molly had always had a way of exploiting a circumstance. Lucy recalled how they had met. After a stumbling fall she'd hit her head on the railroad track in Corrine, Utah, and passed out. When she came to, she found Molly in the process of stripping the gloves off her hands. "They're too small for you," Molly had said to cover her larceny. "See how they bind? Made you lightheaded. I saw you out here crossing the track when you fell. Come to help, I did." Molly had wasted no time in pulling the gloves onto her own freckled paws. "I reckon they fit me perfect. I'll take you to my people and you can ride the rest of the way with us if you let me have them."

The burly abductors forced two tablespoons of laudanum down her throat. After that Lucy had no memory until she came to, tied hand and foot in a closed carriage. She reflected on the jolting ride south that all of her roads seemed to lead to Monterey.

She had spent the time after her transportation pondering the prospect of being hanged, weeping frequently at the idea of it, wondering what her mother would think as she viewed the shameful ritual from her place in heaven, what poor Aunt Agnes would think if she ever found out. Fingering the garnet earring sewn into the hem of her drawers, she felt intensely ashamed that she had lost the mate, and cried fresh tears at the cruel judgment of the world that had despised her for enduring Flynn Talbott and now would kill her for having done him in to save herself. One of the Chinamen had sought to calm her, telling her in makeshift English that she was not the one on trial, only a witness. He'd eased her mind enough that she was able to fall asleep just before dawn for an hour or two.

By ten o'clock on the second day of Chinaman Joe's trial, she was in the courtroom, bonneted and swathed in a veil, seated between the two meaty Celestials who had brought her south. When Judge Nearing settled onto his seat behind the bench in a flutter of black robes, and smacked the gavel with a certain relish, her worst fears returned. She stole a peek at the prosecution table and saw Doc Garrett looking like hell. Pale and hollow-cheeked as a cadaver, he lacked only a hair shirt to fully portray a figure of fleshly mortification.

"Mr. Blake, you may proceed," Nearing intoned. "I assume you managed to find Mr. Foster in satisfactory condition to render testimony this morning?"

Defense council rose to his feet with the precise quickness of a dancer performing a familiar routine. "If the court pleases, the defense would like to call a different witness."

"And who might that be, Mr. Blake?" Nearing asked, looking over his spectacles.

Blake's words sounded over the noise of fans uselessly moving the heated air back and forth. "Defense calls Lucy Strang Talbott."

There was a collective intake of breath in the courtroom. Lucy felt the palpable change. *On the brink of disaster the very air seems to shrink away.*

The bailiff repeated, "Lucy Strang Talbott." The strong arms on either side of her lifted Lucy to her feet. All heads turned to regard the tall veiled form at the back of the courtroom.

"Witness will please take off her bonnet," the judge said, as if in answer to the collective desire of the packed house, "so that her identity can be verified."

She turned slightly as she lifted her bonnet and caught a glimpse of Garrett's eyes as her red curls appeared. She felt her heart pound against her sternum as she began her solitary walk toward the witness box. It seemed she would have collapsed but that her clothes buoyed her up. Stayed and stiff as virtue itself she moved forward with a resolve that defied the slackness in her knees. Aunt Agnes had said once, *If nothing else is left to a sinner there's at least the pride that came before the fall.* And she'd meant to ask about that, why Agnes had spoken of sinners when she professed no religion. Lucy's heart filled with regret, to think of what she might have learned. She felt tears building behind her eyes, threatening to stream down her hot face. But somehow she fought them back, unwilling to let the whole town see her cry.

In that moment of enforced calm it struck her that she was being called as a witness who couldn't speak. What man or woman could be condemned out of his own mouth if no words ever came forth?

The prosecutor shot a glance at the rival attorney as Lucy continued her slow march toward the dock. "Your Honor," he began, getting to his feet, "I protest the defense producing this surprise witness whom they have obviously kept hidden from the people. I request a conference in the judge's chambers."

Nearing raised a jaded eyebrow. "Mr. Blake?"

"Your Honor, this witness is well known to the prosecution. My distinguished colleague unfortunately made no attempt to find her. We will simply ask that Mrs. Talbott respond to questions as to what happened on the morning of her husband's death. I'm sure this line of questioning will come as no surprise to the learned counsel for the prosecution."

"Mr. Langley?"

"Your Honor—" He paused. The fragile string by which he held the judge's attention broke.

"Very well," Nearing said, glancing back to the defense, "Mr. Blake, you may proceed."

As she walked down the center aisle toward the bench, she made out a common thread among the whispered observations of the crowd. "Expect this is the first time she's ever been addressed as Mrs.—Flynn Talbott's wife, my eye." Lucy kept up her steady pace even as her heart cracked. *They begrudge me even that small courtesy.*

When she reached the dock, she peered blankly at the spectators' probing stares as if her own eyes had stopped functioning. She felt a wave of nausea but steadied herself by clutching the railing. She felt Garrett's eyes on her, too, willing her to return his gaze. She did not. Her gaze came to rest on another man, the one who sat behind the row of black-suited Chinese. Of all those present, his face was the one that seemed to hold some shred of sympathy. She marked his spare features and wondered who he was.

"Is the witness ready to proceed?" Judge Nearing asked.

She nodded once, definitively.

The courtroom clock ticked an ominous tattoo.

Lucy felt stifled by her lacing. Heat shimmered the air, coming in waves off a piece of hell heaved up and set down amidst them so each and every one of them—not just she—would have an inkling of what was in store at the end. She remembered Agnes again. *All got to die sometime. All got to die.* When the Bible was offered, she placed her hand on it, thinking what a strange and white hand it was, as if it belonged to someone else. She nodded at the bailiff as he repeated the oath for her.

The attorney before her seemed in no mood to mince words, but he marshaled an elegant slowness to inflect his speech with a note of pathos, almost gentleness.

Jason Garrett looked on with experienced cynicism and spoke to Langley behind his hand. "Good trial lawyer won't risk alienating the jury by bullying a widow. Acts like he doesn't believe in his own case even when the brief is tight as a Jew's purse strings."

"Mrs. Talbott." Blake hitched his thumbs behind the armholes of his vest. "I'm going to ask you some questions about the morning your husband was killed. You can shake your head to indicate no and nod to indicate yes, is that understood?"

Lucy nodded.

"Very well. The day in question is the twenty-third of last month. It that correct?"

A nod.

"You left home that day, did you not?"

A nod.

"And did you see the defendant Joe on your place that morning before you left?"

A shake of the head.

"You had seen him crossing the fields before on other occasions, but not that day, is that correct?"

A nod.

"Now, Mrs. Talbott, you took the train to San Francisco to visit with an old friend of yours, Molly O'Keefe. You had planned this trip for a while since you obtained the train fare by saving a little here and a little there from your shopping money."

A nod.

"I should explain, Your Honor, that the circumstances of Mrs. Talbott's visit to San Francisco were told to us by Mrs. Talbott's friend Molly. Molly also told us that Mrs. Talbott wasn't really just visiting, but planned to stay in San Francisco indefinitely. Isn't that right, Mrs. Talbott?"

A nod.

"The reason is that the deceased, Flynn Talbott used to savagely beat his wife." He glanced at the witness. "Let the court observe that the witness has not shaken her head to deny my statement."

"Continue," Judge Nearing said.

"Your husband beat you with his belt, isn't that correct, Mrs. Talbott?"

A nod.

"Did he beat you the morning of his death, before you left for Salinas to catch the train?"

Lucy lifted her eyes to the judge, the jury, and finally settled them on Doc Garrett.

"Mrs. Talbott?" Blake insisted.

She looked back at the defense attorney and slowly lifted her shoulders.

Blake frowned. "Mrs. Talbott, am I to take from that gesture that you're saying you don't know?"

A nod.

"Mrs. Talbott, may I remind you, you are under oath." Blake strolled toward the jury and then wheeled around. "Let me rephrase the question. Is it not true that on the morning of the twenty-third of last month as you arose to go about your morning chores, you angered your husband somehow? He threatened to take his belt to you, but before he could get the belt off the hook, you struck him a glancing blow to the face with a pry bar. You then struck him again while his back was turned—a much harder blow than your first one, this time to the back of the head—and this time you killed him. That is why you went to the train station—to flee the law. Isn't that right?"

Lucy stood pale as death and raised her shoulders.

"Oh come, come, Mrs. Talbott. Your answer is quite absurd. How can you not know? Were you not there? Did it escape your notice that your husband lay on the floor in your bedroom with his brains bashed in?"

Doc Garrett suddenly rose. "Judge, if it please the court I can shed light on Mrs. Talbott's quandary. Sir, this woman suffers from a malady of the mind which causes her to lose all memory of her actions or whereabouts—sometimes only for a few hours, sometimes for days or weeks. She has no memory of that morning at all. I suspect the only reason she knows she was on a train from Salinas is because she had a ticket stub. It's called amnesia." His voice gathered confidence as he proceeded along the well-known lines of clinical parlance. "I have been studying cases such as Mrs. Talbott's in recent weeks for an article I'm submitting to *The Southern Journal of Medical Sciences*. I believe her muteness is a symptom of her amnesia, that amnesia having resulted from a blow to the head, most likely suffered at the hands of her husband."

"Poppycock!" the defense attorney yelled.

"I would call Mr. Blake's attention to the work of a Frenchman, Paul Broca, a specialist in the anatomy of the brain who proved that a patient who received a blow to the frontal lobe of the left cerebral hemisphere of the brain was rendered speechless though he could still comprehend words spoken to him. In Mrs. Talbott's case the condition of muteness is complicated by amnesia brought on by violent shock. For substantiation of the relationship between shock and memory loss, I would refer the prosecutor to a number of recorded cases of amnesia among battlefield casualties—"

"Your Honor!" Blake interrupted. "Will the court please instruct Dr. Garrett to be silent!"

Judge Nearing wiped the sweat beading his brow with his handkerchief. "Mr. Blake, since we have a mute witness it seems like she's entitled to have somebody speak on her behalf." He adjusted his spectacles and addressed the bailiff. "Have her look at me."

Blake assumed his seat with evident annoyance as the court officer approached the witness and pointed toward the judge. Lucy turned her head and gazed at Nearing.

"Mrs. Talbott," he said. "I take it you have been under Doc Garrett's care from time to time. Is what he said about your memory true?"

She glanced not at Garrett but at the lank figure seated behind the row of Chinese near the defense table. His eyes connected with hers for an instant and then he leaned toward Blake and whispered in his ear. A tight smile appeared on the attorney's face.

Lucy looked back at Judge Nearing and nodded.

"So noted," Nearing said. "Mr. Blake, you may continue your questioning."

Blake rose. "Your Honor," he replied, assuming a patronizing manner, "I see no point in questioning Mrs. Talbott any further. A witness with an unreliable memory is really no witness at all. The prosecution will be the first to point that out. I would, however, like to make this point, as well. Whether Mrs. Talbott remembers striking her husband a deadly blow or not has no bearing on the fact that she committed the crime. The truth is, she had a motive for killing him, she had ample opportunity and she had the requisite size and strength to strike such a blow. It is also true that Mrs. Talbott fled the scene of the murder, an action which speaks much louder than any words. Additionally, she is right-handed, as we noted when the oath was administered and she placed that hand on the Bible. I submit that it is Mrs. Talbott who should stand accused of the murder of Flynn Talbott, particularly if one considers her flight from the scene of the crime and her obvious motive for the killing. In short, I move that the charges against the defendant Joe be dismissed."

A flurry of amazed chatter rose in the courtroom. Nearing beat his gavel to little purpose other than to increase the level of noise he had to shout over. "Silence! Silence in the court!"

In the witness box, Lucy kept her eyes lowered, afraid to confront the confusion she had created. She missed entirely the exchange between Doc Garrett and Mr. Langley, a short urgent discussion between the doctor's mouth and the prosecutor's ear. Langley's eyebrows contracted and he seemed to resist, but only for a moment. Finally he acceded to whatever it was Garrett urged.

Langley rose and addressed the bench. "Your honor, Counsel for the Defense may suggest anything he wants about the witness's involvement in this case, but what about that little bugaboo, proof?"

A furor rose anew amongst the spectators, each of whom appeared to be debating the issue with the person seated on either side.

Nearing hammered the bench. "I'll have silence or I'll have this court cleared!" The noise settled to murmurs. "Mr. Langley, do the people wish to pursue charges against Chinaman Joe in light of the defense attorney's contention that said charges should be dropped?"

"If it please the court," Langley said, "the prosecution agrees to drop the charges against Joe provided we may pursue the line of inquiry with respect to Mrs. Talbott opened by the defense."

Judge Nearing squinted through his thick lenses at Langley. "Mr. Prosecutor, I confess that it gives me pause to continue to question a witness whose mind appears to bear such a defect as amnesia."

"I will seek only to establish whether or not Mrs. Talbott should be considered a suspect in the killing of her husband. I feel that since the question has been raised in open court, we can do no less than this to determine whether new charges should be brought."

"I see your point," Nearing said. He sighed. "And how do you propose to establish this?"

"By means of a demonstration. If Your Honor pleases, Dr. Garrett has agreed to play the part of the murdered man. Mrs. Talbott will step down and take up the iron bar that was used to murder Flynn Talbott, thus reenacting the defense version of the fatal events of that morning."

Nearing squinted harder. "Doc, in your professional opinion is there any point in conducting this so-called demonstration?"

Doc rose to his feet. "It behooves us to see for ourselves if Mrs. Talbott has the physical capability to commit the crime of which the defense attorney has explicitly accused her."

Nearing ran his handkerchief over his sweating head. "Very well. I will consent to the demonstration. Mr. Langley, you may proceed."

Langley pointed to the murder weapon lying on the table in front of him and addressed Lucy. "Mrs. Talbott, please step down and pick up this pry bar."

She left the witness box and picked up the bar.

Doc rose from his chair and stood facing her. The bar sagged from her right hand.

"Now Doc," Langley said, "you must turn your back as we postulate the deceased did, to take his belt off a peg on the wall."

Doc turned around.

"Now when I count to three," Langley continued, "Mrs. Talbott, I want you to raise the bar and advance as if to strike Doc Garrett on the back of the head." He paused, giving the suspense a few seconds to build. "One. Two. Three."

Lucy raised the bar and took one step toward Doc. He whirled around and caught her arm at the peak of its arc, forcing it back behind her head. As he carried her arm out of the socket, the bar clanged to the floor. Lucy sank into the vortex of her skirts. Frenzy erupted in the courtroom. Women fainted, children screamed and men jabbered at each other about how she could "never a'done it," how they'd said so all the time. The judge banged his gavel to no avail.

Chapter Seven

Standing before the mirror in the front hallway of her home, Ida Fleming, Doc Garrett's housekeeper for the ten years he had occupied The Rookery, tied on her bonnet with misgiving. She felt she had been rash in agreeing to take in the Talbott woman, and was annoyed with herself at this latest evidence that she all too seldom took Garrett to task for his faults and acceded to his requests all too often. Still, Ida held it as an article of faith that one should never fail to do good works whenever the opportunity arose. But from the vantage point of a righteous, well-aged widowhood, it rankled to think Doc's motive in urging her to take in the hapless Lucy had more to do with fine features and red hair than with Christian charity.

Ida smoothed the grizzled hair on either side of her wan face and turned her piercing gray eyes on Lucy. "I hope that I can trust you to do as I say. You must, or I'll not keep you. Do you understand?"

Lucy nodded.

Ida wrapped her shawl around her bony shoulders. "I have to visit several of the Methodist Ladies before I go to The Rookery to clean the surgery. I'll stay until I've given the doctor his midday meal. Then I'll come straight home and we will eat. There are some scones in the pantry. You and Alice may have one each if you get hungry. I don't want you fiddling in the kitchen, though. No sharp things. I've left you a basket of stockings that need mending. Doc had said you should do no housework for at least two weeks while your shoulder heals, but you can still ply a needle. You'll find the light is good in the parlor. I expect to see you sitting there by the window when I come home. The stockings are for you, by the way, from the poor box at the church, if that will incline you to the task."

Lucy assumed her place by the window and began threading a darning needle as Mrs. Fleming peered into the glass again and adjusted her hat. "Alice," Ida called, "come here. I'm leaving."

A moment later Mrs. Fleming's sister appeared. She seemed a child at first glance, about the size of a ten-year-old with an abundance of radiant blonde hair, but Mrs. Fleming's sister was younger than Ida by only two years. In keeping with her childlike manner, Alice carried a doll whose smock of pastel blue matched her own exactly.

"Goodbye, sister," Alice said sweetly.

"Will you be all right with Lucy?" Mrs. Fleming asked.

"Oh, yes. We'll make friends. I think Lucy is very pretty."

"Yes. Pretty is as pretty does." Mrs. Fleming's face hardened but softened again as soon as Alice threw her arms around her waist.

"We'll miss you, sister. Come back soon, will you?"

Mrs. Fleming kissed the top of the childish head and then left by the front door. Lucy saw her pass down the walk and waved, but Mrs. Fleming did not look up. Lucy took up a black woolen stocking that was about the right size, but entirely without a heel and began to stitch around the gaping hole. She was aware of Alice gazing at her from the front hall, but pretended not to notice. Mrs. Fleming's sister was very odd and her company made Lucy distinctly nervous. Mrs. Fleming had explained that Alice's stunted growth was the result of a fever that struck her when she was a babe in arms. "Later it become apparent," Ida Fleming added, "that Alice had also suffered some mental impairment." But to Lucy, tiny Alice seemed bright and then some. Within an hour of Lucy's arrival as a guest of indefinite tenure, Alice had shown a wild and mischievous streak of which her elder sister seemed totally unaware. By nature, Alice was gifted in the art of deception, of that Lucy was sure.

From her watch station in the hall, Alice stamped her little foot to make Lucy look up from her darning. "I don't understand," she said. "My sister says you are a tool of the devil and that's why you can't speak. But she says singing and dancing are tools of the devil, too. It doesn't make sense that being quiet and making noise should both be evil, does it?"

Lucy glanced up from her needlework as Alice crossed the room to stand at her knee.

"Tell me!" the blonde imp demanded. Alice threw her rag doll on the floor and stood with her tiny fists on her hips. The wrinkles that etched her crone's face were deepened by a fierce frown. "You know but you just won't tell. You're mean!"

Even though she stood barely four feet tall, the furious little thing was a fearsome sight. "I'll tell *you* something," she said with an evil grin. "My sister says you're Doc Garrett's friend and that he has to take responsibility. She said he should marry you and take you to live with him at The Rookery. That's what they call the surgery. Do you know why they call it that?"

Lucy shook her head.

"Because of the ravens," Alice replied, relishing the words. "A whole mob of them roost on the roof. They're big black birds, black all over. Even their gullets are black. Did you know that?"

Lucy shook her head again.

"There was another doctor who lived there before Doc Garrett," Alice went on. "His name was Old Doc Battle. He passed away—that means he died—one night in his bed and the ravens got in through the window and pecked his eyes out!" She grabbed the doll off the floor and stabbed at the button eyes with her finger. "Peck! Peck! Peck!"

Lucy put aside her basket of socks and took the doll away. She shook her head firmly at Mrs. Fleming's sister.

Alice looked dumbfounded for a moment, then her crone's face puckered up and she began to wail. "My dolly. Is she hurt? I didn't mean to hurt her."

Lucy put her arms lightly around the aged child and whispered "Shh, shh, shh," in her ear.

Instantly her tears vanished and Alice brightened. "There!" she said. "I knew you could."

Lucy let go of Alice and put a finger on her lips.

"I won't tell," Alice said. "I promise. Cross my heart." She sat down in front of Lucy. "We'll be friends now. You can hold Martha."

Lucy clutched the doll to her breast and smiled at Alice.

"Not that way," Alice said. She grabbed the doll back and laid it in the crook of her arm. "Like this. Ida says you have to support the baby's head. Did you know my sister brings babies into the world? She attends all the mothers when their time comes. I sometimes go along because I shouldn't be left alone. Now that you live with us, I won't have to go to any birthings anymore. We can stay here and you can tell me stories while Ida's gone. Ida says you know all about that man who was murdered. You can tell me about that."

Lucy dropped her eyes to the carpet to hide a flush of mortification. The thought of the trial still stung, the wretched things people were saying. Every moment she felt like a skater in the middle of a frozen lake who hears the ice cracking. When would the sheriff come pounding on the door with fresh accusations? How long before she would be dragged away to a dank cell? Who would come forward to save her the next time? Doc Garrett? She found his evident ardor alarming. There was about him something akin to the bald cruelty of men like Flynn Talbott. How easily he had wrenched her arm from its socket. It made her shudder, though she knew he'd done it to save her life. Doc's menace was cloaked in soft manners and a clinician's cool polish, but it was there all the same, hard as the pit at the center of the peach.

Who would bring doom crashing down? Would it be the green-eyed gunman whom people despised for being friends with the

Chinese? She found, examining the question, that Clancy was one of the few men she *didn't* fear. What did it matter to him who'd really killed Talbott, now the Chinaman was cleared? She remembered the way he had returned her gaze in the courtroom, how their eyes had touched. She found, all logic aside, a belief lodged firmly in her heart that he was perhaps the one person in the world who might understand if she were ever to tell the truth about herself.

She felt Alice's arms around her neck. "Don't be sad," the wizened child said. "I won't let anything bad happen to you. We'll be friends."

A sob escaped Lucy's heaving chest. It had been so long since anyone had held her or spoken words of comfort.

Alice stroked her hair. "There, there. Don't cry." When the sobs subsided, Alice offered Lucy her doll again. "Here. You may have Martha for a time."

Alice's tiny hands offering the doll made her think of Aunt Aggie's sugar tongs. That day she and Ellis and Old John had first arrived, Agnes poured out three cups of tea from a gold trimmed pot that matched cups as thin as soap bubbles. Ellis took a cube of sugar in the tiny silver tongs shaped like a squirrel's hands and dropped it into his tea as if he'd been reared with royalty. Agnes stirred her cup. She spoke to Lucy. "Drink it while it's hot. It's good for you, especially after a long journey." Lucy remembered holding her cup with two hands to keep it from floating away.

Lucy got to her feet and turned her back to Alice. She wiped her tears with the back of her hand and tried to tamp down the riot of emotion that the kind words had stirred. Not since Aunt Aggie had she felt a gentle hand stroking her hair. Except for Ellis. Her spine stiffened. *I won't think of him.*

Lucy settled back into the chair next to the window, where a pale square of weak sunlight shone in. The unaccustomed heat of Indian summer had broken and the skies over Monterey Bay that morning were gray and chill. They'd need to be lighting a fire soon, she thought, as she picked up her needle.

Sewing was different from milking, less forgetful. There was always the danger of making a stitch too long or tangling the loop of thread that followed the needle. The muscles between her shoulder blades tightened. Each stitch was a small piece of time that she had to push through before she could gain a reprieve from the pain at the base of her neck. She pretended she was milking, drifting into a daydream listening to the gentle plink of the milk squirting into the pail.

Lucy remembered her stepfather Old John Rafferty saying, "The side of a red cow is hearth and home to the girl." She pictured Rafferty's shaggy beard and his great square head, the scorch mark on his brow where the lightning had struck him. *We all bear the signs of our acts.* She remembered tracing with her fingers the hard leather sign on the cow's haunch where it had been burned with the owner's mark. She felt tears start in her eyes, thinking of how ill it had been used and at such a tender age. *Poor girl. Just like Hester Prynne.* She felt that if she could look in the mirror and see her own soul she would find a brand of shame there as well.

"Shall I sing you a song?" Alice asked. "Here's one I learned from some girls who came out to the tent camp this summer." As Lucy listened to the sweet, pure voice she realized the song was one Molly used to sing on the docks, a right bawdy song at that.

She thought of Molly with a pang of longing. Molly would not hear of reticence or timidity, or even decency for that matter. She used to sing her songs while they were at their laundry tubs, elbow deep in the gray water, scraping the garments of sailors against the washboards. "Just get the crotch," Molly would say. "The soak will clean the rest good enough." Molly would sing louder when there was a boy she fancied idling about.

With kisses and compliments, to her he said
Good morrow sweet honey thou well favour'd Maid,
I think myself happy, I met with you here
As you are a Virgin, and I a Soldier.

Lucy smiled to think of how the boys colored up when Molly spoke to them. "Say what you lookin' at? Hopin' for a bit of leg?"

And she'd hold up the sodden cuff of a pair of drawers and wave it, flicking the suds at them.

She wondered what Molly was doing at that very minute. Had the child come yet? Cramped it would be in her tiny lodgings if the husband was still around, if he'd not gone back to sea. Perhaps Molly would let her stay just one more time, just for a few days until she could find a place of her own with some other girls.

Alice stopped in mid-verse. "You sing too," she said.

Lucy gave Alice a wistful smile and shook her head.

Chapter Eight

On the way back to Monterey from Badillo's rancho south of the Rio Sur, Doc made another call that put him back at The Rookery half an hour late for the noon meal. He left his hat, coat and bag in the front hall but carried a laden flour sack into the kitchen, where he found Mrs. Fleming at the stove stirring a steaming pot. The housekeeper patted the back of her head to make sure no stray hairs had escaped from the tight knot at the nape of her neck. He recognized the gesture. It was what she did whenever she was annoyed. "Sorry I'm late for dinner."

"Shall I dish up? It's beef stew."

"Go on." He put the flour sack on the table and dropped into a chair at the place where the housekeeper had set out a glass of water, a large spoon, and a gingham napkin folded into a triangle. He leaned back and stretched his long legs under the table. "Sorry I'm so late home," he repeated, thinking she still seemed nettled. "I had to stop in to see the Brooks boy. He always seems to have something."

"The mother's Italian," Mrs. Fleming said. "They say north and south European stock don't mix well. That's why the child has a weak chest." She ladled the stew from a cast iron pot on the back of the woodstove into a soup plate held in her hand by the hem of her apron. After she set the plate down in front of the doctor, she took the stew pot off the stove and left it on the drain board to cool.

"Then on the way home, the horse knuckled back and came up lame." He chewed on a stringy chunk of beef and swallowed it mostly whole before he spoke again. "I had to walk him the last couple miles."

"Drink will do that," she said. "Clouds the vision and judgment."

"Horse hadn't been drinking, near as I can tell. Old plug just has a knack for finding squirrel holes."

"I'll thank you not to take a flippant tone with me," she snapped.

"I, on the other hand, had a shot of corn liquor with the boy's father. One shot, which is widely regarded as healthful for the digestion, not that it's any of your business. It was that or come away without a fee of any kind."

She nodded toward the object on the table. "It appears you received something for the larder, God be praised."

"It's a wheel of goat cheese."

"Ah, that would be from Ernesto Badillo." She lifted the edge of the sack where it opened and peered inside. "It smells disgusting. You should have left it in the shed."

"I bet you'd find it delicious if a Methodist had made it."

"You're right in thinking I dislike Badillo. He's Romish and a winemaker besides."

"What's that have to do with his cheese?"

She sat down opposite him and raised her chin once as if her white collar was too tight. Looking down from her drawn-up rectitude, she was the living likeness of the figure in profile on the cameo at her neck, the straight-nosed, empty-eyed goddess with tight carved curls. "It's the animal I don't like when it comes to his cheese."

"You don't like goats?"

"Never did. It's their eyes. The pupils are black boxes. Surely you've noticed."

"I tend to people, not animals."

"If ever you looked into the eyes of a goat you'd know what I mean. Even a man such as yourself."

"A heathen?"

"One who's not been saved."

"What is there to see in the eyes of a goat, Mrs. Fleming?"

"The devil staring back at you."

He couldn't restrain a smile of amusement at her devils and such. "Some say that of cats, that they're possessed by Satan."

"That's an old wives' tale. It worries me that you have no compass in these matters."

"How is one barnyard creature more evil than another?"

"Cats are clean animals, for one thing. They wash themselves. Another thing is they rid the household of mice. But the goat is a lustful beast. It wears the horns of Satan and has cloven hooves and sits on the left hand of God."

"Cows have horns. Are they satanic as well?"

"Scripture does not warn us of cows."

With each bite of stew he sank a little lower in his chair. As he relaxed, his Southern drawl intensified, the words coming out thick and slow and beguiling like the center of a dark chocolate truffle. "My dear Mrs. Fleming, I wish I could believe that evil in the world were so easy to identify. Think how simple it would be if all a body had to do was avoid goats. But it ain't like that. Good people can unwittingly do bad things as easy as bad people can. Or a good deed can spawn an evil one, like as not. And sometimes it's just an accident, like if I was struck by a falling rock coming up the coast road where an evil person had rode a thousand times unharmed. Justice is a fickle dame, and blind."

"Surely you don't believe that."

"Why would I say it if I don't?"

"To annoy me. It amuses you to deride my faith."

"I don't deride your Methodism. In fact I admire it. If evil could be eradicated with a scrub brush, your sisterhood would have rid the world of it thrice over."

"The faith is a joke to you. Always a joke. It's childishness and impudence. I tell you without faith there is no hope in life, no real foundation for home and family. Have you ever asked yourself why it is you're a bachelor at your age? Because you won't stop joking long enough to face up to any sort of purpose."

"I stitch up broken pates and set bones and dose gout and consumption and whooping cough, and am paid for my pains in eggs and potatoes and *cheese*. My cures are brutal, almost worse than the complaint. There enters into it little kindness and less science, but I face up to my purpose, as you call it, every Goddamn day. That's not impudence talking, just the stone cold simple truth."

Feeling in low spirits, Doc stormed out of The Rookery and bent his steps toward Adrian Fiske's quarters on the third floor of the French Hotel. Upon answering the door, Fiske took one look at him and asked, "What in tarnation's wrong? You look like you were killed yesterday."

"The old biddy is more irritating than usual today. I expect the Methodist ladies are ready to give me the ax. And I'll be damned glad if they do. I'm sick of being lectured and interfered with. How any man could have been married to such a nag without everlasting regret is a mystery to me."

Adrian grinned. "You and Ida Fleming are worse than two cats in a hopsack."

"Shut up."

Doc sat down at the table while Adrian rustled about for a bottle and two clean glasses. The apartment was peculiarly cozy, although it was a big barn of a place that could have been let to a dozen tenants. For its exclusive use, Adrian paid a dollar above the going rate. A legendary spendthrift in his younger days, he had given his attic an air of opulence that made Doc imagine the private quarters of an Arabian prince. There was bright sheer fabric patterned in gold draped over the corners of almost everything, objects of hammered and engraved brass, and buckets of iris or lilacs or forsythia, depending on the season, mingling their fragrances with the pungent smell of turpentine. There was an apothecary chest with drawers full of pigments: malachite dust, powdered lapis, earths from pink to gold. Under a ram's head with curling horns like Capricorn stood a tall armoire Adrian had decorated with a scene of Roman ruins overrun with sunspots and wisteria. There were books punctuated on the shelves by amputated plaster limbs—a hand off at the wrist, a foot truncated at the ankle. Pinned and propped and stacked about were the paintings, going back to before the whales went away.

Adrian joined him and poured a modicum of spirits into the glasses.

"No one would accuse you of liberality," Doc said, accepting his share of rum.

"Pour for yourself, you ingrate."

"Your allowance late?"

"Not late. Reduced, it seems. Had a letter from my sister. Very apologetic. They've not been very astute at managing the farms of late. My brother has gambled away most of what we get from the tenants. Dire predictions of want are the order of the day. My personal version of the Depression of '68."

"No chance of your getting rid of those moth-eaten green slippers, then."

"I fear not. Still, I might sell a painting. You never know. Then I'll entertain you with Turkish coffee and we'll sit like princes on curly fleeces on the floor, and play chess on a board made of ebony and the iridescent wings of a particular blue butterfly found only in the Amazon."

From his seat at the table by the window, Doc stared out past a coral mass of climbing bougainvillea. Beyond, the bay stretched like a gray cat across the sill. "You and I've both come to a pretty pass."

"That's what you said the first time I met you."

"I didn't even know what I was talking about then."

"I suppose this means you'll retreat to your attic and drink yourself into a stupor."

Doc tossed back his rum and grimaced. "It would do me good. I hate to waste a powerful sense of indignation, but I think this time I'll pass."

Adrian put down his glass and stared across the table at the morose face he knew so well. "I don't believe it. Wronged and yet committed to sobriety? Why, pray tell?"

"I won't give 'em the satisfaction."

"Who?"

"The damn Methodists." He slapped the table with the flat of his hand for emphasis. "Think they know more about doctoring than I do. Think they can judge my methods and my character. I'm sick of it, I tell you. I've had holier-than-thou crammed down my neck since I could walk and I won't take it here, not from a bunch of withered, hymn-singing bitches."

"Why, I believe what we have here is a full-blown bout of misogyny," Fiske said. "All because of a red-haired gal who's mute and likely mad as a March hare."

"What do you mean by that?"

"You been in an evil temper ever since the trial."

Garrett scowled and considered his friend's assessment of his mood, but refused to acknowledge it. "I don't know as she's mad," he said, "but that leaves an open question as to what she *is*."

"Sorry?"

"The Talbott woman. She might make a rewarding subject of inquiry. Physical manifestation of a mental weakness. It's often the case in women. The womb and its functions drain vital force from the brain, which, as it happens, is smaller than in the male, so less able from the start. I could write it up along those lines."

"Ah! On about the journalizing again. Why is it a particular point with you?"

"My father was something of a writer. It gained him a wider acquaintance than you'd suppose for a small town practitioner, even outside the Confederate States where he was something of a hero to begin with."

"How so?"

"When Sherman was marching through Georgia, my father hung up quarantine signs on the outskirts of Macon. Smallpox, I think. The ruse diverted the Yankees and Macon was spared any damage, save one stray cannonball that pierced the front window of a spinster on the east side. He was garlanded with laurel for an act of sheer cowardice."

"Would that all wars could be fought so sensibly."

"Indeed."

"So I take it you're determined to write about Flynn Talbott's wife?"

"It's either her or something about the surgical cases I had while the insurance company had me investigating railroad accidents. There's been nothing along those lines apart from discussions of hospital gangrene among the Confederate armies." He sipped and mused. "I only hope my straitlaced housekeeper doesn't stand in the way of my getting a good look at her."

Adrian was interrupted in the process of shaping a saucy rejoinder by a loud knock. He opened up to find a spur-booted rider with an urgent look on his brown face. "*Busco el médico*," the vaquero said.

Garrett rose. "I am the doctor."

"You must come to El Llano. Don Felipe, he is very bad."

"I'll need my bag," Garrett said, reaching for his hat.

"I went to the surgery first. Your missus said to come here. She gave to me your bag," the rider explained. "*Por favor.* We must hurry."

Chapter Nine

In no time he was in the saddle, chasing the vaquero downhill. On the rutted streets, they slowed to a more cautious pace, but once beyond the edge of town, the Mexican touched his horse with the savage rowels of his spurs and lit out across the open country at a dead run. Doc quirted his mount and followed.

He wondered at the urgency of this request for him to attend. Don Felipe had been ill for a long time and it came as no surprise that finally he was dying. The first symptom was a palsy that had begun in the hands. He could no longer write. Then he could no longer hold a spoon. His gate had become unsteady. He took up using a cane, then two. Then the strength in his arms failed and he had to rely on a field hand to carry him from his bed to the chair by the window or lift him onto his chamber pot. The last time Doc had seen him, maybe two weeks before, a white nightdress tented bones so poorly fleshed that they seemed about to pierce the cotton.

They raced under the gray scudding clouds along the Salinas Highway within the shelter of the round-shouldered blond hills. The Rancho El Llano Soleado was east of the highway with the hacienda at the extreme north end. He spied bony cows with Felipe Vásquez's mark on their flanks grazing on the dry yellow hillsides. On the west side of the highway there was a stream with a swath of green on either side. It had been Felipe's land once, before the don lost it in a bet to Matt Clancy. Fully half his land he had wagered—the part with the water.

A half mile farther on, Doc passed a shack at the side of the road. With only one room, one window and one door, it was aptly called the little house. Everyone called it that. So many miles past the little house, they would say. He wondered who had built it and why. It seemed a pleasant place, shrouded in live oak trees with one stately sycamore at the southern end.

Not so long ago Felipe would have been sitting at the window of his room watching for the arrival of his doctor and chess partner. He would always make fun of the horse. "I saw you coming. I could tell it was you from the way that bay horse of yours tosses you up in the saddle every time its right rear hoof hits the ground. I think you must have a sore rump after such a ride." The old rancher would smile lopsidedly. "I'll sell you a good horse, a Paso Fino. It moves like a soaring bird. You know, the pain is not so bad today." There were times Doc had dared to hope maybe the disease was on the wane. Maybe it would leave the old man's body like fluff blows off a dandelion, obeying some natural law of its own.

The vaquero didn't slack the pace until they reached the placita of the hacienda. Doc got down off his horse and handed the reins to his escort. He unlaced his bag from the saddle and went straight inside unannounced. He was greeted by the sound of a scrubbing brush rasping back and forth across the wide plank floor. Barely visible in the dim interior, the old serving woman Consuelo was at work on her hands and knees. "*Abuela?*"

"*Sí.*"

"*El enfermo?*"

She rose painfully to her feet before answering. When she faced him she jerked her peaked nose to indicate the ascending flight of stairs. "Up there. But you are too late. She's killed him." Her scrawny hand reached out and grabbed his arm. "It's his blood I'm scrubbing off the floor. His blood. Right there. She murdered him, I tell you."

The arched brows and hooded eyes of Doña Isabel Francisca Vásquez de Costa glared down from the landing on the assemblage of brown wrinkles. "Consuelo! How dare you tell such lies? How dare you accuse me falsely in my own house?" She turned her gaze to Doc. "He fell. I left his bedside only for an instant. I had no idea he had the strength to pull himself to the top of the stairs."

The old woman pointed a crooked finger up at the smooth pale oval that hung above her like the face of an offended angel. "By the blood of him who lies dead, she is a liar. Don Felipe draws his last breath because he has a treacherous wife."

Isabel called out, "Ramón! Ramón!"

"See his blood on the floor," the old woman said. "And what did he ever do to her? Crack a cascarone over her head and shower her with gold dust. And in return she killed him. See the blood on the floor. The blood does not lie. There is truth in the blood." She latched onto Doc's arm with her wizened claw of a hand. "You were his friend. You see his blood on the floor."

A young man rushed in from the back of the house. He looked up at the lady who kept her place at the top of the stair. "Señora?"

"Ramón, take this *bruja* away. Take her to the road. See that she leaves the rancho. Tell her never to set foot on this land again."

The old hag clung tighter to Doc as the young man approached. "Let go, *abuela*," he said. "There is no place for you here anymore."

The old woman clawed at Doc's arm. Her voice rasped his ear. "The blood. The blood." The young man pulled her away.

"Go! Leave my land!" The mistress's words split the air but the aged Consuelo stood her ground one last time.

"I curse you," the crone said, as if remembering an ancient incantation. "I curse this land. The lambs will be born dead. The cattle will drink nothing but dust. Their bones will litter the hillsides. This land will bring you only days full of pain and nights full of bitter regret."

"Take her!" Isabel cried to the young man. "Now!"

Consuelo crumbled into her rusty black skirts without further resistance.

"And then finish cleaning the floor," the señora added, regaining her composure.

Doc crouched and touched a finger to the middle of the pool that had not yet been scrubbed up.

The lady on the stairs spoke impatiently. "I apologize for this scene." She waited for him to assure her it was nothing. He continued to study the blood. "What are you doing?"

"Examining the disposition of the blood."

"If you would hurry you might be able to revive him," she said. "He'll call for the chessboard and you will play with him until he sleeps. Just like always."

Doc finished his assessment and turned his attention to Isabel's petal-smooth skin, the tiny mole at the corner of her right eye and the eye itself, with its hard, gemstone gleam. "Do you take me for a fool?"

She returned a blank stare.

"All this urgency when you took your time sending for me." He nodded to the floor. "It's practically dry."

Her eyes registered no emotion. "I was gone from his bedside longer than I intended. He must have lain there for some time. I sent for you as soon as we found him."

Doc brushed past Isabel as he mounted the stairs and entered the familiar chamber, where the master of the house lay on his white linen. A dry red trickle gleamed dully from a gash on his right temple. The skin was gray, the cloudy eyes unfocused. A thin breath gurgled in his throat. Garrett put down his hat and his bag in the usual place on the nightstand and pressed his ear to the patient's chest. He detected a halting heartbeat.

Doc straightened and gingerly felt the cranium with both hands. He found another wound at the base of the skull, confirming his suspicion that the amount of blood on the floor below could not have come only from the temple laceration. "He's near the end," he said. "You should send for a priest."

The señora left the room to bark another order to Ramón and then returned to her husband's bedside to worry her handkerchief.

"You say he fell down the stairs?" Doc asked.

"*Sí.*"

"Alone? No one knew of it?"

"*Sí.*"

"But he had to be carried from the bed. How did he make his way to the top of the stairs? Did someone carry him?"

"No. Ramón was outside chopping wood. I called him in after I found that my husband had fallen. Felipe must have crawled, pulled himself from his bed across the floor and to the top of the stairs." The eyes she raised to meet Doc's were full of tears. "He was miserable. He wanted to die. It is a mercy it is almost over."

"Señora, in my professional opinion, there is no way Don Felipe could have moved himself to the head of the stairs, much less raised himself to his feet and flung himself off the landing. He's had no use of his limbs for months. I saw him no more than two weeks ago. There was no improvement. No matter how much he may have wished himself dead, he could no more have acted on those wishes than you or I could have taken wing."

"He prayed to Nuestra Señora de Guadalupe," she said. "The Virgin delivered him from his pain."

"Don't trifle with me."

Isabel blotted a tear from her cheek. "Have you no faith?"

"What's that got to do with it?"

"I have seen things stranger than this. When my mother was a girl she had an older sister who was betrothed to a man she did not love. The sister prayed to Santa Librada that the man she was to marry would lose his desire for her. You know Santa Librada? She too was engaged to a man she did not love. Her father insisted that she marry this man anyway. He was a heathen. So Santa Librada prayed that God would deliver her from this marriage and when she woke up the next morning she had a full beard. The heathen would not have her. Her father was so angry he had Librada crucified. She is a very famous saint among women. In the case of my mother's sister, the man she did not love went on a sea voyage. He was never heard from again. So you see, anything is possible."

"What I see is that Don Felipe was carried to the top of the stairs and pushed."

Lucy Lied

"In God's name—"

"In God's name what? Why is it people tend to invoke the Deity when they feed you a lie? Let's put all that aside. I don't need to believe your fool story in order for me to keep your secret. It has nothing to do with God and even less to do with truth. It's simply a practical matter between you and me."

She considered his cold face and steeled herself to do what she must. "I think we can reach an understanding, an arrangement to our mutual benefit." She cast a heavy glance toward the cot at the foot of the Don's bed. "You can think of it as payment for your services and your silence."

He took great pleasure in rebuffing her. "I'll choose one of the don's good horses for my pains. When I'm ready I'll come out with Steadman's boy to look over your stock."

That evening in Simoneau's when he told the story to Adrian Fiske he put a different ending on it. "I said to her, if you make haste and hike down your drawers we can conclude our business before the priest gets here." He pulled at one side of his mustache as his friend chuckled.

"And who got the best of the deal?" Fiske asked.

"Old Felipe, I expect, laughing at what an ass I made of myself."

"As good as that, was she?"

"Cold and dry as snakeskin."

They laughed together and drank to better joss next time, but the image of the serpent left Doc strangely preoccupied. At the ragged edge of memory where reality and fantasy blur, he saw himself as a small child playing on the lawn at his mother's feet. A darkie came running up to her, prattling about a snake in the garden. The boy said she should get the master to bring his gun. But his mama took the shovel from the boy and shot it down to the earth like Jove hurling a thunderbolt and took the snake's head off.

That night in Sally Locke's bed he slept fitfully, trapped in that same dream of his mother beheading the snake, until a wild hammering of his heart startled him awake. He realized that the organ was in spasm. *I'm dying*. His eyes sprang open. Panting, he sat bolt upright and put two fingers on the artery at his throat.

His sudden movement roused the woman next to him. "What's wrong, *mon cher*?" She felt his sweaty brow. "You have a fever. Are you all right?"

"Shut up. I'm counting."

His brain registered the gaps in his pulse rhythm even as it surfaced scenes from the dream.

When he took his hand off his neck the woman asked again. "What is it?"

"My heart—all erratic. It stops for three or four seconds then starts up much too fast."

He stood and paced barefoot across the cold floor until he felt the tight coil of fear leave his body. Sally insisted he change his sweated nightshirt. "You'll catch your death."

"Or it will catch me," he said. "As fast as my heart races, death will still catch up."

He lay down again but never closed his eyes. Dawn began to gray the windowpanes. In the chary light, her face had lost its dusky warmth, but her strong features still bespoke her origin. The bastard of a French aristocrat's daughter and a gypsy, it was rumored, plopped down in dusty little Monterey amongst the bontons and upstarts and broke-down fools. He still found her presence amazing, though she'd been his mistress for nearly seven years.

His stirring stirred her. She stretched and softly spoke. "You're getting up already?"

"I might just as well." He sat up and dropped his legs over the side of the bed.

"Shall I call down for tea?"

"Suit yourself." He began pulling on his clothes, roughly thrusting his legs into pants, his arms into sleeves, trying to shake an eerie foreboding that clung like cobwebs. He fancied himself a man of science, a man who had a mainspring where a pious man's heart would have been. That helped to scoff superstition back to silence, but even the man of science winced at the niggling notion that maybe the churchy crowd were right when they spoke of the devil. And if they were, there'd be hell to pay.

Poignant, those first dawn grays, much more so than the fire rim of a whiskey-yellow sun. The first light was soft-edged, draping every familiar object in indistinctness, weightless and clinging as the ashes on a cold grate. What the eye saw but indistinctly, the mind would flesh out as it wanted. He grabbed his tie from where it meandered across the back of the divan, a stark road crossing a snowy landscape.

Sally stood cupping the warm porcelain of a teacup in her hands after he'd gone, thinking it hard of him to leave her at dawn with soft-edged images of him clinging to everything she called her own.

Chapter Ten

Lucy darned stockings that other people threw out and took in the dresses given to her by several of the Methodist ladies who had, by dint of children or prosperity, outgrown them. It was nerve-wracking at first, to focus all of her attention on her stitches, trying to fend off the urge to look up the way a deer grazing in a meadow must keep an eye out for coyotes. She had to remind herself that she was safe as long as she was in Mrs. Fleming's house.

As she stitched she would think about love: how Ida Fleming loved her strange sister, how she had loved Aunt Aggie ... and eventually she would think of that other love, the kind that had brought her so much grief. Was it purely wicked, what she had felt for Ellis Crane? Was everything she had endured at the hands of Flynn Talbott a punishment for her time with Ellis? If she had never left Aunt Aggie's, all the terrible things that had come to pass would never have happened.

Stitching in the safety of Mrs. Fleming's house could keep her warm and dry and well fed, but it couldn't keep thoughts of Ellis away. *No going back.* She stiffened her spine and sat up straighter.

There was no one to talk to about the right and the wrong of it. There never had been, except for Aggie. And she was too frightened then to speak, afraid Agnes would never understand. She was such a proper lady and a spinster, after all.

Agnes Strang's house was a two-story clapboard set about with elm trees in the midst of a hundred acres of wheat cultivated by a tenant farmer. There was a carriage lane and a wide porch with wicker furniture where visitors might wait in comfort for the lady of the house to ask them in. She was a plain woman of middle age who wore a square of lace pinned to the top of her head, her gray-threaded brown hair parted down the middle and severely pulled back into whorls on either side of her face, a style that resulted in a perpetually surprised expression with eyes wide open. Her dress was a figured calico, plain but for the eyelet border at the neck and the cuffs. The bodice fabric stretched taut, for her aunt was nothing if not well fed. An apron of bleached linen she wore over her skirt suggested that she might go outside at any moment to weed the garden.

The afflicted man was taken straight to the downstairs bedroom off the pantry that was meant for a lady's maid. Agnes Strang had never held with such vanity. She made do with the services of Mrs. Inskeep, her tenant farmer's wife. John Rafferty's feet hung over the end of the narrow cot, but the tenant farmer's wife tucked the blankets in around them before she went upstairs to see to the guest room.

Lucy and Ellis were shown into the parlor. Lucy took a seat on the camelback sofa—nothing like it for refinement or discomfort. Poked by a spring through the maroon velveteen, Lucy tried to situate herself discreetly without appearing to fidget. The overabundance of the house made her head swim, the furnishings crowded together like boiled sweets in a bowl: oil lamps with pink-tinted glass globes, carpets in shades of dark red and blue with all manner of birds and flowers like no birds or flowers she'd ever seen, and circles of lace ironed stiffer than dinner plates, one centered on each polished table. She couldn't breathe for all the claw-foot tables, brocaded chairs and little fancy stuff—needle-pointed footrests about as big as a newborn shoat and little vases painted with tiny scenes of old mills or piles of fruit in bowls. It squeezed her, made her feel like backhanding some delicate object just to listen to it crash on the floor. She thought of her mother and imagined how gratefully she must have fled, at least until she'd caught sight of John Rafferty's hardscrabble farm.

Agnes turned her attention to Ellis. "I'm sure it was a very trying journey for you, what with two charges to look after."

Ellis cleared his throat and spoke louder than usual, as it appeared Lucy's aunt was going deaf. "Nothing more than any hired man would do for a good boss. You know Old John took me in when none around those parts would have any truck with a Southerner."

Agnes seemed doubtful. "What of the expense of the trip, the doctor's bills?"

"I had some money put by." Ellis said it as if modesty forbade taking credit for an act of generosity. "You needn't worry about indebtedness following the old man here." He sat in his gray suit cradling the china cup in his hands and talking to her, an older woman, like a suitor, all dressed up with his face clean-shaven and his steel-gray hair washed and combed. "The old man told me all about you all, his wife's family. Said the Strangs was so starchy they wouldn't even have him in to supper. But I never believed it. I have more faith in human nature than most folks, I reckon."

Agnes raised her chin. Lucy's eyes darted up to her aunt's face for an instant, expecting to be shooed away, exiled to some lesser room with the tenant farmer's wife.

"Now it is plain to me," Ellis continued, "that what happened to John Rafferty was a judgment upon him. I don't mean to speak ill of the afflicted, but John Rafferty could be a lay-about, no doubt dispirited by the loss of his young wife. He was quick to blame anything and anybody for his misfortunes when it was he himself and his idleness that was the source of his troubles. Why, I stayed on out of pity mostly, trying to help him out of his despair." He sighed. "Poor Old John knew nothing of good manners or refinement. Not one to pick up a book and read it to improve his mind." He lifted his teacup and waved it toward the bookshelves on the opposite wall. "Unlike yourself, if I may make a personal remark."

Agnes pressed her lips together into a tight line.

Lucy Lied

Ellis looked rueful. "This young girl picked up a few of Old John's traits," he said. "It's not any fault of her own, but I daresay her moral instruction up to this time has been a shabby one. You can see why I wanted to bring her to you as soon as possible."

The aunt looked sternly at Crane. "Exactly what are you implying, sir?"

"Well, ma'am," he lowered his voice and dropped his eyes, "she takes liberties with the truth. It pains me to say it, but the girl's a barefaced, unblushing liar, the kind many a Christian soul wouldn't tolerate, much less house. She's not fit company for a gentlewoman such as yourself, but I hope to prevail upon your kindness in the name of the girl's dear departed mother, your sister."

"You don't know me at all," Agnes said, and sniffed. "How can you know what kind of company's fit for me?" She peered into Lucy's eyes. "And how, pray, can this child be such a liar? Why she hasn't said a word since she's been here."

The clock on the mantelpiece ticked. Lucy put down her cup and sat with her hands on her lap.

"That's why the good Lord took away her powers of speech. She's—" Ellis pointed a finger at his temple, inscribing tiny circles.

"I daresay almost anyone would be after what she's been through," Agnes said. "She takes after her mother, I expect. My sister was delicate and fanciful. Sometimes she couldn't eat a bite. Her nerves. And she wasn't much of a one for talk, but a nightingale when it came to singing." She paused, then spoke to Lucy. "You're big for your age, my dear. You have your mother's eyes and her lovely red hair. But the length of your limbs comes from your father, I expect. You will grow into a fine woman. Of that I am sure. And someday, when you're ready, you'll speak again. Don't worry about it for now. When the time is right the words will come."

Lucy sank back against the couch and turned nearly as dark a shade of red, as a tide of shame washed over her. Ellis went on. "She's built for work," he said, "but has no head for schooling. Simple is what we'd call her where I come from."

Agnes seized on the reference to his home. "And where is that, Mr. Crane?"

"South of Mason-Dixon, as I previously alluded. Well, you could tell that from my manner of speaking. It was my lot in life to be born on the losing side of the late unpleasantness. But I assure you my family never held slaves. It was against our religion to treat any man different from how we'd want to be treated ourselves."

Lucy tried to disappear into the knobby sofa while Ellis Crane's silky voice held sway. He had a way of holding folks' attention, making them forget what they purposed, and bringing them along to his point of view.

"We can none of us escape the accidents of birth," Agnes said, nodding to Lucy, "but to rise above, that is the sign of a fine character."

"There was nothing left of my family's land after the war," Ellis continued. "It was all sold for taxes, which the Yankees raised sky high, if you'll pardon my saying so. Anyway, I pushed back up North. I worked season to season for this farm and that until I made my way to that part of Pennsylvania where John Rafferty's place was. When I came upon it I felt as if I'd stumbled into paradise. It was fertile and beautiful and hardly bore the scratch of a plow. My Lord, the soil was so black and deep I could scarce believe my eyes. But the fields were fallow. Something was clearly wrong. It was like the farmer had lost the will to get behind his mule and till the earth. When I saw this state of affairs I felt like if I could just meet with the man who owned the land, I could say to him, 'Let me help you sow seed and bring this land to fruition,' and by God it would be a second Eden."

Lucy studied the specks of tea leaves in her empty cup. Agnes replied, "You found my brother-in-law unwilling to work?"

"Yes, ma'am. Fair starved they were, living on wild game and summer berries. But it was because of grief, as I said before. The old man was dispirited, still mourning your sister's passing."

"My sister died seven years ago."

Ellis threw up his hands. "Might just as well have been last week. When I found them that's how it was."

Lucy Lied

"You were able to take the place in hand?"

"Two good years we had. Increased the acreage under the plow from the first year to the second. Thought to go on and increase a bit more the third. But after the second harvest, a funny thing happened. The old man got a lot of big ideas. Wasn't content to just plant a little more the next year. Wanted to double the crop. As if he'd been asleep a long time and woke up hungry—for money. He told me he wrote to touch you for some cash when we was getting ready to buy our seed corn. But he said you didn't send a reply. He said it didn't matter because we'd just borrow the money against the property. We bought so much seed corn we had to clear a new five-acre block. See, he wanted to show all the sodbusters thereabouts that he was as good a farmer as any of 'em. There's a lesson in that, I guess. Sin of pride. Silly old fool. I fear that's why the good Lord sent that storm to ruin the crop and that lightning bolt to strike him down. Don't matter now, I guess. Place is supposed to be sold off for debts."

The aunt set down her teacup. "It pains me for my sister's sake, knowing she poured her lifeblood into that farm and it was all for nothing." She applied her hankie to the lower lid of her right eye. "Sometimes I think it would have been better if she had died in childbirth." She glanced at Ellis. "I'm sorry. Does that shock you? It must sound unchristian."

"I believe I understand," Ellis said. He made so bold as to reach over and briefly place his hand on top of hers.

"No, I'm sure you don't," Agnes said. She pulled her hand away. "My sister bore this child here out of wedlock. She loved a man who promised her a life with him and then left her to fend for herself. She never lost faith in him. That's why it's a mercy she died, rather than endure any more disappointment. My father was so mortified that he arranged for my sister to leave our house. After she left we never spoke of her again. Sarah. That was her name. I haven't spoken it for over sixteen years."

"I think we should never have come here and upset you so," Ellis said. He again extended a solicitous hand, this time it came to rest on Agnes's shoulder. "Please forgive me for reminding you of this sad tale."

Lucy studied her aunt's stern, red-filigreed eyes and could read no sympathy there, nor self-pity. Agnes Strang seemed all starch and stays, just as Old John had always said. "I believe it's time all of us retired," the aunt said. She busied herself calling for the tenant farmer's wife to make sure the spare room was ready for Ellis and the trundle in her own room had been pulled out for Lucy. Lucy stood and took up her candle. She risked one look at Ellis, but he was already following the tenant farmer's wife to his chamber. "Bide here with me a moment," Agnes said, after he was gone. "It's my custom to have a dram of sherry before bed. It soothes the digestion and brings on sleep. Would you care for some?"

Lucy returned to the sofa, this time choosing a spot nearer the end where the springs seemed less aggressive. She listened to the tick of the clock as Agnes went to the sideboard and returned with a tiny green-stemmed glass in each hand. "Little sips," Agnes said. She took up her rocker again and tasted her glass. Lucy's eyes once again took a course about the room, coming to rest on a portrait that hung over the mantle, a pair of fierce eyes glaring down as if outraged at some goings-on amongst the chairs and tables below.

"My father," Agnes said. "He was a great figure in our lives, but he died a shrunken and fearful man, all hollows and raw bones. He was delirious at the end, calling for Sarah." She contemplated the dying embers on the grate. "It took dying for him to show some mercy. But I wonder if God had seen fit to restore his health if he'd have been as mean as ever, still adamant that he'd see her in hell before he'd keep her and her bastard in his house. Yes, he used those very words. He was so afraid someone might accuse him of condoning sin. It was all fear, fear and pride that drove Sarah off. The family was never the same after. I myself never took a beau, much less a husband. Young men were afraid to come near this house. Mother came down with influenza the next year and slipped away without a fight, just sank down between the sheets and disappeared."

Lucy sipped her sherry and felt a bloom of heat in the center of her chest where she supposed her heart was.

"Father was always at his Bible," Agnes said with a small laugh, "stooped with bending for hours over the stand in the library, trying to make out the tiny print. He'd squint through his reading glasses, as if he were trying to see right through the page into something he thought should be there but never was. Huh." Agnes shook her head. "I shunned religion myself, though I still went with Father to church for as long as he was able to plod in all weather to the house of God. He was unctuous before God, a different person entirely. The Almighty was the only one he could talk to, the only one who understood. And yet, on his deathbed, he was as frightened as Sarah that day she left with John Rafferty for the farm outside Gettysburg. So much fear in one house." She paused, looking back to the stormy-eyed father captured on canvas. "I'm a different person now. Now I can feel sorry for him."

Lucy tried to picture the young Agnes, that daughter who had trudged silently beside her father to church, fearful of his anger and immune to the charms of young men lest she wind up like Sarah.

"I sold the business and our house in Philadelphia after he died. It was with a sense of deliverance that I saw him breathe his last," Agnes went on, "a sense, almost, of elation. What a wicked thought, but true. It's not right to speak of, I suppose. But is a thing less wicked just because we keep it to ourselves? Don't we add dishonesty to our sins, thinking we can fool God just as we fool the rest of the world? Surely silence cannot keep integrity if it is already absent from the heart."

Lucy bestirred herself to put the empty cordial glass on the table.

"I see Sarah's features so clearly in your face," Agnes said, "but at a distance, as if she were looking through a curtain. Ah, well. We should be off to bed. The brain is prone to fancies at this time of night." Yet she continued to sit. "I know you've likely heard only unkind things about me, but I want you to know I am your friend. I want to give you the advantages that your mother gave up. And I must tell you that I don't believe you suffer any impairment of the mind as Mr. Crane implied. Someday I want you to trust me enough to speak. In the meantime, I will do all I can to earn that trust."

Almost every evening after that, Lucy would sit with Agnes by the dying fire in the parlor and Agnes would tell stories about Lucy's mother, bringing Sarah to life as a child learning how to ride a snow sled one night, and a young woman meeting the love of her life the next. "He was a Scottish seafaring man," she began, speaking of Duncan Firth, "a captain of his own vessel, the sloop *Indio*. Father's business was in carriages and harness of all types. Besides the carts for tradesmen, Father carried a line of fine items for Philadelphia people. Imported. He dealt direct with the merchant captains to get the best price for transport. Sometimes he brought the merchant captains to the house for dinner, a good meal, then they'd talk business over brandy and cigars. That is how your father first came to our house. He was quite charming, well-spoken for a man of his type, and with a manner so gentle toward my sister it was hard not to look kindly on the connection forming between them. We were all quite sorry to see him leave on his next voyage. We all promised letters. By the time it was clear he'd got Sarah with child, he was ... I think it was Hawaii he was bound for. Well, it doesn't matter."

But it did matter. Very much. She thought of Duncan Firth almost every night as her aunt lay mouth-breathing, sound asleep. *Hawaii*. Such a strange name she would never forget. She wanted to ask about it, think on a way to begin the journey, but her muteness was such a habit that the idea of forming a word turned her mouth to stone. At the very least she could never speak as long as she lived under her aunt's roof. To speak now would be to admit that her muteness had been a contrivance all along, a lie. She dared not risk losing her aunt's good opinion. She'd come to care what her mother's elder sister thought of her. Agnes seemed to see a brighter, better girl than she'd ever been, a self that, with her new clothes and brushed hair, Lucy could almost become, would have, if it weren't for the one great sin of her life that overshadowed all the rest.

Ellis eyed her sidelong these days, mocking her newfound gentility. He would taunt her sometimes, when Agnes was out of earshot. "Watch your step, Luce. You play at being quite the fine lady, but old Ellis knows better." Agnes made him work helping Mrs. Inskeep tend to Old John Rafferty in exchange for his board. It chafed him, being treated like the hired help he was. "I'm no house nigger," he'd say, walking behind her on the way to town on Agnes's shopping day. "You'd best remember that." She had reached to take his hand, but he'd pulled away. "Oh, I don't need no pity. There's a sporting lady in town who's been obliging since you've been acting so spinsterish. She's a big-bosomed gal like those hen turkeys you see roosting in the woods this time of year. Knows what she's about. I might like her a lot better than you. Just think on that."

His philandering made her heartsick, returned her to the sorry state of mind she seemed unable to escape. She lived in fear that Ellis would tell and Agnes would turn away from her. *Not while the living is easy, but someday.*

One morning, toward the middle of October, something happened that was to change everything. Lucy got out of bed and standing before her glass found herself a head taller than when she'd first come to her aunt's house. The hem of her nightgown was so far up from the floor it felt indecent and the sleeve ends were practically at her elbows. "I've been noticing myself," Agnes said, "that it's time we saw the dressmaker. You've come into your womanly form." She put down her teacup and climbed out of bed. "I think it's time you had something of your mother's I've been saving. It didn't seem right to give them to you until this very day."

She shuffled to her dressing table and took a small box from the middle drawer where she kept her pearls and some gold pieces too fine for wearing. Inside the box was a pair of earrings, dark red gems garlanded with fancy work. "They're garnets ringed with gold and seed pearls." Agnes said. She had Lucy sit at the dressing table and held them to her ears. "These were your mother's. Before she left with John Rafferty she made me promise to keep them for her. I suspect she knew that they'd go to buy seed corn if she took them to the farm. It's all I have of hers to give you. Now you're of age, you should have them."

Lucy's eyes in the mirror shimmered with tears. "There, there," Agnes said. "It's little enough. We'll keep them in the drawer with my jewelry and when we have the harvest dance you'll put them on with a brand new gown of the same color. And if that doesn't catch the eye of every young man in the hall I don't know buttons from beans."

They were still admiring the way the gemstones sparkled next to Lucy's red curls when a knock came at the door and Ellis Crane called through, "It's Old John. He's damn well run off."

Lucy scrambled into her clothes while Agnes bent her head close to the oak panel of the door and barked instructions. "Go borrow the horse and wagon from Mr. Inskeep. Look for John in town. Lucy and I will go to the woods and search there."

As she walked abreast of Agnes among the trees, through showers of falling yellow leaves, Lucy almost cried out his name, for it pierced her heart that he should be abroad bareheaded under the uncaring sky once again. The breeze that morning was sharp and scented with rain. She pulled her shawl close around her face and clutched it to her throat. She knew how chill his bony limbs must be, swathed in his thin nightshirt, how blue his bare feet, and felt the sting of conscience, remembering it was over a year since he'd come by his affliction.

An hour later they heard someone calling to them through the dank dripping maze of trees. "Miss Strang. It's Frank Jessup." Lucy and Agnes turned and hurried toward the voice. "It's the sheriff's deputy," Agnes explained, puffing from the exertion. "Here we are, Mr. Jessup!"

"I found him," Jessup said, once they'd met in the middle distance. "He's up at your house with Mrs. Inskeep, none the worse for wear."

"Thank goodness," Agnes said, still breathless. "Let's go in without delay."

As they made their way toward the house, Jessup told an amazing tale. "I was in the barbershop when I heard some fellows going on about a preacher man standing in the street in only his smallclothes, that's what they said, giving out about the Hereafter to a crowd of some twenty or twenty-five people. I told Lemuel to finish me up right quick so I could see what all the fuss was about. When I got there I had to elbow my way through as many folks as you see at a hanging. The object every eye was set on was Old John. I recognized him sure enough, but I couldn't quite believe it because he was holding forth in fine fashion instead of babbling nonsense."

"My lands! What was he saying?" Agnes gasped.

"Talking about how the lightning striking him down freed him from his earthly bonds, and how he communed with the angels. He said he saw his dear mother and his beloved Sarah, both departed from this earth years ago. Tears was coursing down his cheeks and he spoke with such conviction the crowd was all agog. And when I stepped up to fetch him away they protested my interfering. But I was firm with them and told them to move along. Then as I was walking him away, they commenced to throw money. Pennies mostly, but some parted with more. I didn't know what to do about that, so I left it, figured those who might scrounge up the change from the dust probably need it more than Old John does."

"Won't you come in and take some refreshment for your trouble?" Agnes asked as they came to the house.

"Thank you, ma'am, but I'll be getting back to town. I hope you find Old John quite restored to health."

"Improved over what he was, at any rate," Agnes said. "Give my regards to your wife."

Jessup tugged his hat brim and mounted the horse he'd left in the yard. Agnes stood a moment in an attempt to recover her breath before mounting the porch steps. At length she said, "How do you suppose he was so changed all of a sudden?"

Lucy shook her head.

"Well, we'd best go in and see how he's getting on." Agnes rose and held out her hand for Lucy to grasp.

Lucy held her breath as they approached Rafferty's room. If it were true that he was whole again, then a great millstone of guilt would be lifted from her soul. She went along beside Agnes, eager but afraid lest when she looked with her own eyes she would find his recovery some sort of cruel deception.

Mrs. Inskeep had him sitting up in bed and taking nourishment. He was scarcely eating for talking. "Thanks be to God and all His angels in His glorious Heaven. I am but His bell and His trumpet to sound forever His praise and to tell all good people of His loving kindness, that He saw fit to restore to me, the most base of sinners and disbelievers until this day, the sight of my lost loved ones. Sarah! Sarah I see you still, my angel!"

Agnes recoiled on the doorstep of the downstairs room where he had lain for weeks like a mumbling fencepost. She squeezed Lucy's hand. "I am glad of the return of his faculties, but it offends my ear that my sister's name is bandied so."

"It's a stone miracle," Ellis Crane said. He had materialized at Lucy's side where she stood watching her stepfather testify. "He's as fit as an ox team and a damn sight louder. You should have seen all them folks gathered round him. They stopped whatever it was they come to town to do and flocked there dumb as sheep." There was a gleam in his eye as he spoke, that same look he'd worn when he'd first sifted the idea of coming to Agnes Strang's house, like a child with a bright bauble. "They threw down more than a dollar," he whispered, "and he was just gathering steam when the sheriff pulled him away."

"We must fetch the doctor in," Agnes was saying to Mrs. Inskeep. "It may be this is some kind of delirium."

"Or it could be the work of the devil," Ellis said, delighting, it seemed, in raising the specter of evil. "Those possessed sometimes speak in foreign tongues, I hear tell, and beguile the wits of any who give ear. Seducers for Mammon and the fallen host, some folks say."

"Rubbish," Agnes replied. "Mrs. Inskeep, please go for the doctor."

The tenant farmer's wife sprang to her feet, only too ready to quit such talk of seduction and devilry. When the doctor came, he examined John Rafferty with great interest. "I should like to consult my colleagues in Philadelphia on this case," he said. "He seems in all respects physically able, but his mind is unresponsive.

Lucy Lied

As you observe, when I ask his name or some simple question such as whether it is day or night, he makes me no answer, but repeats instead this business of the spirit world, as if he were in the company of those on the other side. You will send word if his condition alters. And please don't let him wander off again."

Mrs. Inskeep would have nothing more to do with Rafferty from that day forward, having taken the idea of possession by the devil to heart, but Ellis Crane was more than willing to be the old man's constant companion. It was light work, Lucy thought, now that her stepfather was able to walk and feed and clean himself. He seemed all too content, did Ellis. Where he used to mutter complaints out of her aunt's hearing, these days she heard nothing from him at all. He was tinkering with some new scheme. She began to wonder if she would wake one morning and find him gone.

She would remember that time at her aunt's house when, in the autumn of the next year, she found herself once again with her forehead planted against the warm, curly side of a red cow on Flynn Talbott's beet farm. She wondered for the hundredth time what had happened to Rafferty, whether Ellis had really put him in the care of doctors or had just disposed of him in an asylum. How had Ellis managed it all, the train tickets and the clothes? Had he tricked Agnes into going to Philadelphia or was it God who had arranged her absence and given Ellis his opportunity?

That day they left her aunt's house she wasn't yet out of bed when he'd bolted into her room as though he meant to fling up her skirt and have her without so much as a civil "good morning." He said, "Get up and get dressed. We're taking Old John and leaving, the three of us. He'll be staying at a teaching hospital in the city. We're going to San Francisco. Now go on and get dressed like I said."

He'd gone to the dressing table and opened the drawer where Agnes kept her pearls and the other jewelry. "Get me that carpet bag of yours," he barked. When she didn't budge, he flung a bottle of toilet water at her. It broke against the wall. "Damnation, when I say get moving I mean it." He stepped over and grabbed her arm. "Now hear me, girl. If you don't do as I say I'll tell the old lady all about you and me, that you're no better than a street whore. How quick do you think she'll throw you out once she knows the history between us, eh?"

Ellis had been nicer after they'd left Aunt Aggie's. He'd taken her to get a suit for traveling, a smart green velvet outfit. She had felt like a new person wearing it, someone with a path ahead, a real life—until he abandoned her in Utah without anything but the clothes on her back and her muteness. She used her muteness as armor against the men who seemed drawn to her red hair like flies to honey. Once they knew she was mute they left her alone, afraid it was the outward sign of a mental defect. Men avoided crazy women like black cats or staring fixedly at the full moon.

From the hallway, Mrs. Fleming stood watching the strange girl who sat so still and looked so sad, as if frozen by some evil enchantment. She crossed the parlor and placed a hand on Lucy's shoulder. "My dear, you've hardly made any progress on that side seam since I went to the kitchen to get supper. I can't find it in my heart to scold you, though. You have the face of a lost soul." The old lady knelt and looked up into Lucy's eyes. "You must find solace in the Lord," she said. "Kneel with me and pray."

Lucy obeyed, imitating the way Ida Fleming clasped her hands together, raised her face to the ceiling and squeezed her eyes shut. "Dear God," Ida Fleming intoned, "help us to find the righteous path in this life, the path that leads us in Your ways of love and forgiveness ..."

Lucy's prayer was slightly different: *the path back to Aunt Aggie.*

Chapter Eleven

Clancy got to the city in good time and made a tour of the docks before arriving at the Grand Hotel. A little before the hour of their appointment he'd planted himself in an armchair behind a potted palm in the lobby. He'd observed Myra Thatcher walk in and take a seat in a straight-backed chair. She peered from under the brim of her bonnet as if she were afraid she might be seen by an acquaintance and reproached. What did she have to look so uneasy about? Was it guilt or was it perhaps merely the manner of one who hadn't yet learned to relax in public places? Whenever he saw her, he thought of a sparrow on a branch ready at any moment to take flight. Why would a widow of thirty and more act skittish as a girl? Clancy wondered if there was more to the affair than she had written to him.

After watching her for a few minutes, he approached her chair and greeted the widow of his comrade in arms. "Hello, Mrs. Thatcher."

She offered her small, gloved hand for him to shake. "Please call me Myra. It's so good of you to come all the way to San Francisco," she said.

"No trouble," he replied. He took the chair next to hers. "I wanted to go by Meiggs Wharf and inquire about the fare to Hawaii."

"My lands! Do you mean to travel there?"

"I've had it in mind for some time," Clancy said. "Only the thought of all that water ..." He left the sentence unfinished, unable to think of a polite way of saying the thought turned all his sporting blood to horse piss.

"Yes, it is an alarming idea," she remarked. "I heard Mark Twain lecture on the queer customs of the savages. He said, as I recall, the men wear a smile and spectacles and the women are forbidden to eat fruit for fear of a second fall. It was a very amusing evening." She dropped her eyes. "I only wish my dear husband had been alive to enjoy it with me." She cleared her throat and raised her eyes again. "How much is it?"

Clancy was thinking of Silas Thatcher who had been beyond all manner of earthly woe since the Second Bull Run. Second Manassas the rebels called it. Silas was a good man, willing and bright behind his merchant's spectacles, but not much of a soldier in spite of all his efforts. He just wasn't cut out for it. Clancy smarted under the reminder of Thatcher's death and reproached himself with fresh bitterness for having failed to save his friend from that fatal bullet, having seen him through a dozen worse scrapes. "I'm sorry. You were saying?"

"How much to go there?"

"Ah," he replied. "Well, one of the seamen who was helping to offload hogsheads said he thought it was about eighty dollars. He said he didn't much pay attention since The Pacific Mail *pays him* to go."

Myra looked thoughtful, as if struck by the possibility of a sea voyage, being in the general vicinity of the docks. "How long is the passage?"

"Twelve days, normally."

"Eighty dollars. Does that include return?"

"No," he said. "I'm not planning on returning."

"You would leave your country?"

"Seems like it left me a while back," he said.

She looked puzzled. "You mean the war? How so?"

Clancy shrugged. "Don't mind me."

"No, really."

"The war changed things. I've felt out of place ever since. Can't say exactly how or why."

She pulled a hankie out of the end of her sleeve and pressed it momentarily to her lips. "You're lucky to have survived the army at all. I think of Silas every day, and so many others who never came home."

"I didn't mean to upset you."

She seemed on the verge of tears. "I should have learned by now to bear my loss better." She cleared her throat and changed the subject. "They put on a nice tea here at the Grand. Would you care for some?" She half raised her hand to summon a waiter, but he shook his head. "No? Well, then I suppose I should get down to it." Her eyes dropped into her lap.

"As you can imagine," she began, "the shock of my husband's death left me quite ill for some time. I never to this day have returned to the state of vitality that I enjoyed before he left me. But several months ago I felt that I was sinking. My doctor gave me several different powders, but none made any difference. My pastor suggested prayer." She shook her head. "Nothing helped. But then I found an advertisement in the paper that offered me some hope. A Brother Elias Croft claimed to be able to cure many of the ailments that afflicted me through the new science of magicology, and for a very modest amount of money. I wanted so much to feel better. I'm afraid my judgment was not what it should have been."

"You answered the advertisement?" he asked.

She nodded. "Yes. I wrote to him at the address at the bottom. It seems so foolish now. But if you could have heard him, how well-spoken he was, so sincere."

"So you met with him."

"Yes. It was the most remarkable thing. As soon as Brother Elias and I began talking, I felt that a great weight had been lifted from my heart. It was extraordinary." She hesitated. "You see, I've been so lonely for Silas. I've had so many questions about things he mentioned from time to time before he went into the army. I forgot so much of importance, like the bonds, for instance, and money he had put aside somewhere. I should have written it all down, but ..."

Myra shook her head and showed him tearful eyes. They were gray, set close to a long nose in a pale-lipped face lacking a focal point. He wondered what Silas, a well-made man if a little on the short side, could have found so entrancing about her. He thought of his own wife, the woman who had left him an empty house to come home to after Appomattox. *Faithfulness counts for something. Not that love ever makes sense to anyone besides the two themselves.* He brought his thoughts back to Croft. "Where did you meet? Here?"

"No. He said it would be best in the home. He said he needed to touch some of Silas's personal things. His gloves, for example. Or a lock of his hair."

"You gave him something?"

"A picture of Silas in his uniform."

"Then what?"

"He said he could help me contact him."

"Contact him how?"

"He claimed he could reach people who've passed to the other side. He told me to invite six lady friends and arrange chairs around a table close enough so our hands could touch. He said it would be best if we met at night. And he said to dismiss the servants so we should not be disturbed."

"And you did this?"

"Yes. It was the most amazing thing I've ever experienced in my life. I don't know how to describe it. It was like a dream. It was as if he'd nodded off to sleep when suddenly the spirits came into his body. He writhed and spoke in strange voices, oaths and odd protestations that made no sense. After a bit when the spirits were calmer, we asked questions and the spirits answered with a knock. Once for yes, twice for no. And all the while both of Brother Elias's hands were on top of the table."

"He came alone?"

"No, there was a young girl with him, an assistant. She was there to help him get home. He became disoriented after these sessions with the spirits. She was an unpleasant drab, always with a brooding expression. He called her his sister, but I scarcely think one as charming as Elias could have come from the same parents as that vile creature. She sat outside the door when we were closed in the library having our session."

"Then what? Another session the next week?"

"Yes. This time the contact came much easier. And the spirits actually spoke to us through Elias about relatives, intimacies, things only the dead person himself could know."

"How many of these meetings did you have?"

"We had a dozen or more. I guess about twice a month. It went from one person's house to the next."

"Anything go missing from any of the houses?"

"I never heard of anything. The objects Brother Elias used to contact the spirits were keepsakes, nothing more."

"Until he asked for money."

"Yes."

"How much did he take you for?"

"Five hundred all together. There were six of us who invested. All widows."

"Invested?"

"He said he wanted to build a sort of college, The Institute of Magicology."

"The Institute of Flim-Flam."

"Yes." She began to tear up again. "What Silas must think of me!"

"He would never reproach you," Clancy said, remembering Silas taking the glasses off his face to wipe his eyes whenever he spoke of his darling Myra.

"When I talked to the city police about it they said Brother Croft had done nothing wrong. He'd stolen nothing, nor made any threats to make us turn over our savings to him. They told me just because a fool and her money are soon parted doesn't mean it's a matter for the law. That's why I asked you to meet me the next time you came to town. There's no one else I can turn to. I hope you didn't make a special trip. I didn't intend to cause you an inconvenience."

"Don't be silly," he said. "It's an easy trip from Salinas. I ride free as I work for the railroad. Does me good to get off the ranch and mingle with the quality."

She smiled at the self-deprecating expression, but her amusement was short-lived given the distressing nature of the matter at hand. "Do you think you can find him?"

"How long since you last saw him?"

"Five months."

"Why did you wait so long to do something about it?"

"We—I felt so ashamed. I felt like I'd betrayed Silas, when all I was trying to do was have a moment with him again. Just a moment to hear his voice."

"Odds are he's left San Francisco," Clancy replied. "I can put out the word to my associates here and alert the train stations along the line between here and San Diego. The ticket masters are pretty good at spotting sharpers. What does this Elias Croft look like?"

"He's slight of build and something of a dandy. He prefers gray silk suits and patent leather shoes. He speaks with a southern accent—South Carolina, I think he said. But his hair is the most distinctive thing about him. It's silver with a white streak over his right eye. He wears it shoulder length. Most of my lady friends found him quite striking."

Clancy glanced around the hotel lobby to make sure they were unlikely to be overheard. "He didn't try anything—make love to you, I mean."

Myra Thatcher colored deeply and shook her head without looking him in the eye.

"All right then," Clancy said, getting to his feet. "You can tell your lady friends I'll try to get your money back."

"You won't hurt him."

"Not unless he provokes me."

Lucy Lied

He saw Myra Thatcher home in a cab, marveling at the mass of humanity that seemed determined to leave wherever they were and travel across town, never content to stay put. He gave himself but little chance of finding the charlatan Croft if he'd left the city, but if the con man was still somewhere in San Francisco, there were people who could ferret him out. He paid a visit to these friends after seeing Myra to her door, smoked a pipe of opium, and talked about the old days laying rails through the Sierras for the Central Pacific. He'd been a boss back then, the man on the upper step. Now they were the ones possessed of wealth and influence in their own sphere. He knew they'd help him find Croft and kill him if he asked it.

On the train heading home, Clancy thought of his first trip to the West Coast, how the far frontier used to be California. On that earlier trip, as now, the engine soot settled on him and occasioned a thought of President Grant, known in his fighting days as the dust-covered man on a dust-covered horse. The discomfort, he had reflected, would be worth it if the layer of grime worked to shield him from others. In fact, it didn't, even though he took the additional precaution of holding a newspaper open on his lap.

In spite of a look of preoccupation bordering on a scowl, females were still apt to strike up conversation. Women gravitated to him, for some reason, and train travel seemed to exacerbate the tendency. Moreover, it seemed, within the confines of a railroad carriage, women were apt to settle in close proximity as if in their own drawing rooms among close acquaintances and erupt in babble without invitation or apparent reason. He was at a loss to explain this lack of decorum, except to speculate that travel at high speeds must affect women's brains with a giddiness similar to that produced by excessive heights.

When confronted with this particular form of female persistence, he found the only thing was to feign deafness while staring out the window mile after mile. Clancy found the monotonous motion oddly soothing. He cast his mind back to coming across the North American continent, back when there was not one visible jot of the hand of man, save the shining tracks that stretched clear back to New York. He had emptied his mind into the tall grass mildly swaying under the blank sky and for the several blessed days it took to reach the other coast found himself untethered, floating free in the to-and-fro of the car suspended between what was and what would be.

On that first visit to San Francisco he'd taken a room and a bath and bought new clothes. His army uniform he had left, spread out on the chair in the hotel room like the remains of a man who'd just up and vaporized while sitting there. He caught another train to Salinas and then went on by coach to Monterey, remembering something he'd read about Junipero Serra and a trail of mustard seed that traced the civilizing progress of the friars all the way up the California coast from Mexico. The Franciscans and Jesuits had depressed the native population to near extinction. *Too much God will do that.*

Now, as the train rattled toward Salinas, he pulled his thoughts back to present day matters and thought about what his boss had said. The company was planning to run a spur on down to Monterey, eliminating the need to take a coach. He tried to imagine a luxury hotel in the old Spanish town that had changed negligibly since missionary days. He bridled at the thought of so much gentility and wondered again about a sea voyage to Hawaii, swells rushing by instead of round-shouldered hills. If only his stomach didn't pitch and roll at the very idea.

Chapter Twelve

When Matt Clancy appeared in the dining room of Rosanna Leese's boardinghouse, the lady herself hastened to greet him, coffee pot in hand. "Welcome, señor. Please take this table by the woodstove. How was your visit to San Francisco?"

He doffed his hat and laid it on the chair next to the one she pulled out for him. "Seems everybody in town knows of my travels," he said, sitting.

She turned up the cup at his place and filled it with steaming coffee. "What will you have? Steak and eggs? We have also bacon."

"Both. I'm starved."

"Bueno." She nodded urgently to the boy who stood waiting by the kitchen door. "Your trip," she said, loitering awkwardly, "it was good?"

"I reckon so. Came back in one piece." He assessed her with his dead calm gaze. "You want to get something off your chest?"

She dropped her eyes, doing her best imitation of bashful jitters. "Oh, señor ... it has been some time since the trial, when we were to have you for dinner. My cousin's husband died, Our Lady protect him, and Isabel is now trying to run a rancho all alone. She wants very much to talk about the water and the cows. What I mean is, we still want you for dinner."

"I might be a little tough."

"No, no, ... I mean ... my English ..."

He continued to watch her without making any move to ease her discomfort or worsen it.

Rosanna continued. "I thought that this evening we might take dinner together, the three of us."

"I'd like to accept your kind invitation," he said, "but I didn't intend to spend all day in town. Should probably go on home. Please tell your cousin that I have long wished to be introduced to *'la Leona.'* We'll have to dine together in future." Clancy glanced across the room. "Sam around? He's been looking after my horse." He eyed the landlady. "Good man, Sam. I've a mind to hire him away from you."

"But you don't keep a household. What use would you have for a hired man?"

"I'm thinking of taking the place in hand," he replied. "Putting up wire fences and maybe building a house on the hill."

She smiled lest her features betray the alarm the news occasioned for Isabel's sake. "Ah well, that is between you and him. I hope you enjoy your breakfast." Rosanna left the coffeepot on top of the iron stove in the corner and retreated to a table on the other side of the room to ponder what she had just learned.

She took a chair near an open casement window in a square of meager daylight. Seeking to distract her mind from worry she listened to the conversation of the two men idling on the porch as she polished knives. It was not wrong to listen, she told herself, so long as your hands were not idle. She glanced outside to see if it had yet begun to rain and saw the two Anglos in the chairs they always occupied, the sight of them as familiar as the back of her own hand. But for his shirt of boiled linen, Doc was all in black from his flat hat to his shoes. His pale face combined the hollow cheeks of a consumptive with the broad forehead and deep shadowed eyes of a Classical bust. She suspected his heavy but well-trimmed mustache disguised a weak mouth, just as his lax posture surely implied a weak will. Doc pared his fingernails with a tiny gold pocketknife he kept on one end of his watch chain. He was as meticulous about his grooming as a cat, Rosanna Leese thought, just the opposite of his companion. The painter's hands were stained with whatever colors he had used on his most recent canvas. His sandy curls were well threaded with gray, his cheeks rosy as a girl's, and his eyes like Chinese blue and white porcelain. Adrian Fiske was as multicolored as Doc Garrett was monochromatic.

The first spatter of raindrops cratered the dust of the Calle Principal, stirring up a scent of cows. Each tiny reservoir cradled the beginnings of a freshet that might well wash away every trace of what little commerce enlivened Monterey from time to time. She breathed in the smell and wondered about adobe and gravity and indolence and ruin.

As if he'd read her mind and shared her apprehension, one of the men sitting on the porch said, "You'd think much as it rains around here they'd build with something besides mud."

Adrian Fiske mulled the proposition for a minute before he replied. Fiske was an artist, a person Rosanna Leese admired little, as he seemed to have no particular purpose in life. And she thought him effeminate to boot. "I thought the white lime kept the damp out together with the overhang of the roof tiles."

"You can see how it sags, the adobe," Doc replied. "It's melting back to street mud before our eyes. We're slipping closer to obliteration every time it rains. And the Mexicans keep slapping up their mud bricks anyway."

"They're a religious bunch. It's Biblical. Dust to dust."

"Can you read that?" Doc asked. His heels dropped off the rail and he sat up in his chair.

Rosanna Leese looked out the window to see if there was something unusual happening in the street. She saw nothing remarkable and returned to polishing knives, sniffing at the way the doctor's conversation had a way of jumping the tracks without warning. He'd evidently lost Fiske who blurted out, "What?"

"In Ortin's window across the way. That sign. What's it say? I swear I think I need glasses."

The painter raised his voice over the drumming of drops pelting the roof. "White Labor Cigars."

"You can read that from here?"

"Well, now, if I were the type to take advantage of a situation, I'd say yes, but the fact is I saw it yesterday."

"White Labor Ceegars?"

"Indeed."

"Now why would I give a hoot who rolls my ceegars?"

"Haven't you heard about the evils of the yellow race—how they've come all the way over here from China just to take white men's jobs? Bronson's got a story in the paper."

"Bronson's an ass."

"It wouldn't hurt you to read about the politics of your own state once in a while. Get a sense of civic duty."

"Politics is an ass."

"What have you got against politics?"

"Politicians. Rabble rousers and demagogues. I got no use for causes."

"You're mighty dyspeptic today. I can see Ortin doesn't stand to make a red cent off you with his white labor smokes."

"I wouldn't buy the turds they make around here if they were rolled by the Archangel Michael. Whoever got the idea you could grow tobacco in Gilroy never tasted a real ceegar. You show me a ceegar from Virginia and I'll smoke it right quick."

"A bit high-priced for a country sawbones, aren't they?"

"Just because my calling has not been lucrative doesn't mean I intend to indulge in items of inferior quality."

The conversation lapsed. For a time there was only the sound of water. The first tentative drops had been joined by a host of others to create a downpour. Rosanna Leese looked out to make sure her two clients were still sitting there.

"If it wouldn't drown us I'd say we should go on over to Simoneau's," Fiske said. "Get a beer. Might improve your mood. Leese's coffee surely isn't doing much for it."

"Why don't you just go out and paint your damn tree, 'stead of sitting here complaining about the company?"

"I was out at the point early this morning, thank you very much. You know, it might not hurt you to get an interest—something besides whores and human ailments, I mean."

Lucy Lied

"I've been considering that very thing," Garrett replied.

"Pray tell."

"As I told you some time ago, I aim to write an article for one of the medical journals, a study of some sort. I used to subscribe to the *New Orleans Medical and Surgical Journal* and the *Southern Journal of Medical Sciences*, and it seems to me I'm as good a writer as any I've read. The question is what to write about. I need a subject. Something others haven't beaten to death."

"Yes," Fiske agreed. "I should think death is the last subject on which a medical journal would seek articles."

"I'm flummoxed," Doc said.

"I thought you'd fixed on the mute girl."

Doc shook his head. "Oh, I don't know."

"Well, as winter draws on there's contagion to look forward to. Maybe the Almighty will send us a good plague. You can get in on it before it reaches more bustling parts of the country. Surprise everyone with the discovery of a cure."

"Well, now what makes you think the Lord would favor me with not only a plague but a cure as well?"

"Why not you? You're not such a bad sort. I've known many a more wicked man and some damn near as ugly. You get out your pens and papers and I guarantee some dread malady will come along. The readiness is all."

"Your confidence is inspirational."

"You mock me, but I can see the wheels turning inside your head," Fiske said. "Already you're feverishly considering the reorganization of the roll-top desk in the surgery, ransacking copies of old journals, listing the topics that have already appeared, the opinions on each, the possibility of taking a contrary view. The idea has infused you with an unaccustomed energy. Why, if we didn't have a meal on order I'll bet you'd find some excuse to desert me right now and go on back to your place to get started. You can already see your name in print, can't you, though you'd never admit to such a foolish and childlike vision."

The painter peered closely at Garrett as a faint blush tinged Doc's cheek.

"Sure as I'm a man of color," the painter continued, "I believe I detect a flicker of hope along with a dose of vanity in your case."

Rosanna Leese saw two plates of steak and eggs emerge from the kitchen and rose to poke her face out the window. "Your food is ready," she said to the idlers on the porch.

The two men hastened to heed the call.

The dining room consisted of a few tables caught between the bar and the desk where overnight guests stood to check in. There was little room to separate the customers, but out of prudence Rosanna Leese put the painter and the doctor as far as she could from her other guest.

Adrian Fiske sat down and said to Doc Garrett, sotto voce, "Matt Clancy."

Garrett glanced up at the gunman then returned his attention to his plate. About half the real estate was occupied by frijoles. "Damn," he said, "Forgot to tell them to keep the beans."

The words were scarcely out of his mouth, when there came a sharp smack from the next table. Clancy had slapped down his copy of the local daily in a fit of rage. "Goddamn Bronson." He stood abruptly and pulled on his hat. "That tears it. He's gone too far, this time."

Rosanna Leese called out as Clancy strode toward the street door. "Señor, what about your food?"

"Keep it warm. I'll be right back."

"What's got into him?" Garrett asked as his friend surveyed the front page of the newspaper.

Fiske cleared his throat and read out loud the start of the main story above the fold:

"*Anti-Chinese Meeting in Salinas.*

"*A grand Anti-Chinese Meeting was held in Salinas City on Saturday the 19th inst., under the auspices of the Caucasian Society, and passed off very pleasantly. It was a crowded affair, and all present were of the male persuasion, as such meetings should be—simply voters. Owing to the late arrival in Monterey of the report of this meeting, we have not space to give even a synopsis of the remarks of the speakers. We will state, however, that* The Californian *endorses the resolutions, the crusade against the saffron-colored tribe, and will rejoice with our fellow laborers when our land is freed from their blighting presence."*

"So?" Garrett asked.

"Clancy's partial to the Chinese. Worked with them putting through the railroad tracks across the Sierra Nevada."

"Let's go," Doc said. He trotted out onto the Calle Principal followed closely by Fiske stuffing a biscuit into his mouth. Rosanna Leese called a maid and had all their plates sent back to the kitchen. Then she followed her customers outside.

She joined a crowd that had assembled within seconds of Clancy taking to the street, tailing him as he headed to The Pacific House where the newspaper office occupied the space next to Jane Krampner's tavern. A man on the street told his son, "Hitch on now," and fell in behind the gunman in anticipation of some free entertainment. As word spread, the saloons along the route emptied and a crowd was soon shadowing Clancy at a safe distance. "Take him by the collar and go right at him!" "Bronson's done like a dinner!" "Put your finger in his ear." If Clancy heard their shouts he made no sign. He just kept heading straight for the editorial office.

Bronson was dozing in his shirtsleeves with his feet on the desk. Clancy flung open the door and raked the rabbit-faced ink-slinger with his cold green eyes. "Do you know who I am?" he growled. That was enough to rouse the editor, not that his being awake could have made much difference. He found himself dangling by his collar from the gunman's fist, nose to nose with a peck of trouble.

"Matt Clancy," the editor stammered.

"I'm one of your readers, and you can consider this visit a kind of letter to the editor." Clancy threw Bronson against the wall, playing to the audience peering in through the windows. "Get your Goddamned pad and pencil and take this down. 'Some folks think that reading something in the newspaper makes it Gospel. Like this beef against the Chinese. Who in hell doesn't know a Celestial who's all wool and a yard wide? But if it says in the paper there's an anti-Chinese meeting somewhere and that's a good thing, then people will forget the good Chinese they know. What's printed becomes public opinion. People will think it's their duty to hate the Chinaman because it's popular. Well, that's hogwash. Think for yourselves. Anybody who takes the word of a pismire like Bronson is more of a damned fool than he is.'" He picked up the editor by his shirtfront again. "Now you print that just like I said it."

A clatter like somebody getting a chair busted over his head reached the crowd on the street. By the time Doc Garrett shouldered his way to the door, the sounds of mayhem had ceased and the gawkers stood breathless. Garrett was on the point of entering the newspaper office when the gunman appeared at the door. They stood one on each side of the threshold eyeing each other like cats on a fence. Rosanna Leese watched the staring contest and gave the advantage to Clancy with his bay-water green eyes.

"If you'll step aside I'll be able to tell if stitches are called for," Garrett said.

"He's all yours, sawbones," Clancy said. "I hope you're as good at stitching as old Doc Archer. He had only one arm. Used to tie knots with his teeth. Always drew a crowd with that trick." He thumbed the brim of his hat as he would to a lady, stepped off into the street, and headed back to the boardinghouse.

Rosanna Leese hastened after him, anxious to preserve order in her establishment by making sure Clancy's plate was at his place without delay. That done, she went upstairs to the room occupied by her cousin to recount all the juicy details of the editor's drubbing.

Rosanna studied her pretty cousin's face and concluded that she looked pale. "What is it? Are you unwell?"

"A headache. It's nothing."

"You should take another glass of brandy."

"No, no. It will make me sleepy. I don't want to sleep."

"Sleep would do you a world of good."

"Consuela used to make a concoction for headache. I wish I knew how the old *bruja* made it. It always worked and never made one drowsy. Do you remember, the old one who used to bleed my father? That winter we all had the pleurisy she made up a tincture of red wine and *excremento del caballo reciente*. Mother said she'd take a beating rather than drink it."

"I think it was bad luck that you chucked Consuelo off the rancho. The old ones, they know magic. She's probably cast a spell on you."

Isabel's face went from pale to white.

"What is it?" Rosanna said. "You look like you've seen a ghost."

"I have," Isabel whispered. "It is as you say. The *bruja* cast a spell. She cursed me before she left. She has summoned him up from the grave to torment me."

"Who?"

"Felipe. He visits me at night. I fear to go to bed."

"He comes to you in dreams?"

"Not always. Last night ... something roused me ... I stood for a while at the open window in my nightdress. I thought maybe the moon was very bright and that it had awakened me, but there was no moon. Or maybe it was the wind that had been moaning. But the air was still. I was sure I had heard a low moan. But then I thought, no, maybe it was a memory from months ago, Felipe moaning."

"I hear things in the night all the time. Always it turns out to be nothing."

"Worse to hear something that is nothing, than nothing that is something."

"Now you're talking nonsense."

"No, I'm not. What I mean is there are sometimes dreams so vivid that when you wake you don't know what is real and what is imaginary. I have been having such dreams since Felipe was laid in the ground. Most mornings I wake confused and distraught."

"It is a spell," Rosanna said, "some charm that is stealing away your sanity. Tell me what you remember about the dreams."

"It's always the same. I wake with my nightgown twisted around my neck and his voice still loud in my ears. He says, "How long since the last rain?""

"Felipe?"

Isabel nodded. "I say to him, 'Is it better now, Felipe? Has the pain stopped?' And then I think about my words reaching down through the heavy dirt and into the pine coffin where he lies with the coins on his eyes. He never answers me. Maybe he cannot hear. Or will not. It's a willful ghost who only speaks and never listens."

"That's all he says?"

"Oh, no. He speaks much. 'You must find my journal,' he says, 'the one that I wrote in every day—the weather, the price of cattle at market, the name of the new hired man, the date I ordered my new saddle. It's bound in dark leather, in the desk in the study.' So I go to find it, but I ask him other things while I am looking through his desk. 'Felipe,' I say, 'please tell me; did we do the right thing? Do you speak to me from Heaven? Do the angels look down upon me and say, 'Ah, Isabel was a good wife to risk her mortal soul.' They know it was what you wanted, don't they?' 'Isabel,' he says, 'You are a good wife, but sometimes not very practical. I do not say this to chide you, only to remind you that in running a rancho there are certain things that must be done. Miguel will come to you—and soon—to ask what is to be done about the stock. And what will you say? It's been ninety-three days since the last rain. In '68 the cattle lasted through two months when not a single drop fell from heaven and they drank only dew.'"

Rosanna regarded her cousin with concern. "Ninety-three days? What are you talking about? It has been raining all month and won't stop until spring."

Isabel rubbed her temples. "I told you, he says these things to me in a dream. He's warning me about the months ahead. He says I must keep the book so I will know how long the cattle have been without water, but all I really care about is whether he is in Heaven or not. He will not tell me if we did the right thing."

Rosanna took Isabel's lovely face in her hands. "Isabel! You must stop talking like this. People will think you've gone mad."

Lucy Lied

"Of course, you're right," Isabel said. "Here with you in the broad light of day the dream sounds absurd. But the matter of the creek, the water, is purely practical. I have to get it back."

"This is absurd. Why are we discussing drought in the midst of the winter rains?"

Chapter Thirteen

Not long after first light on the morning after Crevole Bronson took a letter to the editor from Matt Clancy, Ida Fleming stood at the door of the French Hotel. "It is urgent that I talk to him," she said to the black-browed landlady who opened up only after Ida had beat her knuckles raw. "If you wouldn't mind telling him I'm here I will wait. I'm afraid my heart is too weak to tolerate two flights of stairs."

The Mexican woman regarded the visitor with little sympathy in spite of her stick thin wrists and wattled neck margined with age-stained lace. But in the end, the señora shuffled her ill humor in the direction of the outside stair to summon Adrian Fiske.

Ida Fleming spent the next few minutes trying to imagine what she would do if he were not in. If he were out making one of his interminable paintings of that cypress tree, where might she next inquire for the doctor? The Badlands? God forbid. She then fell to pondering the insanity of it, the offense of such pointless labor to a person with common sense and too many chores to ever finish, among them the task of watching her sister Alice who was deathly afraid of storms. She pressed her thin lips together, a mannerism that habitually accompanied worry.

It was Doc's fault that the red-haired woman was there in the first place, dumped into her lap like a stray puppy that everyone wanted to save, but no one wanted to care for. He had offered a token payment for the girl's room and board, but as with most of the commerce of Monterey it would come down to a share of whatever goods he received in payment for his doctoring. He was rich in corn and stone fruit in the summer, new wine in the fall, fish in the winter, lamb in the spring, and eggs, tallow, and potatoes at all times of the year. A whole ham he'd received once for saving a child from dying of diphtheria; once for setting a herder's broken bone, a whole stinking calf hide. She grew restive waiting. Her foolishness in taking on the charge loomed larger in her mind by the minute.

Ida occupied herself with surveying the height of the sun in the sky and establishing how much longer she would wait. Ten minutes later she was on the point of leaving when his flannel-clad legs came stalking down the steps. He was hatless, and shoeless, pulling on a tattered dressing gown. "Forgive me for making you wait, but I had the deuce of a time trying to find my trousers. What's the matter, my good lady?"

"Mr. Fiske," she began, "I need to find the doctor. He is not at The Rookery and I thought perchance he might be here with you."

"No, I'm afraid he isn't."

"Then you must find him and send him to me right away."

"What is the nature of the emergency?"

"He has lodged the widow Talbott in my house as you know, but I find I cannot keep her. We are being threatened by the Chinese. I am the object of some heathen spell and fear for the safety of my home, myself, and my poor dear Alice."

"Oh, my. Won't you come upstairs and have a cup of tea?"

"That I cannot," Mrs. Fleming replied, irritated at the habit of all British persons of her acquaintance to offer tea in a time of crisis. "I must get home right away. Alice becomes so agitated whenever I am absent. This time of year with the rain, especially."

"But surely she is in the company of Mrs. Talbott," Fiske observed.

Mrs. Fleming shook her head. "One incapable of uttering a word of reassurance. I don't dare risk leaving the two of them alone too long." She took her handkerchief from the end of her sleeve and briefly pressed it to her mouth. "Please assure me you will find Doctor Garrett and tell him I must speak to him directly."

"And so I shall," he said, "as soon as I've properly dressed. But please, before you go, would you elaborate on the nature of the spell? Have you some manifestation of this ill will?"

She removed a small bundle from her handbag, something about the size of an apricot wrapped in a napkin. "You may show him that. It was left on my doorstep last night. I beheld it this morning when I went out to sweep."

The painter gingerly lifted the edge of the napkin and beheld the object and a strip of white paper barely six inches long, inscribed with Chinese script and neatly holed in several places. "Well, this is a puzzle," he said. "But I think we may be able to find out the nature of this writing without the assistance of a medical practitioner."

"I insist on seeing him," she said, "and without delay. The Talbott woman is no longer welcome to lodge with me. It is she who brought this on our house and if I'm not mistaken, she has other recourse in San Francisco or thereabouts."

"I daresay," Adrian agreed, folding away the object of Mrs. Fleming's visit and thrusting it into his pocket. "Leave it to me, my dear lady," he added.

She grimaced at the "my dear", adding to her dislike of the aforenoted tea fixation, a European decadence in the painter's familiar manner of address. "I'll be going home, then," she said, and abruptly set off toward The Grove.

Adrian Fiske returned to his rooms and made all preparations for a visit to Sally Locke. He took a bit of extra care in arranging his unruly locks in anticipation of the audience and set off for Washington Street with the object of Mrs. Fleming's anxiety secure in his coat pocket.

As it was still early morning he caught Sally before she retired for the day. He was ushered into her presence by Rose, the Chinese chambermaid. Sniffing the aroma of tea, he happily anticipated his long delayed morning cup.

"*Bienvenue*, Monsieur Fiske. *Comme tu es gentil de me rendre visite. Puis je t'offrir le thé?*"

Lucy Lied

"*Je meurs de soif,*" he said, and obeyed her hand, outstretched toward the divan, by sitting.

"I suspect you have come looking for Doc," she said, "but sadly I have not seen him of late. He has decided I am a bad habit, something to be given up like chocolate at Lent." She poured out and handed him his cup.

"*Merci,*" he said. "Doc gets very foolish notions from time to time. I suspect he was never loved enough as a child. In later years he has developed a penchant for melancholy attitudes of mind, a sort of self-inflicted martyrdom. I expect one day to see him trot off to a monastery for a hair shirt and a good pout."

"He says he is writing."

"Oh, good Lord, that's even worse. His wretched journal article. You see? It's just as I said. His father wrote journal articles and because Doc wasn't half-witted enough to go to war on the losing side of the recent American debacle, now he finds he needs to make amends by doing something to make the clan proud. Little might they care. They wanted him dead in a beautiful, Southern uniform, tragically doomed to oblivion in defense of human bondage. He thought he'd escape them by coming to California. Guilt, they say, broadens the horizons."

Adrian Fiske situated himself comfortably on the pale green velveteen settee and sniffed the cigar he'd just taken from a box Sally Locke offered. Sally struck a match. He put the smoke between his lips and inhaled as he rotated it in the flame. She blew out the match and tossed the charred stick into an ashtray with practiced efficiency. "Don't drop ash on my carpet," she said.

He blew a puff of blue smoke into the air. "Not every day I get to enjoy the pleasures of a courtesan's company."

She took a seat beside him and adjusted the drape of her saffron-colored dressing gown. "If only your friend were so appreciative." Sally regarded the lively blaze on the grate of her fireplace. "He puzzles me. These spells of sadness, they are very worrisome. It's worse this year, I think, than I have ever seen it."

"The melancholy." Adrian picked up his tea from the table at his knee and sipped. "I daresay he will always be prone to sullen moods. He's a dark, brooding character. It's his normal way of going about in the world. I don't know that there's any sudden cause for concern."

"He hasn't been himself since the trial. In bed he lacks ardor. I think he is bored with me."

He admired her for not mincing words or lowering her eyes when she said what was on her mind. She glowed, not in that damp euphemistic way, but with a sexual impulse bubbling just below her delicious tawny surface. He found himself only half listening, trying to parse where seductiveness came into the mix. Was it due to her frankness that she exuded such sensuality? Was it that the things she said would make most women blench or did her honesty bring the fever down a few degrees, bleeding off pressure? In either case, the idea that Doc might find Sally boring made him doubt his friend's sanity more than ever.

Sally sighed. "You're not listening to me. Why is it that men are so apt not to listen?"

"Sorry, what was it?"

"I want to know what's wrong with him."

"Oh, my dear! So do I. I've asked myself that very question a thousand times. Whatever it is drove him out here to California in the first place, so I suspect we *shouldn't* want to cure him lest, once healed, he might leave for Philadelphia on the next train." He sipped his tea. She didn't prod him to continue, but sat patiently. He liked that. "It has to do with that steamer trunk of his. It's full of letters and oddments that have no particular use, but mean something to him. Mementoes of an unpleasant nature. A collection of slings and arrows."

"*Quoi?*"

"A collection of slights, insults, accusations. When he's tuning up for one of his spells, he goes into that room where he keeps the trunk and begins unpacking it. He comes inevitably to the letters from his mother. There's one edged in black. I've found it in his hand many times when he'd drunk himself unconscious."

"You have read this letter?"

"Oh, no. I've no interest in the sentiments of his imperious Mama. Cowardly, I suppose, but her letters exude dreariness, much like the scrabbling of the ravens on the roof."

"The nuns. I know. He has a particular horror of them," Sally said.

"As if he were a parochial schoolboy terrorized by large women in black."

She laughed. "Yes."

He grew thoughtful. "There's something in that, I think. The notion that his depression has to do with childhood. It's as if he grew into a man physically but in his heart remained a six-year-old."

Sally shrugged. "This is a new revelation to you? I have always thought so. It is what makes men so—" she waved the fingers of one hand to coax a word from the air. "*Toujour ils cherchent le téton.*"

"That may be true, but not all men are prone to fits of hopelessness."

"So what is it about him that brings on these black moods? Why does he not throw away these things that make him despair instead of keeping them in a trunk?"

"You should ask him yourself."

Sally left the settee to pace before the window. "I have tried. He will not talk to me. He said if I keep asking him questions he will go to a Chinese whore, one who knows no English so that even if she talks it will not bother him." Sally considered the chary sun that poorly lit her view of Washington Street. It was empty but for two dogs nosing each other. "Must be why he fancies that red-headed woman, because she doesn't pester him with talk."

"Don't take this personally, *chérie*, but he may have designs on that girl."

She settled on a seat with a tufted cushion before her mirror, and commenced brushing her black curls. "Oh? He has said he loves her?"

He watched Sally's face in the mirror, lovely, urbane, unperturbed. The brush worked with long, even strokes bearing the hair up from the nape of her neck. The black-lashed lids of her eyes seemed to slip down a little as the brush moved. He thought how magnificent it would be to be Sally Locke, gratified by all things in turn, one sensation as pleasing as the next, the feel of the hairbrush as satisfying as sex, insofar as sex was over and it was now time for brushing her hair. She seemed incapable of regret, of longing for the thing that had just passed. She dwelt, he thought, on the surface of time, uninterested in heretofore, having far less use for a fond memory than a dog that lies with his legs twitching in his sleep, chasing a remembered rabbit.

"Not in so many words, but he'd be the last person you'd expect to come straight out with it. He's making noises about studying her case, her muteness. Well, any fool can see through that."

"She won't make him happy. She's not as pretty as I."

"Would be difficult to find any woman walking the earth who is."

"It can't be that he entirely wants to forego conversation. You would never believe what duels of words Doc and I have. Like sparks in the air, the words back and forth. How can he want a mute? A woman dumb as a dog?"

"As I said, he means to try and cure her."

"They say she's an idiot, so even if she could speak what good would it be?"

"There is that," he said.

"He may cure her, but what will she do for him? Give him half-wit children—all with red hair, I suppose."

"I suppose."

She eyed the painter as he sipped his tea. "So, why are you looking for him?"

"Oh, heavens. I nearly forgot." He fumbled the napkin-wrapped object out of his pocket. "It has to do with the Talbott woman. She's staying with Ida Fleming, as you probably know. But Mrs. Fleming is no longer willing to keep her because she found a talisman from the Celestials on her porch this morning. She fears an evil spell."

"A talisman?" Sally looked as he unwrapped the thing he held in his hand. "It's a rice ball."

"Well, yes, but what of the kanji painted on it in red and this strip of paper with more writing?"

"If you like I can get my maid to tell us what it means," Sally said.

"That's the very thing."

She rang a bell and presently a neat little Chinese woman in the plain-aproned dress of a chambermaid came into the room. "Rose, look," Sally said, using the European name she'd given the girl. "This was left on someone's porch. What is it?"

"Good luck charm," the maid said. "Chinese people leave this as a mark of gratitude. Is rice for good luck. Red letter means long life."

"And the paper strip?" Sally asked.

"Is a prayer, also for luck. Holes in paper to fool evil spirits. Evil spirit go into hole and cannot find way out."

"So it's like a note of thanks," Adrian said. "Perhaps Mrs. Fleming will reconsider keeping the girl when she finds out she's not the object of ill will."

"Red," Rose continued, "is very lucky color for Chinese people. Woman with red hair is favored by gods."

"I'm sure everyone will be glad to hear it," Sally said, dismissing the maid. She returned the rice ball to Adrian. "Still, Mrs. Fleming is a Methodist. It may be impossible to talk her out of her mistrust."

"That I'll leave to Doc," Adrian said. "I've done my bit. Now it's up to him to save the widow Talbott from being chucked out on the street."

"Widow, indeed," Sally scoffed. "They called her Mrs. at the trial to keep from offending the ladies, but everyone knew better. I find it more offensive that this woman Doc loves is a milkmaid. An idiot! She probably never owned a pair of shoes before she came to trial. What, in God's name, does he see in this creature?"

Adrian found little in her assessment to take issue with, but out of a sense of loyalty to his friend he refrained from agreeing. "Speaking of Doc, I have to go find him now that the mystery of the rice ball is solved. He'll be walking the beach, most likely, oblivious of the skies above his head and the squirrel holes at his feet."

But Doc was not to be found, and it was Adrian himself who told Mrs. Fleming of the auspiciousness of red hair.

Chapter Fourteen

As the weeks passed, the ebb and flow of mundane ailments depressed Doc's spirits with their grinding regularity. Once in a great while there would be a case that would corner his imagination and captivate it for a day or two. But these were few and far between, leaving his considerable mental capacity to probe a bottomless pit of ennui. Through October, Doc suffered a torment of niggling discontents. The cosmic movement that made for seasons made him feel all the more stuck by contrast. The fine line where the tin-pot sky met the gunmetal bay caused him peculiar anguish, especially as the calendar neared November, the month of his birth. His birthday caused him to reflect on what he'd done with his life, how he'd wound up a foreigner in a dusty California town. It wouldn't leave him alone, a feeling of waste. He thumbed an old issue of *The Southern Journal of Medical Sciences* and reflected that in other parts of the world there was science, people speculating about contagion and such.

With the daylight hours growing ever shorter, Doc's evening rambles along the beach transitioned to late afternoon. He needed what niggardly light there was to study birds with a telescope. He'd put the commercial piers to his back and head past the Chinese fishing village and Lovers of Jesus Point to the southern end of the bay where the lighthouse beamed its white ray out to the horizon.

There he would sit and wait for the keeper of the light to sing some doleful Irish melody as the sun slipped into the sea. Luce was from Martha's Vineyard, and had come to mind the light by way of a ruinous turn at gold digging. But for that one lapse that had led him to California, he was a diligent Yankee, with clockwork habits. Faithfully he kept the gas lamp fired behind the great Fresnel lens and polished the prisms bright so the beacon would stretch far out to sea to fend off ships from the rock-bound shore. Luce had one of only two pianos in town and sang his Irish melodies at sunset about the time most folks were at their dinner and the beach was bereft of good Christians. He had a fine tenor voice that could wring tears from a stone. His very soul seemed to float out the windows of the whitewashed tower at sunset when even his New England efficiency could not disguise a wild penchant for melancholy. Or at least that's how it struck Garrett, being of a melancholy nature himself.

Doc walked at the edge of the water, where the profile of each incoming swell was traced by bits of broken shell and seaweed. Coming to an immense driftwood log, furry gray from the saltwater that had borne it across the Pacific from some Oriental forest, he sat on the sand and leaned into the sun-warmed wood. He studied a tide pool formed in the hollow of a flat rock and from time to time looked up to observe a line of pelicans coasting low over the swells on their broad motionless wings.

As he sat listening to the lighthouse keeper's song, he spied the silhouette of a man coming toward him from farther down the strand. The figure walked with a stiff, long-legged gait like a heron stalking minnows. "Hello, Adrian!" Doc yelled. "Hello, Adrian Fiske!" The gaunt painter waved back and bent his steps toward his friend.

"So how did your painting go today?" Doc asked, when it was no longer necessary to shout.

"Well," Adrian said. He set down his tripod, paint box, and canvas. "The cypress looked remarkably lovely. And how goes it with you?"

Doc pointed to the sea-flooded rock at his side. "I've been studying tide pool society. The snails are Turks. Their shells are turbans. You see? The different seaweeds are Persian carpets just like in the Arab bazaar in one of the storybooks in the nursery back in Macon. The anemones are maidens waving their pink arms at me. And the urchins are villains."

"You're not going to start on one of your melancholy binges, are you?"

"No. Why would you say that?"

"Because whenever you start talking about Macon you tend to get very grave. Bleak, even."

"Why don't you go on back to painting your tree?"

"I'd rather talk about what brings on your spells. Besides one study a day is enough, thank you."

"Never mind my spells."

"Of course. It's just like you to try to figure out everybody but yourself. You have to be a deep, dark mystery. God forbid we should any of us understand what goes on in your tortured soul. You fancy yourself like Hamlet, I'm sure. An enigma for the ages. Why does he not act? Why does he turn on Ophelia? What was there between him and his mother?"

"You remind me that I haven't yet had a drink today."

"You're turning into a sot."

Doc stood and brushed the sand off his backside. "I'm in good company."

"I'll stand you a drink at Simoneau's," the painter offered. "I am possessed of a few forlorn pennies left from my last infusion of cash."

They began the trudge back toward town, stopping now and again for Doc to raise his telescope and peer at a far-off object. He stopped for some time when Point Alones came into view. Adrian squinted with his naked eye at the Chinese fishing village, little more than some driftwood lumber thrown up on top of a crust of rocks standing out to sea. Garrett seemed intent on studying the black-eyed children squatting in the doorways of the shacks.

"Odd group, the Celestials," Adrian said.

"Hmm," Garrett said, thinking he meant their nocturnal means of fishing, using lanterns to draw the squid to their nets. To see their slipper boats by day, bobbing idly on the tide, you'd think you'd come upon the laziest people under the sun.

"Their religion," the painter went on. "I quite admire it, the way they light firecrackers to scare off the evil spirits. You can hardly see the houses for the smoke. It would be nice if everything evil could be scared off with a firecracker, don't you think? What in tarnation are you staring at, anyway?"

"The spot where I first saw her," Doc replied, without bothering to take the telescope away from his eye. "Digging in a pile of abalone shells."

"Some people collect the shells and make buttons of the pearly part," Adrian said.

Still Doc watched. "No, it ain't that."

"What, then?"

Doc chewed his mustache. "Well, on second thought, maybe it is." He lowered the scope and started to walk on. "Well? Come on. I'm parched."

"You're a queer bird," Adrian replied, trudging alongside. "I suspect you fancy her." He considered the proposition for a minute. "She might be pretty enough now that she's scrubbed, but why you'd look further than Sally Locke is beyond me. Now there's an interesting female, a beauty with a sharp mind."

"I've got nothing to say on the subject," Doc said, scowling.

"Suit yourself," Fiske said. "My only objective is to keep you from dwelling overmuch on morbid thoughts." As they ambled toward Simoneau's, Doc found his mood improving, though he didn't admit it. He continued to scowl in silence, trying to think of a way to approach the redheaded woman.

At the Bohemian Café the room was abuzz with talk about an evening performance, the clientele drinking energetically, getting motivated to attend. Doc read aloud from a broadside. "Dr. Elliott Canby, Eminent Clairvoyant and Healer demonstrates the Science of Animal Magnetism tonight at Swann's Theater." He chuckled. "Good lord, I might have known there was something special going on. It's Halloween and Christmas all rolled into one. And that's not all." Simoneau poured him a shot and he swallowed it before continuing. "The gentleman is also pleased to offer for the price of admittance, readings of the past, present and future through the wondrous Art of Magicology."

Bronson threw some money on the bar. "I think I see another whiskey in my future if you don't mind, Frenchie. Drinks all around. Doc's not quite prepared for this evening's event, as yet. But the more he imbibes, the more spiritual he gets."

Simoneau poured out a round of shots. "*Et bien.* So I see."

A squaw who did the cooking, two mongrels who had been whalers, a shoemaker from Illinois, and a Swiss candy-maker all shoved their hands across the bar to take advantage of Bronson's largesse.

After they finished their drinks, Adrian Fiske withdrew his watch from his vest pocket and pronounced it time to be off. "Come on, Doc," he said, "we don't want to miss the opening gambit."

It was a short walk up toward the Presidio to Swann's, a shack that housed sailors and put on shows when the bedding was rolled up and put away. Nearly all the seats were filled by the time they walked in. "It's fitting," Fiske said, "that we skeptics skulk in the back of the hall rather than mingling with the faithful."

Doc pointed to the front of the house. "There's old Ross Spencer. I'll warrant he thinks he'll be walking without a cane by the end of the evening."

"Don't get feisty. It's a curiosity. Folks are just here to see what's what."

"My foot. They think medicine is all hocus-pocus anyway. If they can't get a cure from me, they'll try this trumped-up sharper."

"Good lord!" Adrian said, "is that Mrs. Fleming in the third row? And next to her, the tall woman, isn't that—"

Before the painter could finish his thought, a man in a pearl gray suit with immaculate white cuffs dashed up the center aisle. He bounded to center stage, silencing the crowd with his appearance out of nowhere. He was of medium height and lithe, befitting a spiritual type, with high cheek bones, a neatly trimmed gray beard and pale, pale blue eyes. He had long, shining silver hair with a white streak to one side of the middle part. People whispered the streak was from his being struck by lightning, a bolt that had shocked the color right out.

"Friends," he began, "the Lord be with you." His voice radiated warmth. His smile embraced them. "And all His glorious angels look down on this assembly. Those self-same blessed souls who have guided me on my travels across this great continent, shielded me and showed me the way of healing; the self-same blessed souls who watched over each and every one of you as you left the comfort of hearth and home to come here tonight to share the brotherhood of their spiritual message, a message of healing, healing of the body, yes, and of the soul, our souls that cry out in longing and blind hopelessness for help from our loved ones beyond the veil called death." He clasped his hands. "And why do we long? Because our loved ones have left us bereft and forlorn. And why are we blind? Because we cannot apprehend them in their spiritual guises. We cannot see the loving arms they hold wide open to embrace us, because our eyes have become so used to seeing only the material things of this world. We have lost our capacity to perceive the spirits of our loved ones all around us. But tonight, my friends, will the scales fall from your eyes." He opened his arms wide and flashed his broad smile on the expectant faces before him. "Brothers and sisters, I am Brother Elliott Canby, and I am here with you tonight to bring you together with your loved ones that have crossed on to the other side. For I have been shown the way. I have been made to see that path of light where the spirits dwell on their long journey to Heaven."

He raised his long-fingered white hands. "Yes, my friends, I say I have seen that path of light. I have seen those dear departed souls who stay yet a bit after death waiting for some word from their earthly loved ones. We retain our names and our habits of speech after death; did you know that? Yes, and some of our odd ways, our stubbornness, our affections. The departed have just as much need of brotherhood as the living, my friends. Yes, and hear me now; it is not they who have abandoned us, but we who have abandoned them. Though the body fails, the spirit cries out for recognition beyond the grave! But do the living hear? Do they stop to acknowledge the pining of the dead soul who longs to be among family and friends? What's that you say? You say you put flowers on the burial mound near that lovely marble headstone that cost you a pretty penny?"

He dropped his hands and shook his head at such folly. "Now brothers and sisters, you've heard of the great cemeteries where our dead sons and husbands who fought so bravely in our recent Civil War lie buried. I have walked among the headstones at Gettysburg. I have seen the monuments, the great stone figures nestled in the quiet groves of ancient trees. It is a thrilling sight, a sight that inspires the mind to thoughts of eternity, or perhaps to the brevity of our own lives on earth. Maybe those thoughts incline us to be a little kinder to our families, more generous with our employees. The benefits are many and sundry. But let me ask you this; are they benefits for the souls of the departed or for the living? What makes us think that several tons of carved marble placed over their bones in an expanse of greensward will ease the torment of the departed souls? Do we think their souls benefit because building monuments is easy? Easier than asking ourselves how to bridge that great demarcation between the living and the dead?"

Here Brother Elliott paused to lower the accusatory timbre of his voice and survey its effect on the audience. "Now brothers and sisters, I know some of you came here tonight smitten with doubt. Some of you came here tonight hoping your friends wouldn't see you enter the hall. Then why have you come? Curiosity? Maybe. But maybe it's something more, something you can't quite explain to yourself—something that defies reason. Because scoff as you will at the idea that Brother Elliott can put you in contact with a dead loved one—scoff in your mind with all your faculties of reason as you will—there are still those of you out there tonight who believe in your hearts. You believe with that same faith that the prophets had, that Moses had leading his people through the desert without any rational hope of finding a habitable place. It is your faith that led you here tonight, brothers and sisters. Now I want to see you raise your hands, those of you who have faith! Raise 'em up high for all the scoffers in the back to see!"

A few hands showed timidly at first, then a score, then a sea of hands. Some waved both arms in the air. Others stood and called out, waving letters or hankies. They shouted against one another, clamoring to be heard by the serene figure on stage.

"My God! It's like a political convention," Adrian yelled. "Let's get out of here."

But Doc wanted to stay and watch since he'd paid good money. He didn't move. By then the silvery figure on stage had pretty much quieted the crowd.

"Friends—That's good. Put 'em down now. Friends, let me tell you a little more about myself. I was as much in doubt as any of you and I was no less troubled in my heart. Trouble can hardly describe what I felt, my friends, when the Good Lord took my dear wife Sarah and left me with a child just nine years old." His chin dropped to his chest and he seemed to subdue a sob. "Sarah was ... Well, any of you who have lost a sweetheart, a husband, or a wife know what I mean." When he looked up, his pale eyes glowed soft with tears. "In the seven years that followed her death I was like a ghost myself. Doing the chores, taking the buckboard to town, going in for church on Sunday. I saw nothing and heard nothing and felt nothing. My world without Sarah was bereft of colors and flavors and music and laughter. What I said and did, I seemed aware of only vaguely. I was a man afraid to open up his eyes and see how alone he was."

He paused and leaned toward the audience. "I hear weeping out there. Someone is weeping who understands just how alone I felt because you are feeling that way right now. You are alone and without the will to wake up and see your loneliness in the light of day. And friends, I know that suffering. I have felt the full measure of what you're feeling, but I say to you, do not shed tears tonight because your life is about to change. Just as mine did. Let me tell you how it happened to me."

He paced a bit. "I had a farm in Pennsylvania about two hour's ride by train from the great city of Philadelphia. I was out in the wheat field. The great high clouds of Indian summer were rolling overhead. The wheat baked in the afternoon heat as I went about my harvesting. I swung my scythe alone, for I wanted nothing to

127

do with society. I did not look up nor to the left nor right, but just at the shining blade as it flashed and fell and flashed and fell. I didn't see the thunderheads as they gathered, nor the ominous shadow that came racing across the field before the wind that brought the first spatters of rain. The thunder crashed and the rain came in earnest, driving down the bearded heads of grain. I stood in the unnatural dark of midday and asked God to smite me dead for I had no more use for my life. I remember lifting my eyes to the torrent and seeing a bolt of lightning erupt from the black clouds. Then there was a blinding white flash behind my eyes and I was flung to the ground." He paused and looked at the dozens of eyes riveted to his face. "Presently the sun was shining brilliantly and before me were three figures clothed in radiance, floating above the wheat. I recognized Sarah first. I called out her name and she smiled and opened her arms to me. 'It's all right,' she was saying, 'I'm well. I've missed you, too.' And then I saw my mother and my older brother Seth who died in the cholera epidemic of '38. The three of them made a circle around me and hugged me close. And my Sarah ran her fingers through my hair and told me not to grieve anymore, because they were all with me. She said that she would be there for me whenever I chose to summon her. 'See me as I am now,' she said. 'Close your eyes and see me as I am now and I will be there.'"

A chair creaked in the silence of the hall. "When I came to, the doctors said I'd been asleep for sixty-nine days. They said it was a miracle I was still alive. I had a black mark on my forehead where the lightning struck and my hair had this white streak in it. So I knew that much was true, but I was afraid that my memory of Sarah was a cruel dream. I was desperate to contact her again, but my mind was clouded by memories of our early days together. In that state, I couldn't reach her. I became more and more despondent. What was the key she had given me to unlock that magical door? Had I lost it?" He stroked his brow as if racking his brain for a clue. "And then I remembered. She said I had to concentrate on seeing her as I had that day when I was struck down. I sat in a dark room, utterly quiet, and I conjured up that image of her in my mind. And there at last she was. I call it crossing over when I achieve this state of mind that will allow the spirits to reveal themselves to me." His head dropped in a pulpit gesture of contemplation.

"My friends, I wish I could teach each and every one of you to cross over just as I do. Lord, nothing would make me happier than to see each of you transported by your own powers of concentration. But that I cannot teach. Remember the first time this experience was visited upon me was not of my own free will, but as an act of mercy by those dear souls who saw me in my suffering. And having seen them in their heavenly guise, I was then able to picture them in my mind and visit them again. Without that first sight, however, you have no pictures for your mind to call up. Thus, I cannot teach you to cross over."

He waited for sounds of disappointment. "But don't despair. There is a way as you well know if you have read the bill posted outside. I can intercede for you with the spirit you wish to contact, if you will but trust me to act as the link between yourself and the other world. For since I first began contacting Sarah, I have learned how to call upon other spirits and to receive their answers to the questions I put. All that is needful is some personal token, a lock of hair or a watch perhaps, something that was carried close upon the person in life. With such an object I can begin the process of finding your loved one among all the thousands of souls crowding my mind with messages that they mean for me to convey to the living.

"Tonight I will attempt only one such contact, for under these conditions the crossing over is most difficult. The ideal situation is for me to meet with only half a dozen people in a darkened room around a table where we sit with our hands touching. This is what I would recommend for those who wish, after tonight's demonstration, to fix an appointment to attempt contact at a future date. I also provide private consultations for the purpose of channeling spiritual energy into the bodies of those afflicted with chronic diseases. Remember, it was not our modern medical practices, not the careful science of healing as practiced by trained physicians that led to my recovery from that bolt of lightning. After I regained consciousness, I lay in a state that the medical profession refers to as catatonia. I was taken to Philadelphia to the greatest school of medicine in the land. There I was studied, and poked and prodded. Finally it was allowed that my state was irreversible. The lightning strike, they said, had left me witless and inert. After two months of treating me to no avail, the doctors grew tired of my case and decided that I was to be sent to an asylum. It was then that my dear Sarah bade me return to the material world. On the sixty-ninth day after the lightning rendered me senseless, I got up from my bed with the full use of my faculties and possessed of a vigor that rivaled men ten years younger than myself.

"A cure was proclaimed in the newspapers. Yes, I have copies of those articles from two Philadelphia journals touting the skill of the doctors who brought about my revival. But I say to you, it was spiritual healing. Ask yourselves, brothers and sisters, whether that quickness that resides, not in the muscles and sinews of the body, but in the soul, could have come from any doctoring of this world. And then tell me you do not believe. Who here would tell me, that as I stand before you, I am not proof of the force of spiritual healing?"

Fiske looked sideways at Doc to see if he meant to answer Brother Elliott's challenge with hoots and jeers. There was a sneer on his lips, but he was enjoying the show, waiting for the next revelation like everyone else.

The moment had finally come when the spiritualist called for a member of the audience to provide him with an article from a departed loved one, something he might use to demonstrate his ability to commune with the spirits. From a forest of waving hankies and gloved hands, he chose Mrs. Vidalia Howe, who proffered a lock of her late husband's hair. She had climbed onto the stage and was on the point of delivering the brown curl into Brother Elliott's hand when a low voice boomed from the back of the hall. "Isn't it money you prefer to accept from ladies, Canby?"

Where he stood slouched against the wall at the back of the theater put him squarely on axis with the dumbstruck Brother Elliott. But Elliott couldn't make out his face in the shadows beyond the stage lights. "Sir, whoever you are, you're interrupting this demonstration. If you'll kindly hold your questions until after I've concluded—"

"Wait till you've ducked out the back door, you mean." His boots sounded a slow percussion as he moved from out of the shadow and walked slack-hipped down the center aisle, all unhurried, sure of himself. His face was the last part of him to emerge from the darkness, but only the lower half. His hat brim cast a mask over the eyes. Doc noted the muscles of his jaw working as he passed, the cords of his neck. He was taut underneath that lazy walk, like a lounging cat, feigning indifference before the pounce. He cocked his open cattleman's coat behind the butt of the gun on each hip. There was a scent of something sharp as he strode by, the sort of smell that spooks cattle at dusk.

"Get behind me, Satan," Adrian whispered to Doc, "it's Matt Clancy."

"We're in for a show now."

"Did you bring your bag?"

"No need. He doesn't leave much to mend."

The widow Howe crept off the stage and melted back into the audience. Canby stood to brazen it out. "Sir," he said, "I shall be forced to call on the local sheriff to intervene unless you stop this disruption."

"Sheriff Taylor's already here," Clancy replied.

Taylor stood up from his seat at the end of the third row and poked out his chest where the star was hung. Clancy reached into the breast pocket of his cattleman's coat and pulled out a photograph.

Canby sputtered. "Sheriff, are you going to let this ruffian break up a peaceful gathering?"

"This man stole five hundred dollars from Myra Thatcher, widow of Captain Silas Thatcher, killed at the Second Bull Run. This is the colonel's picture." Clancy passed the photo to Taylor. "You'll find one just like it in Canby's kit. Or should I say Croft. He went by the name of Croft in San Francisco."

"I don't know what you're talking about," Brother Elliott protested.

Lucy Lied

"I'm talking about how you fleeced Myra Thatcher out of her savings to build some sort of meeting house where you were supposed to sit around in the dark holding hands. You had her raise five hundred dollars from her friends and then you high-tailed it out of town. What's wrong, Canby? You're looking a little peaked. Maybe we should take you back to your hotel so you can lie down."

"I don't know any Myra Thatcher. He's making a mistake, I tell you!"

Clancy leaped to the stage and landed a slap across Canby's mouth. "Shut up, you prissy fraud." He commenced to haul and drag Brother Elliott by the collar toward the side door. "No mistaking that pretty hair of yours. Reminds me of another named George Custer, except his was gold, not silver. Counterfeits, the both of you."

Taylor stuffed the photo of the dead soldier in his pocket and followed along. "Reckon we'll have a look in your kit, Canby."

There was a stampede for the exits as the show left the theater for the street. It wasn't clear exactly what happened when Clancy got Brother Elliott back to the hotel. The sheriff was overtaken by the mob of citizens who satisfied themselves as to Canby's guilt without the help of the law. The contents of Canby's trunk showered down onto Alvarado Street from the window of his room and it was generally expected that the owner of the goods himself would follow suit at any moment. Many spectators took a refund on the price of admission to Canby's show by seizing an undergarment or a handkerchief or a boot. One of the men who made it into the room behind Clancy claimed Canby's collection of French postcards. Another got the pearl gray suit, which he put on as soon as Brother Elliott was stripped of it. Clancy found none of the money that Myra Thatcher had been bilked out of, but did claim for himself one trinket, a garnet earring circled with a garland of gold and seed pearls that he judged very fine.

Ida Fleming had Lucy by the hand, trying to lead her clear of the mob, but the girl would lag behind, craning and standing on tiptoe to see what was happening. "Come on, now," Mrs. Fleming said. "It's all over. We must not gawk at the cruel misfortune one man can visit upon another. It's unladylike." The girl's reluctance to come along puzzled her.

The next day, there were enough split knuckles among the hotheads in town to attest to the beating Canby had received before being cast out beyond the city limits. They lost sight of him running bootless in his union suit toward the shelter of the mist-hung pines, heading south with his silver hair streaming madly under the full moon.

Chapter Fifteen

Isabel lay on her side with her face turned to the window. She wearily gazed out at the colorless wash of first light. It promised very little, that light, perhaps escape from the torments of the night, but certainly nothing more. The voice had stopped. She held her breath and listened to make sure. She wanted to say her prayers on her back, but eschewed the bed where she'd wrestled the sheets all night. She went down on her knees against the cold floor instead. The chill of the boards, that was real. Somewhat revived, Isabel rose, grabbed a shawl, and wrapped it around her shoulders. She hastened to the study.

Her bare feet made no noise as she trod down the dark hall. There was no noise in the house at all. Before the double doors of the study she paused. He had been laid out in that room, on a board across the top of his desk, death being an impromptu affair, though it is the one thing that inevitably waits at the end of every life. There he was, washed and clothed in clean linen. She knew these things had been done because when she saw him laid out, every trace of the violent end was gone. She wondered vaguely who had done it, washed him. It was the sort of thing Consuelo would have done.

Isabel walked around the desktop, to the side with the drawers, her hand wary, lingering on the brass pull. She stopped breathing as she pulled the drawer open, half convinced she would see his dead face there instead of the leather cover of the journal.

His friends had filed in one at a time the day of the wake. They came into the study to spend a last moment with him before six of them had put the coffin on their shoulders and carried it out. Sebastián Oreña had come without his wife. She was not robust and had nearly died in childbirth the year before. Had she died, Sebastián might have come as a suitor, not because he loved Isabel but because he loved her land.

She drew the journal out of the drawer and opened it to the first page, closely covered with Felipe's deliberate scrawl. It suited her to look at the writing, not seeing words, but seeing his hand moving, regarding the ink marks as a sign of his having once labored over the page, but without significance in themselves. *Why does he torment my sleep? I did only as he asked.* In her limbs still lived a somatic memory of the enormity of the struggle to get the old man's inert body to the top of the stairs. How he had pleaded with his eyes, uttered incoherent encouragement. He could no longer command his tongue. *I did only as he asked.* Her memory was not of emotion but of being air-starved from heaving. For one so wasted he was very heavy. Only after he was dead did the numbness wear off and the fear begin. *Consuelo's curse.*

She put her dead husband's journal back where she'd found it. She sank into the chair Felipe had used since he'd first come to the rancho. The seat was cracked and stiff, the thongs under the seat all broken down.

She tried to think about Clancy. She considered the lank pistolero with the steel-gray hair and the cold green eyes. How old was he? Was he really as deadly as people said? And was it true, the rumor that he wanted to leave California, go to Hawaii? She had only the vaguest sense of where Hawaii was, but didn't much care beyond the fact that if Clancy had a mind to go there he might just sell the land back. *But why should I have to buy back what is rightly mine, my dowry from my father?*

She dressed in clothes of sober colors, thinking of the gay frocks she used to wear while Felipe was still alive, how he enjoyed seeing her arrayed like a tropicbird. She stood before her mirror and arranged her hair out of habit rather than with any particular style in mind. It struck her, as she looked critically into the mirror, that she had aged. There is a day when the luster leaves the skin and the face becomes a mask. *Today,* she thought, without much regret, *I am old.*

The only thing that mattered anymore was the water for the cattle, the land across which that water flowed. She twisted the wedding ring on her left hand, invoking Felipe's spirit as she did, asking for his guidance, his wisdom. "This is what he wants," she said to herself, "that I reclaim the land." It was the one thing that would placate the ghost if she could achieve it. The first step was to talk to Clancy about the contract to allow Oreña's herd and her own to graze on his ranch for a percentage of the price the beef fetched at market. Then, once the cattle were on the land she would find a way to take it back.

She had Ramón saddle her black gelding and in a little less than an hour she reached the edge of Clancy's property near the Monterey-Salinas Highway, where the one-room shack crouched in the shade of a spreading sycamore tree. She reined the tall horse in, dismounted, and let the reins trail on the ground. She looked in through the window in the north wall and noted a brass bedstead, a tick, a nightstand near the bed. She left off spying on Clancy's goods and turned around to view the high ground to the west. She pictured a herd cresting the hill and running full tilt toward the water. A moment later it was Clancy she beheld cantering toward the little house on his palomino. He pulled his mount up short, stirring up dust, and slid down from the saddle. "Buenos días, señora," he said politely. He grasped her hand man-to-man. "Thank you for coming." He motioned toward the front of the house. "Won't you come in?"

She followed him to the porch on the side of the cabin that fronted the highway. He unlocked the door and threw it open. "Forgive the dust. I'm sorry to say I neglect this place."

"I think it will suit our purpose well enough."

"I daresay," he replied. He ushered her inside and took off his hat, which he threw down on the table near the window.

Isabel plucked at the drape of her habit and flicked a fictitious piece of lint from the sleeve. "I have come to speak to you about this land," she said. "I have long wanted to learn of your intentions."

"I figured as much," he said. His hard green eyes were alight, anticipating what she might say or do next.

"You will wish perhaps to stay here? Establish your own rancho?"

"It's been on my mind, but I've made no decision as yet."

"At dinner at my cousin's boardinghouse you spoke of traveling."

"Like I said, I haven't made up my mind. You'll be the first to know if I do decide to leave. I'll make you a good deal on my property."

"On *my* property, you mean."

"I won't debate you. I'll just point out that the law's on my side of the question."

"I didn't come here to debate," she said. "As we discussed before, my husband's cousin and I need to water our stock. I've come to discuss terms."

"So Oreña has deputized you to make a deal with me?"

"I speak for myself. After you and I reach an agreement I will tell my husband's cousin the details. It is better that way. Oreña is angry. I fear he has little skill for negotiating even when his blood is not boiling."

"What's he got to be mad about?"

"You're putting up barbed wire. Sebastián would sooner tear the wire down than talk business."

"He does and there's vaqueros who'll get shot up or jailed. You tell him he has my word on that."

She shrugged. "There's no need for violence. I'm willing to enter into an agreement if we can come to an understanding on price." She turned away from him, ran her gloved fingers across the nightstand next to the bed then wheeled around again. "We mean to pay by the head."

Clancy pulled out a chair and sat down. "Go on."

"You will need to put in some ditches to carry the water across the fields so the cattle can spread out to drink, and build a bridge for when the creek's too high to cross without swimming your horse."

"Suppose I agree to that. How much are you willing to pay?"

"It depends on what I get at market," she explained. "Our herds will graze here for six months and then when we take them to market they'll fetch a good price. Maybe five dollars a head. I'll give you twenty percent of what I'm paid."

"Twenty-five percent," Clancy said.

"Twenty-five? How dare you!" She took a step toward the door, as if she considered the negotiation over.

"Come on, now. Even at that rate you'll wind up with twice what your beasts will fetch if they were to graze on dry stubble. You should at least talk to Oreña about it."

"I expect I will," she snapped. "I'll tell him about your offer but he won't agree. I might afford your twenty-five percent, but for him it will be too expensive."

"Why's that?"

"Because my husband's cousin must run his cattle across my land to get to your water. I won't allow it unless I receive compensation."

"So you want to tax him for crossing your land," Clancy said. "How do you think that will go over?"

A flush mottled her neck. "What do you mean?"

"It's as you said. Oreña would sooner cut you down than negotiate with you."

She stamped her nicely shod foot. "I'd rather take my chances doing business with my husband's cousin than to bear the insult of bartering with a common thief."

"Be reasonable, señora. You know I won this land off old Felipe fair and square. It was an honest bet. No shenanigans."

"The railroad men cheat. You knew before you bet which coach was going to come in first. Felipe was a fool and you are a thief."

Clancy stiffened. "You call me names and you'll find your rate set higher than Oreña's."

"You don't scare me. I know the truth about you, you so-called gunslinger. You've never shot a man. You're all talk, all bluff. But you've killed no one. Wounded, or knocked down with your fists, but never killed. I don't think I have so much to fear from you."

His face darkened. "There's a few dead rebels might disagree with you. But the fact is, I think you'll find my word carries as much weight as my gun. A reputation for being deadly is more useful than killing, because the reputation keeps most troublemakers on the other side of the street and saves on ammunition."

"You're a practical coward," she said.

"Rational, except where children and animals are concerned. I reckon every man is allowed a jot of sentimentality." He considered the firm set of her mouth. "In view of our friendship I didn't figure you to drive such a hard bargain."

"Friendship?"

"Your husband and I were on good terms."

"Felipe is gone," she said. "Much as I honor his memory I will not be seduced by tall tales of your heroics, as he was."

He considered her, talking tough, and thought of the sodbusters' women, the ones he was sent to roust from their homesteads in the San Joaquin. The sodbusters' wives had a set of the mouth that meant they didn't expect fairness but would get on with their lives anyway, and drag the men along with them. They looked as if they'd never been girls, had been born flinty and clear-headed. Just the opposite of the coddled bitch whose black eyes glanced coyly at the bed, from under eyelids drooping with the weight of her thick black lashes. Yet he sensed that under her haughty bravado she was desperate enough to do almost anything. "All right. You make your deal with Oreña and then the three of us will talk. I'll not drop my fee below twenty-three percent for either you or Felipe's cousin."

She stripped the glove off her right hand and held it out for him to shake.

Lucy Lied

"I'll put our terms in writing," Clancy said. "You'll hear from me soon."

After he grasped her hand she pulled her glove back on and noticed that the button at the wrist was gone. She made a mental note to have one of the maids replace it.

"Next time, then." He walked her out onto the porch and watched her mount and ride off in a whirl of horse-borne taffeta.

Clancy went inside the little house and sat down. He leaned back in his chair and contemplated the change in Isabel Vásquez. He'd attended the odd fandango and noticed her back in the days before Felipe took ill. He pictured her face, smooth and cool and white as a pearl, the mischief shining in her conniving black eyes, full of a childish love of secrets, conspiracy. She smiled with the assurance of a woman who had been rewarded since infancy for her beauty, as if it were something achieved rather than a random gift of nature, the chance combination of traits fashioned in the oblivion of the womb. He wondered what had aged her so noticeably, not that beauty mattered that much. It was just an aspect of her animal nature, like eating with good appetite and then forgetting what it was you had for dinner, or who had cooked it for that matter. Hell, a pretty face didn't give near the satisfaction of a good appetite when you stopped to think about it.

From a shallow drawer below the tabletop, Clancy drew out some blank paper, a pen and ink. The proper writing things seemed to mock him, chasing the intended words from his brain. He sat and thought of the desperate testimonials scribbled with the nub of a pencil he had carried in his tunic during the war. Paper was scarce—a corner torn from a casualty sheet, just big enough for the name and address of the woman some poor sonofabitch meant to marry, a brief sentence to whoever found his body on the other side of the battlefield. "See she gets my watch." Many battles later he'd burned as useless all the declarations he'd been carrying in his pockets. Bodies were pilfered of everything from spectacles to boots. He even saw a glass eye pried out of a dead man's head, a source of instant popularity for the man who recovered it, plenty of humor to break the tension in the twilight hours when a quiet fell over the battlefield, and Death was forced

140

to wait with his sickle for the dawn of a new day's reaping. *Reckon he was a damn poor shot if this was his aiming eye.* Rolls the object in his hand and talks about using it in a game of snooker, turning the iris to the felt so only the white would show until the break. *Give the shooter a turn! Wouldn't soon forget that game!*

Clancy considered the blank page till the ink had dried on the nib, then dipped the pen again. Finally, in cursive stiff from disuse, he set down "Letter of Agreement" across the top of the sheet.

Chapter Sixteen

Oblivious to the time of day, for the sun was nearly at the zenith, Doc was haloed with lamplight where he sat at his desk in the surgery with a pen in hand and a blank sheet of stationery on the blotter in front of him. He made two feints with the pen before laying it down and taking a swallow from the bottle that he kept for anesthetic purposes. Fortified, he picked up the pen again and carefully wrote, *'Dear Mrs. Talbott,'* at the top of the page. He stopped to consider his work. *Sounds like a letter to a Sunday school teacher.* He muttered an oath, snatched up the sheet, crumpled it, and tossed it aside. It came to rest on the floor next to four other balled-up attempts.

He dipped his pen and began again. *'Dear Lucy—'*

He considered this new beginning. *Better. More confident.*

He took another drink. *'I make bold to write to you of my feelings.'*

The pen refused to go on. He scowled down at the line of prose. *You come to it too fast. There's nothing more to say except 'Here's my heart on a plate.'* He crushed the sixth attempt and landed it with the others. He thumbed the dwindling stack of paper on the blotter and found he had only three sheets left. *God.* Worse yet, the bottle was less than half full.

A pecking at Doc's front door saved him from the next assay. He wobbled as he rose and went to investigate, hoping that if it were a medical matter it might be one that didn't require a steady hand. He opened up and found Adrian Fiske standing there in the brash light of broad day. "I am here to ascertain your health on behalf of a lady of our mutual acquaintance," the painter said. "Mind if I come in for a smile?"

"Come in and welcome," Doc said. "Refreshments in the surgery. Exactly which dame have you been talking to?"

"Your dear Sally," Adrian said as he entered Doc's inner sanctum. "She wants news of you." He looked askance at the bottle on the desk. "Barely enough here to wet my whistle."

"True," Doc said. "I'm afraid I've made away with most of the bottle. But it's your own fault. Teach you to come late to a party."

Adrian sat in the chair beside Doc's desk while Doc occupied the seat with the paper in front of it. "The other night when I was out painting my tree, I fell to looking at the moon," Adrian said, accepting a glass from Doc. "And what intrigued me as I painted, was whether I could find words to explain the difference between this moon and all the other moons. If I had only words, as the poets do, would I ever have been able to make the distinction perfectly clear as it was on my canvas? How do you talk about an October moon? The word 'ripe' came to mind, followed quickly by 'tallow,' 'fragrance of dry leaves,' and 'bullfrog notes.' The painting is mute and yet more eloquent than any of these. I sat with my back against a driftwood trunk on the beach and watched the swells heave onto the shore, drunk with moonlight and a sense that I had distilled a morsel of truth."

Doc took a swallow of whiskey. "I appreciate your stopping to tell me," he said. "I'm not quite drunk enough to appreciate the message but damned glad of the company." He looked askance at his dry pen. "Maybe I've been going about this the wrong way."

"What's that?" Fiske asked.

"I've been trying to write something to her."

"To Lucy? Write something! What makes you think the girl can read?"

"Oh. I hadn't considered that." He dropped his head into his hands. "Damn! It's useless, then."

"What the devil are you talking about?"

"I meant to state my intentions, but I couldn't get down to it."

"Your intentions? By that you mean ..."

Garret lifted his head and faced his friend squarely. "Marriage."

"Oh, dear God! I was afraid it was coming to that."

"What's wrong with a man marrying?"

"It's not the estate as much as your choice I object to. I swear you're more bumfuzzled than the old man who went to bed with his boots on and left his wife by the back door. And as far as pitching woo in a letter? You really think that's the way to go about it?"

"A bit cold, do you think?"

Adrian Fiske sighed and shook his head.

Garrett slammed his palm on the desktop. "Damn it, then, you do it."

"Do what?"

"Speak to her for me. Tell her how I feel."

"Me! I'll do no such thing. You've lost your mind."

"Now hang on. Just listen a minute. You told me yourself there's more than one way to put a thing across. Not necessarily words."

"That doesn't apply to proposals. Proposals need to be said flat-out so there's no confusion. A proposal is like a business proposition. The terms must be absolutely clear—the where, when and how of the thing. And you put up your good-faith collateral in the form of a ring. You do that and she'll know how you feel about her."

Doc rubbed his eyes. "Collateral? Now who's being cold?"

"I won't do it," Fiske said. "It would be one thing if I—"

Doc eyed him. "If you what? You approved?" He laughed. "Is that how friendship works? Any woman I might want to marry

144

must suit both of us? Do you propose to join in on the wedding night? Are we to be a threesome?"

"Don't talk rubbish."

"Well, what, then? What is it to you who's my wife? She won't walk with us on the beach or come along to Simoneau's. She'll keep The Rookery much as Mrs. Fleming does and do it without ranting about religion. The minute any wife of mine takes up that topic she'll find herself packed off to The Grove, bag and baggage." Doc scowled and stretched out his arm to point toward one corner of the surgery indicating the direction of this exile.

"But why marry? Why now? Don't you see enough of her as it is?"

Doc lowered his arm and dropped into the desk chair. "In the surgery, you mean, with Ida Fleming hovering over us. It's not enough. I've made no progress at all toward curing her condition, under the circumstances. If she were here all the time, living with me, I believe I could achieve some success."

"You make no mention of love," the painter observed.

"I'm not the romantic you are."

"Don't deny it. You've been morose ever since the trial. Mooning."

Doc sighed. "You're right. I can't deny she draws me strongly." He seemed to ponder. "Her dumbness is part of it, an animal way about her. I want to bring her here, keep her, all for myself." He looked up and pointed a finger at Adrian. "If you were a true friend you'd help me."

Adrian drained his glass and set it down on the desk. "Oh, for Christ's sake. Stop flailing about and tell me what you had in mind. I'm not saying I'll do it."

"I'll have her portrait made."

"Her portrait. You'll commission a painting?"

Doc smiled. "Perhaps commission is the wrong term. Ask a favor is more like it. Just a drawing in pencil."

"Oh, now just hold on. I don't do faces. You know that."

"Just a pencil sketch. Come on, it'll be a challenge."

Lucy Lied

"It'll be an embarrassment."

"Then you'll do it."

"Hell, no. Even if I said I would, I don't see the point. How will getting her likeness drawn get her to marry you?"

"Men sometimes keep portraits of their sweethearts, particularly if they're leaving for the army or a voyage, not that I anticipate an absence."

"Henry the Eighth commissioned a portrait of his third wife, the German one," Adrian added. He weighed the benefit of standing his friend in good stead against the ill of supporting his quest for this idiot woman's hand. *His asking doesn't mean she'll accept. Besides, most marriages mean little more than the title after the deed is done. But an act of friendship is remembered long after a pretty face has faded.* "You wouldn't let marriage alter your habit of walking the beach, taking a drink at Simoneau's?"

"Like one of those weak sisters strangled by his wife's apron strings? I should think not!"

"All right, then."

Doc jumped up from his chair. "You'll do it?"

"For my sins," the painter replied.

"Excellent." Doc clapped a piece of stationery into a medical tome and handed the book to Fiske. "So it won't get wrinkled on the walk over to Mrs. Fleming's place."

"Oh," Adrian said, "We're going to see the old prune directly?"

"Before the booze wears off," Doc replied.

Ida Fleming looked askance at the sight of the two of them, sensing with alarm that they both appeared to have been drinking though it was just midday.

Doc hemmed and hawed, leaving it to Adrian to speak up. "My dear Mrs. Fleming, Doc has come to ask your opinion."

"Oh? Is it about a lying-in?"

Doc found his voice when addressed on a professional matter. "No, nothing like that. I've come to ... actually, may we come in?"

146

"Yes, of course." She admitted them into the parlor where Lucy sat working on a basket of mending, her penny-bright head bent over her darting needle. She kept her eyes down until Doc spoke to her. "Good morning, Lucy," he said.

She smiled at him and nodded.

"On what matter do you seek my advice?" Mrs. Fleming asked, sounding rather pleased at the idea.

"Perhaps we might speak in another room," Doc began, glancing at Lucy. "It's a matter of propriety."

"We can speak in the kitchen." Mrs. Fleming led the way toward the back of the house. "I see you've brought Mr. Fiske along," she said with a glance over her shoulder.

Doc cleared his throat. "Yes. I thought ... that is, I'd like to have him draw a likeness of Mrs. Talbott. I'd like to know if you think it would be fitting."

"A portrait?" Mrs. Fleming's brow contracted with doubt. She whispered even though there was hardly a chance Lucy might hear. "I scarcely think it would be proper for a man to have a lady's portrait unless there were an understanding between them."

"Well, yes. You have it exactly," Garrett replied.

The old dame grasped the significance of the request at once. "Are you in earnest?"

"Couldn't be more so."

She clasped her hands and spoke out. "Oh my lands! Why that's wonderful!"

"Yes, well, it may be," Garrett said, "if the lady consents."

"Oh. You've not asked her yet?"

Doc shook his head. "I thought it best to put it to you first."

"Oh, yes. Very prudent. And now that I understand your intent, I wholeheartedly urge you to put the question to her."

"Well, I ..." Doc stammered, "that is ..."

"I've agreed to act on the gentleman's behalf," Adrian said. "It's rather an Old World custom, but one that I think you'll approve of."

Lucy Lied

Mrs. Fleming glanced from Doc to Mr. Fiske and back again. "You're content to have *him* speak to her?"

"Oh, yes."

Mrs. Fleming whisked her hand at the painter. "Then be quick about it."

Adrian went straight to the parlor and dragged a chair over to the window seat where the girl sat with her mending. She looked up at him, following his actions attentively. He sat before her with Doc's medical book in his lap. He opened up the book and took out the sheet of paper then pulled a pencil out of his pocket. "Perhaps, Miss Lucy, you would put aside your needle for a time. I'd like you to let me draw your portrait now while the light makes your hair shine so beautifully. And after I'm done I'd like you to answer me yes or no as to whether you'll become the wife of my dear friend Doctor Jason Garrett. Doc hasn't much income, but you'll not go hungry, and if it's in the power of medical science he'll find a way to restore your speech. He will be a faithful husband and a cheerful companion, much as he can be, given his penchant for insobriety and melancholy." He saw something like alarm light her eyes and hastened to add, "I find his dark moods one of the more fascinating aspects of his character. Mostly he just sulks although sometimes he gets an ax and decimates a few fire logs. There's really nothing to fear."

"There'll be no more of that," Mrs. Fleming scolded as she entered from the hallway where she'd been listening.

Doc drew the old lady back toward the kitchen. "Let us leave him to do the portrait while we speak of practical matters. Maybe we might have a cup of tea."

"We'll have a cup of coffee but only after you've shown me the ring."

"I have it right here," he said. He dipped his fingers into his waistcoat pocket and produced a gold band with a dark gem. "This is a ring that I have from my mother. It's a bloodstone. I mean to put it on her finger today if she makes me the answer I'm hoping for."

Mrs. Fleming examined the ring that he placed in her palm. "Oh, my. This is very fine. Old, is it not?"

"Then you approve?"

"Of course." She gave him back the ring and filled two cups from the coffee pot on the back of the stove. "Since you already have a ring we can speak of a proper period of engagement. Eight weeks is barely long enough, but a wedding between Christmas and New Year's would add to the festivity of the season."

"Not on your life," Doc said. "I'll not wait that long."

"But there must be time to assemble a trousseau, time for you to walk out together."

"I think she's already got all the trousseau she can afford. As for walking out, she's spent enough time with me to know whether it's right or not."

"In the surgery with you taking measurements of her head," Mrs. Fleming objected. "That hardly counts. And even if she is poor, the girl can't go to her new home without taking something of her own into it. The Methodist ladies always make a quilt when one of our girls marries. That's what we'll do for Lucy. She'll have a quilt for her marriage bed. And that will take a month at least, provided we start right away and all can come together after church over the next several Sundays."

"I agree to wait until the quilt is finished," Doc said. "But you must make it the way I say as to pattern and material. Agreed?"

Mrs. Fleming looked nonplussed. "If you wish."

"Good. Then you'll use the patchwork squares already assembled that I have in my trunk in the attic room at The Rookery. My mother still knew me when she made me a present of them and told me to have the quilt made up when I decided to marry. Though I'm dead to her now, I'm bound to honor her wish."

Mrs. Fleming sniffed. "A wish that's convenient to you, no doubt." She conceded the abbreviation of the engagement period in exchange for his consent that the ceremony would be performed in the Methodist Church. He half-listened and agreed to all of her stipulations, doing his best not to appear impatient. That settled, the two adjourned to the parlor. Adrian had the outline of Lucy's face and was making the first tentative strokes defining her eyes.

Doc came to stand behind Adrian very quietly lest he startle the artist and send the pencil careening across the page. Mrs. Fleming moved a straight chair several inches back from the window seat where she took a position between Doc and his intended.

The sketch took shape quickly now and Doc knew from having observed him at work before that the painter was seeing whatever it was he wanted to catch on paper. Still, there was an unquietness about Lucy's eyes that lingered in spite of the smile on her lips and he became suddenly afraid that she might be contemplating the unthinkable, that she might be thinking of refusing him. He spent the next several minutes in an agony of doubt. "Have you finished?" he said when Adrian set down his pencil.

"I believe I have," his friend replied, "as much as I need do here, at any rate. I can add some details in the studio."

Doc bent to better view the picture over the artist's shoulder. "No," he said. "Not another stroke. It's just right as it is."

Mrs. Fleming rose to come and see for herself. "Oh, my," she said. "I never knew you could really draw!"

Adrian bore her amazement with patience. "It's just a sketch," he said, "not the Mona Lisa."

"Lucy, come and look," Doc said. She rose and came to stand beside him. Her smile when she saw the picture was genuine, albeit brief. He sensed her uncertainty. "Perhaps you and Mrs. Fleming would permit me a private word with Mrs. Talbott," Doc said.

The older woman and the painter left the parlor and Doc clasped one of Lucy's hands just as she was about to step away from him. "I need you to know something," he said, "something I've never told anyone else."

She tensed and waited.

"These past weeks, all the times you've been in my surgery, I felt we never had a perfect understanding because of what happened at the trial. I have to make you understand that I had to do what I did to save you. You see, I know you killed him. I was out on the beach walking one day when I spied you digging in a pile of abalone shells out Point Alones way. I saw you pull that old pry bar out of the sand. I saw you put it into that poke you carry the shells in. When we found Talbott with his head bashed in I knew it was you. I knew all along you were strong enough, but I had to put on that show in the courtroom to make sure nobody else would think so."

She pulled her hand away, paced to the hearth, and stood with her back to him. He followed her and stood so close she could feel his breath on her neck.

"I tell you, you needn't fear. Charges never were brought against you because of that little charade I put on, and once we're married there's nothing the law can do to make me give testimony against you. Husband and wife are one person. It's the same protection as the one against condemning yourself. So you see, you're safe." He put a hand on her shoulder and gripped it hard. "Now I want you to turn around and look me in the face."

She obeyed.

He took her hand and placed the ring on her finger. "This is a family heirloom. I want you to wear it as a token of our engagement. And now I'll have a kiss to seal the deal." He wrapped his arms around her and kissed her hard, forcing her head back against the mantelpiece dislodging a little porcelain bird whose brief flight ended in a dozen pieces.

Mrs. Fleming burst back into the room at the sound of breakage. "See here!"

Garrett left off kissing and grinned at the old biddy. "Settle down. She's accepted me!"

Adrian emerged at the pronouncement and clapped Doc soundly on the back. "Well done, old man. Congratulations! And to the bride, my condolences."

The groom-to-be insisted that all four of them go to The Rookery without delay to collect the materials for the making of the quilt. "I'll not have you dragging your feet," he said to Mrs. Fleming as they crunched along the gravel path above the beach. "She's mine as soon as you take the last stitch."

"I know," the old lady said. She gazed out to sea with what looked like a pleasant memory of the first days of married life.

At that moment Garrett was filled with unaccustomed optimism. "Your thoughts?" he asked her.

"It crosses my mind that maybe the rice ball was good luck, in fact."

At The Rookery, Doc sent the females upstairs to retrieve the patchwork from his trunk. "In the room to the left. You know where it is," he called as Mrs. Fleming led the way. He and Adrian repaired to the surgery where there was a dab of whiskey left in the bottle, a swallow each to celebrate. Presently the women came down carrying the quilt squares. Lucy clutched the lion's share of the material, holding the folded goods tightly to her chest.

"It's going to be a big quilt," Mrs. Fleming said.

"You'll have to get yourself a big bed," Adrian added, once the ladies had left.

"Don't suppose you'd care to lend me a portion of your monthly stipend."

"Maybe the furniture maker will take it in trade."

Doc frowned. "I'd like to buy her a present ... maybe a dress. Something pretty. What color, would you say?"

"Black. Nothing better to set off that red hair. Remember how she looked at the trial?"

"She already has a black dress."

"You might try a different style. Something with bare shoulders."

"Ah, yes. I see. Still, it seems a bit funereal."

"Not necessarily. Black and orange like the butterflies gathered in the grove out near the lighthouse. You've seen them."

"Dull brown like a mob of dead leaves until they fly. Then they're magnificent."

"There's a Chinese legend, something about how butterflies are the souls of lovers who were parted in life."

"They'll have to make up a new story for Lucy and me. I don't intend to let anything come between us. Not ever."

Chapter Seventeen

November 4th, San Carlos Day, was unseasonably warm, the clear blue sky pale and birdless. Without the substance of clouds the air seemed too thin to support winged creatures. Adrian Fiske, with his eye for light and color along with a pure, mystical nature, wondered at the absence of hawks and read in it a divine intervention. The birds of prey, he thought, had given the cottontails and quail a reprieve in observance of the saint's day.

Each year on San Carlos Day, all of Monterey except for the most dire Protestants would come to the brief sandy plain at the mouth of the Carmelo River to celebrate the saint's day in the fretted shadows of the ruined mission. Where once the holy fathers had chanted to the adoring Indian flock in the tongue of dead Romans, a resident pack of dogs and beggars now served in the sanctuary. Each year before the celebration the townsfolk ran the vagrants off, but they always returned, just as sandpipers would fly then settle again around the barrel-stave skeleton of a ruined whale.

Crevole Bronson licked the end of his pencil and pressed it to the pad he always carried to capture moments of inspiration. *Cemetery movement*, he wrote, catching the germ of an editorial. *Restoration not a religious matter but civic. Community must rally*. There was nothing Bronson liked better than to assume the mantle of historian, mediating between the present generation, its posterity, and its venerable antecedents. He would begin by harking back to the missions, the clerical enterprise of Alta California, grown so rich on hides and tallow that the Mexican government found it necessary to secularize the church lands. Settlers possessed the fields and the friars returned to their monasteries in the Old Country. Abandoned, the Indians withdrew within the crumbling mission walls to sing and starve, then moved to the town to drink and die. *Essential to preserve this link to the very founding of our great state heretofore laid waste by squatters and the forces of nature*. The editor chewed his pencil thoughtfully. It would take cash.

The priest from Saint Angela's had brought a troupe of altar boys down from town. He had herded them inside the old chapel walls and had them all in their robes in two rows, with their candle flames guarded behind one hand. He gave the sign for the ringing of the bells and like the faithful of old, the celebrants gathered outside the doors of the church to watch the procession. The children, with their precious lights, came forth from the dark singing the same devotions the friars had taught to their Indian parishioners a century before. They sang with grave, simple faces, free of doubt.

The watchers—they seemed fewer every year—stole glances to the right and left to see who was standing next to whom, or staring at a favorite unobserved. The cousins stood together, Isabel Vásquez and Rosanna Leese, the younger whispering shamelessly, the elder scowling, replying now and again with a terse word. Doc Garrett stood next to Ernesto Badillo, his wife and their eight children, the eldest a taut-skinned girl with dull eyes, Guadalupe, who was betrothed to a Scotsman. The Scot, Robert Tanner, stood a respectful distance away but eyed his finacée brazenly so that she colored whenever she looked in his direction. Ida Fleming, on hand to chaperone Lucy, viewed the pious children pityingly, for they were of such a tender age they couldn't know that their religion was all mumbo-jumbo and idolatry.

Adrian Fiske shifted on his feet, weighing the values of light and dark as the shadows played across the scene, feeling the quality of the composition like the sensation of mud between his toes. He drifted away from the crowd to watch the sunlight dapple the ocean.

The Arguellos, Abregos, Carillos, Alvarados, Ortegas, Pachecos, Peraltas and Estradas stood aloof from the Anglos, holding the center of the tableau as befit their station and the moment. It was, after all, a casting back to the days of their greatness. Matt Clancy, whose own aloofness was less a mark of social status than a sign of destiny, could look upon the gathering from a place removed, a pebbly wash where the river ran wide and his big palomino snorted in the ripples.

"We must speak in privacy somewhere away from the others," Isabel said urgently.

"Hush!" Rosanna Leese ignored her cousin and tugged once at her sleeve, which stood in a starchy puff bellow a deep ruffle of lace and a bare shoulder. The Spanish-descended women wore the traditional garb on San Carlos Day, spanking white full-gathered skirts and blouses of the same stuff, every fiber mercilessly bleached lest another girl's dress look brighter. The men, in short black jackets and slim black pants with beaten silver ornaments, punctuated the groups of girls. Later there would be dancing.

The candle-bearers dispersed at the end of their performance, running off with irreverent shrieks to find sweets among the many baskets of food. The redheaded woman who used to be Flynn Talbott's wife wandered off toward the woods, stooping now and then to pluck a wildflower.

"What do you suppose she is doing all by herself?" Isabel asked her cousin as they watched. "She's betrothed, isn't she? Usually the romance doesn't fade that fast."

Rosanna Leese considered Doc Garrett's bride-to-be. "She never was right in her mind. She proves red hair is a sign of madness."

"I heard of a madwoman once who jumped off the roof of her house after she set fire to her bed."

"The river cuts a gorge back in the woods," Rosanna said. "She might wander far enough to fall in and drown."

Isabel smiled. "Maybe if she fell into the river she would call out for help. I think she might recover the power of speech if it would save her skin."

"She did nothing of the kind at the trial," Rosanna Leese mused.

"Come and walk with me," her cousin replied. "I have thought much about how Clancy and I might come to an agreement about the water. I will tell you my plan."

"Always this talk of water! You exasperate me." Rosanna replied.

Isabel cast a glance at the clear sky. "Is it not as I said? There are no rain clouds in sight. I tell you this winter will be dry. Drought is coming."

"Yes, you're a sibyl where clouds are concerned."

Arm in arm they walked toward the beach. A delta of pebbles marked the demise of the stream where it lost itself in the ocean. Adrian Fiske had left his boots on the dry sand and waded barefoot out to a flat rock where he sat transfixed by the sun-splashed water. He could turn to the west and completely eliminate the crowd in the mission courtyard from his field of vision. There, with the heat from the rock baking his bones, he considered the woman Doc had chosen to wed. Like Isabel Vásquez, he distrusted her. What lay behind those brown, soft eyes, more akin to animal than human?

"Adrian, you slacker! Rouse your worthless self. There's wine over yonder!" Doc called from the place where the painter had left his boots.

Fiske squinted at his friend. "It's uncommon warm for this time of year. I'm enjoying the sun. Must you interrupt me?"

"I must. Badillo and the others insist on it. They've sent me to fetch you. Badillo thinks the wine may sour if it's not drunk up right quick. Get your backside over here. It's plum rude to make me ask you twice. And don't slip and fall. I'd rupture myself laughing if you had to spend the rest of the day in wet pants."

Fiske gave up on having any more peace and waded back to where Doc waited. "Thanks for your concern," he said, as he reached his footwear. He sat down on the dry sand to pull on his boots. "Now if you'll refrain from speaking to me anymore and just lead on to the wine, I'd be obliged."

"You know why Badillo brought a cask of wine?"

"Tradition?"

Garrett laughed. "Tradition be damned. He's trying to marry off his daughters. They're hovering around that cask like flies around horseshit. Thought as you're a single fellow I should warn you."

"Or you could have left me alone in the first place."

They found Badillo encamped in a spot of shade but still sweating profusely, his dark skin beaded and fragrant in a meaty way. He flourished a glass of claret as Doc and Adrian approached. "Ah, it is my friend the painter," he shouted. "Have you painted your tree yet today?"

"No, not yet," Fiske replied. "Thought I'd head back up that way around sunset."

"No! We'll all be drunk by then. Your tree will have to wait for tomorrow. Come. Take a glass of wine and eat the good food my lovely daughters have made us. I would get up and serve it for you myself, but for this cursed gout. I rode here like an invalid in a *carreta*. When I was a little boy I used to go with my mother and my brothers in the *carreta* piled high with linen. We would go to the *agua caliente* where my mother did her washing. It was a great expedition. We took baskets of food and the linen that she had saved for weeks. My brothers and I played in the linen like a haystack while the oxen drew us as slowly as the sun climbs the eastern sky in summer. The hot spring is but a little way farther down the coast from here. If I were a well man, I would go there on my horse, have a soak and be back in time for supper. But Doc's medicine, it does me no good. Doc, you must give me something else. I am too great a sinner to take up the habits of the infirm."

Doc accepted a glass of wine. "If you'd swallow what I gave you ..."

"Bah!" Badillo cut a wedge of cheese and wrapped a warm tortilla around it. "You are a hard man. Even on the saint's day you have no pity."

"Pity for what?"

"For one who sees the robust days of youth slipping away."

"Pity won't cure the gout, my friend."

"You want to know only what you read in books," Badillo complained.

"That's true. I'll not deny I see science as the basis of progress. Healing is a science that has progressed enormously in the last fifty years. Think of carbolic acid and the antiseptic principle, anesthesia, quinine for ague, digitalis for the heart, ipecac for goiter, lime for scurvy. But I suppose you'd rather fast and pray for relief from these maladies."

"Fast? I would never offer such an insult to this food that my daughters have prepared. Come, eat. If we finish what is here they will bring more. Señor Fiske, you are as thin as a new goat. You need a wife to feed you and give you strength to do more than dab paint. And you, my friend the doctor, who knows everything from books, eat and look to the health of your soul."

Doc folded a tortilla around a spoonful of goat stew and bit into it as Badillo's daughters stood and watched, giggling behind their hands. His eyes shifted across the scene upriver, watching for a glimpse of Lucy. He saw Mrs. Fleming, but not his fiancée. It wasn't until he spied Matt Clancy that he also saw Lucy's red hair. Clancy stood in the shallows, sponging cool water over the broad back of his blond horse. A moment later the gunman led the horse to the bank and held his head while Lucy tentatively stroked his white blaze. Doc saw her face break into a childish smile and watched her hand caress the animal with growing assurance. Her whole aspect, her stance, changed as he watched, losing that stiffness the came from distrust of the world. She turned soft before his eyes as if Clancy's horse had thawed her.

"I can almost hear her laughing."

"Who's that?" Adrian asked.

"Lucy. See her there?"

Adrian looked but didn't know what to say.

"I wonder if she'll ever smile at me that way."

Adrian made light of his friend's sad musing. "She might if you were a horse."

Doc continued to watch Lucy as she caressed Clancy's palomino.

"You should buy her a horse," Adrian said, following his friend's gaze. "She's got a way with animals. Anyone can see they have much in common. I'd lay odds you'll find her talking to a horse long before she'd risk it with another person."

Doc grinned but found himself assailed by doubt that changed his view of her as instantly as a cloud passing across the face of the sun alters the landscape. And underneath that chilly sensation, the old wound smarted with this fresh demonstration of a female's indifference. *It's Clancy. She prefers Clancy.*

Adrian felt the melancholy invading his friend's soul and went to fill their glasses at the cask. He caught sight of Isabel Vásquez whispering into the ear of her cousin Rosanna Leese and wondered how Doc could favor a demented Irish slut to the still-voluptuous widow of his old chess partner who was wandering toward the trees with her cousin.

"I mean to travel to Sacramento," Isabel said, noting with a certain pleasure the confusion on her cousin's face. "I don't know how long I will be gone."

"What amusements abound in Sacramento? I've heard of none that compare to San Francisco."

"This is business. It has to do with getting back my land." Isabel hiked her chin a notch higher. "You aren't the only Mexican woman who knows how to beat the Anglos at their own game."

"If by that you mean I got the boardinghouse through a swindle of some kind you are mistaken," Rosanna said.

"Who said anything about a swindle? I merely need to correct a matter of record," Isabel replied. "It must reflect that I have always held the Rancho El Llano as an inheritance from my father, unencumbered by any debts that Felipe might have incurred. Do you see?"

159

Rosanna Leese shook her head. "No. I have no idea what you are talking about."

"The only reason my land was forfeit to Matt Clancy was to satisfy a debt Felipe incurred by losing a bet, right?"

"Yes, of course," her cousin replied impatiently.

"And I had to make over my land to satisfy my husband's debt."

"As everyone knows," Rosanna agreed.

"But what if I never was married?"

"What do you mean?"

"The marriage is being annulled," Isabel said with a gleam of triumph in her eyes. "The bishop in Sacramento will give me the annulment because the marriage was never consummated. Once I have my annulment, then the governor will see to it that the land is returned to me. Clancy will have to give it back since Felipe's debts were never any of my responsibility because we were never married."

"Could such a plan work?"

Isabel shrugged. "It must be done carefully ... and it will doubtless take much time. I only hope I can get a favorable ruling before the cattle go to market. Then I will owe him nothing for the grazing."

"You'll need plenty of grease for many palms." Rosanna gazed at the ground that grew moister as they walked farther into the shade of the trees.

"And it must be accomplished in secret. The governor must recognize my clear title to the land before anyone in Monterey finds out." Isabel stopped and looked her cousin in the eye. "You must promise me."

The painter's eye caught a movement in the trees just beyond the cousins. A second later a youngster came bursting out of the woods screaming, "*Oso! Oso!*"

The child dodged the wide arc of the ladies' skirts. "*Oso!*"

A ruckus broke out among the clutches of men who dropped their cigars and plates to find sharp implements or check the loads in their firearms. They moved together toward the trees like a bloom of kelp lifted by a wave. The women scurried to locate their children and herd them within the walls of the ruined church. A whoop went up as the men trotted deeper into the woods.

Doc ran to the spot where he'd last seen Lucy. He was about to sing out when Clancy's yellow horse came bounding up, bearing the gunman and the redheaded girl riding double. "You'd best get into the church with the rest of the women," Clancy said to the girl as he dismounted. He reached up to lift Lucy down. She leaned toward him and placed her hands on his shoulders. Familiarly, it seemed to Doc.

"Lucy," Doc said. "Where have you been?" Her eyes snapped in his direction, fearful before the curtain of reserve fell once more.

Clancy helped her slide to the ground then remounted. He thumbed the brim of his hat toward Garrett before he wheeled the horse around. "So long, sawbones."

"Wait," Garrett said, seizing Lucy's arm. "I'll have a word with you, if I might."

"I always admired the manners on you Southern boys," Clancy said. "Most people would just come on out with it, whether I was inclined to have a word or not."

Garrett perceived the mockery and bristled. "I couldn't help noticing that you engaged the widow Talbott in conversation yonder."

"Conversation would be something of an exaggeration, since she's not one to talk," Clancy said. "She just came over to pet my horse. She must have a soft heart where animals are concerned. Speaking of animals, you'd best get into the mission with the others. If there's really a bear in the woods these fools are likely to flush it into the clearing here. Best stay within the walls."

"I've taken an interest in this woman," Garrett said, ignoring the caution. "That is to say, she has agreed to be my wife."

Clancy smiled. "Congratulations."

Again, Doc felt the sting of mockery. "Thank you for looking after her. Come along, Lucy." He tightened his grip on her upper arm and began dragging her toward the mission.

Lucy Lied

"You should buy her a horse," Clancy called to his back. "She's got a way with animals."

Garrett didn't turn around to acknowledge the comment, but Lucy did. She looked back once and long.

Garrett's grip clamped down on her arm, hard enough to leave a bruise.

Chapter Eighteen

The Methodist ladies gathered in Mrs. Fleming's parlor around the quilting frame seemed ambivalent. Several rubbed the edge of a square between thumb and forefinger to glean some intelligence from the feel of the material. As they drank their tea they looked askance at Alice, Mrs. Fleming's strange sister, who sat on the floor playing with her favorite doll. Lucy troubled herself to give Alice a cup after Mrs. Fleming had poured out and gone to the kitchen to refill the pot. The ladies spoke in whispers.

"They make a good pair, afflicted as they both are."

"Curious, they both have such lovely hair, copper and gold."

"What God took from them in brains he gave back in looks."

"And took away again with old age in the case of Alice. The first time I saw her from behind I assumed she was a child. What a shock I had when she turned and showed me the shrunken face of a crone."

The conversation took a new course when Mrs. Fleming came back with the teapot newly filled and steaming. Lucy, who had heard all, wondered if Mrs. Fleming knew her friends talked behind her back.

"You say Doctor Garrett's mother gave him the patchwork?" Addie Ross asked. She was the tallest female present, always slightly bent at the waist to blend in. "Will she be coming to the wedding?"

"She lives in Macon, Georgia and I take it has not forgiven Doctor Garrett for his righteous refusal to bear arms for the South," Mrs. Fleming answered.

Anne Fletcher examined the choice of colors and the workmanship that had gone into matching the seams of the patchwork. "The hourglass pattern is simple enough for those with less skill, but this work is plainly that of an experienced hand. It's well crafted, and no doubt about it. I would have worked in more modest colors, though." Lucy considered the many shades of blue and purple that made her eyes swim. "The aquamarine seems like high-sounding brass," Anne said. "So bright, so prideful. I cannot help but think that a quilt in more subdued shades would be more pleasing to the Lord." Anne leveled her keen gray glance at Lucy, who knew it was she, not the bright patchwork that was under discussion and wished for the thousandth time she'd been born with mouse brown hair.

"I think it's beautiful," Addie Ross said. "These are the colors of the bay on a sunny day, a gift of nature. I can't believe God would look with disapproval on them."

"What you ought to be concerned about is how we're to fashion a rectangle out of these bits," Nell Hennessy pointed out in her flat, reasonable manner. "There are nineteen squares of patchwork. Now, twenty would work perfectly. Five rows of four. But nineteen?"

"My gracious," Mrs. Fleming said, counting through the stack of squares. "I had just assumed there was a whole quilt here. Good heavens."

"Wasn't there one entered as evidence at the trial?" Anne Fletcher asked.

"There was, but Doc assured me the sheriff returned that one."

"Well, we'll just have to make a new one to match the rest," Addie said. "We all have scraps."

The ladies continued to examine the patchwork as if they were looking at a pillow with Lincoln's blood on it. "Lucy and I will go to

The Rookery tomorrow first thing and make sure we didn't overlook a square in the trunk, but everyone should bring some scraps anyway, just in case we don't find it."

"I'm sure none of us has any scraps in these bold colors," Anne said.

"Even if it doesn't quite match the colors of the other squares, I don't think it will harm the look of the whole thing," Mrs. Fleming replied. "We can position the new square so when the quilt's on the bed it's on the side toward the wall and hanging down. I really don't think it will be very noticeable."

"You don't suppose they had their slaves work on it, do you?" Marjorie Tenant asked. She had family in Ohio who had kept runaways and was still filled with Abolitionist fervor. "I wouldn't put my hand to it if I thought slave labor had gone into the manufacture."

"As it's cotton," Nell observed, "it could hardly be anything else since it was all slave labor that produced the plants and picked it and ginned it. I imagine you could say the same of the dress you're wearing." Nell could be relied upon to quash any notion that smacked of silliness or misinformation with an opinion as substantial as her weighty person. Lucy realized she had been holding her breath and exhaled, much relieved that the conversation had turned away from speculation about the missing square.

Susan Forest, a slight creature who suffered unaccountably from bad feet, seemed impatient to begin or at least to sit down. "I don't think there will ever be a wedding if we keep on in this manner."

Lucy took her place in the circle of ladies standing around the quilting frame. They took up the matter of who should sit where, considering the left-handed stitching of Addie and the need to put Nell in the brightest light because of her poor eyes, enormous viewed through the thick lenses of her spectacles. They began to stitch together the nineteen large squares of the hourglass pattern, according to Anne's arrangement. At one side, they left a space for the missing square.

Lucy Lied

Though she wasn't a very skillful seamstress, Lucy found herself put to work with everyone else. It seemed like an acre of patchwork before them to be assembled with stitches no bigger than a minute. All the stitches of the quilt added together reflected all the time that remained to her before the wedding. She pictured herself under the quilt lying next to Doc, an image that made her uneasy. She felt nothing for him, though he wasn't unlikeable. As to love, she felt empty as a rattling gourd, except for guilt. The old guilt was always there, ground in, like dirt under the fingernails. Yes, there was always that, but not desire, certainly not that feeling that had swept over her when she first saw Ellis. *He's still the only one who truly knows me, the only one I truly belong to.* Flawed as she was, she could never fail Ellis, never disappoint. With Ellis she would always play the whipped dog, licking the hand of the master who would either break sticks across its skull or offer scraps from his table. She held herself in such low esteem, she believed she deserved nothing better.

As she sat at the quilting frame with five of the Methodist ladies including Mrs. Fleming, it struck Lucy that she had never been very much in the company of women. She wondered whether she would have added her voice to the conversation that underscored their work had it not been so long since she'd addressed a syllable to another soul. In any case, after playing the mute for so long she would be pilloried as a liar if she ever broke her silence.

"You'll not find a handsomer man in the county," Nell said. She sniffed after she said it, as if perhaps handsome wasn't much but it was the only positive thing she had to say.

Addie said, "He's so much a retiring type I scarcely know him. But I've heard he's kind to the poor souls who need a doctor most but least have the means to pay."

Mrs. Fleming said, "You well know, Addie, that Doctor Garrett is mostly paid in eggs and apples if he's paid at all." She seemed a little snappish as if the subject annoyed her, and there was a lull in the conversation after that.

Lucy tensed at each mention of Doc's name, but managed not to falter in the steady push and draw of her needle. It was curious that because she was mute the women around the quilting frame seemed also to assume she could not hear, or perhaps they forgot she was there at all and spoke their thoughts candidly in the confidence that she would never be hurt by their tepid praise of her husband-to-be. She found it surprising, the talk of handsomeness. She'd never really thought of Doc as handsome or not. *Does he know he's admired?* It was, she thought, much like being in the courtroom where she suspected judgments were made before testimony was ever heard, and only the most outrageous evidence in contradiction of the assumed outcome came swimming up to the conscious consideration of the jurors. She was glad for the sewing, for the activity that demanded the attention of her eyes, because it would have been nearly impossible to hide what she was feeling otherwise. Her eyes, she had always thought, would be her undoing.

Anne peered hard at her needle as she threaded it. "My Silas said he saw the doctor down at the Bohemian once talking to Matt Clancy. They'd a bottle between them, he said."

"And what was your Silas doing in the Bohemian, then?" Mrs. Fleming's question ignited a spurt of laughter.

"Delivering beef to the kitchen, I expect," came the reply.

"You may find Mr. Clancy dreadful, but he does come in handy when it's a question of running a pest out of town. Like that charlatan who claimed he could speak to the dead. What was his name?"

"Brother Elliott."

"Matt Clancy took care of him while the sheriff just stood there gawking."

"I wonder whatever became of him?"

"Who?"

"Brother Elliott. No one I've spoken to has seen hide nor hair of him, not since that night. I suspected right from the start he was some kind of charlatan with all that talk of the spirit world. If he was telling the truth about being able to commune with the angels in Heaven, I said, then there would surely be something in the Scripture about ... what was it, the science of?"

Lucy Lied

"Animal Magnetism," Mrs. Fleming replied.

The talk of Ellis made Lucy feel as if she'd been stung, but she tried to keep from altering the expression on her face. These Methodist women missed very little with their darting eyes and sharp tongues. *Just keep stitching.*

"I suspect he'll make his way back to San Francisco. The city harbors sharp customers of all kinds. It's easier to hide amongst the throngs of gold diggers. Sheriff didn't lift a finger to get rid of him so I daresay he'll make no effort to bring him to justice."

"What for?"

"Why, stealing from all those women he bamboozled. Like that widow Clancy said he knew. Five hundred dollars she gave Elliott."

"Sheriff Taylor doesn't take to Clancy. Not by a long shot. I've seen him cross to the other side of Alvarado Street to avoid saying good morning."

"Brother Elliott Canby," Anne said. "I can't believe sensible folk would fall for a line of palaver like that." She shook her head. "Magicology, my foot."

"That kind of nonsense doesn't wash around here. Those San Francisco ladies gave him money but we ran him out of town. That just shows you."

"Too many people display an unhealthy interest in mob justice," Mrs. Fleming said. She shot a piercing glance around the table. "Too many people forget the adage, 'There but for the grace of God'."

"I always heard that Matt Clancy was a regular visitor to Rosanna Leese's. Always spent the night when Rosanna's cousin was staying over, too."

"Those Mexicans! So hot blooded!"

Mrs. Fleming pressed her lips together and cleared her throat, again indicating her disapproval of the conversation.

Addie launched a new topic. "I heard the Papists are trying to clean the vagrants out of the mission—for good, I mean. They found a witch living there during that San Carlos Day celebration of theirs. A *bruja*, they call her. She makes potions, spells and such. Changes men into beasts, they say."

Nell sniffed. "Witches indeed. That's just drunken talk."

"A five-year-old boy came running out of the woods yelling about a bear and all manner of goings-on, is what I heard," Marjorie countered.

"He was drunk, too, most like," Susan explained. "They put their children on wine soon as they're off the tit."

Mrs. Fleming intervened. "There'll be no talk of witches in this house. You'll frighten Alice. I was there with Lucy and saw nothing of the sort. The doctor wanted to walk out with her a bit."

"I'm surprised you acceded to such a request," Addie said.

Nell said. "We must all be careful of the company we keep."

Mrs. Fleming's back stiffened. Several sets of eyes looked pointedly at Lucy, who kept her eyes glued to her sewing, pretending not to have heard, blushing from her neck to the roots of her red hair.

"Lucy," Mrs. Fleming said, "as you have particular expertise in laundry, I think you should begin pressing the seams open with the flatiron."

Particular expertise. Lucy found the iron and set it on the stove to heat. "Lucy," Mrs. Fleming called after her, "Can you light a lamp for us? It's getting dark."

They sewed for an hour more and then it was time for the ladies to go to their own homes to make supper. Lucy finished pressing as Mrs. Fleming saw them out. "I do believe this is the largest quilt I've ever worked on," she said as she closed and locked the front door. "He'll be getting a bed so big he'll scarcely be able to find you in it. Come on, then. Let's have our supper. There are dumplings left from the noon meal. Come along, now. Bring Alice. Don't dawdle so absentmindedly. I can always tell from that expression on your face when your thoughts are a thousand miles away."

Aye, but you can't say what they are. Lucy set the iron on a trivet and led Alice by the hand into the kitchen, where Mrs. Fleming laid three places at the table and then ladled dumplings and gravy onto the plates.

Lucy Lied

"That talk of a bear reminded me of a time not long after I was first married when there was a bear taken live and brought to town for a bull-and-bear fight. They shackled each animal by a hind leg so they couldn't run away and watched the creatures maul each other till one of them died. It's horrible if you ask me, to use God's creatures for entertainment. Half the men's wages in town were lost betting on the outcome, don't you know. Come on. Sit down. Eat it before it gets cold."

Lucy nibbled at her food, aware that Mrs. Fleming was watching her intently. "My dear," the older woman said, "I don't know what experience you've had of men, apart from Talbott, and those times are best forgotten. What I'm trying to say is, I know you must be apprehensive. But you mustn't worry. The first night is always difficult, but at least he's a doctor, a man with clean hands. And I know he isn't ignorant of women. It's likely he knows how to make it pleasant, though I don't hold with the idea that God created the rites of marriage for idle pleasure in exchange for mankind bearing the perpetual curse of original sin. Remember you'll one day be rewarded with a beautiful child and it won't seem so hard to bear." She paused and added, "And even if none of that proves true, remember you wouldn't want to change this station of life for the one you had before. You've been plucked out of the ash heap and plumped down on a velvet cushion. It's a miracle, that alone. Just remember that, if the idea of your future with him frightens you. Just remember where you'd be now, camping with that band of homeless bummers down at the old mission."

Lucy returned her eyes to her plate. *Children.* She thought about Molly as she chewed a fragment of a dumpling. Molly would have had her baby by now. Poorer than ever. Husband more wayward than ever. *Poor little mite.* Frightening, the idea of bringing a baby into the world, even into a doctor's house. It seemed safe with Doc, but still there was the matter of her past, all he didn't know about her. *Perhaps he'd understand. Not likely.* Queer, his endless efforts to make her speak, when in truth he'd never want to hear the tale she had to tell.

"There's plenty who would be glad of that plate you've been ignoring," Mrs. Fleming scolded. She stood up from her place and cleared the table. Lucy rose to scrape the dishes, disposing of her meal in the only way possible. "I shouldn't be cross with you, I suppose," Mrs. Fleming added. "With the wedding only a few days away, I guess you've got a stomach full of jitters. Go on and take Alice. Time for her to get ready for bed."

Lucy helped Alice get into her nightclothes as she did every night, marveling at the white pureness of her finely wrinkled skin, how the sharp ridge of her backbone was bent with age. She tucked her in with her favorite doll and sat on the edge of the bed until she had fallen asleep. Alice would miss her. But it wasn't as if she'd be far away. She'd come often to visit. She tried to picture her married self, walking on Doc's arm, pouring out tea in the parlor of The Rookery. It would be *her* parlor.

After a time, she dressed for bed and crawled in next to Alice. She fell instantly asleep and dreamt of putting on her gray silk dress, the one the same color as her gloves. Mrs. Fleming and Alice each took one of her elbows and led her off to the Methodist Church. There, all the sewing ladies were gathered with other long-nosed matrons and Doc's friends from the Bohemian Café, cheering as if they were at a cockfight. They took her to the front of the crowd and stood her before the black-robed minister. But it wasn't a minister, it was Judge Nearing. It wasn't a wedding hymn that she heard but the crack of the gavel. The pomaded prosecutor stuck his finger in her face. "This woman is a fraud! She can't marry Doc because she's Flynn Talbott's wife!" The blue-lipped corpse of the Irishman with the iron bar sticking out of a red gash in his skull came toward her with his arms outstretched as if he would clasp her in a cold embrace. But his face changed and it was Ellis who leered at her. "She was mine first," he snarled. "I have the better claim." "Very well," the judge ruled, "then you may have the first stone." Ellis picked up a fist-sized river rock and hurled it at her. The crowd pushed in and spun her around, all jeering, taunting, lobbing big round stones. She heard screaming and realized it was her own voice.

She sat up and found Alice clinging and crying. Mrs. Fleming threw open the door and held a lamp over her head. "What on earth?" she said, blinking under her nightcap.

Lucy Lied

Lucy cradled Alice and shook her head.

Mrs. Fleming came to the bedside to soothe her sister and stroke her yellow hair. "There, there, it was only a nightmare," she cooed to Alice. "She knows you're leaving us soon," she said to Lucy. "I expect it's upset her." Lucy nodded and felt the hammering of her pulse lessen some, her secret having once more gone undetected. "Go back to sleep now," Ida Fleming said. She took up the candle and left the room in darkness.

Alice fell asleep again right away, but Lucy lay with eyes open staring at the gray shapes of the leaves moving in the wind, shadows cast on the wall by the moon. She waited a few more minutes before she eased herself out of bed and tiptoed to the dresser. She pulled open the deep bottom drawer Mrs. Fleming had set aside for the storage of her new things: the lightly folded drawers, pressed handkerchiefs, the pink-ribboned corset, and the pearl gray gloves, so much more practical than white, the shopkeeper had said. Three dresses lay like coffined headless ladies with arms crossed. She slid her hands amongst the smallclothes until she found the shift with the earring sewn into the hem. The feel of the gem, all safe and secret, reassured her. If only she had the mate she might sell the pair for enough money to go away, far away. She remembered the night of the magicology show, Matt Clancy at the head of the mob marching Ellis back to his hotel, Ellis's possessions cascading into the street from the window of his hotel room. Clancy would know what had happened to the garnet earring. *But will he tell me where it is? Will he give it back?* She moved her hand deeper into the drawer, as far back as she could reach. She felt the same shock of recognition that she had felt when her hand first came upon it among the quilt squares in Garrett's trunk. She wrapped her hand around the grip, felt the heft of it as she pulled it from the drawer. The barrel shone cold and menacing in the moonlight. For the first time it made sense, what she'd done instinctively, smuggling it out of The Rookery in the patchwork, hiding it away. *If Clancy doesn't give it back I'll shoot him.*

Chapter Nineteen

The sound of a pick clanging on stone carried a few hundred yards to where Clancy sat his horse. From his vantage point on the high ground, the gunman watched a fencing crew: two men digging holes, two men burying posts, and one man stringing barbed wire. A buckboard with a single mule in the traces stood off to the side, bearing more posts and wire coiled at the ready. The breath of men and beast steamed. Frost crystalized the morning air. Under their hats, the men wore rags tied around their heads to keep their ears from freezing off. As poorly covered as the balding ground, they wore pieces of blanket woefully stitched up into jackets or just tied around as if they had no idea when they came to the San Joaquin Valley that they'd be wanting warm clothes. *Probably the railroad advertising: summer year-round land of milk and honey bullshit. Damn foolish, what people will believe.* Clancy glanced at the gray clouds to the east and figured it was still snowing in the high country. His felt his jaw tighten as he thought of snow falling in the Sierra, the railroad gang working in the dead of winter. They'd been blasting a narrow shelf on the rock face just wide enough to lay one set of track. The avalanche came as no surprise to anyone who'd blasted in the mountains before. The bosses just flat didn't care if they lost a handful of Chinese laborers under a pile of snow. The bosses accepted casualties as easily as generals.

Clancy's palomino shifted on his hooves and jingled his tack with a toss of his head. "I know," Clancy said. "You're right. We'd best get on down there." He patted the stallion's smooth neck, but did nothing to urge him forward. He hadn't yet addressed the real issue he needed to think on: Isabel Vásquez's scheme to get her land back. It seemed crazy on the face of it.

"You're sure?" he had asked the Chinese informant.

"Most reliable source," the informant replied. "Maid at Sally Locke's whorehouse has sister working at Rancho El Llano. Sister pretends to be stupid—no English, no Spanish—so Mexican ladies talk in front of her like she cow."

"I can't believe it."

"You no believe, go down to gambling parlor and make bet."

"Christ, if there's odds on it, it must be true. Well, if she thinks she can disappear a marriage, I'll damn sure find somebody who can undisappear it."

Clancy sat composing two telegrams in his head: one to the Southern Pacific's lawyer in Sacramento; the other to the head of San Francisco's Chinese brotherhood asking for the name of someone to bribe in the governor's office.

Then there was the matter of the redhead. She'd come up to the horse with a handful of flowers and stood there petting his nose as if they'd known each other all their lives. Just about the time he thought she truly was addle-brained, she stuck out her hand to shake, some kind of wordless introduction between people who'd never met but who knew each other's names. He'd said "I'm pleased to meet you, Miss ... well, I guess Miss Lucy will do, won't it, at least until you get married to the Doc. I've heard it's to take place soon." She'd dropped her eyes then, had looked less pleased than embarrassed. Then, as if to change the subject she looked up with a question in her eyes and motioned toward the horse. "Oh, that's Jack," he replied. It was remarkable how well she could make herself understood. She stayed there, stroking Jack's blaze, for a long time, as if there were something more, something she didn't know how to get at with her looks and signs. Then the boys came running out of the woods screaming about a bear. He mounted and pulled her up so she sat in front of him, sidesaddle. He could remember the wildflower smell, the gold down on her arms, the wisps of hair that brushed his chin. He rode her back to the mission where all the ladies and the children had gone to take shelter. The men had taken off into the woods to try to drive the bear into the clear. Fortunately their whooping and banging had come to nothing. Whatever it was the boys had seen had gone to ground or never was there to begin with. Doc didn't take it kindly, seeing his fiancée held close in another man's arms, but what was a Southern gentleman to do? He said thanks before he grabbed her arm and dragged her away none too gently. Clancy had to wonder what Garrett would be like once she was his wife, and sighed at such a waste. *Not that it's any skin off my nose. No, but it's something ...* He remembered her long backward glance as she was pulled away to the mission. ... *unfinished business.*

Finally, having thought both matters through without achieving any better understanding of either, he nudged the palomino into a trot with his boot heels.

The men stopped working at the approach of the rider in the cattleman's coat. They watched him approaching on the tall yellow horse and eyed their boss, a man by the name of Martin Bland. Once Bland quit work the others dropped their tools. The two diggers flopped their picks on the ground and planted their hands on their butts to straighten their stiff backs. A Mexican squatted and spat in the dust. A kid blew on his hands. Bland came forward a few paces to meet the rider. Clancy recognized the owner of the property, an Ohioan who'd failed at farming once before. He saw how Bland had shoved his hammer handle down under his belt the way some men carried a six-shooter and knew he was far from welcome. No fool, Clancy scanned the scene for the real thing and picked out the long barrel of a squirrel gun leaning against a pile of posts waiting to be sunk along the fence line forming parallel to the Southern Pacific tracks. He maneuvered his horse so the animal stood between the sodbusters and the weapon.

"Morning," Bland said after Clancy dismounted. "You must be Matt Clancy."

Lucy Lied

Clancy looped the reins around a branch of scrub and left the horse to snuffle the bare ground. "And you're Martin Bland."

"I am," Bland said. He made no move to extend a hand. "We heard you came by Larson's place yesterday."

"That's right," Clancy said. "I guess you probably heard what I had to say to him."

"That I did. You needn't have wasted your time riding out here to say the same thing to me."

Clancy nodded toward the barbed wire. "I thought I best tell you face to face, since it don't look like you took much note of what I said to Larson."

Bland squared his shoulders. "I aim to keep putting up my fence regardless of what you say, if that's what you mean."

"You know the railroad means to evict any homesteader who can't pay the going price for the land," Clancy said. "With improvements like your fence here, it's likely to price out at twenty-five dollars an acre."

"Not once we get our say it won't. We're forming a land league to put our case before Congress. The railroad will have to stand by the price we were guaranteed in '69. The land league will see to it every farmer in the San Joaquin signs a petition."

Clancy took a cigar out of his pocket and bit off the end. He spat the nub of tobacco into the dust and stuck the smoke between his teeth. He reached under his coat. Bland's men tensed. Their eyes shot toward the squirrel gun, but before anyone could make a move for it, Clancy produced the match from his shirt pocket and struck it against the heel of his boot. "You boys are acting a might jumpy," he said.

"You've said your piece," Bland replied. "Now get on your horse and get out of here. We got work to do."

"Every fencepost you drive raises the price of this property," Clancy said. "It may not be fair and it may not be right, but you can forget about two dollars and fifty cents an acre."

"We got the law on our side," Bland said, "so we'll just see about that."

"The law can be bought," Clancy replied. "You're a fool if you think the Southern Pacific will give you a fair fight. How do you think they got this land in the first place? Greased a lot of palms in Washington, that's how. What makes you think they won't do it again when your petition comes up for a vote?"

Clancy heard his horse shy and knew even before the sound of the hammer cocking that somebody had got the drop on him from behind.

"Let me see those hands," a reedy voice said as he felt the poke of the gun barrel in his back.

He flung his cigar into the dirt and lifted his hands. His action prompted a sharper prod between his shoulder blades. "Move over toward the others and face around so I can stand clear of this animal. I got trod on by a mule yesterday. Turned my whole foot purple."

He did as he was told and turned to find a small woman in a billowing calico dress, huddled in a shawl and bonnet, standing behind the weapon. She wore round wire-framed spectacles that magnified her washed-out brown eyes, making them much too large for her narrow face. She stood rigid around the squirrel gun, elbows poked out at a weird angle. She was hugely pregnant. Clancy felt sure she'd probably never fired a gun before and knew he was in big trouble if she got scared and twitchy.

"Liza Mae," Bland said, "what the hell are you doing with that firearm?"

"What you shoulda done, I reckon!"

"You get on back to the house."

"I brung you your lunch." She jerked her head toward a basket on the ground. "Fried chicken and corn pone. Ain't you all gonna get some after I walked all the way out here?"

"We'll get some soon as you clear off. This is men's business."

"I reckon it's your business to do what I say," Liza answered, "seeing as I got the gun."

"Don't you sass me now, Liza. I don't want to have to take my belt to you."

Her pale brown eyes flared behind her spectacles. "You don't dare. Not in my condition."

The skinny man with patches on the elbows of his homespun jacket, one of the diggers, started toward the woman. "Now then, Liza," he said soothingly.

"Back off, Jess," Bland warned. "This is between my woman and me. You got no cause to interfere."

Jess halted in his tracks and raised both hands to fend off his boss's wrath. "Simmer down, Marty. I don't mean to meddle. I just thought to help."

"We don't need no help," Bland said. "We don't need no help, do we, Liza?" He took a tentative step toward his wife. "Ain't we always worked things out between us? Come on, now, honey. Put that gun down and let me get shed of this fella here. Ain't I always took care of you and the younguns?"

"Sure, if what you mean by working things out is making more younguns than I can tick off on one hand. That what you call taking care of us? By God, Martin Bland, I ought to shoot your pecker off right where you stand. You hear me?"

"Liza!"

She leveled the gun at his crotch.

The diggers drew in their breath. Bland's voice quavered an octave above its normal range. "Liza!"

Clancy saw things clear at such times. His gunman's eyes made objects enlarge and movement slow down. He saw how her chapped red hands were white and flaky at the knuckles, how her lips compressed and the hip on the side that carried the gun swung out to steady it. He saw the eye in the profile of her face narrow, aiming. He saw the index finger on the trigger tense and start to pull. He sprang at her an instant before the gun fired, knocking her sideways, pushing the gun barrel off line. He saved Martin Bland's manhood but deflected Liza's aim so the bullet went straight into the heart of the sodbuster to Bland's left. The echo of the gun's discharge still shook the air as Liza sat down hard on the ground. She pushed the hair out of her face and bawled, "Martin! Martin!"

Clancy reached a hand toward the woman to help her to her feet, but Bland sprang between the railroad man and his wife. He grabbed the gun off the ground where she'd dropped it and commenced to bring the butt down hard across her shoulders. The digger named Jess came running to stop the man beating the pregnant woman. "Don't you go hitting on that woman anymore, Marty!"

"Mind yer business," Bland said, but it was only the work of a moment before Jess wrenched the piece out of his hands. The other men stood watching, waiting to see who would tell them what to do.

"Billy!" Bland yelled, "Put Liza up on the buckboard and take her back to the house." He held out his hand to Jess. "There. You satisfied? Now give me that piece back."

Jess handed over the gun.

Bland jerked his head toward the man bleeding on the frosted ground. "Go on, now and see to Tom."

Jess squatted over Tom as Billy helped the heavily pregnant woman onto the seat of the buckboard and climbed up beside her. Clancy retrieved his cigar from the ground and watched as the kid slapped the mule smartly on the backside, sending it off at a run that threatened to bounce everything out of the wagon including the as-yet unborn. The boy's cries of "Whoa!" grew fainter as the wagon clattered away. The Mexican crouched next to the lunch basket and began groping through it. "*Pollo*," he said. He pulled a drumstick from the wrappings and bit into it. "Bueno."

"He's dead," Jess said. He looked up from the prone man. "Shot right through the heart." He stood up and dusted off his knees. "Who woulda thought that little woman could shoot like that."

Martin Bland went pale to the lips. His eyes flicked from Jess to the corpse and back. "You sure?"

"Dead as Abe Lincoln."

Bland's eyes followed the thread of smoke winding upward from Clancy's cigar. "Weren't Liza shot Tom," he said. "It was Clancy. You all seen it."

Lucy Lied

The Mexican stopped chewing and got to his feet with the drumstick still dangling from his hand. The fence gang eyed the railroad man. Clancy clenched the smoke between his teeth on one side. "I got no more business here," he said. He took a step toward the blond horse.

Bland fired a round into the dust at Clancy's feet. The horse reared.

"Grab him," Bland ordered. Jess grabbed the cheek strap and hauled the horse's head down.

"I'll take him." Clancy held his hand out for the reins. "He's young, still a bit skittish around folks he don't know."

"Step back." Bland motioned with the gun. "Esteban, take his side arms."

The Mexican tossed the chicken leg into the dust and relieved Clancy of his cigar and his firearms, two Colt 1860 Army revolvers. He stuck the cigar between his lips and stuffed the six-guns into his belt as he backed away.

"You best think a minute about what you're doing," Clancy warned. "You know the sheriff rode out to the Cutler place to help me see to an eviction. It's just the other side of the ridge. He's probably on his way over here on account of the gunshot."

"When he gets here we'll explain how you shot Tom in cold blood. Tie him," Bland said.

The man holding the horse passed the reins to Bland and pulled a bulldogging rope out of his pocket. He tied Clancy's elbows tight together behind his back. The gunman's fingers splayed ineffectually, groping the air.

"What the hell do you think you're doing?" Clancy said, though there was no doubt in his mind, particularly after Bland took the coiled lariat off his pommel and proceeded to fashion a noose.

"Right handy, your bringing your own rope," Bland said. "Fixing to rope some cows, was ya?"

"Just so I'm clear," Clancy said, "you mind telling me why you're doing this?"

"Somebody's gotta pay for Tom."

"Your woman pulled the trigger," Clancy said, knowing how stupid it was to point out the obvious.

"Think I'm going to let Liza Mae go upriver when I got you here to hang?" He took off Clancy's hat and flung it into the dirt. "Ain't nobody going to ask any questions about how you happened to shoot my best hand. Not a soul will shed a tear over a railroad enforcer who got himself crosswise with a rancher. No sir, not a soul I know will say anything but 'Amen, brother.' Seems to me I'm doing everybody a favor this way." He dropped the noose over Clancy's head. "Let's walk to that plane tree yonder," he said.

It was the only tree of any size as far as the eye could see. *It would be a sycamore.* Clancy loved sycamores. He thought of the one with low, spreading branches beside the little house on the Salinas Highway. He loved the patchwork bark, liked the notion of the tree adding to it year after year like a patient housewife making a quilt with a sewing basket full of scraps.

Bland and the Mexican heaved him up on his horse while Jess held the palomino still. He sat under the spreading plane tree in what would have been the cool shade of the broad-leaved canopy had it been summer. The Mexican flung the bitter end of the rope over a bough above his head. Clancy said nothing, but waited, thinking of Hawaii. As he sat there waiting to die he thought it damned unfair that he would never make it out to the islands. He imagined sweet, flower-smelling air, the soft feeling of it. And coconut. *How does the mind conjure what crosses the tongue?* The blond horse stepped forward and drew the rope tight just below Clancy's jaw. *Don't do me any favors or I'll not let that pretty woman stroke your nose again. What did she want with us, this Lucy? She knew the whole town was watching, whispering.* He thought of Garrett dragging her away to shelter. *She doesn't love him. Maybe she loves me.* He felt in danger of losing his composure. A feeling of tightness in his throat passed off in a second. The upwelling of emotion occasioned by the thought of being loved was tamped down by the grim observation that his neck was giving him a lot of trouble this day. He fixed his gaze on the long lines of shining railroad track running just beyond the fence posts to infinity.

Lucy Lied

Behind Clancy, the men stood wondering which one would have the guts to slap Jack on the rump and launch the gunman into eternity. The Mexican was sweating now in spite of the cold, sweating and smiling. They were all watching Bland. Bland stepped toward Jack. His face was like something carved out of wood, hard, expressionless. He raised his hand. Jack shied out of reach and whinnied. Bland half-stepped closer and then something drew his eyes away. They saw the stiffness leave his expression, replaced by a slack-jawed look of disbelief.

"Shit fire it's Osbourne." He cast a warning look at his men. "Don't nobody say a word. Let me do the talking."

The sheriff rode hard down to the flat but reined in when he saw the proceedings taking place under the sycamore had come to a halt. Clancy turned in the saddle to watch him cover the last fifty yards at a snail's pace. "Afternoon, Sheriff," Clancy called out.

"It's morning, you damn fool," Osbourne called back.

"Is it? I thought you used up the whole morning getting here."

Osbourne reined in and coughed into a crumpled kerchief he pulled from his pocket. He blew his nose and coughed some more and spat on the ground. "Got me a case of the grippe on account of chasing after you. Reckon it would be in my best interest if I let these boys hang you so I can get home and take to my bed." He stuffed the rag back into his pocket and turned to Bland. "Notwithstanding, I don't much care for you dirt farmers horning in on my job."

"This gunslinger kilt one of my men, Sheriff," Bland said. "He told us to stop putting up our wire and old Tom kept on working on account of he was always hard of hearing and this son of a bitch just up and shot him. We all just mean to pay him back what he deserves."

The sheriff followed the point of Bland's finger to the body of the dead man. "I see. Well, I guess I'll just let you get to it, then."

"Best check my six-guns before you leave," Clancy said. "You'll see there's five bullets in each one. I only load five bullets and ride with an empty chamber under the hammer. So's not to shoot off my dick just toting my guns around."

"He used the squirrel gun!" Bland said.

Osbourne eyed the farmer. "Why'd he do that when he had two Colts to hand?"

Bland scowled. "He did, is all."

"Like hell I did," Clancy growled. "Bland's wife shot him. She brought up the lunch and got scared when she found me here talking to these men. She meant to run me off with the squirrel gun, but it went off by accident. Must have a hair trigger or something. It was an accident, pure and simple." Clancy peered down at Bland. "Ain't that right?"

Bland studied the dirt for a second and then nodded. "She ain't in her right mind anyway. You know how they get when they're with child. Half crazy."

Osbourne shifted in his saddle. "The dead man have kin hereabouts?"

"None we know of."

"Then I suspect you all will have to bury him and say some words over the grave. Tell that woman of yours if I ever hear tell of her picking up a gun again I'll hold her down in the jail for thirty days." He turned the bay and added. "Give Clancy back his rope and his pistols. I'll want him to sign a statement in my office. If he don't show up I'll come back out here and hang one of you with a hunk of that Goddamn wire you're stringing all over creation."

The sodbusters did as they were told and let the gunman go. At the sheriff's office he started writing his statement but didn't get far before he asked Osbourne, "You know that sodbuster who got shot?"

Osbourne shook his head. "Just put down 'Martin Bland's ranch hand, known as Tom'."

Chapter Twenty

Clancy thought about that as he rode north; the only epitaph the sonofabitch would ever have didn't even mention him by his full name. He rode to a place known as the Halfway House, where the stage route from Monterey to San Juan Bautista crossed the Los Angeles-to-San Francisco line. For years people had wagered on which stage would arrive first. Felipe Vásquez had bet half his rancho against Matt Clancy's bankroll and lost. Afterward he'd called for more wine. Clancy liked that about the old coot. *God rest him.*

The four men Clancy thought of as "the bosses" had a private train that shuttled between Sacramento and San Francisco mostly, but occasionally headed south. The only car he'd ever been in was a converted Pullman the bosses used as an office. It was richly appointed with dark red Persian rugs, brass lamps, polished mahogany furniture, and a fully stocked liquor cabinet. A coal stove in the corner warmed the car in winter. A painting of a naked lady stretched on a fur hung over the stove, the placement an obvious effort to make sure she didn't take a chill. Four ceiling fans turned lazily on hot days, circulating the air by means of a system of pulleys and belts, truly a mechanical wonder and rather beautiful in its own way. An odor of cured tobacco and leather upholstery served to emphasize the difference between the tastes of the merely comfortable and those of the scandalously rich.

Often the bosses would not be found on board, having relinquished their luxury transport to a second tier of managers, men with less money who wanted more and would take on any sort of unpleasant job to get it. Clancy knew one of these men pretty well, an Irishman named Shaw. Shaw had made a fortune at the Coloma gold fields but had gambled it away. Salted a claim or two in his day. Drank hard. They had a taste for whiskey in common, but not much else. Shaw always stopped at the Halfway House to place a wager. Clancy waited in the private car until the day's betting was decided.

When Shaw came into the Pullman, his face above his starched collar glowed red as Chinese pork ribs. He flung out a paw to Clancy. "Matthew! Put 'er there, old friend. Have you had a drink to wash away the trail dust?" He stepped to the bar and poured two tots of the Irish into two glasses. "Come on, lad. Let's drink to the Old Country." He held his glass aloft until Clancy touched it with his, then he downed the spirits in one go. "Ah, that's the stuff. East-west route won. I collected fifty dollars. Can you beat that?"

"It's quite a mystery how often you win," Clancy said, hinting otherwise with a wry smile. It wasn't beyond Shaw to send a telegram to the train stations along the two routes to find out which ones the stagecoaches had last passed.

Shaw laughed. "I've always been a lucky sod. That's why you won't wager with me. I'm too damn good." Shaw planted his generous ass in the chair behind the desk and grinned. His vest, of a subtly striped maroon fabric that complemented his suit coat and trousers, stretched to bursting across his belly under a heavy gold watch chain slung between buttonhole and pocket.

"If you'd care to try your hand at a test of skill," Clancy said, "I'll shoot you a game of Nine Men Morris. But you'd have to get down on the floor and I fear it might be a question as to whether you'd get up again."

"I haven't played marbles since I was ten," Shaw laughed. "I remember how we used to bargain for the good ones, trade back and forth. Play cutthroat winner-take-all matches down in the schoolyard."

Clancy sipped his whiskey. "Hard to picture you at ten. You have your gold watch and a little banker's hat and a waistcoat?"

"Why sure. Just like you had those two six-guns." He shifted his cigar to the other side of his mouth. "Speaking of that, here's something from the bosses. Little bonus." He took an envelope from his desk drawer and tossed it across to Clancy. "They're happy with the way you've been handling the sodbusters, getting them moved off. No bloodshed. No martyrs."

Clancy opened the envelope and thumbed the bills. "You must have got my letter of resignation," he said.

"Aye, I got it, but I thought maybe you'd gone out of your mind for a spell. I threw it away." He pulled the cigar out of his mouth. "Seriously, Matthew—why in hell would you be thinking a fool thing like that? Have we not been paying you a princely sum right along, even without the bonus thrown in?"

"I'm not fond of throwing settlers off their farms," he said. "'Specially after they've put up barns and fences, dug wells, and scratched out irrigation ditches. Made something where there was just badlands before. Besides, you know as well as I do the railroad promised them that land at $2.50 an acre."

"$2.50 a *nd upwards*. I got copies of the pamphlets right here."

"Come on, Shaw. The homesteaders were led to believe that meant a few cents upwards, not twenty dollars."

"I know no such thing. All I know is what the pamphlet says plain as day."

"They're forming some kind of land league," Clancy said. "Plan on sending a petition to Congress to make the bosses sell them the land at the price set on it, back when the government flat-out gave it away to the railroad."

"If the Southern Pacific had had to buy the right of way, there'd be no railroad today. I guess that would suit you better. I know there's hardship involved here, but it's the way of progress. Individuals have to sacrifice for the greater good."

"Fine. You can be the one to explain that to these people who got nothing but the farms they built up from sweat and blood. I'm through trying to put over what don't make any sense to me."

"Now just simmer down," Shaw said. He puffed his cigar and hatched a new argument as his small eyes moved restlessly across the desktop. "Stop and think about what'll happen if you back out now. I'll hire another gun hand, is all—one who won't have any qualms about shooting your farmers for trespass. Is that what you want? If you really care about any of those poor bastards, what you should do is stay on until they file their petition and the government makes a decision. You keep the peace down there and I'll tell them up the line to go easy until Congress makes a new law. You tell the sodbusters to send their petition to Washington, the sooner the better. Get the issue resolved once and for all." He paused and observed that his argument was receiving some consideration. "Besides, what would an old busted-up gunslinger like you do without this job?"

"I've been thinking of that property I won a while back. It's good land. Has a stream on it and enough grass to fatten half the cows in Monterey County."

"Cows! What do you care for cows? You're no cattleman. Don't tell me you're going to take up a new trade in your dotage."

"On the other hand, I might just sell the whole spread. It won't fetch much, but I didn't pay anything for it to begin with. I could travel on the proceeds."

Shaw chewed his cigar. "You remember what I told you about the rail spur the bosses are thinking about running down to Monterey?"

Clancy shrugged. "Sure. What of it?"

"They plan to build a high-class hotel down on the peninsula, a kind of pleasure spot for San Francisco people. Take tourists right to the hotel doorstep. It'll be an escape from the city. The Del Monte Resort. The best food, elegant rooms. I only say this because for you to sell your spread before the hotel gets built would be a great pity. Real estate values will go up like a Roman candle after the rail's in, and with all the people coming down from San Francisco, there's bound to be some who like it well enough to want a country place."

"When's this supposed to happen?"

Shaw shrugged. "A couple years, maybe. I tell you, you'd be a fool to sell now unless you want to take tallow and hides in trade for your place. You've not entered into an agreement already, have you?"

"Wouldn't be sitting here if I had."

"Good. Now take my advice and keep as you are, at least until the rail spur is done. Let me have your word on it." Shaw stretched out his hand.

Clancy grasped it briefly.

Shaw leaned back in his chair. "Good. Now I want you to go back down south to Goshen. Look up a troublemaker by the name of John Doyle."

Chapter Twenty-one

The part of the jail that was considered the sheriff's office smelled of coffee that had been too long on the boil, but Morris, the deputy, was so used to that particular reek, he didn't notice it any more than he noticed the farts of the prisoners. As he sat with his feet on Taylor's desk, his mind was occupied with the consideration of life's injustices and its scanty rewards. It was a disappointing business, he thought, as he leaned back in his boss's chair. You either died too young to make your mark or you lived long enough to see your dreams wither away, provided you'd had any in the first place. It was this thought that occupied the back of his mind, while in the more immediate consciousness there was a question of whether the dinginess that filmed the front windows was on the inside of the glass or the outside. Was it soot from the lamps or dust from the street? He didn't want to know bad enough to get up and run his finger across a pane. Besides, if he did such a foolish thing Taylor would surely see the finger trace and insist that Morris wash both sides of every window in the place. Morris sucked his wretched teeth. A molar was paining him. He thrust the index finger of his right hand to the back of his lower gum on the right side and prodded the tooth until his eyes watered.

"Get your ass out of my chair," Taylor said, slamming the door behind him.

189

Lucy Lied

"Mornin', boss," Morris said. He dropped his feet to the floor and rose in a gingerly fashion that suggested things weren't quite right with him.

"What's wrong? You get a snootful last night?"

"No sir. Sober as a judge. Gotta bad tooth. Needta go on up to Doc Garrett's and have him pull it."

"Plenty of people in town who'll take out a tooth. Hell, Steadman's boy will do it."

"I ain't goin' to no crazy nigger. Like as not he'd take the wrong one."

Taylor sat down behind his desk. "Suit yourself." He picked up the two sheets of paper he found folded there. "Soon as you finish up the sweeping," he said to his deputy of the wretched teeth, "you might run a wet rag over those windows."

Morris grinned in that mocking way of his that made Taylor's blood boil. "Damn, boss. You sure gotta eye. I declare. Those windows don't look any dirtier than usual to me."

Taylor unfolded the telegrams and pieced together the import. Morris watched him lean back in his chair and wondered why he looked like there was a load on his mind. "Ever'thin' all right?"

"I'll be going out to the valley. I'll need you to stay put here till I get back."

"Whatcha gonna do out there?"

"Something touching on Matt Clancy."

"Clancy?"

"Yep."

"You ain't scared to tangle with the railroad?"

"He don't scare me." Taylor bent to the lower drawer of his desk and pulled out a bottle of whiskey. He uncorked and drank down a belt, thinking things through. It would be Sebastián Oreña who would take care of the gunman as soon as he saw the copies of the telegrams Clancy had sent to the city.

"Want I should ride with ya?"

"No. You stay here and work on those windows after you've finished sweeping up. You got any more time after that, go on and fix that door." He said it knowing the windows would still be filthy and the door latch busted when he got back from Oreña's place. But if the jail ever got to a state of repair that would prevent anybody from walking in and springing loose any prisoner they wanted to, the balance of power in town would be upset and being sheriff wouldn't be worth the aggravation.

Taylor sat and thought of the saint's day celebration, the oddity of that one day's clement sunshine amid a season of sullen skies. Reluctant to leave the warmth of the office, he sat a while longer, watching the meager sunlight shaft through the dirty windows. When he couldn't put it off any longer, Taylor got to his feet. He strapped on his gun belt, dragged on his jacket, and stuffed the telegrams into the pocket where he kept his flask. He thought on his way to the stable how the wind reminded him of the blows they called dry Nor'easters back in Massachusetts. He remembered the rare days when his father would be inside mending nets, plying his marlinspike by firelight as his mother hummed over a pot of fish stew. Most days he'd be with his father at dawn, watching the pier move off into the mist as the wind filled the sail and the nose of the boat bit into the first big swell. Nothing kept out the cold on those days. Clothes would only soak in spray and grow heavier around the arms and legs, the cold meat of hands taking in the dripping lines—why he left off fishing, soon as there was a way out.

The morning breeze was spiked with a salty mist that slipped in under his collar and caused the sheriff to curse the chill of November and the man on whose account he had to take himself out of doors. At the livery stable he waited for the horse to finish its oats.

"Morning, Sheriff. It's a cold one," the boy mucking out observed.

Taylor considered asking the black man his name, but didn't, figuring it didn't much matter. Everyone called him Steadman's boy. "It is," he said.

The horse wanted no part of being saddled. Taylor hauled on the cinch and kneed him in the barrel to make him quit holding his breath. Finally the horse blew out and he tightened the girth. He mounted and turned the gelding out of town. He kicked it into a trot, bearing the rocky gait and the sharper sting of the wind by thinking of the valley. It would be warmer there. Maybe a blue sky.

"So here I am," he said, sharing his thoughts on life and weather with the horse once they were out on the road to Salinas. "Got away from the misery of fishing. Least I thought so. These raw days I ain't so sure I got away at all." The horse flicked his ears as if he agreed with the sentiment. "Farming's the thing," Taylor continued. "Least you don't work once the weather turns bad. There's seasons when the seed's in the ground but not up yet. You take up whittling if you got a mind, or maybe a mouth organ. But mostly you just set. Ever so often get up and throw a log on the fire."

He felt in his pocket and drew out the flask, making sure not to dislodge the copies of the telegrams he meant to show Oreña. These were things of value. He'd make something of them, a good trade. He drank a tot and put back the flask, then kicked the bay to get it to move faster. They came into the valley within the shelter of the hills. Taylor looked up at the sky and found no relief from the gray scudding clouds that hung over the peninsula. Here in the valley where crops and livestock needed rain, the clouds threatened but remained perversely dry, having lost their moisture near the bay. "They say it's gonna be dry this winter," he told the horse, "not a sniff of rain for two, three weeks now."

He was crossing Clancy's land now, brown and dry like the rest except for a green sward by the stream bed. He passed an ancient sycamore tree next to the shack everyone called the little house. On the crest of the hill just beyond, he spied piles of fence posts and coils of barbed wire.

Oreña's spread was east of the Vásquez place. He had several miles to go before he came to the white two-story adobe roofed with terra cotta tiles. In summer it would be splashed with red and coral where bougainvillea clung to the porch posts. A pair of sleek hunting dogs ran out as soon as Taylor turned his horse into the placita in front of the graceful dwelling. They bayed at the horse and nipped at its hocks, but lost interest as soon as Taylor slowed him to a walk. Oreña emerged from a pair of ornately carved double doors and walked out onto his porch. Two small boys ran out after the hounds. Oreña bellowed for the maid. "Hortensia! Come and get these brats. They are supposed to be at their lessons. The tutor will be here soon." He greeted Taylor with a proud grin. "Ah, children," he said gaily. "If you don't teach them any better they grow up to be just like their parents!"

"They could do worse," Taylor said, acknowledging the trappings of wealth as he dismounted and tied his horse at the rail.

"They are spoiled. I indulge them. But it gives me pleasure. Is that not what we live for?" The maid appeared in the doorway and dropped a brief curtsey before heading off after the boys. "Come in, my friend," Oreña said, clapping Taylor on the back. "Come sit by the fire and warm your bones. The air is sharp this morning."

The hounds followed their master as he led Taylor through the foyer to another wide portal. He parted the pocket doors and admitted dogs and guest to a room dominated by a large stone hearth and an equally large desk. The head of a black bull with silver tips on the ends of his horns hung over the mantelpiece. The chairs were all covered in black cowhide, one of which, an uncomfortable looking object, was entirely constructed of polished cow horns. "Here we may talk without interruption," Oreña said, sliding the doors shut as the boys' shrieks sounded in the front hall. "I'm sure you also have such a place where you can find a few minutes of blessed peace." He frowned slightly. "It pains me that I am so little acquainted with you, not even enough to know if you have children."

"I've yet to find a woman who might so oblige me," Taylor replied.

Oreña took one of the chairs positioned in front of the hearth and motioned Taylor toward the other. "So, now tell me why you have ridden two hours on a cold morning to see me."

"On the way out here I saw your cattle grazing on dry land," Taylor began, "and Clancy getting ready to string barb-wire between your cows and the only water for fifty miles."

"Yes, it seems I must make a contract with Matt Clancy. To water my cattle on his land I must pay him a percentage of what they bring at market."

"Who came up with that plan?"

"My cousin's widow."

"Isabel?"

"She must water her cows, too."

The sheriff's eyes darted to a decanter on a table behind the desk and wondered if a refreshment would be offered. "Speaking of which, I'm a mite thirsty myself," he said."

"Let me pour you a drink. Is brandy to your taste?"

Taylor nodded and his host poured two generous glasses and passed one across the desk.

"I take no pleasure in talking about Clancy," Taylor said, after his first sip.

"I'd heard as much." Oreña smiled. "There is bad blood between Clancy and many of the people hereabouts. But I must do business with him. Soon, too, unless we get some rain."

"You got a better hope than that."

Oreña's eyes honed in on Taylor's face. "What are you saying?"

Taylor pulled his trump cards out of his pocket. "The telegrapher in town is a friend of mine. These are copies of messages he sent to San Francisco for Clancy. Your cousin's widow is scheming to get that land back from him."

Oreña took the pages and scanned the content. "I don't understand," he said. "It is something about my cousin's marriage? That it was never consummated?"

"Isabel means to use that argument to assert her title to the whole tract. If she can get her annulment and establish that Felipe's debts had nothing to do with her, she'll have a legal right to throw Clancy off the land."

Oreña threw the pages back at Taylor. "And charge me more for water than Clancy would."

Taylor grinned. "It's uncomfortable having your fate in the hands of an Anglo and a scheming woman."

"Finish your brandy and get out," Oreña said.

"I meant no offense," Taylor protested. "I only meant that I understand what it's like to have a thorn in your side. Isabel is yours, Clancy is mine. We both feel the same pricking."

"What is it you have come to say to me? Speak plainly."

"Just this. If you want to have a say in what happens to that land, you have to establish a stake, a claim."

"How?"

"Before Clancy finishes getting his barbed wire up, you run your cattle onto the land. They can batter the fences down now, but not once the wire is strung. Then, once your beasts are there, it will be up to Clancy to come to terms. Disputes over land. They so often turn violent. Clancy is a violent man. He may lose his head. It will be up to you and your men to see that justice is done."

"What are you saying?"

"Just that I won't interfere. Whatever happens between you and Clancy, or Isabel for that matter. It's no business of mine."

A slow smile spread over the Mexican's face.

Taylor felt the same as when he'd finally been dealt a winning poker hand. Respect was due. "If I find that you've betrayed this confidence I'll hang your balls on the wall next to that bull's head."

"You need not worry," Oreña replied.

"Good. I best be getting back to town."

"Another drink before you go."

Taylor took immoderate pleasure in refusing. "We'll take our next drink together over there by the stream. Till then I wash my hands of it."

Oreña waved from the porch and muttered as the sheriff rode away. "Not one to get your hands dirty, useless bastard that you are." Absent obscenity, it was one of the worst things he knew to say about another man.

Chapter Twenty-two

"I'll be right there with you," Mrs. Fleming said as she met Lucy's nervous glance in the mirror. She smoothed the small white collar around the girl's neck and patted the row of small buttons that ran down her back to the waistband of her black skirt. "You look just fine. The doctor said we must leave your hair loose so he'll be able to manipulate the calipers, but aside from that you look very proper." She turned to address her strange sister. "Alice, doesn't Lucy look nice?"

Alice got up from the floor where she had been playing with her doll. She stood on tiptoe to add her wizened child's face to the two already reflected in the glass. "Oh, yes," she said, touching the sleeve of Lucy's blouse. "Can't I have a dress the same color for my dolly? With lots of buttons? She likes lavender better than any other shade."

"We'll see, my dear," Mrs. Fleming replied. "Now we must go. It wouldn't be fitting for us to be late for one of the foremost throat specialists in the country, would it?"

Alice trotted after the two women as they left the bedroom for the front hallway where a lady of the Methodist congregation stood by to look after her.

"You're off, then," Anne Fletcher said. She helped Mrs. Fleming into her coat.

"Alice, say hello to Mrs. Fletcher," Ida Fleming said. "She's going to stay with you while Lucy and I are at Doctor Garrett's office." Alice stepped behind Lucy's skirts.

"Come, Alice," Anne said. "You remember me. I've been here working on Lucy's bridal quilt. You mustn't be so shy."

Mrs. Fleming pulled Alice away from Lucy and placed her hand in Anne's. "I hope she gives you no trouble." She bent down to look into Alice's wide blue eyes. "You be good, now. I'll be back by lunchtime."

Alice squirmed out of Anne's grasp and ran back to her bedroom. The door slammed shut.

"Don't worry," Anne said.

"We must go," Mrs. Fleming replied. She fixed her hat to her head with a quick tug at the tie and left the house with the mute girl lagging a step behind. "Come, Lucy. Don't dawdle."

Lucy matched her stride to the older woman's as they crunched along the pebbly path toward Monterey. She hunched her shoulders against the shore breeze and clutched her shawl close under her chin, as if that might stave off the dreaded examination. The wind tugged at her hair, lofting it wildly, making it dance to the screaming of the gulls. She wished with all her heart she could wheel overhead with the seabirds, fly across the waves to … anywhere, really … anywhere but here.

"It's a wonder to me how he dotes on you," Ida Fleming was saying. "Sparing no time or expense to try to find a cure. And the two of you not even married yet. Imagine what lengths he'll go to when you are well and truly his." A small smile appeared on the older woman's lips. "He asks me daily how the quilt is coming along. I always put him off. But I think we are close enough to finishing that we must set the wedding date." She cut her eyes over to her companion's face. "What would you say to two weeks from now, the middle of December? Best to get it out of the way before the holidays, I suppose, and—well, my dear, don't look so stricken. I'm sure when I suggest the date your fiancé will argue for one sooner."

Lucy marched diligently toward the Rookery, her mind a stew of worry. *I must find a way. But where can I go? Molly won't keep me again, and even if she would I'm too easily found there. If only I could make my way back to Aunt Aggie. But the train fare!* She began to consider theft for the first time since she'd held pennies back from Flynn Talbott. But how to manage it? *Ida Fleming doesn't drink. How would Ellis have managed it? No, I mustn't think that way. Not ever.* She fought a deep, forlorn hopelessness. If she had been alone she would have started weeping.

All too soon The Rookery was visible with its dark sentinels lofting on the breeze and flapping madly to regain the rooftop. Mrs. Fleming regarded the carrion birds uneasily. "Like dorymen pulling hard for home," she said. Lucy felt the ravens were pure evil and wondered if dorymen were devils or grave robbers.

As they mounted the porch steps, Doc appeared at the front door and opened it to admit them. "Good day, ladies," he said with a certain gentlemanly dash meant to mark a special occasion. "Come on in. Let me take your wraps." He flung Lucy's shawl and Mrs. Fleming's coat on the clothes tree in the hall. "Dr. Leech waits for us in the surgery." Striding past the cane-bottomed straight chairs where the halt and lame would wait on tenterhooks before the terrors of the surgery, Garrett led the way into the room with which Lucy had become overly acquainted of late.

Her eyes drifted from one strange object to the next, avoiding the doctor's—the roll-top desk against one wall, the bookcase with broad-spined medical texts, a japanned tin case, a mortar and pestle, the examining table topped with white enamel. On a towel at one end of the examining table was an array of mean looking knives and graceful S-shaped implements he called "staves" used to inflict God knew what torture. He had told her such objects had been his playthings as a child, that his father had practiced medicine before him. Still the instruments held a lurid fascination for her, as if they were an executioner's tools of trade.

In an armchair positioned near the window with good light for reading, a cherub-faced gentleman with Burnside whiskers and pomaded hair sat turning the leaves of a recent *Harpers*. He cast a glance over the wire rims of his spectacles when the door opened, but did not rise from his seat until Garrett began his introduction.

"Ladies," the local man said, stretching his open palm toward the seated dignitary, "may I present Hannibal Leech, one of the foremost ear, nose and throat specialists in the western United States. His practice is located in Saint Louis and while I was working for the insurance company there, I had occasion to hear of him. I was happy enough to find him sojourning in San Francisco while on my last visit there. Dr. Leech, this is my housekeeper Ida Fleming, who is also the most talented midwife in the region. Her strenuous efforts toward cleanliness have all but eliminated childbed fever among her mothers."

The visiting specialist rose from his chair and took a step forward to briefly grasp Mrs. Fleming's hand with his thumb and forefinger.

"And this," Garrett continued, with a motion toward Lucy, "is our subject, Mrs. Talbott."

Leech advanced on Lucy with no acknowledgement of her slight nod. "She's quite tall," he said to Doc. "Please have her take a chair so I can begin my examination."

"Sit, Lucy," Doc said.

She sat in the straight chair at the end of the examination table.

"I'll begin with the throat," Leech said. He peered at Lucy as if she were a suspect hiding evidence of a crime. "You'll open your mouth please, as wide as you can, and keep it open until I tell you to close." With the knuckle of one index finger, he lifted her chin so far that the back of her head cramped against the bones of her neck. "Now open."

He reached his fingers into her mouth and took hold of her tongue, stretching it down over her lower front teeth. "Bring me a light," he commanded.

Garrett leaped up, lit the oil lamp on his desk and brought it close to Leech's shoulder. Lucy could smell the burning wick, the male bodies, stale breath. Her jaw ached, her tongue felt torn at the root. "Do you see?" Leech asked casually.

"A good color," Garrett replied.

"Except that there's a pale spot on the vocal cord. You see? There on the right."

"Oh, yes."

"This could be crucial."

"Indeed."

"In my experience there is only one way to deal with an abnormality of the vocal cord," Leech began, "and that is to scrape away such irregularities. It's a somewhat complicated surgery as it requires tracheal intubation to allow the subject to draw air into the lungs while we have the airway obstructed. I've had considerable experience with the procedure and consider it routine at this point, though there is always a possibility of—"

"Shall we let the patient relax," Garrett suggested.

"If you've seen enough," Leech replied. Only then did he release Lucy's tongue, letting her head fall forward and her mouth close. "Now then," he continued. "Let us go on to assess the cranial features."

Leech came around behind her and immediately placed both hands on her head. He pushed his fingers underneath her hair and felt of her skull, changing position with short, stiff movements. Pursing his heavy lips and raising his eyes to the ceiling he kneaded the base of her cranium and the cervical vertebrae. He then came to stand in front of her, bent over at the waist and looked straight into her face while feeling both sides of her jaw below her ears. This done, he straightened up and drew a handkerchief from his pocket with which he wiped his fat pink fingers. He turned to Doc. "The head must be sheared before I take measurements, otherwise we can't be sure of our accuracy," he said. "Would you like to manage it or shall I?"

"Cut off her hair?" Mrs. Fleming cried.

Leech set his eyes upon the old woman in disbelief. "I was addressing the doctor, madam." He turned his gaze back to Garrett. "Well?"

"Perhaps you should do it," Garrett said. He opened the drawer of the examining table and withdrew a wicked-looking pair of scissors. "I confess I've never had occasion."

Leech took the scissors and tried opening and closing the blades a few times. "A bit stiff," he said. "Don't suppose you've any oil, have you?"

Garrett frowned. "Perhaps. It might take me a little time to lay hands on a bit."

"Oh, never mind." Leech puffed a sigh of impatience and flashed the blades again. He took a handful of hair at the back of Lucy's head and held it straight out.

Mrs. Fleming leaped between Leech and his victim, protesting to Garrett. "Stop it! This girl's to be wed in less than a month's time. We can't have a bride with no hair! It's indecent."

"Perhaps we can confirm the measurements by comparison with those I've already taken," Garrett suggested. "It would help us spot any inaccuracy."

Leech slung the scissors down on the table. "Oh, very well. I do not recommend it, but if you insist we will proceed as you suggest." He held his hand out to receive the next instrument. "The calipers, please. Are we agreed upon the use of Gall's list of twenty-seven brain organs?"

"Yes, I believe Gall's scheme is the one most commonly accepted."

"Very well."

Lucy, who had sat rigid up till then, flinched at the bite of the calipers.

"Hold still!" Leech barked. He pronged her again, as if he would sink the points clear to the bone, and read out a number. He lifted the tool and sank it again an inch from where her eyebrows ended. The girl jerked her head away. Leech straightened his back and threw up his hands. "If you cannot make her keep still this is a waste of my time!"

Garrett frowned at Lucy. "You must sit quietly," he said. "As you know, Dr. Leech has put himself to some trouble to consult with me. The least you can do is cooperate." He nodded to Leech, who then bent forward to bring the prongs into position. But as he was about to touch her, Lucy pulled back again. "Oh, really!" the specialist exclaimed. "You might remind her that if she moves like that when I'm taking facial readings she might put out her eye!" He pursed his lips. "Perhaps we should put a collar on her."

"A collar?" Garrett asked.

"An immobilizing device. I'm sure you must have one."

"I've not seen one used since I left the plantation," Garrett said, "and then it was applied as a punishment."

"Very well," Leech replied. He bent toward her with his instrument once more, muttering, "Now you damn well better not —"

Before he could finish, Lucy was on her feet. She jostled him on her way out of the chair, causing him to jab himself in the hand with the caliper and cry out in pain. "Damnation!"

"I *beg* your pardon!" Mrs. Fleming cried in outrage.

"Lucy!" Doc yelled after the patient fleeing into the hallway.

"I never!" Leech fumed. "Well, don't just stand there gawking, get some bandages!"

"Will you see to her," Garrett said urgently to Mrs. Fleming, who gave a curt nod and scurried away.

Garrett fumbled as he wrapped a length of linen around the spot where the caliper had grazed Leech's hand. "I sincerely apologize for Mrs. Talbott's behavior," he stammered.

"Outrageous!" Leech fumed.

"We might proceed with the diagnosis based on my measurements."

"I couldn't possibly base a diagnosis on another practitioner's measurements," Leech said. "There are very few who understand how to apply the calipers correctly, with sufficient tension. I should start back to San Francisco at once."

"That would be a great pity," Garrett said, "particularly since I had planned an evening's entertainment at the house of a particular friend who is adept at providing female companionship for my out of town colleagues."

"Yes. I have had occasion to hear something of Sally Locke. I had a distinct feeling of anticipation..." Leech hesitated.

"And you will not be disappointed," Doc assured him. "Surely we can spend a few minutes in discussion of Mrs. Talbott's case, if only on a theoretical basis." He tied the bandage and then gestured toward the chair by the window. "Why don't you sit comfortably. Peruse my notes." He handed Leech a sheaf of papers.

At the end of a few minutes, the visiting professional looked up from Garrett's list of figures. "These measurements clearly indicate two areas of considerable concern. I am referring to area two and area seven."

"Yes," Doc replied.

"Perhaps I should congratulate you on area two, as you're betrothed to the girl. Amativeness bodes well for a happy marriage. But when combined with a prominence in area seven, the diagnostic picture becomes less sunny. I believe that the contours of the patient's skull leave no doubt that she indulges in female onanism. This pernicious habit has resulted in unhealthy excitement causing hysterical symptoms, including a malady of the vocal cords resulting in muteness."

Leech paused to let his colleague absorb the information. "I know this may come as a shock to one's personal sensitivity, but as a physician you must see the logic here. I trust you've read Dr. Edward Clarke on the subject. If not, I can recommend several fine essays, one I have in mind as recent as 1873."

"I know Clarke's work," Garrett replied.

"We will want to do the procedures in my offices in the city. I insist on having my own staff around me when I operate, and I will want to control all aspects of the patient's recovery. You may of course assist, if it would not be too upsetting, considering your tender feelings for the girl."

"What procedures do you specifically ..."

"You're aware of Dr. Isaac Brown Baker's surgeries in Britain over the past dozen years or so. He's shown his treatment to be quite effective against epilepsy and other nervous conditions."

"Yes," Doc said. "I am aware of that treatment. It seems rather extreme."

Lucy Lied

"Take heart, my good man," Leech said with an avuncular lightness. "She will be your vessel all the same. Make no mistake." He made reference to specific parts of the female anatomy, concluding that, "the loss of this tiny bit of flesh is but a trifle that need not impact married relations."

Leech put down Garrett's clinical records and got to his feet. "Perhaps we might find a spot of dinner somewhere in town and then repair to the pleasures of that particular house you alluded to earlier."

"Indeed," Doc said with a hospitable smile. The two physicians struck out presently, speaking of various new techniques and therapies. Doc was only half engaged in the conversation with Leech, truth be told. He was preoccupied with thoughts of how he might go about explaining to Lucy the surgeries he and Leech had agreed upon. He would put it to her with the promise of a reward in advance, as if she were a child who needed to be cajoled to eat greens.

I've got you a nice little filly down at Steadman's. She's not entirely yours yet, but you can get to know her and let me know if she meets with your approval. If you get along and if you can govern her properly I'll finalize the sale. I chose her because she's the same shade of red as your hair. Her name is Zorra. It's the Spanish name for a female fox. Someday soon you'll be able to call her to come to you. Won't that be fine?

Chapter Twenty-three

The next day, after he had seen Dr. Leech off on the stage to Salinas, he found Adrian Fiske and they headed to the beach.

"I hear you took my advice about getting a horse for Lucy. Bronson said he saw it down at Steadman's. Said it's a damned fine filly," Adrian said, as they set off. "Where'd you come by such a pricy piece of horseflesh?"

"Old Felipe Vásquez promised me a horse for tending to him all those months."

"And his widow was happy to pay up? Or did you have to make love to her again to get her to look on the proposition favorably?"

"I'll thank you not to refer to adventures from my bachelor days," Doc replied.

"Not as if there was much in the way of adventure, as you put it. I expect my conversation won't suffer from the omission."

Doc remained silent as they walked, thinking his own thoughts while the painter prattled. He was thinking of Lucy, remembering the first time he'd ever laid hands on her that day Flynn Talbott had appeared at his door shouting about his wife. He'd assumed it was a maternity case. "You'll be needing Mrs. Fleming," he called out, careful not to show his face. His experience was that to make eye contact was to inherit responsibility. "She's seeing to Millie Ross down at the Methodist camp."

"It ain't labor," Talbott yelled back. "Girl got herself round the wrong side of the horse here." He pointed to the animal's rump. "Kicked what little sense she had right out, sure as shit."

"I don't attend women," Doc replied.

"It's her arm, not her female parts," Talbott said. "Her arm's no different from a man's, just a mite smaller. She's no good without the use of it."

Garrett's father had taken the boy along sometimes when he treated female slaves. Staunched the blood from their backs after they'd been lashed, set broken bones, always stripped them to the waist, had them sit up straight, allowed not even a slouch of modesty to hide those goose-prickled, dark-skinned breasts. He had seen his father suck down a mother's milk and one time drink a tear before it crested a lower eyelid. Later on at supper his mother would say, "You'll be working on horses and cows next." His father always replied, "A cotton picker is a cotton picker."

The recollection of treating Lucy was of a piece with those older, deeper memories. How she'd stood at the threshold of the doctor's house, the fine red hair around her face drenched brown in sweat with her right shoulder concave where it should have been convex. Her face ashen with pain, she reeked of fear. She wasn't much more than a youngster, though she was large of frame. She made no noise, but her large brown eyes followed his smallest movement, wary, ready to flee.

What he did to address the injury took a second, no more. With one hand in the axilla, he grasped her wrist with the other and yanked hard, stretching the arm full out, and it was done.

She made an inarticulate noise. Or perhaps he was just remembering the way the darkies had yelled when they had their injuries tended.

She sat shaking in her thin clothes as his hands moved over her. "Feeling for broken ribs," he said. With urgent excitement he remembered running his hand down her throat, his fingers following her sternum through her thin cotton clothing, how the incidental contact of his sleeve against her breast had made the nipple bunch and stiffen.

"All sound," he said. "You're lucky. I would have expected more damage if you were kicked by that horse outside."

He felt he knew her, much as he used to feel he knew the field slaves at home just by the way they squatted, resting at the side of a building. "How old are you?"

She made no reply but looked straight into him with her bovine eyes.

He watched her as she bore the procedure, thinking she took it much the same as the rest of her life—the food-crusted crockery, the cups with greasy prints of lips and fingers, the mucking out, the milking, the farmer's foul breath, and the wretched couplings. Not to mention the beatings. She kept silent, but he felt he understood her, with her brown eyes closed against the pain, the dirt, the day.

"Can you get to your feet?"

She made no move to acknowledge his words.

"Have you come from Europe?" he asked. "No English yet?"

He moved to the surgery door and held it open as he would for a cat that wanted out, but was loath to let her go. She rose and passed into the hall. "I'll make up the fire," Doc said to her, ignoring Talbott. "Try to warm you some before you start off home." He took her into the shallow warmth of the parlor to a low chair. She sat and shook and said not a word. Her muteness intrigued him as he placed kindling on the grate. "I don't light a fire unless I'm expecting company," he explained. She shuddered. The grandfather clock at the foot of the staircase tocked with hollow decorum. He balled the front page of Bronson's paper and stuffed it under the kindling. He glanced at her as he rose to take the matches from the mantel. "Some people say you're one of them pushcart people. Mennonites, or some such." He struck the match and ignited the paper under the kindling. A blaze flared up and caught the sticks. He crouched there and fanned the flames with an old magazine kept on the woodpile for that reason. He eyed her analytically. "You don't look like a Mennonite. Can you say your name?"

Lucy Lied

She wouldn't look up from the rug until he'd turned to his fire again. From the stack next to the hearth he pulled out a split log. The wood was light and dry and went up like a heathen in hell. He stayed in his squat and fed the fire two more logs big enough to keep it burning for a while. Then he stood and clapped the crumbs of bark from his hands. "Stand here where you can feel the heat. I'm going upstairs to get you something to use for a sling. Mind a spark don't catch your skirt."

He went as far as the parlor door and turned to find her large eyes following him. He thought particularly of her eyes, so dark in her waxen face, beseeching in the way of a homeless cur.

Adrian Fiske watched the worried expression on his friend's grim face as they marched along the firm sand above the surf line. "You seem unwell," the artist observed. "Was the consultation less than successful?"

Doc's conversation was enlivened by a certain excitement brought on by his memories. He explained the procedures Leech had proposed then sighed and squinted across the sparkling ripples toward the horizon. "It's a source of much anxiety."

"I daresay. It all sounds most drastic."

"No, not really. My concern isn't for the procedure. It's about Leech. My guess is Leech aims to publish the results of the surgery himself, which is why he insists on performing it in his own offices. And I'm damned if I'm going to let that happen. That means I'll have to do it here with the assistance I can get locally."

"So your chief concern is for the journal article you propose to write?"

"Of course not," Doc back-pedaled. "My chief concern is to correct Lucy's problem. But I can't let this chance slip away. Surely you understand."

"Not really." Fiske frowned at the latest wave making a dash up the beach. "I can see the efficacy of the one procedure on the vocal cord, but this other you propose ... How can that be remotely connected to her muteness?"

"Pathological conditions in women nearly all have a basis in hysteria, a nervous excitement stemming from the reproductive functions that can be exacerbated by too much mental or physical activity, or by a tendency toward over-amativeness."

"Over-amativeness?"

"I am referring to area two of the skull. Area seven is secretiveness. Lucy has significant prominences in both areas. Together these traits suggest that Lucy's particular hysteria is caused by ..." He seemed to have trouble bringing out the word. "Masturbation, to speak frankly."

"Ah." Fiske plodded on. "Have you discussed any of this with Mrs. Fleming?"

"Mrs. Fleming! Why would I? This doesn't in any way involve matters of Mrs. Fleming's particular expertise. I assure you that when Lucy is brought to bed with our first child, I will call on Mrs. Fleming to effect the delivery, for there is no one like her for making a successful lying-in, but until then I am the sole practitioner on this case."

"Apart from this Leech, you mean."

"If I decide this course is correct I will not involve Dr. Leech any further," Garrett said.

Adrian stopped dead in his tracks. "Are you serious? You would perform this—what do you call it?"

"Clitoridectomy."

"—on your own fiancée?"

"No, never. That would be completely improper. It will have to wait until after we are wed."

Adrian walked with his eyes fixed on the toes of his boots, encouraged to delve into the subject by his friend's seeming detachment. "Does it not occur to you that this may have a chilling effect on your married relations?"

"It's the removal of a piece of flesh about the size of the end of your finger. I am assured that it would have no effect on the birth canal or urination. It is a largely extraneous bit of the anatomy, but once discovered by those given to this particular vice, can lead to that most damaging of personal habits. At any rate, it's hardly worthy of the concern you might have for an amputation."

"Except for the site from which the flesh is excised! I don't suppose you'd feel it was hardly worthy of concern if that amount of flesh were coming off the end of your prick."

Doc stopped in his tracks. "What choice have I got?"

They walked on again. Adrian ventured to speak his mind. "You could accept her as you find her. Seek another subject for your journalizing or give up your notion of writing articles altogether. It seems to have had nothing but a pernicious effect on your wits." He paused, wondering if he dared to say the rest. "Or you could give up the engagement. Content yourself with your life as it is."

Garrett seemed not to have heard. "I can't give up on it now. I have to make her speak or I'll forever suffer a qualm that I didn't try." He stopped again and turned to look Adrian in the eye. "You're my dearest friend on earth. You must understand."

Adrian threw his arms around Doc and held him close. "I do," he said. "I always will."

Chapter Twenty-four

She entered his room without knocking, unclosing the door and slipping inside so quietly he didn't even wake up. She was able to eye him at her leisure. He sprawled low down in a copper tub, knees jutting out, feet planted on the braided rug in the middle of the room, arms folded across his belly, slack pectorals with a skimpy growth of hair turning gray, head thrown back against the side of the tub, mouth agape and snoring. Accustomed to observing closely, she took in every detail of his appearance unabashed and unjudging. His cock, curled and maggot white, hardly worth consideration in its drowned state. She lifted her gaze above the waterline. It wasn't an easy face. The creases were deep, here and there running crosswise to the care lines, almost as if the skin had been torn and patched. His hair was about the color of road dust, shot through with gunmetal gray. Any sculptor would have been proud to have made his neck and shoulders with the balls of smooth muscle, which made her think of that first summer Ellis had split cordwood with his shirt off and talked to Old John about all the great things they'd be doing come spring. Clancy was bigger than Ellis, with wider hands, hands that tended to make a fist even in his sleep.

There was nothing she found surprising, except perhaps the utter surrender of his pose, the completeness of his oblivion. She had always suspected that a gunman would be vigilant, afraid to relax his guard lest one of the friends or relatives of the multitudes he'd slain should catch him unawares and exact revenge.

She was habituated to observing in this way, having, as a rule, little claim on the attention of others. Her hair often attracted attention, to be sure, but she'd cultivated a vacant stare and left her face unwiped so as to suggest mental defect. Together with her muteness, this made her invisible, or at least so repugnant that the sight of her made no impression, nothing more than a freak of nature that most people would want to put out of mind.

She heard a sound of water. Clancy was awake. He had moved, sending a tide of water rolling out of the tub. She saw him jerk up straight as if a bluebottle had stung his butt. The splashed water darkened a wide arc across the braided rug. His green eyes seized on her dress at about the level of her knees and then climbed upward, finally connecting with her stare, sending another jolt through his body. A second tidal wave of water crashed out onto the floor. "Mrs. Talbott, I believe," he said, after clearing his throat.

She curtsied, smooth as the way on to sin.

"You're a bold one," Clancy said. "Any woman who'd gawk at a naked man like that might well be called loose. You got something on your mind of an unchaste nature? Unless you do, you might toss me that pair of Levis off the chair there." He hauled himself to his feet, grabbed the towel folded on the bed and applied it to his limbs. That done, he held out his hand for his trousers.

She tossed him the blue jeans.

"Quit staring," he said, buttoning his pants, "or I'll think you're just plain brazen." He took up the towel again and began drying his armpits. "Anybody see you come in here?"

She shook her head.

He smiled, as if he had begun enjoying the novelty of the situation now that he was over the shock. "Business of a confidential nature," he went on, "otherwise you'd have waited for me in the public rooms below, or at Steadman's where I keep my horse. You spend a lot of time there with your filly. You probably saw my palomino and knew I was in town." He pulled on his shirt and buttoned one cuff then the other. "Your fiancé being of some standing in the community, I am surprised that you would risk the injury to your reputation that would attend your discovery in a strange man's hotel room. From that it seems clear you have something of importance on your mind. A matter that probably doesn't involve your intended— something you would not particularly want him to know about. Anybody ever tell you, you have exceptionally pretty eyes?"

She kept her eyes locked to his, gratified to note that it was he who first looked away. He apparently needed to see to tucking his shirt.

"If I may say so, you're a woman whose name has been linked with scandal before." He looked up at her again. "In any case, it's a question of considerable interest as to how you intend to state your business. I insist that you do state it, by the way."

She made it a point to look only at his eyes, to study them as if to commit their shape, size and color to memory. His were a particular shade of gray-green, a seawater shade with bright rays of emerald and gold. The lids sloped down at the outside corner, a wanton slouch. His lashes were tawny and all about his eyes the fine white lines crossed his tanned face at odd angles, showing where it creased when he squinted. It was by minutely studying his eyes that she put across the impression of being unafraid.

He grinned. "We seem to be at an impasse."

From the basket she carried over her arm she withdrew a square of paper from underneath a gingham napkin. It was a newspaper cutting. She handed it to him.

He held the piece of newspaper as far from his face as his arm would reach and still had to squint to make out the small type. He read out loud.

"When you visit San Francisco, visit Brother Elias Croft, the eminent Eastern clairvoyant and healer now stopping at 214 Kearney Street who makes the following propositions: Reads Past, Present and Future—Past to be correct or no fee; Service given in reference to lost friends, property, love, business—satisfaction or no fee. If in poor

health, will locate your disease, describe its symptoms and particular effects without asking a question! The health examination is made by the wonderful art of Magicology, without any visible examination of diseased organs and is given as a test of power—FREE to ALL! If your disease is curable he will guarantee to restore your health without a drop of any drugs, by a method of treatment essentially his own. Particular attention given to nervous diseases, consumption, female diseases, sore eyes, deafness, rheumatism, neuralgia, mental weakness, loss of memory and all diseases having their origin in the back, kidneys, & stomach. Fees moderate averaging from $1.50 to $3.50. Call for a Health Examination or a Reading of Character. Full health examination sent to people at a distance who enclose 35 three-cent stamps and a photograph or lock of hair. People at a distance wishing the Past and Future read must enclose correct Date of Birth with lock of hair and $5 in gold. Upon receipt a written Destiny will be sent by first mail."

He flung the cutting on the table. "What's this Croft got to do with anything?"

She dropped her eyes to the braided rug.

"None of that now," Clancy said. "Answer me. I know you can. I've been on to you for some time."

She looked up again, trying to keep the shock out of her eyes, wondering if she'd heard right. *How could he possibly know?*

"I know you have voice," he said. "So you can drop the act." He grinned and took a step in her direction. "What is it? You must want something awful bad to come to a man's hotel room and interrupt his bath."

"How?" she asked. Her voice sounded like someone else's, sharper than she remembered. She took a deep breath and tried to manage the sound of it. "How do you know?"

"That night the Chinese took you from your friend's house in San Francisco. They dosed you with laudanum to take the fight out of you. Under the drug you talked a good bit."

"The Chinese .... the men who took me from Molly's. How do you know about that?"

"I'm the one who paid them to find you. I have connections among the Tong. They know what goes on. You weren't hard to find."

"But why?"

"Why, what?"

"Why did you want to find me?

"Because a friend of mine was going to get strung up—strung up for a murder he didn't do. And I knew you could convince the jury of that. At least give the defense attorney enough doubt to work with. It was a near thing, though. That crowd had been promised a hanging and they weren't happy to be deprived. I thought sure they'd accept you as a substitute for Joe. But then Garrett put an oar in."

"You won't tell," she said.

"About your voice? Hell, if I was of a mind to give you away I'd have done it before now. Could have said something at the picnic on San Carlos Day when you came by to visit with my horse, but ..." He shook his head. "I've often wondered why you keep it up, especially when it causes you so much pain."

"Pain?"

"Good lord, at the trial Garrett had to wrench your shoulder from the socket to save you, when you might have just spoken your piece. Don't tell me it didn't hurt."

She didn't comment.

"You're tough," he said. "I don't think I could do it myself, keep my tongue through all that. Don't you hanker for the sound of your own voice?"

"Maybe. If I did I expect I could walk down by the lighthouse where the surf crashes against the rocks and give vent to it there where no one could hear. But mostly I'm content not to talk. It's what makes me a plain brown bird in the midst of orioles, not worth the notice, all but invisible."

"Except for that red hair."

"So why *haven't* you said anything?"

"What? Put it out that you can speak?"

She nodded.

He shrugged. "It's nothing to me if you play dumb." He sat down at the table by the window where there was a bottle and two glasses. "You want a drink?"

She stood rigid.

"Come on. You can trust me."

"I trusted a man once and look what it got me."

He poured two shots and pushed one across the table toward her. "It's just a drink."

She picked up her glass. "To the day," she said.

"The day," he repeated, before tipping the glass to his lips.

She drank it in one gulp that took her breath away for a second.

He picked up the clipping from the table and regarded it. "So tell me, was it Elias Croft you trusted?"

"Ellis Crane. Elias Croft. Elliott Canby. Called himself by other names, too. Always kept the same initials, though."

"You trusted a man who changed his name at each whistle stop?"

She nodded. "Till I learned my lesson."

"What'd he do to you?"

"He ... took something from me."

"He was good at that, taking from women. Robbed a widow I know. I beat him to a fare-thee-well and ran him out of town for it. But I didn't get back her cash. I reckon yours is gone, too." He handed the clipping back to her. "That how you wound up washing sailors' smallclothes on the docks?"

She accepted the clipping and crumpled it in her fist. "Yes."

"Well, ma'am," Clancy said, "if he weren't quite so far off I'd beat him a second time just for you."

"You know where he is?"

"Why? You thinking of putting in with him again?"

"No! I told you I'm finished with him."

"What, then?"

She reached into her basket and brought out the garnet earring. "What he took from me. The other half of the pair. It's a family heirloom. I need to get it back. You must have come across it the night you spilled his goods into the street and ran him out of town."

He took it from her and held it up to the light to examine the seed pearls and gold leaves garlanded around the gemstone pendant that gleamed like a dark passion in the late afternoon sun. "I did," he said. "It's a right coincidence you having the other. How would a penniless scrub woman come by something so fine?"

She saw his cool stare taking her apart, assessing the good clothes, the ring on her finger, the things a woman can put on to make herself seem a certain way. She held out her hand for him to give back the earring. "The one you found is mine. I need it back."

"It's at Ortin's on consignment," he said, "and I could reclaim it but I don't believe I will. I think I'll telegraph my friend's widow in San Francisco. See if a pair like this went missing after Brother Croft and his assistant visited. I never got a real good description of his assistant, except that it was a girl. I'm thinking maybe it was you." He grabbed her wrist and pulled her close. "Look at me! Were you with him? Did you help him steal from all those innocent women? You want me to go after him to get you your share of the take?" He studied her face, digging into her with his brutal green eyes, so cold and pure. Then he flung her away.

Something like a fist closed around her heart and made her breath come short. "Canby—Crane—he worked for my stepfather on the place back in Pennsylvania. He took me one night in the barn. It stormed that night. My stepfather was out in the field—I ... We were ruined. Had to go to live with my aunt. Ellis took us in the wagon. The earrings belong to her."

"So you robbed her after she took you in?"

"It was Ellis. He said if I didn't go along he'd tell her I was ... he'd tell her about that night in the barn."

"So you lit out for California?"

"Yes. He bought us fine clothes for the train. He told everyone I was his sister. There was trouble one day as we pulled into the station at Corrine, Utah."

"What kind of trouble?"

"I was sullen, angry with him about how he was treating me. I ... That morning he slapped my face and tore off one of my earrings. Then he told me to go to the station café to get him a biscuit with marmalade. It was very hot. I had to hurry. It was a short stop. My skirts were heavy, made it hard to walk. I was running back after I heard the whistle. I slipped and fell. Knocked myself out. The next thing I knew Molly was kneeling beside me, taking off my gloves."

"So the train pulled out and you got left behind."

She nodded. "Molly's family was on an immigrant train. I came on the rest of the way with them. They let me stay with them in San Francisco. Molly and I scrubbed sailors' skivvies down on the docks. It wasn't so bad. Better than being with Ellis anyway."

"And you never said a word about him to anybody?"

"Not since that night in the barn. I couldn't speak of it."

"You couldn't speak of it, so you stopped speaking altogether?"

She nodded.

"It's a damn sad tale, but nothing to do with me. Go on and marry Garrett. He won't make you any more miserable than you've been up to now. And I see he's already got you some more fine clothes." He turned and gazed out the window.

"I can't marry him."

"Why the hell not?"

"He intends to operate on me to give me voice." She paused. "It's too horrible to speak of. I have to leave right away. I need that other earring. You have to give it back to me so I can sell the pair and buy a ticket."

"And if I don't?"

She reached into her market basket one more time and drew upon the argument of last resort. She pulled back the hammer.

That pinpoint of sound brought him round to face her again. He looked at her and smiled coldly. "Now, ma'am, I think you'd best go before it gets any later. I don't want to be accused of taking liberties with another fellow's woman, even if the other fellow is Doc Garrett."

She met his hard green gaze. "Give me back that earring and get me the other one you took from Ellis."

"Or what? You'll shoot me where I stand? Anybody ever tell you it's low carrying a concealed weapon and then getting the drop on the other fellow?"

"Give it here."

"Oh, stop trying to be a bully. It's ridiculous." He tossed the earring so it landed neatly in her market basket.

"Promise to get me the mate," she demanded, "or—"

"—or what?" He stepped toward her deliberately, to within a hand's breadth as they stood face to face. "If you've a mind to shoot you'd better do it now. Say, you know, you flush a right pretty shade when you're armed."

"Take care."

"Why? Is there danger about?"

"You'd best believe it."

He laughed. "Sister, there's a difference between drawing a bead and pulling the trigger. If you can't do both you should never do either." He backed her up to the wall, took hold of her wrists and splayed her arms wide. "You had your chance."

The heat of his closeness, the insistence in his eyes made her heartbeat quicken, her head feel light. "Let me go," she whispered.

"No, I can't do that. You told me yourself you're dangerous."

"I won't shoot you."

"I know."

"Then why?"

"Because I mean to kiss you."

"You can't."

"Oh, but I can."

"You mustn't."

"I insist."

"And if I say no?"

"Come on, now. Not likely Garrett will miss what he's never had."

"How do you know that?"

"I know. And I find it puzzling why you'd agree to marry such a cold fish."

Her eyes shifted under his scrutiny.

"Oh. I see. It was convenient at the time. You've only recently made up your mind not to go through with it."

"I won't marry him. Not on this earth."

There was a hardscrabble edge to her voice he hadn't heard before. "I don't understand. He'll give you an easy life. And if I don't mistake he'll keep his whore, so the demands on you will be few. Why would you run from that? This operation you spoke of .... Is it really that bad?"

"I don't intend to belong to a man ever again."

"Third time's the charm. Where's your spirit of adventure?"

"Not all the slaves were freed in '63."

"Who'd have thought such a pretty one as you would have a head for dates!"

She squirmed and scowled at him. "Let me go!"

"I've never forced a woman in all my long days." He eased his grip on her arms but he didn't step back. He just waited for her resolve to melt.

The gun weighed like an anchor in her hand as he touched his lips to hers. As it began to slip, she squeezed her fingers around the grip and the trigger. The explosion sent Clancy reeling back though the bullet never touched him. Instead it tore through the copper bathtub and started a stream of water pouring onto the floor. Clancy twisted the weapon out of her hand. "What the hell'd you do that for?"

"I—"

He grabbed the gun and stuck it under the bed pillow, then thrust her market basket into her arms. "Come on. We need to get you out of here right now."

He dragged her out of the room and flung her toward the back stairs as the desk clerk came pounding up from the lobby. In a second Clancy was back in the room. He ran to the window and threw open the sash. He was standing there with his head stuck outside when the clerk burst into the room. "Señor! Are you all right?"

Clancy pulled his head in. "Somebody climbed up to the window and took a shot at me. You'd best go get the sheriff."

Outside in the alley, Lucy stepped aside as the Mexican came bolting past her on his way to fetch the law. She felt strangely calm now that she had faced him and lived to walk away from it. But she'd left the gun. What if Doc should go to the trunk in his spare room and find it gone? She supposed he might think they'd picked it up by mistake as they'd gathered up the patchwork squares. But if that had been so, Mrs. Fleming would have returned it by now.

An early rising winter moon was already up, its cold face peeking through the wind-tossed pines. She clutched her shawl tighter around her and fastened her eyes on the path immediately ahead, now and then looking up to glimpse the flat, waxen face. It seemed amused at the plight of such a girl who used to dream of living in town in a nice house with initialed stationery and ladies coming to call for Destinies, asking for the Reverend Mr. Crane. She burned with shame, all the old memories tumbling together: the stolen kisses, the rutting, the earrings, the pretty boots, the Pullman car and Flynn Talbott lying in a puddle of thick blood. She wiped her eyes on her sleeve and plodded on.

At Point Alones she stopped to watch the Chinese fishermen oar their slipper boats out into the bay. She knew Mrs. Fleming would be worried but she was far too excited to return to the house in the Methodist settlement just yet. She kept walking down the beach, beckoned by the beam of the lighthouse.

Alan Luce was singing one of his heart-wrenching tunes.

She thought of the new mare, the copper horse named Zorra, and wondered how much money such a fine mount would bring, how far the money might take her. But Doc might put the law on her for horse-stealing. Not might. Would. Her only hope was Clancy, the earring. "He'll get it for me. I know he will." Though her words were quickly swept away by the wind, it was good to hear her own voice again, outside her body.

She thought of Clancy, how he'd kept her secret, how his touch had made her pulse pound. "I trust him." *But when will I see him? How will I get word?*

She looked up at the moon and wondered what Clancy was thinking, if he was wondering what manner of girl she was, if he cared. She could hear his voice again. *I mean to kiss you.* She remembered the thrill of it on her lips, how she'd felt as if her body had boiled off into the air. *A wondrous kiss, the kind that might lead to disaster.* "Maybe so. I don't care."

Chapter Twenty-five

The writing closely covering the front and back of the page was extravagantly elegant, done by a person with leisure to polish her hand. *"Dear Sir, my Son,"* it began.

Your father and I are well pleased with your progress in the medical profession thus far. In fact, we believe that you are in all respects as qualified as ever your father was when he started his practice here in Macon. I am sure you are sensible of the urgent hour that calls for all of us to act as true and loyal Southerners. I am sure you realize that duty and honor require your presence here where your home is. I cannot urge you strongly enough to come and take up your place with your brother in the militia of our beloved state of Georgia. If you come now as soon as this letter reaches you, I have no doubt your father can obtain a commission for you. But equivocation will cost you dearly, as it costs us in reputation. Ours is an old and venerated family, one to which others look for civic spirit. In this time of turmoil they look to us to lead them in right thinking and demonstrate right action through selflessness and valor. I ask you with that iron hoop that binds the heart of a mother to the heart of her son to come home to us now and save us from a shame too infamous to bear. If this letter does not produce your immediate return to Macon, my only recourse is to know you no more. For only by disowning you, can we save the rest of our family from disgrace. From this day forward your absence will taunt me with reminders of your base cowardice if I keep the memory of you in my heart. Because I cannot endure such a galling cancer in my bosom, I will think of you no more, draw a shade down across all our history together as if you had never been, and never again speak your name. Even to write this, wrings bitter tears from my eyes ...

Over fifteen years old, the sting of her words had not dulled with the passage of time nor had its tone of urgent pleading diminished by being so long ignored. The wound, as fresh as the day it was cut, smarted anew. And time, if it were measured by the words of that letter, would have pressed forward barely as many minutes as it took to read. *How sad that we keep our slights like buried treasure, valued over any measure of praise, and ironic that we know ourselves by our sins, even when we have no religion.* He stuffed the page back into its envelope edged in black, chucked it into the trunk, and threw down the lid. Then he stood for a while, considering whether he should go to see Lucy in spite of the late hour. She had seemed so remote the day before. He wasn't sure she had understood the treatment he had proposed. A loud knocking at the front door brought his musings to an end. Doc yelled down, "Come on in."

Adrian Fiske's scuffing step sounded on the stairs. "I'm off to the Bohemian," he called, halfway up. "You'd best put all that rubbish back in your trunk and come along."

Not one to refuse a trip to the tavern, Doc complied.

Simoneau looked up at the opening of his door, and reached for the bourbon when he saw Doc. "*Bonsoir, mon ami. Et monsieur?*" He waited with the bottle poised over a second glass until Fiske replied, "The same."

Crevole Bronson put down his beer and inquired after Ernesto Badillo. "Is he still gouty?"

"I expect so, although I haven't seen Señor Badillo since San Carlos Day." Doc tossed down his drink. "More's the pity. He's the only *ranchero* I know who isn't mortgaged up to the eyes to David Jacks."

"I beg your pardon?"

"A paying customer," Doc replied.

"I heard somebody took a shot at him," Fiske said. "Jacks, I mean."

The newspaperman grinned. "Hey, Doc. I'd like to see you try to bleed Jacks sometime. I don't think the leeches would suck on one of their own."

Doc ignored the comment. He made no attempt to hide his dislike of Bronson. Adrian Fiske responded out of courtesy. "I don't know how Jacks stays in business. There's no one left to put the squeeze on. He can't even loan to the city." He turned to Doc. "Did you realize when you moved here that the town had gone broke?" Fiske raised his glass. "I give you Monterey. No longer capital of California, nor county seat, nor even incorporated city. To her insolvency. I congratulate us all for gravitating to such a disreputable locale."

"No disgrace in being out of pocket as long as you have pride of place," Doc observed.

"In my case that would be a place at the bar," the painter added. He tapped two fingers on the rim of his glass to get Simoneau to pour two more shots.

"Then poverty must be no virtue," Bronson said, "as it commits the sin of pride."

By the time he'd downed his second drink it suited Doc to argue. "But if there's no virtue in poverty and the rich man would as soon get into Heaven as a camel through the eye of a needle, then who is left to populate Paradise in the Hereafter?"

"All of us who repent our sins on our deathbed," Simoneau said, the good Catholic.

Bronson snorted. "I should live so long!"

225

Lucy Lied

"Ah, that's why we employ Doc, here, to keep us in breath long enough to say our Hail Mary's," the painter said.

"Mr. Fiske," Bronson answered, "for you to say sufficient Hail Mary's will take a long while. Maybe you should start dying now, so by the time you have your three score years and ten, Doc here will have saved you long enough for you to complete your prayers."

"I'm wounded you think me such an evil man," Fiske replied. "In fact, I think you do me an injustice."

"Oh?"

"Name me one sin I've sinned today, if you can."

"You went out to paint that tree of yours today, didn't you?" Doc asked.

The painter shrugged. "Of course. What of it?"

"There's the sin of idleness, then," Doc said. "For isn't it idle to paint the same picture every day? No one will buy it because you can go to the point and see the tree itself for free. Now, you could get somebody to go out and chop it down, but then you'd have to pay a few bits for the labor."

Bronson put in his two cents. "But isn't it true that every man and beast and object has a function under heaven?"

"I reckon," Doc agreed.

"And doesn't each creature's excellence lie in the fact that it fulfills its function better than that function can be done by any other? For example, excellence in a horse lies in its being able to carry a rider better than a chicken or a cat."

"I would agree to that standard," the painter said.

"And that as far as the horse exhibits this excellence, it is good and just."

"Just a good horse," Doc observed.

Bronson pointed at the defendant for emphasis. "Then Fiske here cannot be idle."

"I say he is an idler."

"But idleness is sinful, is it not?"

"Oh, yes."

"And the sinful are unjust?"

"Lamentably."

"But Mr. Fiske, in painting his tree every day, does that function better than any other man. So that practice makes him good and just, doesn't it? Surely you can't tell me that Mr. Fiske is both just and unjust at the same time!" Bronson crossed his arms over his chest, content that his point was unassailable.

Garrett pinioned the editor with a look that might have etched stone. "Surely you don't mean to tell me you've ever known a man who was anything but. We are all as bad as we are good, sir. Only the dead are saints, because their sins die with them while their goodness lives in the hearts of those who mourn. On that somber note, I wish you all a good evening."

"Now don't go away mad," Bronson cajoled. "You hardly got a good start here. Give him another, Frenchie. I need to enlist these gentlemen in my latest civic cause."

"Enlist? That has an unattractive ring to it," Doc said.

The editor seized this moment to lay out his big idea to the boys. "I have it from reliable, confidential sources that the Southern Pacific wants to run a spur down from Salinas. Not just for freight, either. There's good money to be made hauling city folks to visit the peninsula for pleasure trips."

Someone sniffed. "Jacks would have to be in on it. And Huntington, Stanford, Crocker and Hopkins."

"I've heard talk of a grand hotel," Simoneau added.

"The Methodists may lose their Pacific Grove Retreat," Bronson continued. "They rent the land from Jacks, you know, and he might take it into his head to develop it in other ways—if the time was right to speculate. Now, the mission could be the centerpiece of tourism at this end of the coast. And the Chinese fishing village. People will line up to pay for the pleasure of seeing the heathens casting their fortunes at the joss house. There's money in it, I tell you. Think of all those city gents and their ladies flocking in by train. Only one thing, though. The mission is inhabited by rummies and varlets, degenerates of the worst sort. It's in need of a thorough housecleaning, if you know what I mean."

227

"You should be talking to Taylor," Adrian Fiske observed.

"The sheriff says there are jurisdictional issues," Bronson said, without bothering to explain. "Still, if enough able-bodied men were willing to go along, I'm sure he would lead the charge."

"I'm for it," a former harpooner yelled. "Any excuse for busting heads."

"You need to go back to sea," the man next to him said.

The harpooner was about to rise to what he heard as a challenge when the telegraph office messenger burst in, gasping for air. "Doc Garrett here?"

"I am," Doc replied, straightening up from his elbow lean on the bar so the man could see his face.

"It's for you," the messenger said. He handed over a twice-folded telegram transcription and watched while Garrett opened it and absorbed the news. "Any reply?"

Everyone in the bar strained to hear.

"Not now," Garrett said bleakly. A change like a killing frost had come over him, lending a bleaker cast to his already joyless expression. He thrust the telegram into his breast pocket and downed the drink he'd left standing on the bar. He left without providing any inkling of what was up. Adrian Fiske had to run after him to find out.

"My father," Garrett said when the painter caught up with him. "Dying. I'm for Macon first thing."

Chapter Twenty-six

Early the morning after the telegram had arrived, Adrian stood in the front hallway of The Rookery. "We'd best get down to the wharf," he called up to the second floor. "Sometimes when the tide's about to turn the packet pulls out a bit early."

"I'm ready," Doc called down from his bedroom. He extinguished his candle with a weary sigh and descended the stairs. In front of the hall mirror he stood and settled his hat on his head before taking up his satchel. "I should have visited Lucy this morning, I think."

"Too late now, old man," Adrian replied, holding open the door. "We must hurry."

The two started down the gravel path to the front gate. "I confess to feeling a mite unsettled where she's concerned," Doc said. "She's never given me any real sign of affection. I'm used to women behaving quite the opposite way, apart from the likes of Mrs. Fleming. The ones who aren't too old or too concerned with their immortal souls are normally fawning and brimming with vapid conversation mainly engineered to elicit praise of their hats or their hair ribbons, as if their female finery were meant to please anyone apart from their silly selves. Lucy, on the other hand ... well, it goes without saying that she doesn't prattle."

"So I've noticed," Adrian replied.

"Oh, damnation. What I mean is she's got a sober way about her. She's not one to go all pale and whimpering at the sight of a man, or indulge herself in daydreams about spooning under the harvest moon, or sigh and swoon and lose her appetite because she's got a bad case of storybook love. I tell you I hate all that."

"This is quite a change since you told me you were determined to use surgery to make her speak. Can it be you've reconsidered performing that horrible operation? Have you finally come to your senses?"

"Confound you, Fiske." The gravel seemed to crunch more aggressively than before as he strode on. "I'll need you to watch over her while I'm gone. Read her my letters. I'll address them to you. Observe her from afar from time to time, especially if she goes out on her own."

They had reached the end of the wharf where the packet's sooty breath tainted the pure pale dawn. An orange sun heaved itself over the eastern hills and a whistle sounded with steamy insistence. Doc embraced Adrian. "Keep to painting your tree and all will be well," he said. Then he climbed up the gangway and found a spot on deck where he could watch the milling water near the side wheel and feel Monterey slipping away after the jarring engagement of gears.

The crew went about their work with brisk indifference, coiling the mooring lines into tight spirals on the deck and disappearing either by way of a ladder up or a ladder down. The wind picked up as the vessel gained steerageway and churned out into the northern reach of the bay. Doc took a wide stance and stood with his elbows fixed on the rail, staring across the water as the color of day blued the sky. The rolling of the deck beneath his feet gave him the sense of doing something as he stood, meeting each swell with his own counter-motion. It pleased him, this being at sea, in a simple unthinking way, as few things did. The motion of the swell seemed to answer its own questions. Amid the water noise, the machinery growl of the steam pistons and the crisp flap of the ensign in the wind washing across the bow, the voice of a nagging spirit harrying his soul like a hawk swooping the fields for mice had been momentarily drowned out.

Aft of the boil of foam at the wheel, the iridescent sheen of oil patterning the water gliding down the side of the vessel reminded him of the marbled endpapers of an extravagantly bound edition of Gray's *Anatomy* his mother had given him on the eve of his departure for medical school. As unwieldy a tome as ever a dilatory scholar hesitated to open, it eventually was sold to buy a trio of more practical volumes, seeing as Gray's was available in the library. The immaculate condition of the book, the gilt-edged pages still stuck together in places, brought more cash than he'd dared expect. He chuckled and corrected his first recollection. The sum had gone to ether and not to other books, every penny. "Trading heavy for light," he muttered, "or at least trying to."

It was a small sin compared to the one that got him chucked out of the family. He'd always believed in that one moment when life went wrong, the fork in the road, steps that couldn't be retraced and corrected. And yet it seemed he was doing that very thing, going back East for the first time after so many legs to the West. He nourished a germ of hope that maybe she would forgive him, soon to be the only man of the family left. He promised God, the God of his most craven and hypocritical self, that if he were forgiven he would never deny Him again. He closed his eyes to strengthen the conviction of his vow and repeated to himself the promise. *I'll be your prodigal returned if just this once she don't look at me like she wished it was Cal standing before her.*

Once on his train journey he started his letters home to Lucy. At a water station halfway across the country he scribbled:

> *Dear girl,*
>
> *I write this while waiting at a stop not far from Chicago. You must think it hard of me that I didn't come to see you once more before leaving. I do so hate goodbyes. It pains me that you may take it that I was too busy to think of you as I was preparing to leave. This is certainly not so. I think of you with each tick of time. As I write this I realize how ridiculous my errand must seem in light of what I have written above, as this whole journey is undertaken to say goodbye to a dying father. Please*

accept such incongruities as you find them, in the character of your most imperfect but loyal
  J Garrett.

His old connections, established when he was employed by the insurance company to investigate railroad accidents, stood him in good stead and he made it back to the rebuilt hub at Atlanta in less than a week. He rode straight on to Macon and arrived at the family home at twilight, thinking, as he stopped the horse, how fitting was the hour. Scarcely had he untied his satchel from behind the saddle when the two women of the house came out on the porch to greet him.

At first sight his mother looked well, nearly the same as the last time he'd seen her, except that her coffee-brown hair had gone silver-gray. Her posture was still defiant of age and gravity, but the stern look in her eyes had given way to an absence of expression. She clutched a bedraggled sheaf of flowers in her hand as proudly as if it were a cotillion nosegay. Violet hovered at her elbow, whispering in her ear, "Say hello, now, Maudie. It's your son, Mr. Jason."

"Where have you been?" his mother demanded. "Everyone is waiting inside. You must change your clothes. Hurry! Violet! Where is my veil?" She groped at the top of her head. "What have you done with it?"

Violet was the only house slave who had stayed on. He'd recognized her right off ,though the last several years had worried most of the flesh off her. Her frame that he remembered as so robust had shrunken, her bosom just a sad remnant of the taut-skinned, vanilla-smelling breasts he'd mouthed and fondled at every opportunity back in the days before he'd left for medical school. Her face had lost its luster, though her eyes were still quick to see the slightest shadow of every mood that crossed his face. He realized she'd never aged in his dreams. When he tossed in the tangle of his sheets, he never imagined her but in the full blossom of her twenty-fifth year. He tried to put it in concrete terms. *She must be over forty now. Not that she isn't still fine.*

Violet held on tight to his mother's arm. Maude began to struggle and cry. "Let go. Where have you hidden it?"

Doc stood drop-jawed as Violet, with an apologetic expression, let her wriggling charge go. Maude ran back into the house. "I'm sorry, Mr. Jason," Violet said mildly. "Her mind is fixed on this being her wedding day. Every day the same."

"How long?" he asked.

"Oh, my," she said, "some time back. 'Bout the time she heard her family's land was all sold for the taxes. It's just a blessing your father was with us long as he was or this place would have gone, too. He still made a living doctoring folks right up until his heart give out."

It was then Doc realized he was too late. "He's gone?"

"Yes, sir. Left us two days ago. Right soon after your telegram came saying you was on the way home. It gave him some relief, I think, knowing your mother wouldn't be at his funeral all alone. I think he left us once he was quiet in his mind."

Doc thought of that expression. Left us. As if the dead were all congregated somewhere, a destination the living were unable to reach, a party they weren't invited to. He thought of a notion he'd had as a small lad in Sunday school, of the sky as a vast sheet of blue paper that he one day punched a finger through. He had torn a piece away and there were the faces of his grandparents and a host of long-dead relatives smiling down at him, beside the face of Jesus as he appeared haloed and rosy-cheeked in the colored plates of the New Testament. Now, from the sour perspective of adulthood, he felt that behind the blue paper was just another blank page.

Maude came tottering out of the house with a white dinner napkin pinned to the top of her head and the withered flower stems still clutched in her hand. "I found it," she sang out gaily. "I found my veil."

Violet showed him to his old room. There was still a narrow boy's bed, but in every other respect it had been transformed into a sewing room. "Two hours till supper," she said. "Not much more than collards with a little fatback. We didn't know you'd be here tonight. I'll call you."

Lucy Lied

He lay down on his old bed as he heard the door close. Being there affected him with a kind of lassitude, a slowing of the blood, to the point that he wondered if he cut himself whether it would drip out of the wound at all or just ooze a bit. A physical sensation, almost anything would be a relief, something like the report of a gun to wake things up. He found some paper, a pen, and ink in the desk where he used to work on his Latin translations. He shoved aside some dress patterns that cluttered the top. He sat down in the chair that seemed still to inspire squirms and fidgets and began a letter.

Dear Lucy,

His pen stopped as he envisioned the whiteness of her throat, imagined stroking its length, caressing the hollow above her sternum. He imagined planting kisses on the baby flax at her temples, his lips moving inevitably lower on her body, reaching the nipples. And then .... A crowd of goblins gnawed at the edge of the dream, consuming delight and spitting up doubts. Was she anticipating the consummation as he was? He picked up his pen with a renewed sense of discontent.

Coming home after many years is difficult.

He opened wide the window of his old room and listened to a bullfrog, somewhere in the reedy marsh at the bottom of the yard, and wondered if his steady calling would ever be answered. The twilight was soft; the moon was full. A wrought-iron bench sat empty near a centuries-old pine just as it had when he was a child. In spite of the war nothing in Macon seemed to have changed, except that people had left, having sold out to new rich or Yankees. But the white clapboard houses, the rose-garlanded, falling-down pickets, the cloth-wrapped heads of the Negro women who refused to leave their mistresses, and the occasional gator appearing in somebody's backyard—all that was the same. All outside of town the fields had been fired, but had by now come back under the plow. To see any real destruction you had but to go to Atlanta, but in Macon you'd be hard pressed to see the heel print of war at all. This he translated into a rationalization that the whole conflagration—all the killing and strife and one-legged men—had been meaningless from the start. They'd been wrong to shun him, wrong to judge him. He assured himself that he'd been right all along, but in his heart he still didn't feel it. In his heart he still ached with the forlorn despair of a small boy who'd been spanked and sent to bed without dinner. He picked up his pen.

It is still unseasonably warm here. In days past in such weather Mother would sit outside with her tatting in the evenings as if it were springtime. Father died some time before I arrived. It is good he did not linger. Tomorrow I'll see to settling his debts. More worrisome is the matter of Mother. I must be sure of her resources before I can start back to California.

The lawyer who had been his father's friend for years would in all likelihood pass away before his mother, but there was no one else to entrust with her will, hardly enough to warrant the expense of ink and paper, but still .... All the years he'd lived at home they'd prospered in cotton. But in the end it had come down to what his father could make doctoring, another reminder that it had been for nothing, all the fighting to preserve property, wealth. Foolish. You really don't own a plot until you're in it, and then who cares? The ink had dried on the nib of his pen. He dipped again into the inkwell.

Of course the prospect of returning makes me miss my Lucy all the more.

She alone gave him hope, gave him reason to think he could affect the outcome of some small business under the sun, some small part of the eternally uncaring universe. He wanted with all his soul to save her, reach into her silence and pull her out of it. It was his one ambition, the thing that he felt would give his life meaning, to hear her speak his name, to write the article about her recovery that would pluck that name from oblivion.

I hope you have been well and that you know you are constantly in my thoughts.

Gazing on the lawn bathed in moonlight, listening to the bullfrog calling for its mate, he wondered how she had entrenched herself in his soul. What was it about her that couldn't be found in another woman—in Sally, for example? Ah, but Sally was so self-sufficient, so cynical. There was no comparison. Sally needed nothing from anyone, beyond the payment of her hourly charge. On occasion her company left him feeling lonelier than ever. So what was it? The large long-lashed equine eyes, seeming to reflect only his own face when he looked into them? The slender stem of her neck, dusted with faint traces of red curls at the hairline, so delicate, so childlike? Her haunting clavicle, lost to sight below a maddening swatch of calico. Her scent was of a disembodied warmth like the whiff of a ripe grain field. If he closed his eyes, Doc could dispel the moonlight in his imagination and come up with that smell, red if it could have a color, the same red as her hair.

You and the ladies have probably finished the quilt by now and I confess I have often longed to see it spread on our wedding bed.

It was the closest sentiment to the longing in his gut that he could write without plunging into vulgarity of the worst sort: her milk white thighs and other imagined glories that sounded like a barker for a whorehouse. He thought of Adrian reading such tripe out loud and had to laugh, picturing Mrs. Fleming swooning away with a thud on the plank floor.

There's things I would say to you, but as they are for your ears only I will refrain. Just know that my silence doesn't mean I have no thought of words to further my wooing.

He considered the page, nearly full, and wondered if he might best end it there with a large closing flourish. Perhaps in saying nothing at all he'd said too much already.

This must stand me in poor stead until I can press you to my heart. Your faithful
J. Garrett

He folded the page and stuffed it into an envelope. Then he rose from the desk and went to fetch a bottle from his satchel. The liquor burned its way up the back of his neck, turning off sensations. The tightness at the base of his skull, the throbbing in his temples, sank beneath an amber wave. But if bourbon blunted physical discomforts, it also sharpened the dumb show of memory. He wondered if this was yet another night when sleep would never come.

Violet called to him from downstairs. "Supper time, Mr. Jason," she sang, with that sweet dark voice.

"Come on up here a minute, would you, Vi?" He poured another drink and waited till she knocked softly on the door. "It's open."

She pushed at the door and peered in at him.

"Come on in here and close it after you," he said. He wondered if she remembered those were the exact words he'd always used. "I was just thinking about the old days. When you first came up to the house to tend to me. Mother was sick with her monthly courses. I had no idea what that meant."

"You were just a little child."

"Who made your life a misery."

"You were fussy because you missed your old mammy. You didn't want nothing to do with me."

237

"Remember the day you took me out to see the snow? Remember how sparkly it was in the Spanish moss?"

"I remember you sat yourself down and commenced to wail. And I said, "Go on and cry. I'm not about to carry you. You either get up and walk beside me right or there you'll sit and there you'll be till your bottom freeze solid to the ground." She laughed. "After that you behaved better."

"But Mother was angry when she found out you took me down to the quarters. She made me watch while you got your ankles switched."

"And after that if I caught you stealing a fist of gingerbread you'd say to me, Don't tell Mother or I'll say you took me down to the quarters again. That was bad of you, Mr. Jason."

"You gonna make me some gingerbread now I'm home, Vi?"

"If we can come by some molasses I will."

"And the other? We don't need no molasses for that. Why don't you come on in here and get into my bed right now."

"Now, Mr. Jason," she began. "I can't leave Maude alone these days. I need to get back downstairs right now and dish up the supper."

"After supper, then," he said. "After you put Mother to bed. We can take our time, not be afraid of disturbing anybody."

"Sir—"

He got to his feet and came to the door, took her in his arms and gave her a bruising kiss before she could say another word. When he let her go her eyes were glazed with tears. "Just like old times, Vi," he said. As she retreated he felt sure he'd sleep like a babe with Violet next to him. And he did.

Chapter Twenty-seven

Lucy stood at the side of her filly running the curry-comb over the coppery coat, as she did nearly every day as soon as her chores at Mrs. Fleming's were done. She liked to ride out on the Salinas Highway and would have done today except that Mrs. Fleming had gone to a lying-in and didn't want Alice left alone too long.

She leaned into the horse's warm side, into the heavy contentment large animals seemed to exude, but took little solace from it. She'd been on tenterhooks since the meeting with Clancy at the boardinghouse, but the gunman had yet to keep his side of the bargain. Not long after Doc had left for Macon, Clancy had left town to attend to railroad business in the San Joaquin. With the passing of weeks, Lucy couldn't help worrying. *What if he got himself shot? How would I go about the business then? If it's Doc who comes back first I'm lost.* She stood with the horse for some time, until Zorra's hide shivered and Lucy knew someone had come up behind her. She composed her face into a blank slate and turned around.

It was Sam. He gave her a gentle smile. "Howdy, Miss Lucy. You have a nice ride out to the valley?"

She smiled back and didn't bother to correct his assumption.

Lucy Lied

"I got a wire from Mr. Clancy. Said he should be finished with his business soon. Said he'll wire again when he's on his way home."

She laid aside the comb and nodded carefully. *Thank God.*

"You got her coat looking really good." Sam ran a hand over Zorra's flank. "Don't you worry now. He'll be back soon," he said kindly before bidding her good day.

She tied on her bonnet and kissed the blaze that streaked the red hide between Zorra's eyes. *I'll see you tomorrow, pretty girl.*

Out on the street it was windy, but sunny. When she got to the top of the bluff overlooking the pier she could see whitecaps on the sun-sparkled water. She stepped lively to the south, hugging her shawl tight around her, resisting the temptation to run. *He'll be back soon.* She kept her eyes down, lest she encounter one of the Methodist ladies and something of the giddy anticipation she was feeling show on her face. She tried to rein in her hopes. *Soon. What does that mean?* But then the giddy sensation came over her again, stronger than ever.

She loved to walk below the fringe of pines on the shelf above the shingle beach. The sea rocked and clattered the round stones as it pulled away from the land, only to beat shoreward again. That steady to and fro reminded her of squeezing cows' teats, first right then left, regular as a tick-tock. She walked on steadily crunching across the yellow gravelly sand that topped the bluff. She felt the sting of the salt-smelling breeze on her cheeks, sharp and fresh. She paused on the outskirts of the Chinese fishing camp where a Celestial was kneeling before the joss house. The Chinaman was shaking long sticks out of a narrow tube, and from the way they fell, so Lucy understood, he would divine the will of his gods. Throngs of shiny black cormorants crowded the white-crusted rocks just inside the shore break. The sampans bobbed and a red-billed oystercatcher skimmed the surface of the water. Smells of wood smoke, incense and fish cleanings drifted up to her as she passed by a school of drying jacks, beheaded, gutted, and strung out on lines like scalps on lodge poles pictured in a Western romance.

Farther on she spied a pair of mergansers diving in the lea of Lovers of Jesus Point, seeking the still medium below the chop, out of sight and beholden to no one. A gull wheeled overhead and shrilled a piercing note of mockery at the poor earthbound woman. She picked up a stick of driftwood and flung it as high as she could. *Get off, you.*

She walked on until the lighthouse came into view. The beam that pierced the gray curtain toward the horizon made her think of truth and what black stains would be revealed if God's illuminating beam should ever pierce her soul. *I can't think about sin now.*

The bluff on which the lighthouse at Point Piños sat was mantled thickly with cypress trees. Doc had brought her there once to observe a roosting screech owl. Lucy made her way to the edge of the dark green boughs. There she closed her eyes and lifted her face to the sun, drinking it in as if she had not felt it for a long, long time, as if she'd just emerged from a time of imprisonment. She had to cement her plans, all the details. *He'll forget me. He barely knows me anyway, and if he did ...* She put the thought of Doc out of her mind. *It's not you I want to think about. It's Clancy. He'll be here soon. Soon.*

She hugged herself, told herself she must be content to wait, scanned the beach with an eye to its beauty. *As deserted and perfect as upon the morning of the fifth day of Creation. A world before beasts and men.* She wondered why God had persisted beyond that pristine state. *And women made later, only to satisfy a longing of Adam. We are lower than the beasts.* There in the seclusion of the pine verge, she spoke aloud. "The last shall be first and the first shall be last. The Bible says that, too."

She was suddenly aware of another, someone walking toward her out of the trees. She whirled.

"Morning, little Luce. I didn't mean to give you a fright. Just thought I'd watch you a bit. You're a pretty sight in your nice, new clothes. I ain't fared so well, as you can see. It's a sad tale."

He looked a sight; a front tooth gone, all unwashed, bearded and roughened all over from exposure day and night. His clothes were ill fitting and caked with dried mud or worse. He smelled filthier than the whiskey-soaked Flynn Talbott on his worst day. He stroked her cheek with a grimed paw. She recoiled. His hands used to be so elegant, long-fingered and softly fleshed. His touch had been luxury.

"Oh, now. Don't be that way. Don't you love old Ellis anymore?" He flashed the grin that had once made her heart skip. Now it only served to frighten her. *What has happened to you?*

"I know I'm not pretty like I used to be. But I can get me a new tooth soon as we get some money and get out of here. Just like old times, little Luce. Remember when we left your aunt's place? How nice we had it? I hear you're engaged to a fancy doctor. Oh, yeah, old Ellis knows all about that. There's this old crone down at the mission where I been staying. She knows how to get rid of babies with ergot of rye. Does business with some of Sally Locke's girls. You're the talk of the whorehouse. How I knew where to find you. I seen you at that San Carlos Day picnic, too. Bright as a penny. I said to myself it's time old Ellis and little Luce got together again."

She shook her head at him and started back toward The Grove.

"I guess you'd rather stay here now you're engaged. Well that's fine," he said, coming after her. He grabbed her arm. "But I got something coming," he hissed. "The people of this town robbed me of all my money and my possessions. Stripped me bare and turned me out. You think I'm gonna forget that? I mean to have some of my own back, something besides a few rags stolen off clotheslines."

It struck her that it offended his vanity to have to wear secondhand trousers. *Still proud and vain, and such a ruin.* She almost smiled but knew better than to appear mocking. She still feared his swift backhand.

"So here's what we're gonna do," he continued. "You're gonna get me some money so I can get on my feet again."

She felt his grip ratchet on her arm and flinched in pain.

"I know you won't leave me in the lurch," he said. "Because if you do, I won't go away. I'll be right here amongst all these fine folk who think you're fit to marry their highfalutin doctor. All these friends of yours are so godly, so pure. How do you think they'll feel about you once I tell them how we used to carry on, how that first time in the barn you wanted it so bad you didn't even try to bring your old father in out of the storm? You let him lie there half-dead in the mud between the cornrows, all out of his head and lightning-struck. You think he'll marry you when he hears all that? You think you'll be welcome amongst the righteous old biddies then?"

Everything he said was true. She shivered, aware of the wind breezing through her dress, the vulnerability of a woman alone on an empty beach. She tried to pull away. *They've heard worse about me.*

He squeezed her arm harder. "What I want is enough for a train ticket to Saint Louis. Never been in that part of the country aside from passing through. I'll need a decent suit of clothes and some personals for shaving and such. Soap. A comb. And I'll need some cash for getting my teeth fixed and then some over."

She pulled free and raised her hands. *How would I come by all that?*

"Oh, you'll figure it out," he said. "You can sell that ring on your finger for starters. And what about that garnet earring? I reckon you still got that. It'll fetch a price. Hell, you got plenty of ways to go about it. But you better get busy. I can't go on living down in that ruined mission much longer. You got one week. I'll be waiting close to that house where you live, watching for all the lights to go out. You come out and find me or I'll be coming in."

She shook her head at him and started to walk away.

He called after her. "What if I tell the sheriff you're wanted for murder. Not the one here. The one you done in Pennsylvania."

She stopped dead and turned around.

"You heard me right. Your own aunt. Cracked her skull just like you did that Talbott fella. Now I got your attention. She caught you stealing money. Money she had stashed. Said she was going to get the law. Get you put away. You grabbed the first thing to hand. Poker on the hearth. One good swing. Not a sound. You took her body into that little room Old John used and closed the door. Then you come to get me and tell me we had to git."

243

Lucy Lied

It all made sense. Why he'd looked so strange that morning. How he had enough money for the clothes, the train. She flew at him, flailing with her fists.

"You hellcat. Don't you raise your hand to me!"

He cuffed her and she fell. She sat up, tried to clear her head. *Aggie! Oh, Aggie!* Her right hand found a limb of driftwood. She got to her feet and charged at him with the heavy piece of wood raised high over her head. He ran, but she came after him, laying the wood about his head and shoulders, would have beaten him bloody had her skirt not tripped her up. As it was, she fell and he kept running till he was out of sight.

She tried to stand up and give chase, but sank to her knees. Shot through with grief and panic, she covered her face with her hands and wept. After a time all the tears had dried on her face. Then she sat, growing colder and colder. She sat with her hate. *My word against his. But the sheriff will side with Ellis. He couldn't hang me for Flynn Talbott, so he'll see that I hang for a murder I didn't do. I can't let him do this to me. Ruin me all over again. I can't.*

She stayed until her mind went numb and her limbs were stiff with the sitting, her every fiber cold through from the damp coming off the wintery bay and her nerves raw with the keening of the gulls overhead.

When she rose from the ground her mind was heavy, overwhelmed. She brushed at the spots of sand on the front of her skirt. Her voice sounded as if from far away. Yet it was her voice, loud and clear. "I'll kill him," she said. "I'll kill him."

She had scarcely ceased speaking when she heard him coming again. Panic squeezed her heart. She turned suddenly, ready to fight. But it wasn't him at all. It was the painter.

Encumbered with a canvas, his easel and paint box, Adrian Fiske emerged from the copse of cypress trees. "Hello, Miss Lucy. Hope I didn't frighten you."

She shook her head though she quaked with dread. *Had he heard her?*

"You'll forgive me intruding on your solitude. There's talk around town of some rough characters loitering hereabouts. Sheriff's been rousting vagrants out of the mission. It isn't safe, your walking by yourself in these lonely parts."

She dropped her eyes.

"I have news from Doc," Fiske continued. "It was my intention to stop by Mrs. Fleming's house to seek you out and impart it. Perhaps you'd like to walk along with me that way."

They plodded off toward The Grove, crossing through the graveyard to reach the tent lots of the Methodist settlement by the shortest route. All was deserted at this time of year, where in summer families of the faithful would be crowded in cheek by jowl.

The painter spoke of trifles lest silence persist between them as they walked. "We won't see Sam at the stable or at Leese's much longer. He's off to work for Clancy at that spread out on the Salinas Highway. I guess Clancy is tired of living in that shack. Plans to put up a hacienda and string barbed wire around his land to keep the neighbors' cattle from drinking at his creek. No good will come of that. I can tell you." He paused to regard her. "You know the place?"

Lucy kept her face a blank and shrugged.

"No matter," Adrian Fiske said. "I don't expect you ever ride that far. Do you?"

She shook her head and wondered why it seemed a particular point with him.

"You really don't look well, my dear," Fiske continued. "A tot of brandy by the fire is what you need."

My gun is what I need.

Chapter Twenty-eight

Beyond the tent lots were a few clapboard dwellings. Mrs. Fleming's residence stood among a handful of others, like white hens clustered around a sprinkling of grain. Through the kitchen window, Mrs. Fleming was clearly visible, stirring a cast iron pot on the stove. Alice, who looked like a blonde china doll from behind, sat at the table folding laundry. Fiske insisted on going around to the front door and knocking.

Mrs. Fleming answered with a look of prim disapproval directed toward Lucy. "I little thought I'd get home before you had returned from the stable," she said, adding, "Good day, Mr. Fiske." Then, as an afterthought, "Please, come in. We were just about to drink a cup of tea."

The painter put down his things in the hall and followed Lucy into the parlor.

Ida Fleming excused herself and returned a moment later with her sister and a tray of tea things. Lucy stood at the mantel rubbing her hands together, her back to the others lest they observe signs of her distress. Adrian Fiske occupied a chair near the hearth. Alice dropped to the carpet to play with her doll. The painter found it hard to take his eyes off the strange creature with the glorious cascade of blonde hair, a face as shriveled as a dried crabapple, and pink-rimmed, vibrant blue eyes with lashes as pale as bleached bones. "I've never seen such a combination of youth and age as your sister exhibits," he said.

Mrs. Fleming sat down across from Fiske. She poured out four cups and handed them around "Have I never told you about Alice?"

The painter shook his head. "I've heard this and that. She is most intriguing."

"Alice is my younger sister by two years," Mrs. Fleming began, in a way that made him think she'd told the story in exactly these words many times, "but she was afflicted with a high fever when she was an infant. She was always sickly after and never grew beyond the size of a ten-year-old, as you see. Her mind is that of a cunning child, not retentive of facts, but full of imaginings, some of them quite fearful. My father tried to break her of some of her worst fancies, but only terrified her more in the process, especially when he tried to rid her of her fear of thunder. We'd tried reading Scripture over her and prayer circles, and even the water cure, but nothing would stop her screams. And this was odd because Father was uncommonly upset by noises himself. When we were very young my father had a new house built; this was back in Salem where we grew up. It was a very handsome house and pleased my mother greatly, but the floor in the parlor squeaked whenever Father crossed the room. He found the noise exasperating. Finally one evening he brought in his carpenter's box and set about driving a nail into the floor whenever he heard the squeak. First he took care of the boards by the window, then over near the fire and then by the hallway door. It went on and on. Bang! Bang! Bang! Alice hid upstairs under the bed with her hands clamped over her ears."

"The poor thing."

"Yes," Mrs. Fleming said, smiling at her sister fondly, "She's terrified of crawling things, and the out of doors and sometimes she's even been known to scream at the portrait of Father hung over my bed."

"Alice, you're looking fine today," he said to the wizened child on the floor.

Alice lifted her shriveled face and grinned at him. "Thank you."

"She speaks very politely," Adrian said to Mrs. Fleming. "Not at all shy."

"Oh, indeed. She's fond of company. Inseparable from Lucy. I suspect it will upset her when Lucy goes to live at The Rookery. I intend to make Lucy promise to come back and see Alice regularly."

Mrs. Fleming and Adrian Fiske both turned to gaze at Lucy, as if they expected her to add her agreement. She could but smile and wonder why he was taking so long about reading the blasted letter.

Adrian withdrew a small packet from his pocket. "Does your sister care for butterscotch?"

Alice abandoned her doll before Mrs. Fleming had time to reply. "Yes, please," she said. She came over and stuck out her hand for the treat. "Thank you very kindly," Alice said and returned to her place on the floor with the candy bulging in her cheek.

"What is your doll's name, Alice?" Adrian asked.

"Martha," she replied.

"She's very pretty."

Alice rocked her doll and sucked her sweet.

Mrs. Fleming cleared her throat. "Have you been out painting your tree?"

"Why, yes." Adrian rose from his chair and fetched the canvas from where it stood against the easel near the front door.

Mrs. Fleming screwed up her mouth. "This one doesn't look anything as much like a tree as some of your others," she said.

Alice rocked her doll in her arms and began to sing to her with a rapt expression on her queer old face.

> *"At last with a deep sigh, these words spake she,*
> *I pray thee good Soldier wilt thou marry me:*
> *Else my hasty pleasure, sweet Sorrows will bring,*
> *And I may repent I heard the Nightingale sing.*

Oh no, quoth the Soldier, I may not do so,
Along with my Captain, tomorrow I must go,
But if I come this way, again the next Spring,
We'll walk once more to hear the sweet Nightingale sing."

"What an interesting song. Quite like the ones Alan Luce sings," Adrian observed. "Did you teach it to her?"

"I don't hold with music apart from hymn singing," Mrs. Fleming said, "but poor Alice has so little amusement I can't find it in my heart to silence her."

"Where do you suppose she learnt it?"

"I suspect she heard the keeper."

"While out walking?"

"No, Alice does not walk the strand. She fears the out of doors, as I said. I suppose on a windless evening the sound carries from the lighthouse."

"Ah," Fiske said, though he didn't for a moment believe it.

Mrs. Fleming got to her feet. "I beg you to excuse me while I go out to gather the sheets off the line. The way the wind has been blowing all day I fear it may rain any minute."

"I hardly think so," the painter replied. "All the talk around town is about how this is making up into a dry winter. Everyone is saying it's the start of a drought."

"In any case," the old dame replied. She looked pointedly at Lucy. "Mind Alice," she said. Then she left the parlor for the backdoor.

Lucy caught Adrian's eye and mimed reading a letter, running an index finger across the open palm of the other hand.

"We should wait for Mrs. Fleming," the painter said. "I'll talk with Alice in the meantime." He rustled the bag of sweets pulling it from his pocket. Alice immediately looked up from her doll. "Tell me, Alice," he said, "where did you learn that pretty song you were singing? Will you tell me if I give you another candy?"

The yellow-haired creature jumped up and ran to Adrian in response. "Oh, yes please," she said.

"Ah," he said, holding the bag of candy out of her reach, "you must tell me about the song first. Who taught it to you?"

Lucy rose from her chair and stumbled into the tray with the tea things, sending the metal tray, the teapot, the sugar bowl, and several teaspoons clattering and clanging to the floor. Alice froze for an instant then clapped her hands over her ears and dropped to the floor, rolling like a dog having a fit and shrieking in distress.

Adrian leapt to his feet. "Mrs. Fleming!" he cried.

Lucy dropped to her knees next to Alice and tried to put her arms around the hysterical girl to stop her flailing about.

Mrs. Fleming ran into the parlor dropping an armful of sheets as she passed through the kitchen. "What's happened here? Lucy! Who upset the tray? I'll see to Alice. You get this mess cleaned up."

"I'm terribly sorry," the painter said as Mrs. Fleming comforted her sister. "I honestly don't know how Lucy managed to upset the tray. What can I do to help?"

"Please sit down and be quiet," Mrs. Fleming replied. She continued to hold her sister, rocking more and more gently until Alice, having forgotten what had upset her, broke away from the confining embrace and sat down to play with her doll as before the ruckus had occurred. Lucy had by then mopped up the floor and returned from taking all the offending objects back to the kitchen.

"Well," Adrian said, hastening to put the unpleasantness behind them, "I have news of Doc. Why I came to find Lucy in the first place. Came back here to read it as I thought you'd want to hear, too."

Mrs. Fleming's jaw untensed. "Indeed I do. High time you mentioned it. You ought not keep us in suspense." She called toward the kitchen. "Lucy, come to the parlor."

When Lucy had rejoined them, Fiske produced the envelope from his breast pocket with a flourish. "A telegram," he said.

Lucy held her breath as Adrian pulled a square of paper out of the envelope and unfolded it.

"My work here over. Put quilt on bed. Doc."

"Oh my lands!" Mrs. Fleming cried. "He must be coming home! Does he say anything else? Does he say when?"

"No," the painter lied, as he folded the telegram and put it back in his pocket. "I expect he'll let us know the details soon enough."

"You must send back to him and tell him we need to know. We have to make all the necessary arrangements. There's cleaning The Rookery, then carrying all of Lucy's clothes and things down, not to mention all the baking if we're to have food for the wedding celebration." She sank into a chair and began to fan her face with her apron. "Just the thought of all the preparations makes me feel quite overwhelmed!"

"Is the quilt done?" Adrian asked.

"Oh, yes. Let me just go get it." She scurried from the parlor and returned a moment later to spread out the finished piece for his inspection.

"My, my," Adrian said, running his hand over the patchwork, "I had no idea. The colors are dazzling."

"It's a bit bright," Mrs. Fleming said, "but very pretty all in all."

"Yes, it's perfect. The aqua with the lapis and malachite ... and that lovely plum color is splendid."

"Well," Mrs. Fleming said, as her wan cheek took on a pinkish color, "yours is high praise indeed, but it will look better once it's been spread out flat on the bed for a while. When they're new, it seems to take some time for the seams to relax, if you know what I mean. My thought is that you might take it up to The Rookery and spread it on his grand bed. I heard the bedstead and the tick were delivered some time ago."

"Aye. Steadman's boy had a hell of a time getting everything up the stairs. But now it's all put together and quite handsome."

"I'll thank you not to swear," she replied, though she did so less vehemently than on occasions when she wasn't quite so happy.

He bent closer to inspect the needlework.

"It's easier to see the stitches on the solid backing," she said.

"This one square doesn't match the rest, does it?"

"No, we had to invent that one ourselves," Mrs. Fleming admitted. "There were only nineteen squares in Doc's trunk. One must have gone missing. But I don't think it takes away from the whole, do you?"

"No, not at all," Adrian said.

"Then you'll see that it's spread on the bed."

"Yes, of course." She began folding up the quilt.

He ignored his cue to leave. Mrs. Fleming sensed he wanted a private word. "Lucy, take Alice to the kitchen and stir the stew. I'll be back there directly and we can dish up our supper."

Lucy took the strange sister and led her by the arm to a kitchen chair, but then crept back along the passageway to listen to the rest of the conversation in the parlor.

"Touching on Doc and Lucy ..." Fiske began. "You know, I don't think she's quite well. So pale. And such a strange expression on her face all the time we were talking. Positively grim."

"She is perhaps a little run-down," Mrs. Fleming agreed.

"Are you still sanguine about the match?"

"Sanguine?"

"Does Lucy still seem eager to wed?" he explained.

Mrs. Fleming put on a flustered expression. "Well I ... I surely don't know what you would mean by that. I've noted no change in her demeanor, nothing that would signal a change of heart."

"Ah, yes, you hit on the expression I was searching for." The painter paused, as if he were considering whether to pursue the issue. "Then you would say that it's true, the old saw about absence."

"Yes, I would say it makes the heart grow fonder." Another pause. "Are you sure there's nothing else on your mind?"

"I hope you don't think it was I who upset Alice," he said. "I'd like to come around again to visit her. She's an enchanting creature. And she sings beautifully. I'm still curious as to how she came to learn that song."

"She's been known to capture peoples' fancies, I daresay." Mrs. Fleming sounded a note of finality to signal that the subject of the song was closed.

He picked up his canvas and his painting things. "Does it ever occur to you that Lucy may have taught it to her?"

"Lucy? Lucy who doesn't speak?"

"Are you so sure about that? Perhaps Doc had some success with her. Maybe she made some progress unbeknownst to us. Imagine how delighted Doc would be if there were some evidence that Lucy could speak, after all his efforts!"

Mrs. Fleming's eyes blazed. "What a crack-brained suggestion. I won't have you saying such things in my house. It's as much as saying that she lies every time she fails to answer a question. That's what it amounts to. You're saying her muteness is a ruse, a trick."

"No, that's not what I—"

"It is! You're trying to undermine this marriage by finding a new fault with her—and I won't have it. Now I'll thank you to take your insinuations and—"

"Don't boss me, woman!" Fiske exploded in a self-righteous rage. "Don't presume to take me to task! I'm not one of your men sicklied-over with religion whom you can berate like a stepchild!"

"I trust Doctor Garrett will take you to task on my behalf once he learns what you have been up to! Mark my words, you won't stand in the way of this marriage much as you fear that a woman has displaced you in Doc's affections."

"We'll just damn well see!" With that, the painter stormed out and slammed the door behind him, setting Alice off again.

Chapter Twenty-nine

Upon beholding Adrian Fiske at her door, Sally made him a mock curtsey with a sweep of one hand toward the sofa. "Please make yourself comfortable." Her chamois colored dressing gown hung loosely about her. As she crossed the room she tied her sash. "Please sit down." She took a seat opposite him and studied his cheerless face for a minute. "You have business with me?"

She smelled of something floral, maybe jasmine. He pondered that lovely scent for a few seconds before he spoke. "I've come to talk about the Talbott woman," he began. "I've come to suspect things about her—such things as a man would want to know before he marries."

"Unless he's so besotted as to be blind," Sally said.

"It's up to his friends to make sure the blinders are off."

She looked at him with renewed interest. "What is it you propose exactly?"

"This redheaded woman isn't what she seems to be. Of that I'm sure, but I lack the means to prove it to Doc. She's a fraud. The proof exists in a number of small incidents. Only if you put them all together can you see it. The question is, how can I make Doc face the math?"

"I'm puzzled," Sally replied. "How is it you have come to oppose his marriage after you lent a hand with the engagement?"

"I always had my misgivings," Adrian said, "but when your friend asks a favor one cannot refuse. Naturally I had no idea that the flaws in the lady's character ran so deep. Now that I do, I cannot, as a friend, fail to warn him off."

"I see," she said. "Perhaps you should first tell me of these incidents. Then we can discuss how to put them together for Doc to see."

"All right. First is the business at Leese's, the attempt on Clancy's life," he replied. "There are rumors that shot didn't come from outside."

"Have you also heard that she was seen coming from Clancy's room?"

"By 'she' you mean ..."

"Doc's Lucy, of course. The widow Talbott, as people politely call her. What do you suppose she was up to?"

"I wish I knew." He leaned back and ran his fingers through his unruly locks. "Doc asked me to keep an eye on her while he's away. Lately I've taken the duty more seriously as she sometimes stays at Steadman's rather late. She always takes care to start back to The Grove before dark, but often I take the precaution of walking her back. On the day in question she had left the stable by the time I got there. I saw Clancy's horse."

Sally smiled. "Ah, so that is how she knew Clancy was at the boardinghouse. She saw the palomino and deduced that Clancy was staying at Leese's as usual. She's not guileless. To think of her as innocent as a dumb animal is to underrate her. I have always thought so. Her muteness makes fools of us."

Adrian shook his head. "I've been trying to find some way to explain that very thing to Doc, but with no success at all. He's as deluded as she is dumb."

"Then they deserve each other."

"Nonetheless, a friend must do what he can to avert disaster."

"Then why do you think she had an assignation with Clancy?"

"I've heard she was seen running from the back door."

"You believe this rumor?"

"I do. It's a gut feeling," he said. "You think I'm wrong?"

Sally smiled and shook her head. "I happen to know you're right. My maid Rose spoke to one of her sisters who works at Leese's. The sister saw the red-haired woman bolting down the service stair just after the gunshot. She saw her run from the kitchen door and make for Pacific Street."

"I suspected you might know the facts."

"I know more than Bronson has to put in his paper. He doesn't talk to the Chinese."

"So was it Lucy who tried to shoot Clancy? Why would she have done such a thing?"

"We'll never know. Sheriff don't like Clancy much. Probably hopes the shooter has better luck next time."

Adrian considered the glint of amusement in Sally's eyes and wondered how many times she had been privy to backdoor escapes. It struck him that she had more knowledge of the world than he did, knowledge that was passed down through generations of independent women who found the antics of men and their paramours entertaining, in the same way it's entertaining to watch a swarm of ants discover a crust of bread, disassemble it grain by grain and bear it away. "Why do you think she went to see Clancy?"

Sally shrugged. "Why do you suppose? You should have followed her inside and put your ear to the door."

It irritated him to hear her speak so simply of it, as if anyone with common sense would have done as much.

"What else have you found out about her that you intend to tell Doc when he gets back?" she asked.

"I believe she isn't mute at all, that it's an act."

"And there is proof of this?"

"I'm trying to come up with it. Nothing yet."

"And?"

"That's it."

"That is nothing." She propped her chin on the heel of her hand and considered the matter. "We must prove that she has betrayed him," she said at length. "Only then will he break off this idiotic engagement."

"Prove?"

She sighed impatiently. "If she has fallen in love with Clancy there will be other meetings. You must follow her more closely now, find their meeting place and what time they see each other. Then when Doc comes home, you must take him to see for himself."

"It's an ugly business," Adrian said.

"If you don't want to do it, don't bother me with your suspicions. Just go and paint your tree and let Doc marry this imbecile."

Sally's maid knocked discreetly at the door of the apartment before Adrian could say more. "Now you must go," Sally said. "I have a client."

"Perhaps one of your people might be employed to follow her," Adrian suggested as he rose.

"All right," Sally said. "I confess I had already resolved to send one of my people from the scullery."

Adrian reflected on the expression she used, 'one of my people.' "They'd do anything for you, wouldn't they?"

She nodded. "Of course."

"What inspires such loyalty?"

"Kinship," she said. "We are none of us white, all of us smart and useful but never given our due. It is up to us to bind ourselves together for the mutual good."

"You sound like a politician," the painter said.

"If I were a politician your kind would be clearing beet fields."

"Then I'm glad you run a whorehouse."

"As I enjoy your company and those of others weaker than myself, I am glad also." She paused and dropped her eyes to the carpet. "What have you heard from Doc?"

"His business in Macon is all but concluded. I haven't let anyone know yet, but he's due to arrive in Salinas on Friday. Please keep it to yourself."

She lifted her eyes and smiled. "When I hear it from the telegrapher I'll act surprised. Tell Doc when you see him I have cognac and cigars, the kind he likes."

"Miss Sally," the painter said, "if he don't know by now that you have what he likes then he's not the man I took him for." He lifted his hat and walked out into the evening, more pleasant now the wind had died.

The dust of the street softly powdered the toes of his boots. He thought of evidence, of secret trysts, animal lust, naked bodies seen through a crack in the window curtain, the shock and pain on the deceived man's face, the act of vengeance. The thought occurred to him that he'd best go to Doc's house, find that gun in the sea chest and take it away. As he started up Alvarado Street toward the Custom House it occurred to him that there might be another way to bring the woman down, a way that wouldn't depend on him peeping through keyholes. Fiske took a detour by the sheriff's office and poked his head in. Taylor was perusing the newspaper at his desk. A miscreant of some sort was asleep in the cell behind the desk.

"Evening, Mr. Fiske," Taylor said. "What can I do for you?"

"I'd like to speak with you about the incident at Leese's."

"Oh?"

"I don't suppose you've heard, but the widow Talbott was supposed to have been in Clancy's room about the time the shot was fired."

Taylor dropped his boots off the desk. "You have proof of that?"

Fiske shrugged. "Just the story of some Chinese gal who cleans the place. I don't think there's anything in it, myself, but the maid went on and on about red hair."

"I see. You think there's any reason why Flynn Talbott's wife would try to shoot Matt Clancy?"

"I'm not saying she did. There's not a shred of proof, just the word of a Chinese charwoman, so don't go around saying I'm accusing Doc's woman."

"When's he due back, anyway?" Taylor asked, though he already knew, since he was also a confidant of the telegraph clerk.

Adrian shrugged. "Any time now. Tomorrow, for all I know. Well, I'm off to The Rookery. Doc asked me to keep an eye on things."

"I heard he got himself a great big bed," Taylor remarked. Adrian caught a sidelong glance of his canine tooth gleaming behind a lubricious grin. "Heard it come from one of them big San Francisco hotels. I wouldn't mind taking a look."

"Come on, then, if you don't mind a walk. It's a sight worth going a good bit out of your way," Fiske replied, with only a momentary qualm about treating his friend's bedchamber like a circus attraction.

Taylor stood and grabbed his hat. "I don't mind a stretch of the legs."

As they set off, Adrian was the first to speak. "You still feel like she got away with Talbott's murder?"

"Whole town thinks that," Taylor replied. "Just no way to get at her now. Judge told me after the trial he wouldn't listen to any more accusations against her unless there was new evidence."

"Best forgotten, I expect," Fiske said.

"I'd have hanged that Chinaman if it wasn't for Clancy," the sheriff said as they trudged to the top of the bluff where The Rookery sat silhouetted against the dark sky.

Adrian led Taylor through Garrett's front door and up the stairs. At the foot of the grand bedstead Taylor finally spoke again. "Damn," he said.

"Indeed," the painter replied.

"Where'd he get the money? Why, just the freight alone." The sheriff paused as if he were calculating. "How many's this thing supposed to hold, anyway?"

Lucy Lied

"The Methodist ladies sewed the quilt," Adrian said abruptly. He touched the coverlet toward the foot of the bed, ran his hand across the square that didn't match.

"Huh," Taylor said. "I'd have thought they'd have done a better job. That piece there looks odd."

"Ida Fleming said there were only nineteen squares in Doc's trunk. He brought the patchwork with him from back East. Someone in his family made it for him, though why anyone would think you could make a rectangular coverlet out of nineteen squares surely beats me. I believe he must have lost one somewhere."

Taylor grinned again. "I cannot imagine he'll notice it much once he gets his bride up here. There's some men would give an eyetooth for a woman who can't speak, and she's a looker to boot."

"It's odd because I know the one that was used as evidence at the trial was returned," Adrian rattled on.

"That piece of goods Chinaman Joe was peddling," the sheriff said.

"Yes. So let's assume there were twenty squares in the trunk originally," Adrian mused. "Doc gave one to the Widow Talbott for a sling, but she wore it to San Francisco and left it there. That could only mean that a second piece—the one used for evidence at trial—was put in Joe's way, so he'd be sure to find it."

"You mean somebody salted a claim?" Taylor peered into Adrian's eyes. "Who might have done such a thing?"

"I hardly know."

"Then what are you saying?"

Adrian shrugged. "What do you make of it?"

"What do I make of it?" Taylor chewed his lip. "Somebody may have rigged the evidence to save a pretty face. Seems like I ought to see Doc as soon as he gets back from Macon. We'll get to the bottom of it. You wouldn't know when he's due back, would you?"

"Surely you don't think ..." Adrian let the presumption of Doc's guilt lie there and stink.

"Folks still feel like they was done out of a hanging," Taylor said. "Makes people restless and ornery." He contemplated the state of the citizenry and thought of a topic touching their thirst for justice and amusement. "You know, there's to be a meeting of the Civic League tomorrow. You ought to come."

"The Civic League?"

"Group of like-minded men who want to see the riffraff run out of the old mission. We were down there not long ago and ran off a gaggle of ragamuffins. But we're thinking of going down at night. We'll find more of them sleeping, I'll warrant. Should you want to lend a hand I can promise you a lively affair, if you take my meaning."

"Yes, I understand. Such doings don't draw me strongly, though I'm sure you'll find many among our townsfolk who will gladly pitch in. Sorry to have to decline."

"I found one of them devils of interest in particular," Taylor continued. "Brought him back to town after I recognized him. That sharper with the white streak in his hair, the one who said he could contact the spirits of the dead. You were there, weren't you, at Swann's that night?"

"The one Clancy ran out of town?"

"The same. He was talking all out of his head when we found him. I thought I'd sober him up and see if I could make sense out of his jabber. But he didn't improve any after he'd been dry a couple days, so I let him go. He'll be down at the mission if I need to find him again."

"What's the difference?"

"Kept raving about some girl. Called her Luce. Seems like they was in cahoots. I reckon it's worth my while to find out." Taylor's porcine eyes gleamed. "More than one way to skin a cat, if you know what I mean."

"You think he's talking about the Widow Talbott."

"Now I see you got my drift," Taylor said. "You tell old Doc when you see him to come on over to the jail when he's a mind."

"I'm sure he'll attend with great interest."

"I bid you goodnight, then," the sheriff said. He turned on his heel and took a few steps toward the stairs. "Oh, by the way, I heard you got a wire of recent. Came from St. Louis. I'd guess that means Doc Garrett is on his way back to Monterey."

"Yes, I imagine it does."

Taylor grinned. "You wouldn't know a date for certain, would you?"

"I'm afraid he left the details to a future message."

"Right." Having assessed the painter's steadfastness on the point, the sheriff took his leave.

Adrian lingered at the foot of the bed after Taylor had gone. "That cursed redheaded daughter of Eve," he muttered. He felt a fool to have impugned Doc's truthfulness only to find out the woman was likely lashed up with Canby, in which case she could be condemned for other crimes altogether. The whole episode left a bitter taste in his mouth. He hastened into the other upstairs room and lifted the lid of the steamer trunk. "I wash my hands," he said, rummaging through the odd assortment of things Doc had laid in there. And he would have said more had he not been stunned by the realization that the gun he meant to spirit away was already gone.

Chapter Thirty

Sam leapt off his lathered mount and burst in. "Mr. Clancy!" he said, gasping for breath. "There's some Mexicans driving their stock onto the place, up the north end."

"I gotta put my boots on," Clancy said. "Bring Jack around front." As Sam went outside, Clancy thought of leaving a note for Lucy—she was due any time now—but decided not to take the time. Better to just hurry up and get back. When he emerged from the little house, shod and gun-belted, Sam was waiting in the saddle. Clancy took Jack's reins from Sam and mounted up. They whipped the horses into a gallop as they climbed the rise to the north. Once they crested the high ground, Clancy pulled up and drew the scope from his saddlebag. He snugged the optical piece to his right eye socket, sitting bolt upright in the saddle. "Goddamn double-crossing bitch," he growled. "She's taken down the wire. I got cattle on my place from fifty miles around."

Lucy tied Zorra in the copse of live oaks at the back of the little house and came out from the shelter of the trees only after she'd looked up and down the Salinas Highway, just as Sam had cautioned her to do. He'd told her twice just to make sure she took it in, what with the excitement of hearing the news. *"He'll be up at the little house on Friday if you think you might ride out that way."* Remembering his delicacy of expression made her smile.

Lucy Lied

She made sure no one was approaching before venturing to the front porch. Her heart fluttered as she raised her hand to knock on the door. *His door. Shall I throw my arms around him as soon as he opens it or wait to see what he does?* She knocked again. Then it occurred to her that the big palomino was nowhere to be seen. Two days ago at the stable Sam had told her Friday. And this was Friday. She'd checked Mrs. Fleming's calendar to make sure. She tried the door and found it open. She stepped inside.

She glanced around the place. With its unfinished plank interior and spare furnishings, it reminded her of Old John Rafferty's house. But on the bed was a lace coverlet and two pillows in fresh linen. She untied her bonnet and placed it on the table by the window where there was an oil lamp, filled and trimmed, light to read by. He'd even picked daisies and put them in a jar on the table next to the bed.

The blossoms reminded her of how Ellis used to appear with a handful of wildflowers for her, how the open barn door framed the pinks and lavenders of sunset and her younger self would be singing a melody her mother had taught her as the shots of milk hit the side of the pail. The hired man who called her "Luce" would lean against the post where she hitched up the cow's head. She could tell he was watching her, admiring her hair. She had taken to washing it almost every day since the first time he'd said how pretty it was. He'd said she had milkmaid's skin and she blushed even though she didn't know what he meant exactly. Ellis never spoke much above a whisper. She had to listen hard to make out the words, and sometimes she didn't bother because it was enough to hear the tone of his voice, the soft caressing sound of it. Often after she had finished milking and taken the jug to the springhouse he would still be standing next to the cow when she returned. *Are you fond of cows?* She knew he wasn't waiting around because he liked the beast, but she asked anyway, shy and brazen at the same time, looking him dead in the eye and asking such a fishing question. He pushed a wisp of hair away from her cheek. *It's you I'm fond of.*

Damn you, Ellis, and damn me for a fool. Those days are gone; all your days if I ever meet up with you again. She looked at the bright bars of sunlight that penetrated the shack's one window to slant across the plank floor. *Clancy! Where are you? He's been called out on railroad business at short notice. That must be it. But then why didn't he send Sam to let me know?* She felt her stomach turn. *I shouldn't have thought he'd be any different. Damn me for a fool.* Yet she lingered, her heart unwilling to accept the stomach's opinion.

To the north of the little house just over the rise, Clancy shoved the glass back into his saddlebag. Sam watched him mull the situation. "What you aim to do?"

"Go see whoever's driving that herd, I guess. Tell them to clear off. They won't, of course."

"You aim to draw down?"

"If it comes to that," Clancy said. He considered Sam for a minute. "You'd best ride into town and tell Sheriff Taylor there's trouble out this way."

"Taylor won't care. Reckon I'll stay and back you up," Sam said.

"Thankless job," Clancy replied.

"Better than washing dishes at Leese's."

"Okay." Clancy spurred Jack and the palomino sprang into a canter with Sam's black gelding on his flank. They rode up on the mob of cows that were crossing onto Clancy's spread, following their noses to the water. Clancy hailed a man dogging strays. "Where's the boss?" he called. "*El jefe?*"

"Señor Oreña," the cowpoke replied. He pointed to the east. "He's there."

"Gracias," Clancy said. He headed in a wide arc to the south, keeping his distance from the herd. Sam followed. After the horses splashed through the creek that cut Clancy's land on the diagonal, the gunman held up one hand, a signal to whoa. He nodded toward a knot of mounted men silhouetted against the morning sun. He took out his glass again and studied them.

"Oreña?" Sam asked.

Clancy nodded. "The biggest man on the tallest horse," he said. "No mistaking him. Come on."

Lucy Lied

They rode at a walk so as not to seem either aggressive or fearful toward the four men. A fifth galloped up, the man Clancy had spoken to. He was delivering a warning, pointing.

"Wouldn't take much to stampede the cows back the way they come," Sam said.

"They're mad with the smell of water," Clancy said. "I'd rather not try to turn them."

"You'd rather kill a bad man than a cow, I bet."

"Unless it was a bad cow," Clancy replied, "but to be honest I never came across one of those."

They approached Oreña's contingent at a lackadaisical pace, impassive as shadows, as if it were a matter of indifference as to whether they got their heads blown off or not. The wind shifted, bringing a hint of freshness from the west. The stench of cattle and the din of their excited bawling underscored the silent action of the two riders coming up slowly to where the group of five sat and waited.

Clancy was the first to speak as he and Sam came to within a stone's throw of the others. "Buenos días, Don Sebastián. Your visit surprises me. I've had no time to prepare the ditches to divert water across the grazing ground as I discussed with Señora Vásquez."

"Good day to you, Matt Clancy," Oreña replied. His mount shifted its stance, nervous at the approach of the other stallion. "My cousin's wife sometimes forgets to tell me things. She would rather flip through catalogues of the latest dress patterns than talk business. I've told her so myself. I've said to her that she ought to leave the running of the ranchos to me, both hers and mine. But she is young and headstrong. She likes to pretend she is as able as a man." He smiled broadly at the absurdity of the notion.

"She is, as far as I can tell." Clancy watched with pleasure as Oreña's smile withered away. "Came up with a good plan for getting your stock watered. She didn't tell you about it?"

"I know nothing of it," Oreña replied. He put on the expression of a man at a loss. "I know only that she has applied to the governor in Sacramento to review your title to this land. She told me that she anticipates a favorable ruling. So she told me to bring my cattle down to the water rather than waiting for the formalities. It is cruel, is it not, to deny the beasts water that is so abundant only a few miles to the south, water that goes unused for any other purpose than to provide a pleasant view to a man looking down from his yellow horse?"

"It was never my intent to deny your herd the water," Clancy said. "Isabel and I agreed on terms. She said she would convey them to you. That if the terms were acceptable to all, we'd all sign an agreement. That's where it sat when I went down to the San Joaquin."

"Ah," Oreña said, "but this is what comes of doing business with a woman. She said nothing of an agreement to me. Perhaps she forgot. Or perhaps she never understood what it was you proposed. She probably nodded, smiling, and seemed to comprehend, but all the while her brain was leaking the details like an unseasoned barrel leaks wine. She meant no harm, I'm sure."

"When she told you to bring your cattle here because she's contesting my title to the land you found her brain seaworthy enough."

"*Qué?*" Don Oreña leaned forward in the saddle as if didn't trust his ears. "Forgive my poor English."

"You heard me," Clancy said. "Now hear this, too. I'll take this up with Isabel. You can water your stock in the meantime, provided you put that barbed wire back up the way you found it. The price for grazing and watering your cattle is twenty-three percent of what they fetch at market. That's the agreement I made with Señora Vásquez. That's what she was supposed to convey to you. If you don't like those terms you can clear out now. Otherwise I'll have an agreement for signature in hand next time you see me."

"Very well," Oreña said. "I will talk to my cousin's wife and the two of us will sign such a contract with you. When will it be convenient for us to meet at your casita? Say four o'clock? I think that will give my cousin plenty of time to pick out a frock and arrange her hair."

"I'll be there."

Oreña smiled. "Bueno," he said.

Clancy and Sam rode back the way they'd come.

"Dodged a bullet there," Sam said, wiping sweat off his face.

"At least until four," Clancy replied.

Sam retied his kerchief around his neck. "I was meaning to take the wagon into town for supplies today, maybe slip over to The Badlands and find a bed for the night, if you know what I mean. Maybe you'd rather have me come straight back here after I've loaded up."

"No, no. You go and stay till tomorrow. It's nothing but putting signatures on a couple papers." They rode to within sight of the little house together before Sam split off to go about his errands. He caught sight of something. "I believe you got a visitor," he said, with a sly grin.

Clancy spied the red horse tied amongst the trees behind the shack. "I'm late for an appointment," he said. "A matter of some urgency. Concerns a filly," Clancy said, returning the smile.

"Horses and whores," Sam said, as Clancy made for the little house. "Horses and whores."

It seemed she'd been standing in the middle of the room half the morning by the time she finally came to the conclusion that he wasn't going to show. With legs that felt mired she went to the table. With unwilling hands she picked up her bonnet. With fingers that didn't want to work she tied it back on.

She heard the horse whinny before she was aware of the approaching hoof beats. She held her breath. *Is it coming from Monterey?* She closed her eyes to listen but couldn't tell. The sounds of horse went quiet. And then, magically, the door opened and he walked in.

"You came," he said.

His hands moved to caress her face, but she fended him off. "Where have you been?"

It took but a second for him to adopt his usual sardonic tone. "Why so frosty?"

"I've been waiting here an hour. I was afraid you weren't coming."

He stiffened and the softness went out of his eyes. "Simmer down. I came as fast as I could." He slapped his hat down on the table and peeled off his gloves.

She doubled down on his remoteness. "Do you have my earring?"

He unbuckled his six-guns and hung the belt across the back of a chair. "I went to Ortin's to check on that earring of yours, but I got bad news for you there. It's not at Ortin's anymore. Sally Locke came in and bought it." He pulled off his jacket and slung it over the gun belt. "I haven't had any coffee yet today. If I was to make some would you drink a cup?"

"How can you think of coffee?" On the verge of tears, she turned her back to him.

She seemed so stricken. At the sight of her standing there, so distressed, all his resolve to stay aloof vanished. He approached her softly, gently put his hands on her shoulders. "We'll get it back. I'll help you." She let herself be taken into his arms and poured out her tears against his chest. "Here now, all this over such a small thing. I'll get it from Sally for you. Don't worry."

"You don't understand," she said, wiping her tears with the heel of her gloved hand. She told him about Ellis and her dear Aggie. "I want to kill him," she said. "I need my gun."

"I would, too, if I were you," he said, "but first I'd make sure what he said was true. He may be lying about your aunt to make you feel threatened. He'd say anything to get what he wants, wouldn't he?"

She raised her face and looked him in the eye. "Yes. I hadn't thought ... oh, if only that were true! If I knew for sure Aggie was still alive ..."

"Why not sit down. We'll talk about it over a cup of coffee."

She dropped into one of the chairs by the window and took off her bonnet as he went about making a fire in the stove, grinding beans and filling the pot. He spoke to her as he worked. "I don't expect it will be too hard to find out. Send a telegram to—where did you say she lived? It's not a common name. Then if it's true, we'll put the law on him. You can't do it yourself. For one thing, it's not that easy. Most people can't look a man in the face and pull the trigger. You don't deal death like a hand of poker. The other thing is that five-shooter of yours is a misfire waiting to happen. If you're smart you'll never load it. If you do load it, keep an empty chamber under the hammer."

"What do you mean?"

He set the pot on the stove and got the revolver out of the drawer in the table. He broke it open to show her. "You put four rounds in the tumbler and rotate the empty chamber into the firing position."

"Where are the bullets?"

He opened the drawer again and scratched around for the ammunition. "Promise me you won't use it, at least not until after we know about your aunt." He dropped the four rounds into her hand.

She nodded and put the gun and the bullets into her handbag.

"If you want to use a gun you should let me teach you with a decent weapon," he said, "one less likely to blow up in your face."

"I'd like that." She unbuttoned her gloves and pulled them off.

"Course, I'd rather we occupy ourselves a different way; but truth is, I'll do anything you want as long as I can spend time with you."

She broke the connection of their eyes. "I like this little house," she said. "It's pleasant."

"Sam's been busy civilizing the place. He's the one put the sheets and such on the bed. Dusts and sweeps the floors. I'm the one who brought in the flowers, though. Reminded me of the ones you picked on San Carlos Day. I started to fall in love with you that day." He placed his hand on her arm. "In the San Joaquin not too long ago I thought I'd had it. Had a rope around my neck and Jack was skittish like he can be sometimes. I thought of you, how much I want you. I've wanted you from the first time I saw you in court, but I never thought ..."

She rose from her chair and settled herself in his lap, twined her arms about his neck and kissed him long and slow.

"Lucy, I—"

She put her finger across his lips. "No talking."

She unbuttoned her bodice. He pushed the dress and the underclothing off her shoulder and mantled the exposed flesh with kisses.

Lucy touched the lace of her shift and the ribbon trim of her corset. "I'm meant to wear these on my wedding day, but I thought ..."

He set her on her feet and carefully drew her sleeves off her arms. Skirt, corset, shoes, stockings, shift, drawers. Piece by piece he laid all of her clothes on the table next to her blouse, bonnet, and gloves. He turned her, meaning to take down her hair, and caught sight of the marks on her back. He traced each long scar with his fingertips, wordless acknowledgement of her pain, her past. Then he let down her glorious red curls and carried her to his bed. He climbed in after her, the same man she'd beheld in the bath, but with one remarkable difference. Lucy smiled. *You do want me, then.*

He took her hand in his and kissed her palm with maddening slowness, made her wait. *Whatever I've done before doesn't matter. It's different with him.* The waiting made her throb. *The part Doc wants to cut away.* She pressed her face against his neck, put her arms around him and held him close and hard, as if she would merge their skins and bones. He unwrapped her arms so he could see her face and entered her, looking into her eyes nakedly, the contortions of ecstasy drawn plainly on his features. *He's not afraid for me to see the whole of him. He wants me to keep my eyes open.* They moved with an urgency that reduced time itself to the cadence of their bodies. As long as they were locked together, time was their slave, ticking back twice for every tick forth, forced to keep lovers' hours instead of running headlong to the end of days. They spent themselves inevitably, panting, sweating, erupting. She who had been silent for so long found this state more profound. The voice inside her brain went silent. Rolling apart with sighs, they rolled together again to sleep.

When she woke, she lay with her back pressed against his belly, their heads on the same pillow, his one arm curled around her neck, the hand holding her breast, the other hand now stroking her thigh, now playing with the small curls near her ear. "I thought I might speak now," he said. "Ask what you're thinking."

"Of the old place where I grew up," she said. "The cow. Ellis used to say he'd never seen anyone fuss over a cow as if it were a prize saddle horse."

"He was your first?" Clancy asked.

"Yes."

"You feel you must tell me about him?"

She nodded.

"The past is gone. All behind you. It's nothing to me."

"I know," she said. "The problem is I feel it clinging. As if I'd walked through a doorway where there was a spider web stretched across."

He nodded. "I understand. You can tell me if it will make you feel better."

"Promise you won't think ill of me?"

"I never could."

She changed position to lie on her back and worried a hank of red hair between her fingers. "I was just a girl. At the beginning Ellis was sweet to me, like no one I'd ever known before. He had a fund of stories. Listening to him made the work light."

"What kind of work?"

"The first fall he was with us we cleared stumps with pick and shovel, and a team of oxen to yank the roots from the earth once the men had dug clear under and passed the rope through. The field was pocked with holes. Ellis said it reminded him of the war, shell craters. I was too young to know much about it. Ellis said he was glad that I'd not been spoiled by the war like everyone else."

"He was a good talker."

"That winter he and Old John sat inside putting an edge on the shovels, polishing away the rust, mending harness. Ellis sewed up the holes in their underwear. Old John said a fresh girl ought not be fingering a man's smallclothes. But when they were out of the house I used to go to Ellis's room and run my hands across his spare union suit where it hung on the clothes peg. I tried to see the impressions of his body." She stopped abruptly and blushed.

"It's all right," Clancy said. "I like it that you're honest about it."

"That spring we turned the earth as soon as it wasn't too stiff with ice. I trailed the plow with as much seed corn as I could carry in a sack hung over one shoulder, bulging in front of me as if I had a child in the womb. Ellis came after folding the earth over, putting the seeds to bed. It was the two of us who impregnated the soil while John Rafferty whipped the mule. Ellis used to tell me all manner of foolish things as we went about the sowing." She imitated his Southern drawl. "Did you ever hear tell of a three-legged pig?"

He watched her face through a long pause.

"We were happy for a while."

"But then ..."

"The corn tasseled out and Old John Rafferty in his cups of a summer evening mumbled about the greatest crop the county had ever seen, counting his chickens. He figured he'd finally get some respect among the other farmers come harvest time. Truth is, he was a terrible farmer. People made fun of him, about how he'd bought the rockiest piece of ground in Pennsylvania and how he never did get the knack of it. Either he planted too early and the shoots were all frost-killed about a week after they sprouted or he'd buy a kind of seed that wouldn't grow good in our part of the country." She half laughed. "That last crop we put in was the one lost during the storm when John Rafferty got struck by lightning. We left the farm after that."

"You miss it?"

"Some. The barn. The animals. Used to dawdle out there of an Indian summer evening, waiting for Ellis to come from the cornfield. I brung you an ear of corn fresh from the field, he'd say. Bet you never seen one so fine and fully growed."

Clancy waited through another pause while she cleared her throat. "And then he slipped it into my hand and showed me how to hold it and ... I slouched against the cow because if I didn't I'd stand taller than he. I knew he wouldn't like that." She shifted her gaze to the rafters. "He said he always knew I'd like kissing because of my red hair, that red hair is the devil's favorite color."

"Is that true?" Clancy asked.

"I wouldn't know anything about the devil, but as far as Ellis Crane, my eyes are open now."

He saw her tears and caressed her face. "What?"

"I was so caught up with Ellis I left Old John out in the field. We might have saved him from being lightning-struck if we'd gone to find him. It was my fault, leaving him there."

"Your stepfather should have been the one to save you, not the other way around."

His words created a new flood of tears. "What?"

"Why did Ellis take me then cast me aside?"

"You said it yourself. You were too tall."

The ghost of a sad smile flitted about her lips. "He was a bad man even then, but I wanted him to love me. I would have given anything. How can it still hurt, what he did, someone like that?"

"You haven't had time to outgrow some of those old feelings yet. You've barely hit your prime."

"I felt I was past it until I saw you that day at Leese's. I thought I'd lost all appetite for a man."

"Why did you accept Doc Garrett, then?"

"I couldn't refuse him after the trial, what he did for me."

"Yes, I can see how you'd feel it was your duty to marry him after he saved your neck. A loveless match is akin to life in prison, but it's preferable, I suppose, to execution by hanging."

"He said as my husband he could never be made to testify against me even if I was charged with the murder someday."

"I shouldn't think that likely. That would require Jedediah Taylor to get off his fat ass and put together some evidence in the case." He gently turned her chin so he could see her eyes. "You can't go through with it. Not now. We'll leave," he said, "before Garrett gets back to Monterey. We'll go to San Francisco. Put up in a hotel. Send our inquiries about your Aunt Aggie from there. You needn't face him ever again."

"Could we?"

"Well sure. Why not? After we settle any dealings with the law we'll book passage on a China trader. Go as far east as the mood takes us. Stop in Hawaii first. I've been wanting for some time to go there. Do you think you'd like that? To sail across the ocean?"

"I would if this bed were our ship."

Jack whinnied. Clancy got up and went to the window to take a look around. Seeing nothing, he climbed in next to her again. "I thought there was somebody coming." Ordinarily he would have gone outside to check around the little house, but this time he was more interested in the visitor inside. "We'd best get up and dressed. There's the chance some rider on the highway will spot your mare."

She slipped out of bed and dropped her shift over her head. "There's still the matter of the earring. The pair was all I ever had of my mother's, and now Aunt Aggie, too, if she's really gone. I'm going to see Sally Locke directly as I get back to town." She stepped into her drawers.

"You can't just waltz in there unless you're on Louis's list." He pulled on his Levis then sat down to think for a minute.

"Who is Louis?"

"A big muscular type she keeps by her front door. About four times your size. Carries a long knife. Some kind of Indian from up north. His face will give you a turn, all tattooed across his chin and a tall black hat like Lincoln used to wear. He's there to make sure Miss Sally sees only people she wants to see."

She finished closing herself up in her corset and reached for her skirt. "You'll talk to him?"

He opened the drawer in the table and took out his writing things. "Here's how we'll manage it. I have some business here at the ranch having to do with my neighbors putting their cows on my land. We're to meet in a couple of hours so I have to stay here. But I'll give you two letters. One is a note to my banker in Chinatown. I'll put the address on the outside so you'll know where to take it. He'll give you some money, enough for the earring and for us to travel on. The other note is one you can show to Louis when you get to Sally's. I'll put in that you need to see her about buying the earring."

She watched as he wrote out the banking instructions. "Here." He handed her the first note after waving the page in the air to dry the ink. "You can read, can't you?"

"My mother taught me when I was a little girl. The Reverend Parks told Old John to put a stop to it. He said being brought up with all manner of books was bad for me because a female's brain is too small for supporting procreation and book-learning, too. So I had to hide the books my mother had brought with her from Bucks County. She was especially fond of Hawthorne. The books were kept in a trunk. I'd scramble out a volume when my stepfather was in the fields and take it to the barn." She paused to remember the illustrations: winged creatures with hawk bills and lion bodies or a naked swordsman holding aloft the severed head of a woman whose hair was all writhing snakes. "I hid the books one by one in a place where the cat had a nest for kittens. When Old John eventually got around to fetching the books out of the trunk to burn them there was only one left, and that he could not burn as it was a Bible."

"Look that over," he said, as he started writing again.

"A lot of money," she said when she'd read it. She folded the note and put it into her handbag then sat down to pull on her stockings.

"You'd best keep the bulk of it on your person rather than in your handbag," he said. "Think you can manage that?"

"I will," she said.

"Soon as you get through dealing with Sally Locke you come straight back here. If there's any need for you to go to the house at The Grove, do it first before you go to the bank, but it would be better if you don't go back there at all."

"I don't need to," she said, touching the lump of the earring sewn into the hem of her drawers.

"Here's the other." He shoved the second note across the table for her to read. "Does that state it plain enough?"

She read, then nodded. "Yes. Perfectly. I can always show her mine if she's in any doubt as to the earring I want." She put the second note next to the first in her bag and they stood.

He took her in his arms. "Be careful," he said. "Come back to me as quick as you can."

"Don't worry," she smiled. "I will."

He pushed open the door and walked her out to where the horses were nose to nose.

She took up Zorra's reins but couldn't bear to mount until they had kissed once more. "I nearly never knew you," she said. "I nearly decided not to go to Leese's that day. It seemed so rash, so improper."

"Sometimes it's luck," he said. "What the Chinese call joss." He held his hands for her foot to help her into the saddle. When she was up they locked eyes one more time.

"Godspeed," he said. He slapped the red filly's rump and sent Lucy on her way.

He stood for some time stroking Jack's nose and thinking of how pretty she was as she rode off on her filly, all that red hair flying out from the back of her bonnet. He walked into the house, still daydreaming of coconuts and papayas and red curls. His six-guns, holstered in the gun belt slung over the back of a chair, seemed to argue for the other life, the old way. *The twins. You never hugged me back, but then you never let me down, either.* Out of habit, he checked the cylinders, five rounds each. Always one chamber empty. Gave you a chance to chamber a round as a warning. He did it now and felt that same fine edge of anticipation on hearing the ominous fall of the cylinder. He took his time handling them both once more, because he needed to test himself against the notion of finality. But he knew he wouldn't change his mind. This decision, sudden as it was, had never been in doubt. He knew he'd never risk another face-off like the last one at Mussel Slough. Death would come soon enough without inviting it by way of a regular occupation. *Hawaii.*

Chapter Thirty-one

Doc Garrett sat on the rock-hard bench of the dusty car second back from the engine, wearing a brand new pair of spectacles, and glad of it because of the dust and soot sifting in, even though the windows were closed. The man opposite had tied a bandanna over the lower part of his face and looked like a bank robber. Do this long enough, Doc thought, and you'd have respiratory damage, kerchief or no. *It's a modern problem. People didn't have to worry about choking when they followed oxen. Every benefit has its price. You take advantage of speed and convenience at the risk of your health. You possess a woman at the risk of your sanity.* He sighed deeply and wished the train trip were over and the ride to Monterey as well. He wanted only to be near the interminable breakers again when the mists rolled in, soothing as a cool hand on your brow when you could just close your eyes.

All the risks and complexities inherent in progress would perhaps be worthwhile, he reflected, if you could be sure of it. The mails, for instance. Mail came by train now, faster than by sea or stage. And telegrams were even more reliable. Still, he didn't feel confident that Adrian had received the message setting out the time of his arrival. Think of how many opportunities across a whole continent for a few clicks of a transmission to go astray. Sheer lunacy to plan on being met at the station, he thought, naïve anyway. He'd sent the telegram, reluctantly in the first place, knowing if it was received, the wire agent would publish the contents to the entire populace of Monterey. Another modern problem: privacy. He sat a bit straighter in his chair and pulled out the tiny gold-cased pocketknife at the end of his watch chain. He opened it and ran the blade carefully under each fingernail.

The conductor strode up the aisle by and by, absorbing the train's lurching as he came, as if one of his legs was a good deal shorter than the other. "Sa-a-a-linas," he called, "Sa-a-a-linas."

Doc pocketed his knife and grabbed his bag. He stood and scanned the faces on the platform as the train slowed to a stop. He looked for Adrian, though he'd convinced himself that his appearance would be a miracle on a par with the loaves and the fishes. But wonderfully, there he stood under his ridiculous hat, improbable as ever. Garrett sprang down from the door of the carriage to the platform as soon as the train was reasonably stopped and ran to embrace his friend. "Mr. Fiske! By God. You're a sight for sore eyes!"

"Damnation, Doc. I thought this train would never get in."

Doc laughed. "People will think we're veterans of the same unit, slapping backs and hugging like this. Dear old Adrian. I hardly thought you'd come."

"Turns out I should have brought my paints and easel," Fiske replied, "long as the damn train took to get here."

"And what would you have painted?"

Adrian looked around, intrigued by the question. "Impatience," he said. "I would have drawn everything orange, an irritable color. Impatience has a gritty feel, difficult and unrelenting as a blister on your heel, especially if you keep treading on it. Orange. Everything saw-toothed and orange today. You got new eyeglasses while you were back East, didn't you?"

"You don't miss much," Doc replied. "How do you think I look?"

"Like a sawbones."

"By God, I'm glad to see you. I didn't think you'd be here."

"Tell me then, do you think me too much a fool to remember the time and date, or such a skinflint that I'd neglect a friend?"

Garrett laughed, delighting in the old familiar way between them, everything easy and no explanations to make. "Ah, son. Would that you had gone with me to Macon. Life would have pleased me a damn sight better."

"I missed you, too. And the custom at Simoneau's dropped off most drastic."

"They'd no one to revile and ridicule while drinking, so they gave it up?"

"So I hear, but I couldn't swear to it as I never drink a drop myself."

"More's the pity. I've a nip of the creature in my pocket to sip on the way home."

"Do you now. And here I thought you were a practicing Methodist."

"You have me confused with somebody who died, I think."

"This all the bags, then?"

"The rest is coming by freight," Doc replied.

"Good, then we're off." Fiske led the way to where the horses were tied. Doc took the flask out of his pocket and handed it to Adrian. "I sore missed you, friend, and I'm glad to be home."

Adrian drank and passed the flask back. Doc took a pull. "That's welcome, that is. Should ease the pain in my backside."

"What's wrong with your ass?"

"Too much sitting."

"A ride on one of Steadman's nags won't improve your condition any."

"No," Doc said and took another swig. "Best get it over with." They mounted up. "Now, tell me; who missed me most of all?"

"I don't take your meaning," the painter said.

"Don't be an idiot. Tell me; how is she? Pretty as ever?"

"I'd forgotten how much I enjoyed getting drunk with you," Adrian said. "Good thing this nag knows the way home."

"She knows the way to her stable and I've no intention of sleeping there, so look to her. I'm sleeping in my own bed tonight if I have to walk."

"Your new bed, you mean."

"That's right. I plumb forgot. What do you think of it?"

"It was the scandal *du jour* when it came in. All the old biddies saying, 'How many people you reckon he's going to have sleeping with him?' Mrs. Fleming wouldn't even go to put the quilt on it. She made me do it to save herself embarrassment."

He looked up at the western sky. "We don't have more than a couple hours of daylight left. Can't you make that nag of yours go any faster?"

Adrian's jocularity failed him. "You'll get there soon enough," he said.

Doc noticed the merriment had gone out of his voice. "What's wrong? You sounded just then like something was wrong. What is it?"

"Nothing. Steady on."

"Is it Lucy? Is she all right? You've said nothing about her at all."

The painter revived his smile. "She's fine. You should see how she dotes on that filly you bought her. I believe not a day goes by that she isn't in the stall with the animal, always currying."

"And she rides?"

"More and more, these days. I think the exercise agrees with her. She likes to ride out to the valley where the air is drier."

"I thought she would," Doc said. "I've been concerned about her developing pleurisy living near the sea where it's so often chill and damp."

"So tell me about Macon," Adrian said. "How is it between you and your mother now?"

"She loves me."

"What? All is forgiven?"

"No, she's lost her mind. Believes I'm my father. I'd think it was funny if it weren't so damned depressing. I'm like to end up that way myself. It runs in families, you know, diseases of the mind."

"Diseases of the mind? You mean madness. Call it what it is."

"You got a burr under your saddle all of a sudden?" Doc passed the flask. "Take a drink. You need to improve your mood."

Adrian drank. "Sorry ... it's just that ..."

Doc reined in. "Just spit it out."

"There's a thing or two you need to hear before we get back to town. Touching on Lucy."

"Good. You haven't told me near enough about my girl. Is she still eager for her wedding day?" Adrian stole a guilty glance at Doc. Doc's skin began to prickle. "You'd best tell me whatever it is you've got to say."

Adrian cleared his throat and began. "You remember back on San Carlos Day when she went off picking wildflowers. She fell in with Matt Clancy. I think that must be when it started."

Doc flushed a dark red. "What started?"

"She met him at the boardinghouse. Stayed for the better part of an hour in his room."

"How do you know this?"

"Sally's maid is friends with a gal who cleans up for Rosanna Leese. I spoke to the woman myself to make sure. It's true."

Doc didn't speak immediately. "What else?"

"I had her followed about town and when she went riding. Trailed her myself a time or two. Spied her this very morning out at Clancy's shack. Saw her on my way to meet the train. Another time I came upon her out by the lighthouse."

"With Clancy?"

"No, that time she was by herself, but she was—talking. She's lied to you from the start. She speaks."

Doc's eyes went hard. "You have heard her speak?"

"I didn't believe it at first. Thought it was a trick of the wind in the trees. And she's taught Alice songs, some of the ones Luce sings. The tunes don't carry as far as The Grove. No way Alice could have heard them except ..."

Lucy Lied

"But why?"

"It serves some nefarious purpose. How should I know? You need to ask her." He paused to peer at Doc's face to see how he was taking the news, but his friend's features were unreadable in the shadow of his hat brim. "I know how much she means to you. I'm fond of her myself, but ..."

"No, you're not," Doc shot back. His jaw worked. "When I think of all the hours I spent trying to coax a word out of her—the mesmerism, the phrenology—conjuring with every means I—God, what a fool! What a .... And she's betrayed me, too?"

"Likely more than once."

Garrett clenched his fist around the reins. "Is Clancy in town?"

"Judging by her visit to the little house this morning, I expect so."

"When we get to his place I'll stop and talk to him."

"Now Doc," his friend cautioned, "That might not be a good idea. You might want to talk to Lucy first. Hear what she has to say for herself. He's a gunman, for God's sake. You can't be serious."

"I'll see him. You'll ride on toward town. I'll catch you up."

"If he doesn't kill you first. You're not even armed."

"All I want to do is talk. I just want the truth of it from him. I'll deal with Lucy when I get back."

They rode on in silence until they reached the point on the highway where the little house was visible off to the right. "Go on, now," Garrett said.

Adrian began to reason again. "I hope you know what you're doing ..." But seeing it was no good he spurred his mount, leaving Doc alone to contemplate the shack next to the sycamore tree and to plan his next move.

The window at the north end of the dwelling was dark. After a few minutes of listening to the creak of saddle leather as the horse shifted his weight, Doc rode down slowly so as not to alarm anyone who might be sitting inside without a candle. He tied his horse in the shelter of the live oaks behind the cabin and took a look around. The boards had shrunk since the place was built, leaving good-sized chinks. He put his eye to one in the back wall and was able to see enough of the dim interior to know it was empty as he'd first surmised. Stars were beginning to wink in the twilight sky. He took out his flask and downed the last swallow. Then he left the horse and went around to the front of the shack. He found the door unbarred and went inside.

As his eyes adjusted to the dimness he surveyed the Spartan room. Next to a half-burnt candle standing in a holder was a bunch of daisies in a jar on the table next to the bed, a bright spot in the gloom. He imagined his Lucy nosing the flowers, sprawling there on the bed with its coverlet, so carefully made up. He found a matchbox in the bedside table drawer and lit the candle. He held the light up over the bed, drawn by some fatal urge to examine it for any sign of her. He drew down the coverlet and observed that the pillows on both sides had been plumped and smoothed. He felt disappointed that he could see no impression of her head, or better still, her face. For surely she had been there, he knew it. He took the left pillow away and brushed his hand across the linen underneath, finding only cool emptiness. He walked around the foot of the bed and examined the right side just as he had the left, hoping to spy a strand of long red hair, curling languidly. Finding nothing, he sat for some time on the edge of the bed, thinking that it was just as likely to have drifted onto the floor between the headboard and the wall, never to be seen by anyone ever. *Maybe it wasn't true after all.* His second thoughts carried little weight, a protest of her innocence amid a whirlwind of conviction to the contrary.

As he replaced the candle on the nightstand he saw a tiny object next to the vase and a little behind, as if hidden on purpose. He felt, as he picked it up, that all his suspicions had been vindicated. *A button from a lady's glove. Adrian was right.* He thrust the little object into his pocket. A wave of wrath surged through him. Suddenly warm, he drew out his handkerchief and blotted his upper lip. *Calm down.* When he returned the handkerchief to his breast pocket, it seemed to pulse against his heart, a silent witness to his suspicions. He rose and put the pillows back in place, drew up the coverlet and smoothed it, making everything as it had been. Then he blew out the candle and crossed the room. He pulled out a chair at the table by the window and sat down to wait.

Chapter Thirty-two

For Lucy the hours since she'd left Clancy had crawled by. There was the long ride back to Monterey, normally such a breezy trot, then the waiting for Clancy's Chinese banker to assemble the cash. Once she had it, she'd stepped into the deserted alley to stuff the cash into her bodice, all except for twenty dollars. That was as high as she'd bid for the earring. She nearly broke into a run as she approached Franklin where she turned to the right. Sally's house was two blocks farther on Washington.

With its cut-glass chandelier, the many gilt-framed mirrors and fancy wallpaper, Sally Locke's house of ill repute was by far the grandest place she had ever set foot inside and, insofar as it was a place of cultivated sin, she considered it by far the most dangerous. The man who greeted her at the front door was, if not the devil incarnate, at least a close approximation of what her imagination had always pictured. His giant stature alone would have discouraged most people from entering. Add to that the black tracery that covered his chin, his black brows and the fiercely gleaming and perfect teeth. Had she not been in character as a mute, Lucy was sure she would still have been tongue-tied. Hard enough to just stand there and wait for his nod to pass in.

Once inside, she found that all her haste up to that point had been useless. The mistress was abed. Louis told her he would not carry the note to her until four, her normal hour of waking. Then he seated her in Sally's parlor and resumed his lugubrious watch over the front door.

She passed the time sitting in the silence of Sally Locke's front room trying to imagine the clients who would come to wait for a certain girl, wondering what it would be like to bed with several different men in one night. It struck her that they were all men from town, the husbands of women she knew, perhaps, men she might nod at in passing on the street. *How queer.* She thought of Doc and wondered if he'd sat where she was sitting, waited as she was waiting. Why wouldn't he? Even the most genteel men had their appetites. She felt hot, thinking of Clancy, his kiss.

Finally a clock in another room somewhere struck four. A few minutes later, Louis came to summon her. She started toward the staircase. Louis laid a firm hand on her arm. "Down here," he said, and pointed to the door of a ground floor apartment. She could hear a lovely melody issuing from inside as she knocked. It abruptly stopped and a striking woman opened the door. She'd heard Sally Locke was a beauty but she'd never expected such a magnificent creature. Everything about her seemed exotic: the raven ringlets, the maize-colored dressing gown, the sumptuous bosom. "Ah, *bonsoir*, Lucy! I have long wanted to meet Doc's little friend."

It struck her as odd. *Only Ellis has ever called me 'little.'* There was something of Ellis's charm about Sally Locke, something beguiling. She moved with a certain grandeur, as if she were on stage, sweeping her hand from the doorway into the room as she spoke.

"Please come in and make yourself comfortable on the divan, *chérie*. I just had a pot of tea brought in. It's still fresh and hot if you care for a cup."

Lucy sat down and shook her head, wishing she were already gone from this place.

Sally sat next to her, a bit too close.

"It pleases me that we meet at long last. Ever since the trial I have wanted to make your acquaintance. I hope maybe someday after Doc has restored your power of speech you will tell me everything about yourself."

Lucy smiled at the bizarre suggestion. Even after only a minute in the madam's company, Lucy was aware of a current of something dark and unsettling underneath the friendly words.

"There is so much I find curious about you. You've heard, maybe, about the man the sheriff found at the mission, the one who claims to know you. He is deranged, *n'est-ce pas?* How could it be otherwise?"

Lucy kept her face a studied blank under Sally's close observation.

"I'm sure there are other women who go by your name. He must be speaking of one of them." She made a dismissive wave of her hand. "He is a drunk. He makes no sense."

Lucy studied the tea service on the table in front of her.

"But we should speak of your business," Sally said, producing the letter from her pocket and unfolding it. "I see Matt Clancy writes on your behalf." She paused and her dark eyes flicked at Lucy, who felt as if she'd just seen a snake query the air with its forked tongue. "I wonder how you know this man. Why he would do your bidding?"

Sally smiled. "But no matter. You are Doc's fiancée and no doubt this brings you a wide acquaintance. Still, I don't think there's much love between Doc and Matt Clancy. I wonder if Doc is quite content to have Clancy as your confidant. That is, assuming Doc knows you and Clancy are friends. Does he?"

Clancy had signed his name to the note in order to make sure Sally Locke would take the matter seriously, to hint that if she refused, there would be the gunman to deal with. Lucy felt herself blushing at the thought of him, a telltale sign she could not suppress.

Sally's eyes gleamed with pleasure. "Well, it's usual for a wife to know very little of her husband's affairs. I suppose sometimes it is the husband who is in the dark."

Lucy pulled open her purse strings and took out ten dollars. She put the money on the table and waited.

Lucy Lied

Sally rose from the couch and returned with a small marquetry box. She sat down again and held the box so Lucy could see inside as she lifted the lid. There lay the garnet earring, the mate to Lucy's.

"This is what you came for," Sally said.

Just as Lucy was reaching for the gem, Sally snapped the box closed and placed it on her lap under her folded hands. Lucy felt herself go cold.

"It occurs to me that we each have something the other wants," Sally said. "You have Doc and I have your earring." She paused to see if Lucy would respond. "If we could but trade two objects there would be no problem. But Doc is a man, a foolish, petulant man with no more understanding of what is good for him than a child who will not eat his supper."

Sally summoned Louis by means of a dainty silver bell, so petite and musical it hardly seemed possible it would draw forth the brute who guarded the door.

"He wants you," Sally continued, "and there will be no changing his mind, not while you're still here for him to pine for."

Then it hit her. She was in danger. Lucy sprang to her feet, knocking into the table at her knees. A teacup hit the floor. She took several quick steps toward the door only to find Louis suddenly before her. He seized her and covered her nose and mouth with an ether-soaked cloth. She struggled wildly, until her limbs refused to obey her. Before her eyes, the colors of the room went muddy, as if a cloud of brown dust had gathered at the corners, pulling in toward the middle until she could see only the brightness of the chandelier, and then that, too, was drowned in sepia.

She could hear Sally Locke's voice, sounding far away. "Go quickly. Take this bag of hers. And send Rose up here. That woman spilt tea on my carpet."

Rose, always the prompt and willing servant, took an inordinately long time to appear. It was she who bound Lucy's hands and feet, tied a silken kerchief over her eyes and made sure she was breathing regularly. While Louis counted the money she'd given him for his silence, Rose waited at the back door for two friends, two Chinese who came in place of the one who had been contracted to dispose of Lucy's body after Louis had cut her throat. Before laying hands on the unconscious woman to carry her out, they each spoke an incantation in their particular dialects, only one of which Rose knew, but she understood both all the same. They were speaking to the woman with the auspicious red hair, asking her pardon for the necessity of restraints and for carrying her like a bag of rice. "Give her opium when she wakes," Rose told them. "It will keep her quiet until the ship is at sea."

Chapter Thirty-three

Doc stared out the window at the silhouette of the hills. It wouldn't be long before the last bit of evening light drained from the sky. Riders appeared coming down the highway from the north. Five or six, riding hard. He jumped from the chair, slipped out the front door, and made quick and quiet around the south end of the cabin to where his horse stood tethered in the deep shadows of the live oak trees. He untied the reins, ready to mount in a flash. Doing his best to exude calm, he stroked the mare's nose and whispered, "Shhh, shhh." Perhaps the riders wouldn't stop at the house. If they did, perhaps he could remain undetected. Failing that, he hoped the old nag had one good run for the barn left in her. He saw the animal's ears pitch forward as the horsemen pulled up on the other side of the house. *Damn!* He held her head close to his chest and whispered, "Shhh."

A few moments passed as the riders tied their mounts out front. He heard their boots on the porch, the door scraping open, a woman's voice. A wavering light came through the chinks between the boards of the back wall. They'd lit the oil lamp.

Another rider came up fast, from the south this time, and reined in out front. There was some commotion among the animals. Garrett's mare twitched her ears and tried to pull away. "Shhh. Shhh."

A second later, he heard voices from inside. "Ah, here is our host. Buenas noches, Señor Clancy. I thought maybe you had forgotten our meeting."

"Sorry I'm late."

Doc let go of the mare. She dropped her head and began to crop grass. "Good girl," he whispered. He stepped slowly to the wall, got down into a squat and pressed one eye to a chink to peer inside. Besides Clancy, he saw Isabel Vásquez and four men.

Clancy unfastened his gun belt and wound it around the holstered weapons, a sign that he wasn't expecting to have to use them. Doc thought of dead men he'd buried, how their sidearms were often bundled that way before being laid down in a casket where the action would rust and the leather would molder away along with the deceased.

Clancy laid his rawhide gloves on the table. They copied the curl of his fingers even after he'd taken them off. Garrett thought of personal belongings, things that took on the character of the owner. He fancied Clancy's gloves took that form because they didn't believe in a life apart from what they'd always known, railroad work, no starting over.

Oreña and the others stood aside as Isabel came to the table with a dispatch case. "I have the agreement here," she said. "I hope you have not changed your mind."

She seemed tense, probably piqued by Oreña's boorish presence, Garrett thought. Or was it fear he saw, her ivory cheek a little more pale than usual? He couldn't be sure.

"Let's get down to it," Clancy said.

"Yes," Oreña said, approaching the table. "Let us."

Three other men came to stand behind Oreña, causing Clancy to ask, "You brought enough witnesses, you think?"

"Oh, them?" Oreña grinned again. "We have some new cattle to brand. There's supposed to be a full moon tonight. Good for working."

Clancy grinned. "Good for rustling, too, I've heard tell."

Oreña ignored the provocation. "They will get started as soon as we have signed the papers." Oreña's cowhands fingered the bulldogging ropes hanging from their belts.

"I'll sign your agreement," Clancy said, "or we can talk about a price for the land if you want to buy it back. I'm prepared to be very reasonable."

Isabel's lip curled in a sneer. "I should buy what is mine by right?"

"Now, señora," Clancy said. "You know it isn't yours. You've had both the church and state in Sacramento examine your claim. And they've not found in your favor. The best you can do now is to buy it back for a token sum. If you consider the price you're prepared to pay just for grazing, a purchase might be more reasonable."

"Say what price you are thinking," Oreña said.

Clancy pulled out the drawer of the table and found a pen and a bottle of ink. He took a small notebook from his shirt pocket and wrote a figure on one of the blank pages. Isabel looked at the number.

"Why have you not said before that you want to sell? Are you not building a house?" Oreña nodded west toward the rise where the frame of the new structure stood.

"I've recently thought of travel," Clancy said, "maybe leaving California altogether. It's as simple as that. I don't care what the land will be worth in two years or five. I don't intend to wait around that long, so I might as well sell up now." He tore the sheet out of his notebook and penned his initials next to the dollar figure. "I'll stand by that price," he said, as he handed the slip of paper to Isabel. "If you don't want the deal, I got a man up north will snap it up right quick."

She passed the slip of paper to Oreña. "Sebastián, what do you think? If we put our assets together we wouldn't even need a note. You said yourself you thought the grazing fee was too dear. This is surely a much better arrangement."

He flashed a dismissive smile at her before pocketing the piece of paper. "What would you know about notes and deals?" He raised his chin at one of the men standing near Clancy. Oreña's man seized Clancy from behind and dragged him up out of the chair. The pen clattered to the table.

"What kind of double-cross—" Clancy cried out.

Oreña drew his sidearm and shot Isabel Vásquez in the chest.

Garrett's horse pulled free and hightailed it at the sound of the shot. He considered chasing through the live oaks after it, but couldn't take his eyes off the scene in the house.

Isabel had staggered backward two steps into the wall. Her eyes dropped to the white lace showing at the front of her dress, now ragged and red-stained. She looked up at Oreña. "What have you done? Why?"

Oreña took Clancy's guns off the table. "For my cousin, an innocent old fool who loved you better than you deserved, you murdering bitch."

With one hand pressed to the hole in her chest, she slid down the wall and came to rest in a heap of tulle on the floor.

"Tie his hands," Oreña commanded.

"You'll never get away with this," Clancy growled. He nearly struggled free but the other vaquero rushed to assist in restraining him.

Oreña removed the two six-shooters from Clancy's gun belt. He waited until Isabel's eyes had closed and then fired a round from one of Clancy's guns into her chest. He passed Clancy's sidearms to his vaqueros who fired rounds into the woman until both of the guns were empty. That done, they hustled Clancy outside.

Garrett moved away from the house and into the trees. A minute later he saw one of the vaqueros lead Clancy's horse to stand beneath the sycamore. The other men followed, wrestling Clancy toward the tree.

"You won't get away with this," Clancy bluffed. "I expect Sam has heard those shots and is already heading over at the gallop. He'll be here any minute."

In the darkness Garrett could see the white flash of Oreña's teeth as he smiled. "Any minute? In that case, he will be too late."

Lucy Lied

As Oreña spoke he strolled toward the sycamore tree. "By that time you will be dead. He will look at your corpse swinging from this tree and at the woman inside there and think that you and my cousin's wife had a disagreement while discussing the sale of the land. You shot her in anger. So much anger to empty both guns into her. The rope!" he snapped to one of the hands.

They settled a noose around Clancy's neck and lifted him onto the saddle of the tall yellow horse that stood patiently under a stout limb of the sycamore tree. Someone tossed the bitter end of the rope over the bough. Oreña and the others climbed onto their horses, bringing the last mount over to the man taking tension on the rope. Once astride, he tied the rope off to his saddle horn. Oreña continued to narrate his version of events. "These two vaqueros, they decided to take justice into their own hands. They strung you up and took the money that Isabel had brought to make the deal. I'm afraid they are going to disappear with their loot. They will be seen riding toward Mexico." Oreña reached into the saddlebag and took out two bundles of cash. He tossed one to each of the two men who had opted for a trip south. They spurred their horses and took to the highway.

"You forgot there are eleven slugs in Isabel Vásquez," Clancy said, trying one last ploy. "One doesn't match the rest. How does that square with your story?"

"You think the sheriff will try to find some other killer when he's got you to pin it on, all tied up and hanged for him, nice and neat? I think not. I think he's going to dance on your grave."

"But the whole thing's crazy. Why would I shoot her eleven times?"

Clancy's mount took a step forward, tightening the noose. At Jack's flank, Oreña held up his hand as if he were signaling the start of a race. "You got any last words? Something you want to say before you see God?"

Clancy began to speak as the wind rose. His words were lost in the rustling of the sycamore leaves. Then the breeze abruptly ceased and Doc heard the last of what Clancy had to say. The abbreviated epitaph would always stick with him, maybe because the very last word out of the gunman's mouth was "picturesque."

Oreña chose that moment to slap the horse on the rump. The blond stallion leapt forward, leaving his rider swinging in a wide arc that grew shorter and shorter till it stopped.

Chapter Thirty-four

The moon was up, flooding the landscape with pale light that turned grass and trees to pewter. As he reached the top of the rise where the skeleton of Clancy's new house stood, he saw the horse nibbling the grass twenty feet down-slope on the other side. The nag raised its head and snorted, as if pained that it had taken so long for Garrett to come and find her. "Shut up, you," Doc said as he came slowly forward and made a grab for the dangling reins. The mare jerked her head and ran off just as Garrett thought he had her. "Damn you, you faithless bitch!" There was nothing to do but walk down to where she stood sniffing the air with defiance in her eyes. Again he crept up slowly to within a few feet. Again she bolted seconds before he could catch the reins. How long the comedy went on he could not tell precisely. Suffice it to say, the only reason the mare eventually allowed herself to be caught was that she'd grown bored with the game.

Having succeeded in his last lunge, Garrett wound the reins around his hand and drew the animal to him. "God help the next rider who neglects to hobble you. Don't think I won't tell Steadman as much." He mounted and turned her head toward Monterey. He gave the corpse in the sycamore wide birth as he traveled on an arc to the highway. Having reached it, he turned south. He had his story down pat by the time he saw four riders coming fast in the opposite direction.

Taylor and his posse reined in as Doc approached. "Evening, Sheriff," Doc said. "Looks like you're chasing some miscreant."

"You see anything wrong up at the little house? I had word from one of Sebastián Oreña's vaqueros who was out branding there was trouble at Clancy's place. He rode right into town to tell me, but I was attending to some business and didn't get the word till just about an hour ago."

"My horse got spooked and threw me on the other side of his place. I followed the worthless plug off to the west a ways, then she got the smell of home and turned south. By the time I caught her I found myself down this way a good bit. Didn't get close enough to the little house to see any goings-on there."

"You best turn around and come with us," Taylor said. "May be a body or two." Doc joined the group that set off again, but at a slower pace than before, as if the sheriff no longer had a sense of urgency. "You coming home from Macon?" Taylor asked.

"Got into Salinas today," Garrett answered. He omitted the details, knowing Taylor would think it odd if he said Adrian had gone on ahead halfway home.

They pulled up in the yard, noting the hoof prints of several riders in the dust. Doc dismounted carefully, thinking as he did that he must take care to look shocked, as if he were seeing the business at the little house for the first time.

"You all right, Doc?" Taylor asked.

"Yeah," Doc said. He joined the posse standing slack-jawed around the body hanging from the sycamore branch.

"New rope," Taylor said. It had stretched almost far enough for Clancy's inert toes to touch the ground. "Looks like it took quite a long time for him to die."

Garrett nodded with the detached air of a man of science. He examined the corpse, noting the distortion of the facial muscles, set in rigor after the airway had finally squeezed shut. "I'd have him down," he said after he'd finished.

Lucy Lied

Taylor addressed his men. "Okay, boys. Cut this one down." He turned to Doc. "If there's somebody shot they must be inside."

Doc followed Taylor to the doorway of the little house where the lawman paused. "Good God," the sheriff said, as he took in the body sitting against the wall, the soles of her shoes pointing to ten and two o'clock, her head lolled to one side. Isabel Francisca Vásquez was beautiful, even in death. Her lips were still full and red, as red as the blood soaking her chest that had obliterated all the white of her blouse. The lawman stood back and let Doc get on with it.

The amount of blood on the floor made it difficult to examine her without getting it on his shoes. Gingerly he moved close enough to put his fingers to her throat to confirm that life was extinct. "She's cool," he said. He sat back on his heels and surveyed the wreckage of her bodice. He faked a rough count though he distinctly remembered the number of shots as they had rung out in the night. "Eleven holes," he said. *That's a trouble*, he thought. Taylor would surely ask if he'd heard the shots. He called to mind something he'd read about shadow zones, that during the war there were spots very close to the battlefield where spectators would gather to watch. Occasionally they would report in amazement that not a single sound of the battle raging could be heard. That was why he'd heard nothing as he ran after his horse. That's what he would say.

But Taylor never asked what Doc had heard.

Taylor examined Matt Clancy's two six-guns where they lay on the table by the window. "Both guns empty of rounds," he said. "Presumably discharged by Clancy—but why? What had Isabel Vásquez done to deserve such a dose of lead? Don't figure. Not if you believe half the stories you've ever heard about Clancy. The man was a womanizer—not one to waste a nice looking female."

Doc reflected on whether or not Taylor was likely to come up with a theory of the tragedy that lay close to home. *Could I have done such a thing if I'd found him with Lucy?* He tried to imagine how it would have played out.

Taylor continued to sketch out his version of events. "Both Clancy and Isabel are fully clothed, so they weren't surprised in

300

bed. Would have been more logical if they had been, easier to disarm the gunman if he was enjoying some horizontal recreation. But Clancy with his boots on? Easier said than done. Bastard didn't get a reputation for invincibility based on letting other men relieve him of his iron. Men. Okay, so there must have been more than one. Then it couldn't have been a love triangle. Isabel was a widow, anyway. No husband to betray." Taylor sighed, pulled his hat off and scratched his head. "Well, not my job to explain the why of it." He put his hat back on and turned away from the corpse against the wall. "You ready? Let's load her up with the one outside."

"Drop them both at the undertaker's," Doc said. "Say I'll be up there directly to do the autopsies."

"I'll take the slugs you dig out of the woman," Taylor replied. Need to make sure they all match Clancy's shooters."

Doc nodded. "I'm not averse to collecting my fee from the county."

Taylor looked at the tracks in the dust under the sycamore then lifted his eyes and squinted toward the rise beyond which lay the stream and the cattle. "Reckon I'll go on over and talk to the vaqueros. See if anybody has a notion about what went on over here."

Taylor and Garrett mounted up and rode off in different directions. The doctor followed the buckboard back to town while the lawman went to seek Sebastián Oreña's men among his cows. Taylor was surprised to find the boss working alongside the cowhands, stringing barbed wire by moonlight, finishing the job Clancy had begun with the objective of keeping the cattle inside rather than out.

"You got quite the work ethic," Taylor said to the Mexican.

"Will be easier to round them up when it is time to take them to market," Oreña said by way of explanation, since he'd always maintained the wire was the work of the devil. "Besides, it's my land now. What I do is no business of yours."

Taylor nodded back toward the little house. "Two birds with one stone. How'd you manage it?"

"She came to discuss the land. Apparently they could not come to an agreement on price."

"I'd have liked to be there when you put that necktie on him. I'll bet he wasn't so cocksure then."

"He said he wanted his hired man Sam to have his gloves. They are good gloves, he said. I think I will keep them for myself, though. I, too, take pleasure in such things." Taylor watched the leather stretch tight over Oreña's knuckles as the Mexican made a fist.

"What else?"

"He said many other crazy things, about when he was with the Chinese in the Sierras, cutting through a mountain of stone with chisels and mallets. He said something about how you risk blowing yourself to hell with dynamite or getting buried under sixty feet of snow in winter so some fat Eastern bankers can sit in comfort in a Pullman car crossing the mountains. So they can look out the windows and call it ... picturesque. That was the word he said. Picturesque."

"What in Sam Hill does that mean?"

Chapter Thirty-five

Doc remembered that cot at Felipe Vásquez's footboard, how the icy Isabel had invited him to bed her there as the old invalid lay dying. He dug his forceps into the meat of her chest and pulled out another spent round. He examined it briefly before dropping it into a porcelain vessel. So far only one slug didn't match; only one had come from a gun other than Clancy's twin Army Colts. Popular lore had it that she'd had lovers, but only while her husband lived. Once the old man died, she had assumed a different identity, that of a woman in need of no man, at least that's what people said. And it was true she stayed less often with her cousin at the boardinghouse once she became a widow. Perhaps her own house had become more of a home with the male presence expunged.

He sighed and looked at the slugs in the porcelain bowl. All of her plans, whatever they were, had come to this. It was discouraging in a more profound sense than any disappointment having to do with land or pride. Maybe only because it was a woman he was digging lead out of instead of a man. Or maybe ... He thought of Lucy and how much he had trusted her, how she seemed a different species, not a woman capable of cheating and lies but something purer, like a dumb creature, a good dog. *God damn.* He flung another spent round into the bowl. It clanged and rolled like a roulette ball before settling. *She was just like the rest. Maybe worse. More resourceful, coming up with the mute act.*

He was putting off seeing her. He didn't know what to say, how to communicate his rage, formulate it into action. His hands were steady as granite as he asked himself what he would do. The next spent round clanged against the side of the porcelain pan. "Damned if I know," he said.

When he was satisfied that he had extracted the lump of lead at the bottom of each hole in Isabel Francisca's body, he counted all the .44's and came up with ten. There was only the one of a slightly smaller caliber, ironically the kill shot that had shattered her heart. After that bullet had found its mark, the rest were just for show, just to give Bronson a gripping tale of blood and blame. He dropped the smaller round into the pocket of his vest and touched the glove button stashed there next to the pocketknife at the fob end of his watch chain. *Has she been told? Does she know about her lover?* He dropped his forceps and stripped off his apron. *She must hear it from me so I can watch her face. I'll see the truth written there when she hears Clancy is dead.*

He marched to Peabody's front door, put on his hat and coat, and stepped outside. It seemed the whole night had passed away while he had conducted the two autopsies, stopping often to sit stunned, draining cup after cup of the undertaker's weak coffee. As he made his way to The Grove, he saw nothing of the daylight-dazzled bay, nor did he note the acrid scent of the burnt offerings rising with the smoke from the Chinese joss house. He heard neither the screams of the gulls as they tore bits of blubber from the carcass of a beached whale, nor the insistent rattle of the surge retreating from the shingle beach. He felt not the warmth of the sun nor the sting of the salt spray, only the tattoo of blood in his throat under the starched whiteness of his collar. *Damn her. Damn her. Damn her.* The curse echoed in his brain all the way to the Methodist camp, all the way to Mrs. Fleming's door.

The old woman opened up to his raised fist before he'd had a chance to knock. "She isn't here," she said, before he'd had a chance to speak.

"Where is she?" he asked.

"Gone," she replied. "You'd better come in."

He entered and followed her to the hearth in the front room.

"Stay and warm yourself a minute. You look like death."

"Where is she?" he said again.

"I have no idea. I didn't see her leave. I was out hanging the laundry on the line first thing yesterday. When I came back inside ... I thought perhaps she'd gone riding. I didn't think anything of it until it was close to suppertime. I never saw her before I went to bed. She never came home last night. This morning I looked through the room she shares with Alice to see if she'd left a note. There was none. I don't know if she even knew how to write. She took nothing with her, not even smallclothes. I don't know. I just don't know."

"Clancy's dead," Garrett said. "She comes back here, you tell her that and send for me."

She nodded, asked nothing as if she already knew.

He turned to leave.

"Where are you going?"

"Steadman's."

To the stable he went forthwith but upon arriving learned nothing except that Lucy had not used the red filly to make good her escape. Finally Doc arrived at Sally's Locke's, where he should have gone in the first place, since Sally always managed to learn about everything that was going on in town, especially matters of stagecraft or stealth. Louis met Garrett at the street door and didn't hesitate to direct him to her apartment even though it was well past that time of day when Sally Locke was normally in bed alone and asleep. "She's expecting you," he said.

Sally Locke was sitting at her dressing table, admiring her image in the glass. She wore a dress the color of red wine with a neckline that bared her handsome bosom and her shoulders. The burgundy frock tinted her skin the way a setting red sun hues the landscape. When she saw him in the mirror she set down the bauble she was playing with and rose from her seat. "Ah, *mon cher!*" she said, her skirts whispering as she came to greet him. "Forever you have been gone. Now finally, finally you have come back to me."

Lucy Lied

He went straight to her sideboard and poured a brandy. "You?"

She nodded and accepted a crystal snifter from him. "*Merci.* We must toast to your safe return."

He downed his drink in one swallow. "Don't play with me. You know what I want."

"Of course," she purred. "I know what you want to know and what you want to know I know."

"Where is she?"

Sally stepped back to her dressing table and picked up the gem she had been fingering when he came in. "There is a proper way to tell this story." She hung the garnet trinket in her earlobe. "If you would hear it you must sit down and not interrupt."

He complied wordlessly, flopping onto her green velvet divan.

"Yesterday," she began, "it was late afternoon, not long after I had arisen. Louis sent me word that your Lucy was waiting to see me."

Doc scowled. "What did she want?"

"This *bijou* I bought at Ortin's store." She pulled back her hair so he could see it plainly.

"She spoke?"

Sally shook her head. "She had a letter to explain."

"What the hell!"

"I was as surprised as you when she came in here and threw off the hood of her cloak. She was wearing traveling clothes. And she had money. I don't know where she got it. Seemed like a lot of cash." Sally smiled. "She didn't say, though she could have if she'd had a mind to."

"Adrian told you he heard her speak?"

"He did. Came here to see what I thought—should he tell you or not, about that and the other thing."

"The meeting with Clancy."

"Not just one, *cher*. She was seen out at the little house, too. That red horse is hard to hide. Even when it's tethered in the bushes that color draws the eye."

"You had her watched?"

"It seems like you might thank me."

"For what?"

"Saving you from marrying a faithless liar. Of course, you could say it wasn't me who saved you, since she left town."

"When?"

"This morning's packet, I suspect. I really don't know for a fact. But it stands to reason."

"You didn't sell her the earring."

"No. Considering who it was wanted it, I decided to keep it for myself." She turned from the mirror to face him. "I took pleasure in denying her. She seemed to want it so badly. Apart from that it means nothing to me." She took the jewel from her ear and threw it at Garrett. "Take it. Keep it against the day she comes back. Tell her you pried it out of my hands. It will perhaps warm her." She moved to a sideboard and took a revolver from the top drawer. "You can have this, too." She handed him the sidearm, grip first. "I was lucky to get it off her before she used it on me. Little fool didn't have a round in the chamber."

"This is mine. Lucy had this?"

"Yes, she had it! She threatened to shoot me with it if I didn't hand over the garnet. After I took it away from her, I shouted for Louis and he put her out."

"Without a thought for her welfare? Where she might go?"

"I don't care. I hope she goes straight to the devil. And you're a fool if you feel any different. I tell you she lied every time she looked at you and said nothing. She took up with another man as soon as you left for Macon. She stole that piece and used it to threaten me in my own house. I suppose you wish she had shot me, then you would say, 'Oh, my poor little Lucy! Did that nasty trigger bruise your finger?' Why don't you go and find her if you love her so much! Search the world over and see if you can find her. Such a fool deserves a fool's errand."

"That's a lousy thing to say. Even for a green-eyed monster like you."

"At least I'm honest. You know where you stand with me."

He tossed the gun aside and laid his head against the back of the divan, suddenly very tired.

Sally felt that his wrath was spent. "Why don't you stay here a while? Let me play for you."

"I'd like that," he said, "but I have reports to write on two corpses up at Peabody's. I should have done them before I left there but he was knocking together pine boxes with a vengeance. I feel like he was hammering inside my skull."

She gave him a look of incomprehension.

Doc put on a look of amazement. "What? You haven't heard yet? Your spies are letting you down. It's Clancy and Isabel Vásquez. They had some dispute over the land Felipe gambled away. The two of them met at the little house and one way or another Clancy shot her dead. Then I guess some vaqueros heard the shots and came running. Found Clancy standing over Isabel's body and strung him up."

"*Mon Dieu!* And your Lucy will be waiting for him in San Francisco as we speak, or wherever it is they'd planned to meet so they could run away together. So farce turns to tragedy."

Doc ignored her reference to Lucy. "On my way in from Salinas I ran into Taylor riding out to investigate. He had me go with him to the little house. They were both long dead by the time I got there."

"The land will pass to Sebastián Oreña now."

"I suppose." He poked the garnet earring in his vest pocket where it nestled against the glove button, the gold pocketknife and the spent round he'd dug out of Isabel's chest, the one that didn't match the ten .44's from Clancy's Colts. He rubbed his eyes. "I was up all night. Brandy seems to have gone to my head."

"Write your reports later on, after you've slept. We'll have a dinner brought in. And a bottle of my good wine. I'll tell Louis to kill a capon."

"All right, as long as you don't let the cook go stuffing it with cornbread. I ate enough cornbread at my mother's house to be stuffed with it myself."

"*Bien. Pas de* cornbread."

Chapter Thirty-six

He felt some better after a few hours of sleep at Sally's and a decent meal. Still, he wasn't quite himself. There was an eerie tinge to the evening, as if all the familiar places along Alvarado Street had turned ghostly in the long, low rays of the late afternoon sun, The Rookery most of all with its sentinel ravens on the roof. He felt as if he'd come full circle in the last ten years, arcing back to that first day when the town was all new to him. He cast his mind back deliberately, thinking, as he made his way slowly and a decade removed, about fate and inevitability.

He remembered, having stepped off the stagecoach into the sun-baked intersection of two dirt tracks that passed for the middle of town, how he badly wanted ether, inhaled oblivion that produced no hangover. But the only option within the dusty precincts of Alvarado Street was ardent spirits. He pulled his hat low over his eyes, imitated the expression his father used to wear when he wanted no part of an argument, and entered a grimy saloon. Despite this expression, the barman couldn't resist, as he obliged Garrett's request for a shot. "Where you coming from, stranger?"

"Saint Louis."

"What I figured. You got that look of a man just come in on the stage. Am I right?" The barman glanced conspicuously at the carpetbag near the customer's feet on the floor. "We got a boy at Steadman's livery who carries freight if you got any baggage needs hauling."

"I have a trunk to go to a place they call The Rookery."

"Thaddeus Battle's old place?" The barman shook his head. "Steadman's boy may not want to do it. He's a mite suspicious. Heard old Doc Battle died in the house and had his eyes picked out by crows. Must be he fears the Grim Reaper's still lurking about up there, or the spirit of the dead man."

Back then, on that first day, he'd had no idea what to expect as he crested the bluff. He'd seen the gap in the mantle of pines and caught his first glimpse of it, from the close-in chop, all steely gray, clear out to the pale edge of the world where it merged with sky. He remembered running through the trees to the brink of the bluff in a state of anxious anticipation as if the water might drain away over the horizon before he could stand close enough to hear the swash rattling the shingle and smell the tang of brine and feel the salted edge of the breeze. When he came to the brow of the headland, there it lay, the expanse of the bay equally impossible as the thought of its absence. It pushed slowly shoreward and, running shallow up the beach, sank into the sand. He wanted to possess it as his own. Others may have regarded the bight of Monterey a thousand times, but not with his discovering eye.

It was the same thing with her, he thought, twenty-four hours after learning of her betrayal. As he made his way to the front gate and up the sandy walk to the front porch, the memory of her pierced his soul with longing. She became at one stroke the new matriarch of his misery, each sin of hers an irritating impurity that would pearl over in time with constantly being worried the way a bad tooth is constantly tongued. From the roof the ravens scoffed at him as he pushed open the front door.

He entered and without taking off his hat or coat, went straight to the room to the left at the top of the stairs. The trunk seemed rather empty now that the quilt pieces were no longer folded inside. He lifted the edge of the boat cloak left from his grandfather's time in the navy and stowed the glove button, the spent slug, the garnet and the gun underneath. Then he lowered himself to the floor in the diminishing square of sunlight that briefly warmed the boards at this time of the year and sat with his loss. He sat still and long as if the life had gone out of him, his brain consumed with the idea of emptiness, the fancy that all the steamy viscera of his body had been replaced by sawdust and that he could no more rise off the floor than if he were a rag doll. He teased himself that he could be the first of his kind. Since rag dolls were always female, he could be the rag Adam, guilty of rag Original Sin—hardly possible with only an upturned crescent of chain-stitched yarn for a mouth, but surely the religious tribes of the world would find a way to explain it all.

He heard a scraping of the front door opening and heard, "Doctor? Are you here? It is Ida Fleming."

He gathered his stiff joints under him. "Coming."

Mrs. Fleming waited at the bottom of the stairs with her pale gray eyes lifted to the space at the top where she expected him to appear. He noted they were more bloodshot than usual. As he approached her, he saw a new tide of tears rising within the lower lids. "I thought you might like me to make you some supper, or maybe just coffee. I brought some bread and currant jelly as I thought there would be nothing in the larder."

"Good of you to come," he said. "Things are much changed since we last saw each other here."

She nodded. "I confess that I had intended to take the quilt off the bed before you came home, knowing the sight of it would be upsetting to you."

"The quilt?" He grinned and uttered a bleak, barking laugh. "Would that were the only reminder of my folly."

"Folly? That strikes me as a strange word to use."

"No doubt it's the word the whole town applies to me." He glared at her. "Everyone knew she was playing me false, it seems, but no one bothered to tell me. It occurs to me that maybe you never wanted the match to succeed, that it might have interfered with your notion of what my service to the Methodist ladies should entail."

"I have no idea what you mean!"

"I suppose I owe you all my bachelor hours, my undivided attention."

"How dare you!"

"A wife would have displaced you, so when you saw your chance, you let my sparrow fly without raising a hand to catch her."

"It was not me who chased her away," she said, straightening her spine and raising her chin. "It's only yourself you have to blame. Look in the mirror if you wish to assign guilt."

"For leaving her unattended. Oh, pardon me. I trusted my friends to look after her till I returned. I was guilty of too much innocence."

"I think not," Ida Fleming retorted, her sense of outrage having reached full flame. "You drove her away with all your poking and prodding, measuring her head with calipers, examining her teeth as if she were a horse you thought to buy. You never wanted to know her, only to cure her, to work a miracle of science that might gain you a name in this world. Don't I know from sweeping up all the crumpled pages of your writings, flung all over the floor of the surgery?"

"To cure the infirmities of my fellow man is now a sin in your straight and narrow book?"

"The sin is in trumpeting your so-called cure. That is the sin of pride. And God has seen fit to punish you for it."

"Only you would see the hand of Providence in the small doings of a whore."

"You think a woman less fit for God's attention than a man? Even in sin you would assign a higher place to yourself than to her? Let me tell you this. If you had once paid an ounce of attention to that woman instead of seeing her only as a means to your own glory you would have known she was never mute to begin with. Think on that, you great man of science. Even I knew. Everyone knew. Think on that as you try to close your eyes in sleep tonight."

"You knew nothing."

"It was you who scared the poor creature away, drove her from you with your cold instruments—calipers where anyone with a jot of sense or tender feeling would have put his arms around. Write about that, why don't you. Write about the effects of steel caresses on the human heart."

"This from prudish Ida Fleming? A primer on love?"

With that she made for the door, but turned once to add, "I hope she never comes back. I hope she has more sense than that."

The old biddy swept out with a fierce rustle of her skirts. He was not sorry to see her go apart from the consequent withdrawal of the bread and jelly and the prospect of coffee. "Ain't the first time I've supped on whiskey," he said to the ticking clock and the empty row of chairs flanking the surgery door. He paused a minute as if they might answer before admitting himself to his inner sanctum.

Fear gripped his heart in that second it took to yank the lower drawer of his desk open. Then relief, upon discovering two full bottles lying close together like lovers. "Thank God," he said, reflecting that in the past Mrs. Fleming had sometimes made a sweep of his drawers when he'd been careless and left them unlocked. Things had evidently been in too much upheaval of late. His resources had remained untouched.

He took a glass from his drug cabinet and blew dust from the interior. He poured it exactly half full and admired the sparkling tawny draught before he poured it down his throat. Ah, the old familiar burn, but not the longed-for lift. Another pour, this time a bit above the halfway mark, and down the hatch. He paused a bit after that one, to look around the surgery. His gaze came to rest on the graceful S-shaped staves lined up largest to smallest on a clean white towel on the enamel-topped table. He remembered explaining to Lucy that they were used to explore the urinary tract for obstructions. Her brown eyes had flashed up and met his at the mention of this rude subject. He had apologized for offending her, but then added that in his work all manner of bodily ills were his constant concern. He had said, by way of making the idea more palatable, "The Methodist ladies say that God made all parts of us and the functions thereto, so it cannot be evil that I make it my work to delve into them as it were." Some expression of interest in her eyes then led him to broaden the subject. "What about you?"

Lucy Lied

he continued. "Do you believe the Lord looks out after things on earth, keeps his eye on the sparrow?"

She had cast down her eyes and shrugged.

"It is a thorny subject," Doc went on. "Perhaps the Celestials have it right. Maybe their heathen religion is the straight and narrow way to Heaven. They have a white square building they call a joss house. They go there and burn incense and pray to their heathen gods. Every year there's a big celebration where they light firecrackers to scare off the evil spirits. You can hardly see the houses for the smoke. It would be nice if everything evil could be scared off with a firecracker, don't you think?" He remembered quoting Adrian Fiske on the subject, then expanding a bit. "Odd to think maybe the secrets of the universe might be unlocked in that white shack of theirs, but then appearances can be deceiving." He had paused to see if this commonplace would receive some sign of approbation. Instead she clasped and unclasped her hands. He had thought it a charming gesture, evidence of her nervous excitement at being alone with him. Now, he reappraised it as a sign of guilt.

Had she ever made him a sign of her actual thoughts, her true nature? He searched the album of his memory finding only Lucy of the downcast, bashful glance, the delicate hands raised to hide her face as she turned away, or covering her mouth as she stifled silent mirth. All childish gestures, suggesting only innocence, vulnerability.

He poured himself another whiskey, this time full up to the brim. He knocked it back and chased it with another. "Damn her once and damn her again," he said through clenched teeth. He threw the glass across the room and left the surgery for his bedroom. Furious, he stood for a time regarding the magnificent bed, all made up and awaiting the bridal night. Then his anger burst forth in a surge of activity. He tore the quilt away and stripped off the bedding. He flung the mattress aside and the supporting slats away. He stood, surrounded by the bed frame, intent on tearing it apart with his bare hands. After a few tries at taking off the side rails, he had to descend to the garden shed out

314

back for a mallet. But once he'd so armed himself, he had the whole structure reduced to pieces on the floor in no time.

Chapter Thirty-seven

He stood sweating and breathless amid the wreckage of his bedroom for a moment, the mallet still clutched in his fist. It felt good. He wanted more. He wrenched open the window and made short work of tossing all the linens, the quilt, the slats and the side rails out onto the ground below till all that remained of his bride bed was the headboard, the footboard and the tick. These he hauled down the stairs. The tick and the footboard were easily removed. When it came to the massive headboard he had to drag it a few inches at a time, pause, and summon up fresh anger to move it a few inches more. Finally all was collected in an impressive heap on the ground. He paused to survey the destruction as his heart hammered in his chest. He'd not neglected to bring the whiskey bottle out also, the second of the two. As he raised the bottle to his lips it came to him what he would do next.

He went again into the surgery and emerged with an armload of papers: all the notes of his examinations of Lucy, the observations of her manner, the measurements of her skull, the results of all the tests and experiments with opiates, Mesmerization, audiometry, reflex action. Notes on her acuity of hearing, her responses to loud noises—he'd been looking for a scream there, any sign that she had voice. *Hadn't occurred to me to ask her to sing me one of Allen Luce's melodies,* he reflected acidly.

All the paper he dumped on top of the wrecked bedstead in the middle of the yard, to one side of the sandy track that led from the gate in the white picket fence to the front door. He went inside one more time to secure a lighting taper from next to the pile of kindling on the hearth. And almost as an afterthought, but most important of all, he seized Adrian's pencil portrait of her from where it was propped on the mantelpiece.

On that moonlit night, the sight of black smoke coming from the bluff above the Custom House alarmed all and sundry including fishermen plying their trade in the bay. An evening that had started off calm had grown blustery by midnight when the blaze at The Rookery had reached its peak of ferocity. Townspeople came to watch in case the flames started to blow toward their homes, or so they said. Mostly they came to eye Doc Garrett as he stood close to the inferno. He faced each explosion of super-heated wood, each shower of sparks as if daring the flying embers to brand him with a mark to remember the occasion. The townsfolk whispered to each other that his wits had turned as they reveled in a display that no Fourth of July could rival. Had he built his pyre higher up on the promontory, it would have been better still, but he'd not given any thought to showmanship.

It was Peabody who first had the notion of adding to the blaze as it began to die down. He ran to his shop and came back with a load of pine scraps he'd had piled out behind his place for years but never had the gumption to get rid of. Like a bucket brigade, a line of men formed to pay out the fuel from the wagon to the fire. The flames sprang up with new life, expanding the charred territory within the fence. When the scraps played out, they were followed by the wagon itself.

Silas Fletcher fetched a cradle with a broken rocker. Steadman brought several bales of molded hay. Martin Ross brought a jug of wine, as the work had them all parched. The Tenant brothers found some busted fencing. Kevin Hennessy came with an armchair that looked reasonably sound, but must have offended his butt somehow. His wife Nell chased after him crying, "You bring that back right now!"

It was Nell who came within the fence line among the men to take them to task for their folly. "What is the meaning of this willful destruction?" she demanded of the blackened faces. "It's a pure waste of winter fuel, of good furniture, things of use. An offense to reason as it is to God. You'll rue the day—"

"Back off, woman!" Nate Forest warned, waving a flaming brand. "Go tend your hearth!" He helped Kevin heave the chair atop the remains of a load of barrel staves that would never know hoop nor head.

Nell was beaten back by a thundering male chorus of "Go home! Go home!" Several other women who had come to stare shrank away back to their inglenooks to establish battle lines of silent disapproval.

The men went teaming forth like soldiering ants to find more combustibles. Bronson, who had already cranked out his latest edition of the newspaper, regretted that he had missed the opportunity to report the great conflagration, but took comfort in the fact that he was able to save his morning edition from being confiscated for burning. During the night several buildings in town were stripped of shutters and a couple even lost sections of plank siding. It was reported that in the midst of the rampage of destruction, men were seen in weepy embraces like brothers long estranged who had just buried the hatchet. Judge Nearing heard a case against Henry Tenant and Brick Forest for chopping down an apple tree and bearing it off to the pyre, but he went easy on them as it had been barren of fruit for many years. "I dare not ask what got into you," he said before he dismissed the charges with a bang of his gavel, looking as downcast as one who'd missed out on Saint Crispin's Day.

On his way to The Rookery the morning after the fire, Adrian Fiske threw down a nickel and took a copy of the paper from the stack on the porch at Leese's. He took it out from under his arm as he opened Garrett's gate and approached the smoldering pile of detritus, using it to fan a gust of smoke away from his face. One elegantly turned post of the bedstead, a headless hobby horse, and the frame of a once-gilt harp were still identifiable amid the ruins burned black and felted with gray ash. Embers glowed cherry red with each breath of air, lost their brilliance when the wind dropped, then flared again at the next puff. On the top step of the porch Doc squatted like Hephaestus at his forge, soot-smudged and wild-eyed with the memory of the inferno. There was an inch of whiskey in the bottom of the bottle he held out to the painter.

"Been tidying up the place, I see," Adrian said.

"I hate useless clutter," Garrett said.

Adrian took a drink. "Reckon you got her burned out of your soul?"

"Don't know as the soul can be cauterized, but I gave it a good shot."

"You're well singed, I'll say that. You mind if we take our ease farther from the rubble? I'm reminded of the gates of hell."

"Will you ever in tarnation stop complaining? I swear! From now on instead of talking about all the things that don't sit altogether right with you, just tell me when everything's perfect. That'll save you a lot of breath."

"My God, you stink worse than a burning horse turd."

"I been working."

"Working man would have better sense than to set to in his best bib-and-tucker."

"Hand me that damn bottle. I don't know why I ever share my liquor with you, annoying as you are."

"I'm the only society you got, I reckon. All the other citizens of Monterey was put off once the sparks died down. They all got tired of you and wandered off home."

"Suits me. Why don't you go on and do the same? I find the company of most people onerous. What brings you up here anyway? I hope I'm not keeping you away from your tree."

Adrian snapped the crease out of the paper. "Thought you might want to know what Bronson saw fit to print about recent doings. He put out a special edition."

"Let's hear it while I'm still drunk enough to take it straight."

Lucy Lied

Adrian cleared his throat and read:

"Life for Life

Yesterday afternoon, Sheriff Jedediah Taylor was summoned to a scene of murder and retribution just north of Monterey in Monterey County. The murder victim, Isabel Francisca Vásquez, was found dead of several gunshot wounds in the house of her neighbor Matt Clancy. Evidence suggests that Señora Vásquez had come to the cabin on Clancy's property near the Salinas Highway to settle a disagreement over property rights. They apparently argued, which argument having got out of hand, ended in the fatal shooting of Señora Vásquez. A number of vaqueros who had been branding nearby said they heard the many shots. By the time Sheriff Taylor came upon the scene, Clancy had been taken by unknown avengers to a tree outside the house and there hanged. The hanging party must have been thoroughly drilled and the details systematically carried out as the act of retribution was accomplished before the alarmed ranch hands arrived on the scene. The sheriff has confirmed that the evidence in the case conclusively proves Clancy's guilt in the murder of Señora Vásquez. Thus it may be said that the actions of the anonymous band served the interests of justice. Taylor added that the rope used to execute Clancy was a new one and had stretched almost enough for the gunman's feet to touch the ground before he was strangled. Likely Clancy would have lived to stand trial if anyone had come upon the scene a few minutes sooner to offer assistance."

Doc seemed riled. "What's he accuse me of?"

"What?"

"Stop muttering, would you please? Stop muttering and make sense. Pass me that bottle."

"It's empty. We'd best be off to Simoneau's, then." Fiske looked at his friend's grimy face. "You want to wash up?"

"Wash up for those clods?"

"Fine. I'll try to keep to the upwind side of you."

"Anything else in that paper of yours?" Garrett demanded as they set off down Alvarado Street.

Adrian perused the front page. "Story about plans for a luxurious wallow going up after the new railroad spur from Salinas is built. Bronson runs it side by side with the story on Clancy. Then he puts in a piece about how conditions in Monterey are looking up."

"Read," Garrett said.

"*Better Late Than Never; Citizens Regain Carmelo Mission,*" Adrian began.

"By the time the Civic League had formed up and resolved itself to root out the disreputable and worthless types who sheltered in the Mission, the sun-dappled season of San Carlos Day was but a memory and the men sitting their horses in the fringe of the woods saw their breath steam in the early morning air. The horses stamped the rime ice on the undergrowth and rimpled their hide in the raw mist. Their nostrils flared to catch the scent of campfires rekindled after the long night. Sheriff Jedediah Taylor listened and watched, not sure what signal he was waiting for. At his right elbow Deputy Morris said, "Reckon we've come before they've turned out of their bedrolls. What say we shoot off a few rounds and watch the commotion?"

Taylor raised his hand and made a forward motion to alert the others that they should follow. He nudged his mount with his heels and the horse stepped out of the woods, splashing through the shallows of the Carmelo River and heading toward the tumbledown wall of the mission compound. The men advanced soundlessly, twenty in all. The leader of the party hoped there would be someone within the mission with whom he might parley, but feared that between those who were liquor-addled and those too sick or old he would never make his conditions understood. Nevertheless, once the message was delivered, the rest of the plan would be set in motion and the sand would be running through the hourglass.

To the squatters, Taylor delivered this ultimatum: Their occupation of this place is at an end. The citizens of Monterey are reclaiming their mission. It is no longer possible for them to camp here. The church is soon to be restored to its former glory as a house of God. People from San Francisco will come to see it and hear how the Franciscans and Jesuits first tamed California by dint of faith. It follows we cannot allow a gaggle of vagrants to occupy such a jewel of our heritage. You are hereby put on notice. If in a few days you have not vacated this place, you will be driven out without mercy. We will spare no straggler a bullet to end his slothful life. Those who would stay alive must pack up now and be gone.

With that, the horsemen were on their way. All vowed to reassemble to execute the threat of eviction in a week's time."

"Cleaning house on all fronts," Garrett commented.

"Not the least of which is yours."

At Fiske's comment Garrett halted. He nodded toward the Bohemian Café. "What is it they've been saying about me?"

"They've beatified you and accorded you a black letter saint's day."

"I mean about her putting horns on me."

"That she was a devil who killed Flynn Talbott and then played everybody like a Stradivarius with that mute act. She was never liked. You know that. Truth is they wish they'd seen her hanged just like Clancy. That's the gist of it."

"And you? You see it that way?"

"I never understood why you saved her from the gallows to begin with."

"Then it's nothing to you that I've had my very heart torn out, that I've lost the one woman in the world who ..."

"You're a fool if you believe that. Why, you never even had a conversation with her. And don't tell me you had some kind of telepathic connection. I don't believe in all that. She was a pretty face. Nothing more. You're well shed of her and if you weren't of such a confounded ornery nature you'd admit it."

"I'm alone now."

"You've never in your life been alone. For one thing you've got me. And you've got Sally. You never credit her with much, but she's solid as they come and a beauty, too. It galls me you don't see past her profession."

"You mean that I should consider myself something more than a client?"

"You're an ass. I don't know why I even bother talking to you."

"Perhaps you'd best take up with Jedediah Taylor," Doc said. "He seems to be the hero of the hour."

Having just made this observation, Garrett pushed open the door of Simoneau's only to be stunned by a rousing cheer from the battle-grimed veterans of the great blaze assembled at the bar. He was clapped on the back by a bummer he knew only as a sometime miner from Pennsylvania who exclaimed, "Get thee in here, son! I ain't seen anything like that since we made the crater at Petersburg."

"Look what we got us in return for that damn fancy man that left here for back East," one of the Portuguese said. "Those Methodist ladies won't talk to you till you've washed your hands and face!"

"To hell with the Methodist ladies," Doc declared, to the hoots and shouts of his new fast friends.

"You showed 'em, Doc. You got 'em good!"

"Honest sweat never served a better purpose. Tell those stiff bitches that!"

Simoneau, who had contributed a quantity of beverage to the festivities of the night before, was out of beer. "Whiskey is on the house today!" he said with a broad grin. The band of sooty brothers toasted each other and celebrated Doc as their beloved general until the whiskey ran out, too. Having galvanized the male spines of Monterey, the heroic bed fire gained a place in local lore as an unparalleled achievement, which could have been greater only if Doc had managed to roast the redhead alive in it.

Chapter Thirty-eight

Sally Locke was annoyed to find Adrian Fiske and Doc Garrett on her doorstep during her normal business hours, but when she realized the condition they were in she told Louis to admit them without delay.

"He was feted with unusual diligence," the painter explained.

"He's filthy. Put a sheet down," Sally said to Rose before Louis dumped Doc onto her couch. "Louis, bring the tub and hot water. Rose, I'll need an apron."

"I believe I'll be going," Fiske said, as if he had visions of himself in hot water, too.

"You're both absurd," Sally said, by way of goodbye, "just like children."

Once she had everyone scurrying in different directions per her instructions, she perched next to Doc and gently stroked a piece of lank hair off his forehead. He opened his eyes and grinned. "The boys don't hate me anymore," he said and closed his eyes again.

She and Rose pulled off his clothes and Louis lifted him into the tub. "Boil everything," Sally said, as the maid carried the laundry away, "and if they still stink after that then burn them."

Sally tied the apron around her waist and dismissed Louis with a nod. Then, kneeling at the side of the tub, she dipped a washcloth and lathered it with a bar of her best imported soap. She began with his face. "*Mon Dieu.* I've seen men home from battle who weren't this dirty."

"I heard of a man was so dirty he died when they washed him off. Mud was caked in the bullet hole, see. Water opened it up. Odysseus returning from Troy. So grimy no one in the household could recognize him, not even his wife."

"I could have used that bed. Did you ever think of that?"

"That's a hard thing to say, as if it were just a piece of furniture. I swear, you women have no sense of honor whatsoever."

"No. What we have is just plain sense." She pushed him forward in the tub and began to scrub his back.

"Oh, lord, Miss Sally. You have a heavenly touch. Remind me to have you bathe me again some time."

"Oh, you have another bath in your future? How very decent of you."

"Cleanliness is next to godliness."

"What would you know?"

"Don't be so sharp now, Sal. You know you love me."

"Yes, just like the boys down at Simoneau's."

"They bought me drinks all afternoon. Did I tell you?"

"I figured it out for myself."

She soaped his limbs methodically, went over his privates especially well, and then told him to stand up and be dried off. He stepped out of the tub onto a mat and endured a toweling that left his skin bright pink. By the time Sally dropped a fine, soft cotton nightshirt over his head he was asleep on his feet. "Walk with me," she said, taking a firm hold of his elbow. He did as she said, content to be bossed by a dark-skinned woman again, fussed over, and put to bed.

She sat in a low chair by the bedside and wondered how it would all turn out. Would he wake in a black depression or still giddy with the heroics of the night before? Would he have a splitting head or would he call for more whiskey? Would he still be consumed with the redhead or would he want to take her into his arms and put her to use as the sporting woman she was?

After he'd been snoring soundly for a time she rose and undressed and joined him between the sheets, enjoying an unaccustomed night of slumber next to him. It was not until the first gray light of dawn paled the sky that he stirred and sat up suddenly. The abrupt motion woke her. She waited to speak until he had stopped checking his pulse and dropped his hand from his throat. "What is it, *cher?* The old dream?"

"No—" He had to stop and clear his throat.

"The one with your mother chopping the head off the snake?"

"No, not this time," he said. "I thought it was when it started. But then I was walking on the beach, walking out to Adrian's cypress tree. And I came upon a lake. It was a lake on the edge of the town where I grew up. In the dream I thought how odd it was. I'd been transported from Monterey to Macon."

"In dreams that sort of thing is usual," Sally said.

"Anyway, it must have been winter because the lake was frozen. And I walked out on the ice. It was very thick but crystal clear. I could see a whole tree submerged, sealed like a specimen in a jar ... airless, silent and still. A body was caught on a branch where her skirts had tangled. She hung there with her eyes wide open as if she were looking through a windowpane up at the sky. Her eyes were brown. The water was black around her face and there was a silver bubble under one nostril and the sash of her dress rose up behind her like a ribbon of smoke torn from the top of a chimney. There were men with axes crowded around me chopping at the ice. They worked by lantern light. The echoes of the axes woke the townspeople who came down to the lake to watch, still clad in their nightclothes with blankets clutched around their shoulders. But somehow the ice never broke and we could all see her red hair floating up around her pretty face and the more the men chopped at the ice the more she seemed to get only farther and farther away."

"A woman drowned with her red hair floating up around her face," Sally said.

"It's Lucy," he said, "don't you see?"

Lucy Lied

"How is your heart? Still the palpitations?"

"She's dead."

"We don't know what happened to her," Sally said. "Perhaps she is dead; perhaps not. It's a dream about death, not about her."

"It's my conscience makes me think I see her dead face."

"Why would you say such a foolish thing?"

"I had it in mind to kill her. I was going to put my hands around her throat and ..."

"Thoughts don't kill people. Whatever happened to her she did herself. You had nothing to do with it."

"I think it was evil intent killed her."

"Don't be foolish."

"Then why do I see her corpse? It's a punishment."

"Stop it now, and listen to me. That's not it at all. It's the idea of death that upsets you. Not her death, your own. All men fear death. But what can we do? We all shall live our three score years and then life is no more. We die and our possessions end up in Ortin's store." She paused to consider the thing a different way. "It's always water in your dreams, *toujours la mer*, the sea."

"She was so young ..."

She saw he would not give up the idea that haunted him. "You saved her once, you know. How is it you feel such a sharp pang of guilt? It is foolish of you to carry on so when you are blameless. Besides, like as not she is sleeping sound herself next to a rich man who will give her a house full of children and a bright red filly just like the one you gave her before she ran away. Now go to sleep."

She settled him back down under the covers and wrapped him inside the iron circle of her arms, rocking him and humming a tune she recalled from her own childhood. Once more, soothed and comforted, he fell back asleep, thinking of history, old tales that had aged into fact, but most of all secure in the belief that what Sally said was stronger than his fear, more powerful than any medicine, perhaps even true.

Epilogue

Thirty years later Doc Garrett retired in his own bedroom at The Rookery on an autumn night, leaving the window next to his bed ajar, as it was mild, only to succumb to heart thrombosis sometime during the hours of darkness. He never stirred the next morning, nor the next, but no one noticed until a sister of the congregation came the following Wednesday to clean. She saw that Doc was absent from his surgery and as it was late morning, slap in the middle of normal office hours, she called upstairs. Hearing nothing, she called again and finally plucked up the courage to go and look into his bedroom.

The instant the door creaked open, her curious gaze was met by a furious flapping of wings as the ravens she had startled rose off the corpse and flung themselves against the window. Their frantic efforts only served to shut off the escape route. The window was side-hinged and opened into the room. The good woman screamed and fled as the black birds cawed and flailed and beat themselves senseless against the panes. She went for the sheriff who, along with a deputy, managed to rid the room of birds. The undertaker was sent for, as it was abundantly clear that Doc Garrett had been dead for some time. After the body was removed in a box the story was repeated around town that the birds had pecked out his eyes just like they'd done to the body of Doc Battle before him.

The obituary that ran in *The Californian* bemoaned the loss of a "healer who had come to Monterey for the benefit of the children. Many had died of diphtheria in prior years and the Methodist churchwomen felt that they had to act to preserve their offspring. They sent letters out into the wide world to procure the services of a new physician, hoping to find that compassionate soul who would not mind the sleepy seclusion of Monterey and would apply himself assiduously to its sick and injured for little compensation apart from the reward of virtuous toil. Jason Garrett came all the way from Saint Louis where he had worked for an insurance company after completing medical school in Philadelphia. He was but thirty-four when he arrived two years after the end of the war and was seventy-four when he died." The piece was conspicuously silent with respect to Garrett's role in the infamous trial of Chinaman Joe for the murder of Flynn Talbott.

Though Doc Garrett's possessions were thoroughly tattered and ordinary, each item of furniture and household goods attracted a mob of onlookers as they were carried off to Ortin's Store. Will Ortin had bought the lot sight unseen as his family's enterprise had thrived for three generations in the secondhand trade. It was he who opened the cedar chest and found a collection of objects at the bottom that made him scratch his head and ransack his brain for certain childhood memories that remained elusive. There was a letter edged in black with writing so faded that Ortin couldn't make it out, a broadside for a magicologist show, and folded into an old boat cloak a spent bullet, a lady's glove button and an old five-shooter. But the object that most intrigued him was a pendant earring consisting of a large oval garnet set in a garland of gold leaves and seed pearls.

He knew as soon as he laid eyes on it that his father had acquired this earring once before. As a child playing in the shop he had seen it in one of the glass-sided display cases. And he knew there was a story behind the bauble, an explanation of why there was only one, a singular tragedy. He couldn't bring the details to mind, but no matter. He had the earring restyled as a pendant to be worn about the neck on a golden chain. He pinned an exorbitant price on it since it was old and very fine, and because the city people who toured Monterey would think nothing of dropping a pile of cash to obtain a keepsake of the trip to the old Spanish town by the bay.

Ortin showed the remounted pendant to his wife Muriel, who was older than he, though she denied it. She remembered having seen the earring in the store when Ortin's father Dan had been the proprietor. "There was a charlatan they ran out of town one night," Muriel Ortin said. "Matt Clancy and them. Then when they ransacked his things they found this earbob. Clancy had something to do with that mute gal with the red hair. You know, the one who murdered her husband. Everybody knew she done it, but she got off scot free." She worried over the missing name, tapping her fingers on the table.

The events his wife vaguely recalled jogged his memory. "Oh, yes," Will said, "Flynn Talbott's wife."

She was called that just as if she'd been Talbott's horse, or his dog or his boots, as if she had no claim to life but through him, poor soul.

"How do you suppose that sharper came by such a fine piece of jewelry?" Muriel held the polished garnet up to the light and saw the fire flash from its heart. "Probably stolen," she said and handed it back to him.

As often happened, Muriel, being of a pragmatic and logical bent, was right.

But Ortin didn't hear her comment. As he polished the ovoid dome of the gleaming stone with his handkerchief, he was imagining a pretty woman who would beg her husband to buy it, only to display it on her bosom to delight another.

The End

About the Author

M.J.Daspit

M.J. Daspit was born in Princeton, New Jersey in 1951. After graduation from Cornell University in 1973, she became managing editor for The Writings of Henry D. Thoreau in association with Princeton University Press. She subsequently joined the Navy and served in the anti-submarine SOSUS community and in the Navy Recruiting Command.

During her naval career she had two tours in Monterey and fell in love with its historical treasures and natural beauty. Retired as a Commander in 1994, she taught English at Southwestern College in Chula Vista, California and later moved to Oregon to pursue a career in writing. She currently lives in the vibrant theater town of Ashland with her husband Gary Greksouk.

Daspit's other published works include a nonfiction book titled ROGUE VALLEY WINE, co-authored with winemaker Eric Weisinger, (Arcadia Publishing, 2011). She is also the author of a forthcoming collection of short stories, THE LITTLE RED BOOK OF HOLIDAY HOMICIDES.

If You Enjoyed This Book
You'll Love Everything
That Has Ever Been Printed
Or Ever Will Be Printed
by

FIRESHIP PRESS

www.fireshippress.com

All Fireship Press books are available directly through our website, amazon.com, Barnes and Noble and Nook, Sony Reader, Apple iTunes, Kobo books and via leading bookshops across the United States, Canada, the UK, Australia and Europe.

Peregrine

by

Mary Ellen Barnes

The true story of one woman's indomitable spirit, and her love for the hawks she raises in the time of King Charles I of England, Cromwell's War, and the forming of the New Colonies.

Frances Latham, daughter of the royal falconer, is expected to tend her brothers and marry a farmer's son, but she yearns for freedom to study in London, to hunt with hawks, and to marry for love. Her spirit will carry her from a stifling country life to the bustling streets of London, through the harrowing hell of the plague, and eventually to the shores of the New World, where Frances struggles to raise eleven children and pass on a better legacy than the one she endured.

History buffs will become immersed in this panorama of the English court, country life, the grueling voyage to colonial America, the harsh life settlers endured on its shores, and encounters with Anne Hutchinson and Miantonomi, the Narragansett sachem.

WWW.FIRESHIPPRESS

HISTORICAL FICTION AND NONFICTION
PAPERBACKS AVAILABLE FOR ORDER ON LINE
AND AS EBOOKS WITH ALL MAJOR DISTRIBUTERS

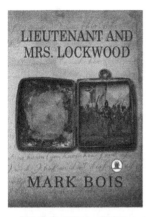

Lieutenant and Mrs. Lockwood

by

Mark Bois

"Captain Barr desperately wanted to kill Lieutenant Lockwood. He thought constantly of doing so, though he had long since given up any consideration of a formal duel. Lockwood, after all, was a good shot and a fine swordsman; a knife in the back would do. And then Barr dreamt of going back to Ireland, and of taking Brigid Lockwood for his own."

So begins the story of Lieutenant James Lockwood, his wife Brigid, and his deadly rivalry – professional and romantic – with Charles Barr. Lockwood and Barr hold each other's honor hostage, at a time when a man's honor meant more than his life. But can a man as treacherous as Charles Barr be trusted to keep secret the disgrace that could irrevocably ruin Lockwood and his family?

Against a backdrop of famine and uprising in Ireland, and the war between Napoleon and Wellington, showing the famous Inniskilling Regiment in historically accurate detail, here is a romance for the ages, and for all time.

"… Bois' meticulous research and command of historical detail makes this novel a must read. He sets the standard for research and understanding… and the audience will demand more novels from this new author. Historical fiction welcomes Mark Bois with open arms." – Lt. Col. Brad Luebbert, US Army.

Fireship Press
www.FireshipPress.com

www.Fireshippress.com
Found in all leading Booksellers and on line
eBook distributors

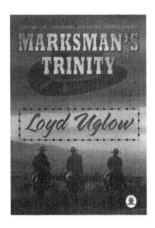

Marksman's Trinity

by

Loyd Uglow

When Captain C.W. Langhorne, 4th United States Cavalry, takes a green lieutenant named Harry Bennett and a trio of Apache scouts on a hunting trip along the Rio Grande in the summer of 1916, he has no idea that their real quarry will turn out to be Mexican bandits and a kidnapped child. Although the rescue attempt goes sour, Langhorne captures a plan by extremists to ignite a bloodbath in the Border States. While U. S. authorities decide how to react to the threat, Langhorne and Bennett have their own troubles with the glory-hunting Major Philip Cobb back at Fort Bliss, including Bennett's unconventional romance with Cobb's young daughter. Finally assigned to stage a preemptive military strike against the plotters, Langhorne and Bennett find themselves battling not only Mexican revolutionaries, but also treacherous civilians, hostile terrain . . . and Major Cobb.

Fireship Press
www.FireshipPress.com

www.Fireshippress.com
Found in all leading Booksellers and on line
eBook distributors

Wings over Cairo

by

Simon Herbert

When Jack McClelland joins the Advanced Flying Unit at RAF Ramsey in early 1941, he takes to the air to defend Britain in the new Bristol Beaufighter. But he finds out the hard way that a thwarted senior officer can carry a grudge, especially when a beautiful woman is at the heart of their rivalry. McClelland is sent to Egypt, and as love and war collide, he finds himself in a desperate situation: follow orders on a suicide mission, or disobey his commanding officer to accomplish the objective.

Set in the early, desperate days of World War II, here is a tale of courage, romance, and the struggle to win over adversity, based on the actual exploits and misadventures of the men of the RAF's 272 Squadron.

Fireship Press
www.FireshipPress.com

www.Fireshippress.com

**For the Finest in
Nautical and Historical
Fiction and Nonfiction**

WWW.FIRESHIPPRESS.COM

Interesting • Informative • Authoritative

CPSIA information can be obtained at www.ICGtesting.com
Printed in the USA
BVOW11s1452230814

363952BV00006B/16/P